SHADOW CRUSADE

SHADOW CRUSADE

PRIMORDIALS OF SHADOWTHORN

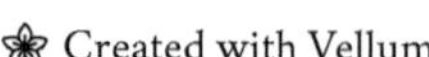 Created with Vellum

ARCATHAIN
Arcathain Capital
Drayfil Shore

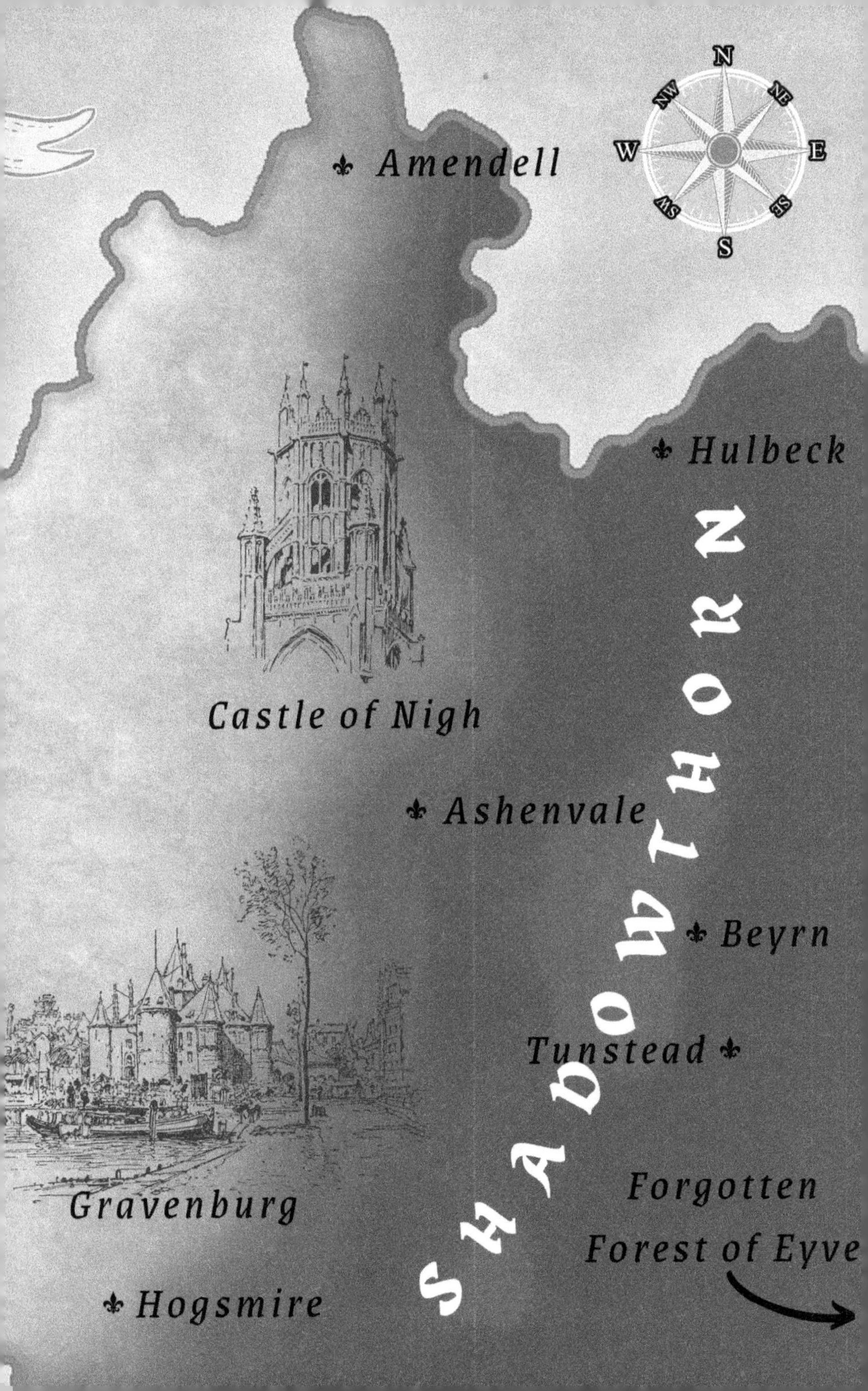

Amendell
N
NW NE
W E
SW SE
S
Hulbeck
Castle of Nigh
Ashenvale
SHADOWTHORN
Beyrn
Tunstead
Gravenburg
Forgotten
Forest of Eyve
Hogsmire

To Kieran,

*Whose demons I will always strive to vanquish,
and whose world I will always try to brighten.*

PROLOGUE

Monster and human once walked the earth together, if not in harmony, with an understanding that each deserved a place in the world.

However, such an existence is easier to accept when you're the predator in the equation.

As the human population grew, as they built their villages and towns, encompassing more and more of the land they had previously shared with the ancient beings, they became suspicious that a different balance was possible than the one they had adapted to.

Why live as the hunted, when you can become the hunter?

Of the shadowcreatures, they feared the Primordials most of all. And so, as humans do, they set aside their differences with each other to face the giant beasts as one.

They killed every Primordial they could find, until only one remained.

For each life a Primordial took—be it human, demon, mage, or otherwise—it only grew stronger, engorged with darkness and death. Over time, none had claimed more lives than Qaeus. Qaeus was the most powerful of all the Primordials. No matter how diligently the humans fought, not even shadowsteel could pierce the creature's flesh, and for each failed attempt, they were only feeding it and stacking the odds against themselves.

With no other option, the humans turned to the mages. The two races had long since been at odds, however, realizing just how powerful the Primordial Qaeus had become, the mages agreed to isolate the shadowcreature in the farthest corner of Arcathain, in what became known as the Forgotten Forest of Eyve.

And though Qaeus was quiet for centuries, it wouldn't remain imprisoned for long.

In time, the mages' magic failed. The barrier keeping Qaeus in the Forgotten Forest of Eyve shattered. On that day, the Primordial bellowed, an earth-shattering and malicious cry. All who heard it swore it meant death to them all.

Once again, the creature began walking the lands of Arcathain, only this time, it brought the Blight with it. A blackness crept across the land like a plague and mangled everything it touched.

The mages, fearful of the beast's vengeance and of what the Blight would do were it to reach the magical soil of West Arcathain, used their powers to split the continent and flee across the ocean, creating the new country of Illashore, and leaving the humans on their own.

The Arcathainians were abandoned, utterly outpowered, and left with nothing but their shadowsteel to comfort them.

But, as is often true in the face of adversity, humans discover their strength. When one has no other option but to die or fight, many choose the glory of battle rather than the shame of awaiting an inevitable and visceral demise.

And thus, the Shadow Crusade was born, a legion of warriors sworn to find the Primordial Qaeus from where it dwells inside the blighted lands of the Shadowthorn and slay the creature, once and for all.

They are humanity's only hope.

COMETH, THE BLIGHT

THE WALLOWS, GRAVENBURG, ARCATHAIN

*E*very time I leave the cottage, it's like wandering straight into a demon's maw.

From our doorway, darkness stares back at me from the forest yonder, eerily quiet for a place that I know to be crawling with danger. Our front door is east-facing, and as such, the encroaching Shadowthorn will soon be at our front doorstep. For now, at least there is still a few houses between us and the blackness, and a few Crusaders patrolling to keep us safe, but judging from the rumors we glean from the neighboring villages, and the refugees who have flooded our own, not even the Shadow Crusade can protect us.

I stand, frozen in the entryway, wrapping my cloak around my arms as I fix my eyes on the spaces between the blackened trees. The creatures that live there are too quick, too skillful at ducking between the shadows for me to spy any of them with great detail, but I feel their presence all the same.

Malicious.

Malevolent.

And always, *always* watching, waiting for an opportunity to strike.

"Does this mean I won't have the pleasure of your company today, daughter?" my mother, Evelyne, calls from behind me in her usual singsong voice. From the safety of our home, sometimes it's easy to forget what's outside of these walls, especially since it's been approaching for so, so long.

I close the door a crack to give her my full attention, careful not to allow any of the creatures easy access inside—not that cottage doors or thatched roofs have ever stopped them before.

I find my mother buzzing around like the bees we keep outside. The braid hanging over her shoulder is as frosted and glistening as the snow that coats every inch of the Wallows outside, the poorest part of Gravenburg where we reside. Defying the laws of how much a single person should be able to hold in their two slender arms, my mother gathers a large spindle of wool string, a knife hanging from the wall, an iron pot, a ladle, and the other usual assortment of tools she'll need for making her candles today.

And thankfully, I won't be joining her.

"Sorry, mum. I promised to accompany Dimitri to the town square. The Shadow Crusade is coming through and—"

My mother stops so abruptly she nearly trips over the hem of her skirts. The tools in her hands fall to the floor like they are sinking in water, like time has slowed their descent just to give me long enough to realize how careless I've been with my words. They clatter against the floorboards, the spool of string unraveling before me.

I rush across the room to her side, the frayed edges of my cape billowing behind me, and bend down to collect her things.

"Don't worry," I say, trying to sound reassuring. "I have no interest in joining the Crusade. It's Dimitri who's enlisting." When my arms are full and the floor cleared, I stand back up to face my mother. Seeing her cheeks are still pale, I offer her what I hope is a comforting smile. "I promise, Mum, I'm not going anywhere."

It takes her a moment before the color returns to her skin, another two before she's able to find her breath again, and longer still before she finally takes her supplies from me.

"Yes, well," she starts, clearly miffed. "Dimitri shouldn't be enlisting either, Halira. You know as well as I do that it's a death sentence. He should already know that too after what we've all been through these past few years."

I nod, and when my mother continues on her trajectory across the room, I step aside to let her go, but I'm not completely unscathed. Of course Dimitri knows how dangerous a Crusader's job is. We all do. But his options are limited. He's been fortunate enough to find work after his family died, but soon the Blight will engulf Gravenburg just like it did every other village and town before it. Our home, all of the Wallows, will be among the first to go, and the butcher's place—*Dimitri's* place—won't be too long after. If the Shadow Crusade doesn't stop the Primordial, soon all of Arcathain will be consumed by the Shadowthorn.

"He knows that, Mum, but few orphans have better choices. If the Blight spreads any farther, everyone here will lose their homes. Unlike us, Dimitri doesn't have any other family to turn to, not that our options are plentiful either. He wants to do what he can to protect Gravenburg while it still stands, before we become refugees like the ones freezing in the streets outside."

My mother sniffs, a haughty, disapproving sound. "Then he'll die."

It's not just fear in her voice, nor a healthy dose of pessimism. Few Crusaders live long once they've been inducted, and our family is unfortunate enough to know first-hand just how short their lives can be.

"He'll die anyways if the Blight reaches us," I argue softly, biting back the sting of tears in my own throat.

Our front door swings wide before she can respond with

the same counterargument she's thrown in my face a dozen times before. My mother believes that there is always an alternative choice, that no one has to *choose* death, which is what becoming a Crusader is. And though I'm no longer eager to join them myself like I was when I was younger, back when I believed in the glory of heroism and the optimistic outlook that we might stand a chance against the evil devouring our lands, I think my mother still doubts I've had a change of heart. I think she fears that the reality check of my brother's untimely death is waning on me, no matter how many times I reassure her otherwise.

My father blows through the doorway like the winter wind. He stomps the snow from his boots at the entrance before throwing back his hood to frown at us both. "It's too early in the day for morose talk of the Blight," he says. "If it's work you're in need of, Halira, you can join me out at the shop. You can help me deliver more soup to the refugees we're housing there. I'm sure they'd rather be served by a beautiful young woman than this ugly, old man."

My mother and I both snort, for my father is anything but ugly and old. Though he's not as roguishly handsome as his youngest brother—my uncle Adrien—his gentle heart is visible through his umber eyes. There's no rigidity or coldness to him like most of those who live in the squalor of the Wallows, and despite the hardship he had to endure after his parents died during the Great Rift when he was still just a boy, he still managed to carry himself with kindness, benevolence, joy. The same can't be said for his other brother, Esmond.

Before I can politely decline his entirely unappealing offer, my mother interjects for me.

"She's headed to town with Dimitri to watch him sign his life away."

I scowl at her as she walks by me to give my father a kiss on the cheek. He leans down into her lips, but his mind is at work behind those dark eyes. He props the door open for her so she can start her day, but instead she stops, spine straight, clearly waiting for him to agree with her and give her some vindication.

To my mother's disapproval, my father shrugs at her before saying to me, "Then may bravery fill his heart and protect his soul."

Rolling her eyes, my mother starts to walk out the doorway, but she's stopped by a raven chittering in the window. As the three of us turn to it, it belts out a single deafening squawk that grinds at the back of my neck. Most animals, I adore. I'd spent much of my childhood wandering the forest and observing the many woodland creatures I came upon.

I have no love for this fowl though.

"Oh look, Kalli's sent a raven." My mother races back to the table to set aside her candle-making supplies before jogging over to the window. She unravels the twine around the bird's ankle. "Do you think she's coming home for a visit?"

"In the middle of winter? With the Blight so close?" My father barks a laugh, steam carrying it out into the cool open air by the doorway. He closes the door behind him and shrugs his cloak off. "I doubt it. Maybe she's sending word of Esmond's most recent heinous plans."

"Oh stop," my mother says, fanning him off. "You shouldn't talk of the Magistrate that way, even if he is your brother. If anyone heard you—"

"What? They'd call me a traitor? Accuse me of treason? Bah!" my father bellows. "Would a traitor sacrifice his arrow shop just to house the refugees fortunate enough to have made it out of Ashenvale? Would a traitor have sent his only son to fight in the Shadow Crusade to protect all of Arcathain? *Or*"— he adds emphasis here, mischief hiking his thick eyebrows—

"would a traitor, perhaps, anoint his son as a general just so he wouldn't have to see battle, and then flee to the westernmost side of the continent, taking his elite army with him, and abandoning the people of Arcathain?"

"Oddo!" My mother's voice is shrill, her eyes bulging. "You can't say such things about the Magistrate—"

He throws his hands in the air with an exasperated sigh. "Piss on a mage, Evelyne. You'd think I was talking to one of his advisers about my plans of killing the bastard. I'm in our home, dear. I'm allowed to besmirch my selfish, greedy brother under the protection of my own roof. It's not as if Halira is going to travel all the way to the Capital just to tell her dear old Uncle Esmond how I feel about his politics, are you, dear?"

Groaning, I flip my hood over my head, making sure to roll my eyes at them both before turning my back to them. "Dimitri is waiting for me. I have to go."

"Be careful out there," my mother warns when I open the door again, another gust of winter flurrying in. "Remember to keep as much distance as you can between you and the—"

"I know, Mum. I don't have a death wish. I won't be caught anywhere near the Shadowthorn—no nearer than we already are, anyway. I'll be back in time for lunch."

"Wonderful. You'll be just in time to help me with dipping the wicks."

I can hear the goading smile in her voice, so I say with a smirk of my own, "Maybe make that suppertime."

Outside, the frigid morning air blows through the threads of my cloak, making me feel as if I'm not even wearing one. I tug the worn fabric closer and glance through the fog of my breath. Winter has sunk its teeth into Gravenburg, and it's not even a week past solstice. It's too cold and too early for most of my neighbors to be outside right now, not unless they have to be, but I'm not entirely alone.

Crusaders patrol the Shadowthorn border, clad in their black leather and shining, silver breastplates, shadowsteel weapons close at hand. They're a new addition to the Wallows, one I still haven't grown accustomed to. It's an odd feeling to grow up knowing of the Blight's existence but never having to confront it. It always seemed like some distant threat, one that I thought the Crusaders would've dealt with long before it ever reached Gravenburg. But with the increasing presence of the Shadow Crusade at our border, and having watched the black sickness claw its way through the forest that I used to frolic in as a child, it's impossible not to face the hard truth that the Blight has arrived, and it's unlikely anyone will stop it before my family loses everything here.

Ducking around the corner, once I've put some distance between me and the Shadowthorn, my gloomy disposition fades. It's rare that I get a day off. Although I'm not as beholden to my work as most seem to be, my parents keep me fairly busy helping them with whatever they need. This past fall, my mother assigned me to harvesting her beehives, ensuring we had enough wax and honey to barter with for the year. My father, too, had his assignments around the shop—I think I fletched over a hundred arrows one week—but since last month after Ashenvale fell, we've been busy arranging the best accommodations that we can for their refugees who fled into our town. I suppose I should feel guilty for taking myself away from the hard work that there is to be done, but I relish every moment I can away from that shop, my mother's beehives, and all the other responsibilities that feel more burdensome than fulfilling.

Besides, there's no company that could compete with that of Dimitri.

The winter wind howls, another flurry blustering through my fraying cloak. If only we could afford new ones this year, ones made from bear pelts or wolf, rather than the scrap of knitted wool that's stretched out over my back.

I groan as the snowy gust assaults me. In my frustration, I even blow at it as if I can prevent the wind from reaching my already freezing skin.

To my surprise and great dismay, it actually works. The winter air had pressed down on me like a blanket of snow. Even clothed, there'd been no escaping its bitterness. But with one breath, I've blown the cold away.

Of course, a deep chill penetrates me then: dread.

Panic swells inside me, wild and desperate. It's not the first time my surroundings have seemingly...manipulated at my will. When I was a child, I'd managed to run through a rainstorm without any wetness reaching me. Just this past autumn, I went into the garden to find that our potatoes were rotten to the root, only to then watch as those same plants became verdant again right before my eyes.

The mind has a way of toying with memory. That rainstorm, it's likely I returned home as wet and dripping as the laundry we'd left out on the clotheslines, but my childlike mind made a game of it, and chose to believe otherwise. The plants in the garden? I must've just not seen them correctly to begin with. After all, I'd been staring out at the Shadowthorn all morning, thinking about what the Blight does to the trees and bushes. I must've still been imagining it when I first gazed upon the potatoes.

And now? Who wouldn't want to believe that they could prevent their bodies from being cold when the chilling pain is already bone-deep?

Yes, there is always an explanation for these oddities, there has to be, for the alternative would be far too horrifying. After all, only the mages possess magic, and they are just as abominable and wicked as the demons that Dimitri will soon be hunting.

And to be a mage is punishable by death.

The moment I inhale, the arctic air reaches me again, and I sigh with relief. I grip my feeble cloak and continue stomping through the snow until I reach the familiar home.

Compared to the rest of the year, when the sun bakes the butcher's hut, and the raw stench of blood and flesh permeates the entire road, during the winter months, the odor is dulled all the way until I reach their doorstep. Once I'm at their front door, spying a freshly slaughtered deer in a cart beside me, I have to fight the urge not to cover my nose.

"Finally!" a man grumbles from inside the modest cottage. His familiar lean shadow crosses behind the window, and a second later, Dimitri shoves the door ajar. There's a scowl etched in his grimy forehead, his long face seeming longer. But when he sees me shivering before him, my nose already pink and raw from the short walk, he sighs and gestures me inside. "Come in before you freeze to death. I have to change now anyway."

Ducking through the doorway, I cock my eyebrow at him. "You're giving me a hard time for being late and you're not even ready yet?"

He scoffs, closing the door behind us. "I *was* ready. But time is money, and I couldn't very well just stand around as my master bled a bull and sectioned the meat for the day while I waited for your always-running-late ass."

I smirk, but he fails to find it amusing.

"Where have you been? I don't want to miss them."

I turn around, my mouth queued with a retort, just as Dimitri lifts his bloodied tunic up and over his head. It catches on his chin and the back of his head, and despite telling myself to look away, my eyes have a mind of their own. They flick to his taut shoulders, trail down his chest slick with sweat from the effort of his morning work, and plunge deeper still down his flat stomach.

We've been friends all of our lives, and it's not the first time I've glimpsed his body—in the summers, we used to dive nude into the lake behind my home—but this might be the first time I've flushed looking upon him. He's not sculpted out of stone or anything; he has the body of a poor laborer, someone who's had to fight and hunt for every meal on their plate. But for a single, fleeting moment, part of me wonders what his chest would feel like beneath my touch.

At the same time as he tugs the dirty garment the rest of the way over his head, I finally fix my nonchalant gaze elsewhere—which unfortunately happens to be on a thick knife lathered in blood on the table and a few hacked hocks beside it.

"Want a bite?" he asks wryly, catching me staring at the butchered meat.

My stomach churns. I'll eat meat, don't get me wrong, but I'd rather not have to see it like this. "Ha-ha. Just put some clothes on so we can go already. You know how much I can't stand the smell…"

"Don't be such a mage," he says, crossing the room to grab a fresh shirt hanging in the back window.

I bristle at the accusation, my voice lowering with lethal quiet. "Don't call me that."

He glances over his bare shoulder before ducking into the clean tunic. "It's just a saying, Halira. Calm down."

I know he's right, but either I'm still riled from my stint with the snowy wind, or I simply enjoy arguing with him. "Yeah, well, save it for the girls who aren't already chastised and ridiculed for being of the Eyve."

"You're not Eyvi." He laughs, the sound rich and warm. "Your mother is. You were born here, in this pigpen of a town. You're more *wallow*ing Arcathainian than anyone I know."

His rare usage of a pun finally gets my lips to bow. Unintentionally, my eyes fall back to the table, my smile fading as soon as it arrived.

"You get used to it; you know?" he says.

"Hmm?"

"The carcasses."

I shake my head. "I'm not sure I could ever get used to the smell of blood, but maybe that's why you're joining the Shadow Crusade, and I'll be stuck here making candles the rest of my miserable life."

Out of the corner of my eye, I see him open his mouth to retort, but he clamps it shut.

"Say it," I insist.

Exasperated, he shakes his head. "It's nothing."

"It's obviously not *nothing* or you wouldn't look so somber about it. Just say what's on your mind. Get it over with."

He stares at me, his jaw twitching as he does his best to keep whatever thought it was to himself. But it's clearly more pressing than he tried leading me to believe. Eventually, running a hand over his freshly shaven chin, he caves. "If you don't want to make candles for the rest of your life, then don't."

My eyes graze the top of my skull "And what? I should just join the Shadow Crusade, like you? I've already told you, I can't—"

"Yeah, so you've said." He shakes his head, turning his gaze out the frosted window. "Just forget it."

We stand there in silence, amid the carnage and decay, and I'm sure he's thinking the same thing I am. I don't want this to be the way we say goodbye. If I could, I *would* join him, just to have him by my side a little longer. But even if my brother hadn't died as a Crusader, my mother would never allow me to join them, and Dimitri knows that. This is another conversation I've had too many times to count, and if we are to say our farewells soon, I don't want our last interaction to have ended in an argument.

Dimitri crosses the room to me. He stands so close that I can feel the heat radiating off him and warming my snow-kissed skin. But as I gaze up into his sage-green eyes, prepared to insist he drops the topic, he smiles and ruffles my hair.

"Come on," he says, making his way toward the door. "The Crusade awaits me."

THE MARKET

TOWN SQUARE, GRAVENBURG, ARCATHAIN

The farther we walk into town, the easier it becomes for the sun to seep through the dark sky. Instead of the ominous dark teal that I've learned to associate with daytime ever since the Blight reached our borders, a brighter blue shimmers above us. I'd almost forgotten what sunlight was like, but the farther away from the Shadowthorn we get, the more I remember and long for clear skies, soaring birds, and the ability to distinguish a rain cloud from the evil that festers over our lands now.

Regardless of the darkness cast over Arcathain, hundreds of people flood the streets as if nothing is wrong. Vendors push their carts of goods and set up their stalls. Eldest children roam the streets with their coin pouches, setting about purchasing the food and wares that their parents have sent them for. Everyone goes about their day as if danger isn't just on the other side of these stone buildings.

"A cloak for the lady, sir?" a woman asks as Dimitri and I walk by her stall. "We can't have the missus walking around in that tattered thing this winter, can we?"

"Not interested," Dimitri replies, his sage-green eyes fixed distantly up ahead.

"Come, now. She's freezing. That scrap of fabric will be wasted by the fortnight. Our cloaks will last years, made from the finest wool you can find, at prices you can afford—"

"Do we look like we're made of money to you?" I snap at her.

The vendor's eyes cut down to the dagger at my hip. "Shadowsteel like that can fetch for a high price. Say, two cloaks, one for you and your husband?"

Protectively, I clutch the blade. It had belonged to my brother, Tor, before he had died. Upon officially becoming a Crusader, each warrior is allowed to select one of the shadowsteel weapons to wield. My brother, having preferred the quicker arts of battle, had selected the dagger. He believed it gave him speed and stealth that would prove imperative when fighting fiends and demons, when so many of the other weapons hindered the Crusaders.

"It's not for sale," Dimitri growls, deadly warning etching his words until they are as sharp as Qaeus' teeth.

Before the woman can take a different approach—and, as a vendor, I'm sure she plans to in hopes of making a sale—Dimitri takes my hand into his and pulls me back into the crowded marketplace.

"Every time, with her," he seethes. "You really ought to get a new cloak, just so she'll shut up already."

I snort a laugh, but my eyes catch on a young girl with hair the color of cider at the stall up ahead. She's being reprimanded for stealing, from the looks of it, and she gives me the perfect fodder to add, "The only way I'm getting a new cloak is if I try my hand at her line of work."

"You'd make a terrible thief," he says, flashing me a dubious grin. Even smiling, there's still years of pain edging his features.

"You have no control of your hands. Or your feet for that matter."

My jaw falls wide open. "Says who?"

"Says me."

Without warning, he spins around and launches an apple at me. The scarlet thing smacks me right in the face, my hands fumbling somewhere in the air behind it, before it tumbles to the ground and rolls beneath a cart of bulging burlap sacks.

Dimitri breaks out into a hysterical fit of laughter as he reaches for a coin and tosses it to the apple vendor who, of course, apparently has quicker reflexes than I do.

Glowering at my friend, I storm ahead. He yells after me, muttering something about how I should at least retrieve the apple he purchased, but I don't lose haste, especially not since if I turn around, he'll see that I, too, am smiling, and I wouldn't want to give him that satisfaction.

When he finally catches back up to me, with an apple half-eaten in his hand and some of it glistening in his chin, I'm standing before a stage where a leather-clad Crusader is just beginning to recite the next round of his appeal to his potential recruits.

"The foul reach of the Primordial Qaeus has already spread across much of Arcathain. The Blight has taken Tunstead; it's taken Hulbeck. The Shadowthorn has even spread past Beyrn and to our brothers and sisters in Ashenvale. Think not for one moment that Gravenburg will go untouched, not unless we stand to defend it! My good brothers and sisters, today I ask for you to join our ranks. As you know, Magistrate Esmond has stationed most of his legion to defend the western shore from the mages, but the Shadow Crusade remains here, committed to the people who need protection the most. We fight for Arcathain. We fight to put an end to the Primordial's reign.

"Qaeus sends its demons to feast on your young; it sends its fiends to lure your friends into the Shadowthorn where they are lost and tormented forever. But the Blight stops here, with you, Gravenburg!"

At Dimitri's beckoning, we sink deeper into the crowd until we're able to touch the stage. From this close, I'm able to see just how young the speaker is, hardly twenty, no more than a couple years older than us, even though the badge on his chest identifies him as high ranking—a captain, if I'm not mistaken. It shouldn't be surprising. Crusaders die quick, and the ranks fill fast.

The man crouches down low so that he's practically at eye level with us. He looks through the front row, stopping at Dimitri to stare him straight in the eyes.

"I see it when I look among you. You are a people of bravery. You are a people of duty and valor. The Shadow Crusade would flourish with you among our ranks." In a fit of theatrics, the recruiter stands abruptly and bellows so that all nearby can hear. "Join us in bringing peace and honor back to Arcathain, and your loved ones shan't live in squalor any longer."

Most of the people around us are young. They are the impoverished children of farmers and blacksmiths, the brothers and sisters of the dead, the refugees of the towns already consumed by the Blight. If Qaeus' reach seeps any farther, they are the ones who will lose their land, their homes, their livelihoods, everything.

So I do not fault them for charging forward to sign their lives away.

But Dimitri and I are different. My family has connections, even though we ourselves are not well-off. My sister works in the Senate, my uncle Esmond is the Magistrate and governs all of Arcathain, and despite his tumultuous past with my father, I'm sure he would arrange for our safe departure, should we need it, and I'm surer still that my family would gladly take Dimitri and his master with us, should it come to that.

As Dimitri marches forward, sheer determination rippling off his every step, I snag his arm and pull him back.

"What are you doing?" he asks, thick brow furrowed beneath his unkempt hair.

I release his arm and instead hold him with my gaze. "Are you sure this is what you want?"

He throws his arms up in an exaggerated display of frustration. "This again, Halira? How many times do I have to tell you? It doesn't matter what I want. The Shadow Crusade needs able bodies and it is my duty to join them."

"It's not your *duty* to do anything. You don't owe it to anyone to sacrifice your life. And becoming a Crusader…y-you could die."

He stands even taller, his chest puffing with infuriating pride. "Then I would die fighting. It's better than doing nothing and just letting the Primordial win. For too long our people have suffered. Those bastard mages retreated. The Magistrate, he's focused on other matters on the coast. No one will protect us but ourselves. The Crusaders are all we have, and they need more men." He pauses, his stony expression softening a little as he stares into my eyes and adds, unconvincingly, "And women."

"I'm not joining the Crusade," I snap.

"Why not?" When I open my mouth to recite my usual retort, he points a finger close to my face. "And don't say it's because of Tor. I know he died, but so have other brothers and sisters…so have mothers and fathers…"

Pain flurries behind his eyes, dimming the resolve that was once there. We both know the people he's talking about aren't nameless nobodies. My brother and his sister were slaughtered by demons during the same expedition into the Shadowthorn. His mother was lost in one before that, leaving just his father and him to take care of each other. But as the Blight crept closer, Qaeus' fiends grew restless inside the boundaries of the Shadowthorn, as they always do. Any chance they had at beckoning unsuspecting victims closer to their borders, they took, and soon Dimitri lost his father as well, never to be seen again once he stepped across the dark boundary.

At least my family was fortunate enough to have Tor's body retrieved and returned to us. Dimitri never so much as saw any of his family members again.

But Dimitri's momentary visit with the dark memories of his past fade almost the moment they arrive.

Returning to the present, to me, he steels himself. "If everyone refuses to join their ranks, more will die. We owe it to the families who remain to fight for them."

His conviction can be so exhausting, especially considering I bear none of it. What I wouldn't give to feel so fervently about something the way he does about his duty to our country. But that's not me. My life is mine, not the Magistrate's, not Arcathain's, not my mother's and father's to pawn off their dreary professions, but mine.

I just haven't figured out yet how to spend it, and the fact that he has, drives me mad.

"Not all of us have nothing left to lose!" I yell, cheeks heating. "I can't just abandon my parents like Kalli did. They need me."

"Then do what you think is right—" He scoffs, watching me with contempt. "And let me do the same."

After turning his back to me, Dimitri leaves me in the emptying street and approaches the table with the sign-up. He nods to the Crusader standing there like they are the oldest of friends, picks up the quill, and I swear the winter wind howls its distress the moment he writes his name down in ink.

Only, the more the snow flurries around me, I realize, it's not just the wind I'm hearing.

A muffled cry hollers from down the street, frantic and severe. It draws the attention each person in the square one at a time as it draws nearer, the harsh sound clambering its way up the road until I can finally make out a woman panting just ahead.

"Demon scourge! Demon scourge!" she yells, warning us all.

Everyone bristles. Nervous eyes dart to the shadows between the buildings. Mothers reach for their children and pull them into their skirts. It takes them longer than I am comfortable with, but even the Crusaders ready themselves for the worst, drawing their shadowsteel and sheltering the people nearby the best they can.

"Demon scourge!" the woman continues to cry, until one of the Crusaders catches her in his arms.

"Where?" he demands. "Where is the breach?"

The homely woman extends a shaking hand to the east, down the road from which she fled, and with a flood of icy fear washing over me, I realize that's the same road Dimitri and I took to get here.

Trembling, the woman answers. "The Wallows."

FOREVER GONE

THE WALLOWS, GRAVENBURG, ARCATHAIN

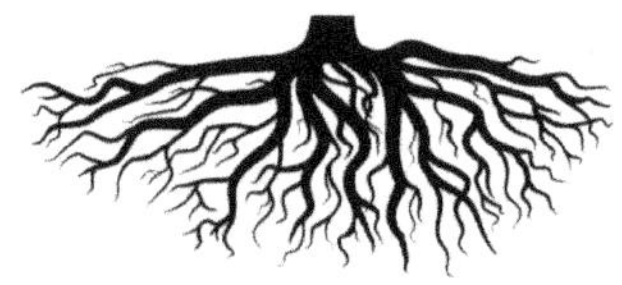

My heart pounds in time with the pumping of my footsteps as I race and slide back down the streets of this doomed, dreary town. The snowflakes are like glass against my skin; the wind in my face sharp enough to cut right through me. But I still run. I run like I never have before, like I have the lean muscle of a gazelle who's only purpose was this moment.

My parents. I have to reach my parents.

Most of the streets have emptied, the denizens of the city having retreated inside upon hearing of the demons that are pouring out from the Shadowthorn. Not that any of the people here have anything to worry about yet. Demons never wander far from their home. They cross over only to feast before retreating back into the safety of the black forest where no human, aside from a Crusader, would dare chase them.

I shove aside the few people still left in the streets who are unfortunate enough to cross my path as I sprint all the way back to the Wallows.

"Halira!" I hear Dimitri shouting behind me. "Wait up!"

But there is no time for waiting. I push myself harder, the

screams of my neighbors filling the narrow streets and urging me on as I bluster into our derelict neighborhood.

The sight of my community being ravaged is worse than anything I've ever imagined. Doors are splintered to pieces. Black, hulking masses pounce across the streets, their poisonous claws digging into every person they encounter. They rip my neighbors limb from limb, tear out their hearts and guts, strewing them across the street.

I only falter for a moment when I see the tanner's daughter being cornered by one of the snarling demons. Its hunched back is just as mangled as the rest of it, but regardless of its knobby legs, or the way its neck looks twisted—broken, even— nothing seems to hinder the speed with which it strikes. Its jagged, black nails pierce through the girl's stomach before I can think to do anything. A burst of red spews from her lips. Her eyes meet mine, a silent plea sputtering from her mouth and an image I will never be able to erase from my mind, but although I want to help her, I know it's too late. The demon sinks its fangs into her shoulder as I turn my back to her and dash toward my home.

As our cottage comes into view, all I can see is darkness. It's like the sun has disappeared just for me. But the closer I race, the more I realize that it's not just darkness I'm looking at, but shadows. Demons prowl in every corner of this block, some bulging, some small, some with misshapen heads and bodies, and some still that look almost human in form. They are all too oblivious to notice me though as each of them are busy mauling one of the dozens of refugees who'd been seeking shelter on the streets. My heart aches for them. They escaped the horrors of Ashenvale or perhaps Beyrn, only to meet the same fate they had outrun here.

But now's not the time to dwell. My ears burn for the familiar sounds of my parents' voices, even though I'm not sure I'll be able to distinguish their agonizing cries from the others.

We lived a peaceful, mundane existence. I never knew what terror sounded like, what death smelled like, what true fear felt like.

Tor's shadowsteel dagger feels useless in the sheath I always carry on my hip. What good would this small blade do when I am entering a hive of vicious killers? If I am spotted by any of them, it will mean my death.

Still, I can't just leave my parents. I have to find them. And so, I round the side of the house.

I freeze before our doorless frame.

Panting and shaking, I cross the threshold with my heart solid and wet in my throat.

"Mum?" I whisper, my voice thick and watery. "Pa?"

No matter how soft I try making my steps, my boots sound like hammers against the floorboards. Any second now, the demons outside will finish their meals, but they won't be satiated, not when there's a live snack just waiting for them inside this sepulchral home.

I swallow the impulse to call out for my parents again, and instead slink my way into the cooking area.

I nearly slip on the pool of blood waiting for me there. When my eyes fall to my father's lifeless face, his chest cavity ripped open like a black abyss while a demon feasts on his heart, it takes everything inside me not to wail, not to crumple where I stand.

But I lose my hold when I notice my mother beside him.

The scream swells from deep inside me, scorching me from the bottom up until the fiery thing bursts from my inconsolable lungs. If I had just been here like she'd wanted, instead of wasting my time going into town, I could've protected her; I could've offered a distraction so that she and my father might've escaped. They gave far more to this world than I ever will. My father with his heart of gold and my mother with her sage wisdom.

Instead, now they're both dead, and all that they've left behind is me.

At the sound of my cry, the black creature's bloodied jaw twists over its shoulder. Its ravenous, red eyes find mine and I sob all the harder. Dying here, like this, it's what I deserve for never amounting to anything. I couldn't even master how to dip candles correctly, and my fletching, despite years of practice, is still mediocre at best. Regardless of what I deserve, still, I am afraid. I never wanted this death. I wanted to live a long life, see blue skies again, become more like my gentle parents with hearts as big as oceans.

And maybe it's the thought of them, dying with disappointment that they'll never get to see their youngest daughter amount to anything, that has me raising my brother's shadowsteel dagger in my shaking hand.

The demon snarls, teeth gleaming and dripping.

Then it lunges.

I stagger back, fear consuming every notion of bravery I thought I had mustered. I close my eyes and turn my head away, but I keep my dagger up, hopeful that it will do the work for me. If I'm to understand the legends correctly, all it takes is a single nick of shadowsteel and a demon is doomed. If the creature is to attack me, at least I will take it down with me and it'll be one less monster to ravage Arcathain.

But as I press myself up against the table, prepared for the hulking beast to crash into me, a new snarl sounds from the doorway. I pry my burning eyes open just to watch the figure slam into the demon before it can reach me.

The two beings blur into a brawl of shadowy limbs and growling maws. I've never heard of demons fighting each other, but for creatures who have no humanity, I should've known. They are starved in the Shadowthorn. Only human flesh and blood can fill their bellies and quench their hunger, so of course they would fight each other for a meal.

Blinking out of my frozen stupor, I realize this is my chance to run. Once a winner rises between them, it will waste no time in diving for me and finishing the job that the first demon started.

Even knowing that though, I still can't bring myself to sprint for the door. My gaze returns helplessly to my parents, to the bodies that are still warm because I was just a few seconds too late to—

My mother's fingers twitch. I blink, trying to force my head to clear. She's dead, I remind myself. A demon killed her—

She coughs, a splatter of blood frosting her lips.

"Mum?" My voice cracks under the pressure of hope, and I slide through the blood to kneel beside her, cradling her head in my arms. "Mum."

But as my eyes search hers, I see no recognition. She stares right past me like she doesn't even see me. Her skin is so cold already, the wounds in her chest and abdomen pulsing red.

"It's all right," I say between sniffles, my voice hitching. "I'm going to get you out of here. You just have to hang on."

She coughs again, a crimson fountain spraying us both, but I swear on her next sputter she mutters something I can't quite make out. I lean in closer, blood be damned, until her slick lips brush against my ear.

"What was that? What are you trying to say?"

She swallows, the movement taking everything she has left, and with one last dying breath, I hear her clear as any summer day before the Blight's existence:

"Imryll."

In my arms, my mother's head becomes lead, her neck limp.

"No," I wail, burying my face against her neck. "Please, don't go."

The tears flow from me like an autumn rainstorm. With my head pressed against her bloodied skin, I can neither distinguish the wetness of my tears from her blood, nor do I care.

My father is gone, as is my mother now, and her last words are nonsense to me. Not confessions of her love, or hopes for my happy and long life, but a jumbled, incoherent word that has no meaning. It's a mockery of the full life she led, and an omen for the nothingness that will now befall me.

In the distance, a raven calls, reminding me that I'm not entirely alone, even if I might as well be. Kalli has her life at the Capital, and sure, we will always be sisters, but she and I share no life apart from that.

The floorboards creak behind me. I stiffen.

Pulling away from my mother, eyes raw, heart unsteady, I set her lifeless form down onto the cold floor and stand to face my maker. But behind me I find the first demon lying in a heap of oily blood in the corner of the room. The second creature is hunched over it, using its thick arms to rip the other demon's head clean off its body. I've never seen such ferocity, such grotesque rage, but I suppose I should count my blessings that I didn't walk in to find my parents decapitated and limbless.

The victorious demon must have eyes in the back of its skull because it straightens when my gaze befalls it.

Slowly, the muscled creature stands, carelessly tossing the demon head aside and turning to face me. I almost gasp at the peculiar sight. If I had any emotional stamina left, I would. Because, although I saw some demons as I raced through the Wallows who walked upright like humans, or bore humanistic traits like two arms that extend from their torsos, I've never seen one that *actually* looked human.

The man before me could almost pass as just that: a man, an undefeated warrior whose muscles are as thick as trees, his stomach carved from the hardest stone. Like most demons, he's not wearing a shirt, but he is, however, in trousers, ones as dark as death itself.

With nothing covering his torso, I'm able to see the demonic thing he has for an arm, the Blight that encompasses every inch of his skin in black tar. His fingers are claws, his biceps scaly and prickly. The darkness continues to wind up and over his chest like ink beating through his veins. It crawls up his neck but stops just below his chiseled jawline. And though there is a demon-like glow behind his russet eyes, they watch me with the sorrow of someone who's lost family before. Someone human.

But that can't be right. It must be a ruse, some trick of demons that I'm not privy to, because the black horns tucked amid his midnight hair, and the dark wings stretched down his back show me his true nature. And if that didn't do it, the way he turned his vicious eyes on me does.

The demon throws his human head back, chest exposed, and roars. A guttural, shredding sound that sounds exactly as I feel, devastated and destroyed.

I see my opening, feel Tor's dagger warm and heavy in my hand. My knuckles ache as I coil my grip tighter, and charge.

The demon's gaze snaps back to mine, lethal rage flickering behind those cataclysmic eyes. My heart beats so wildly that my chest seizes. I halt in my tracks, no more than a dagger and my shaky arm to separate us. He dares a step closer, the tip of my blade denting the skin on his firm chest, but not quite enough to puncture it.

A challenge. One I should eagerly oblige. But this close up, it's even more difficult to deny what he is, what he looks like. Tainted but flawless. Wild but observant. Demon but...something else.

Shaking my head, I scan him again to see if I've made a mistake, but my eyes trail his black scales, the claws at the tips of his hand, and I know without a doubt that he is, in fact, of the Shadowthorn, and thereby deserves to die.

But just as I'm about to muster the courage to sink my shadowsteel blade inside him, someone clambers through the doorway at the other end of the cottage.

Dimitri stumbles forward with some random rusted pitchfork he must've grabbed from outside. It takes him all but a breath to spy me standing within danger's reach in the middle of the room, with what must look like seconds away from my own demise. Without hesitation, Dimitri tightens his grip on the splintered shaft of his futile weapon, bares his teeth with a throaty roar, and thrusts himself toward the demon in front of me.

The anomaly twists around with a roar of his own, one that sends shards of ice down my spine. I stagger out of the way just as his black wings sprout wide from his back with a gust of air, and he leaps up and through my roof, splintering it to pieces, and disappears into the gloomy sky.

Dimitri stumbles to a halt beside me, watching the hole in the thatched roof like more evil is about to descend down from it.

"Did you see that—" I breathe, but Dimitri throws his arms around me.

I'm too stunned to do anything but stand there.

After a few moments, he finally releases me. "Fucking demons. They shouldn't have been able to attack like this. We have Crusaders at our borders now. They should've—"

"That wasn't just a demon," I say pointedly.

Dimitri raises one brow, tilts his head up to the destroyed ceiling. "Sure looked like one to me."

My mouth hangs open, a protest in my throat, but he crashes me back into his embrace. "It's all right. You don't have to worry. I'm here now. I'll protect you."

My thoughts start to reel then.

If what I saw wasn't real, then maybe none of this is. Not the demon anomaly. Not my mother's slurred nonsense. And certainly not the deaths of my parents.

If I turn away from Dimitri now, part of me almost believes that I will find my mother and father smiling back at me as if none of this ever happened. My father will ask Dimitri how enlisting went, while my mother stirs one of her stews and slyly sneaks in a remark about how his life is more precious than throwing it away to the Crusade.

Perhaps it's hope that makes me look, or maybe I'm just more masochistic than I ever knew, but every false notion I had crumbles when I lay eyes on my parents again.

This time, it's me who buries myself into Dimitri's chest. There's something about knowing my sobs are muffled that make them flow all the more freely.

"I'm so sorry, Halira," he says into the top of my head, one of his hands stroking the length of my pale hair. "You're safe now. The Shadow Crusade is outside," he adds hurriedly before I might get the wrong impression that he's referring to his presence. "They've either killed or chased every last demon back into the Shadowthorn, so at least we're safe for now."

I nod and sink deeper into his warmth, but my mother's eerie final word rings in my ear, the sight of the demon anomaly has my mind in knots, and somehow, I know that Dimitri is horribly mistaken.

WHAT REMAINS OF BLOOD
THE WALLOWS, GRAVENBURG, ARCATHAIN

My fingers tap against the wooden table while Dimitri dishes up some supper. The plate of venison he sets before me steams with the juicy aroma of salt and herbs, but beneath it all, I still smell the blood. I tell myself it's just the deer's, but my mind is convinced it's that of my parents'.

Three days since the slaughter, and I still smell their blood.

"Eat," Dimitri insists, taking the seat next to mine.

I shake my head. "I'm not hungry."

"It doesn't matter," he says flatly. Taking a fork into his hand, he stabs the slab of meat and tears a chunk out with a toothy bite. "You haven't been eating and you need the sustenance. Now eat."

Out the window, I'm saved by the flutter of white I see walking by. I've been waiting for her for three days, even though her letter said exactly when she'd arrive.

I shove my plate forward and stand. "I'm not staying for supper. Kalli's here."

Dimitri swallows the mostly unchewed bite and leans

forward to peer out the window. "That was quick. The Capital is a month's journey, at best. You only just sent the raven—"

"The raven was precautionary. She was already on her way. She sent word of a visit the morning of..." The rest of that sentence is too bitter for me to put into words, and the weight of it hangs in the air enough that it can go unsaid anyway. "She'll be heading to the cottage. I'll meet her there."

Dimitri wipes his mouth with the back of his hand. He shoves his chair back to stand. "I'll come with you—"

"No," I say too sharply, my words landing visibly in his expression like I've just twisted my dagger in his gut. I wasn't trying to be hurtful, especially not after everything he and his master have done for me since the scourge—housing me, feeding me—but this isn't something I want an audience for. "Sorry, I just...I need to speak with her alone. It's been... months. And our parents just..."

Once again, I let the silence say what I can't bring myself to. The unspoken reality settles in the room with us like it's a living being who is hogging all the air and leaving none for the rest of us. I grow dizzy. I need oxygen, fresh air.

"I understand," Dimitri says at last. "Go then. Greet your sister. When the two of you are finished, let her know that she is welcomed to join us for dinner."

"Like that will happen," I scoff, but then I catch myself and wince. "No offense. She's just—"

"She's Kalli," Dimitri says, waving his hand and rolling his eyes, and it's a relief to know that there's still someone in this world who gets it, who knows my difficult sister like I do.

But before I leave him to finish his meal, I catch the muscle flickering in his jaw, see the shadows that have cast themselves over him.

A raise of my eyebrow is all the invitation he needs to speak.

"If she won't lower her standards to be here tonight—" He pauses again, eyes fixed on his plate. They refuse to look up at me, but he finally musters the courage to speak. "Then I hope *you'll* at least return. I leave with the Crusade tomorrow and—"

"I know," I say quickly, cutting him off to leave yet another unbearable truth unspoken:

After tonight, I will have no one left in Gravenburg.

My voice is hoarse when I murmur, "I will see you soon," and make my way to the door before he can see the glint of sorrow in my eyes.

As I charge out into the snow, I do nothing to stop the frost from settling over me. Instead of clinging to my cloak, I let it ripple behind me, and although I could pull my hood up, I'd rather feel the sting of winter on my cheeks, let the chill freeze whatever tears are left inside of me so that I might face my sister with dignity.

By the time I reach our home, I feel just as raw as ever. The walk was too brisk, the distance too short, to allow for any real hardening of my disposition.

But it becomes clear that I never stood a chance at matching her resolve anyway, not when I find my sister just inside our childhood home, standing taller than I've ever stood a day in my life, let alone in these recent ones when grief has thoroughly consumed me. If her unwavering stance wasn't intimidating enough, the large raven perched on her shoulder is. At least I know she received my message and that I don't need to bother telling her where our mother and father are.

My boots sound on the wood as I enter behind the two of them. Only the raven deigns to glance at me. Kalli stays where she is, in the middle of the ransacked room, with her hands clasped before her. The longer I wait to be acknowledged, the more I start to remember why she irritates me so much. Leave it to Kalli to depart years ago for a fancy job with the Senate, to have visited only a handful of times and only to do so to gloat about how important her position is for the welfare of Arcathain, then to come here after our parents have been slaughtered, and to hold her head up high like she is above it all, unfazed by the anguish.

"I didn't expect you so soon," Kalli says, tone as cold as the winter's breeze. The bone-white ropes of hair heavy against her spine barely move when she finally glances over her shoulder, one slender brow raised. "You came alone?"

My knee-jerk reaction is to remind her that I *am* alone now. With Mother and Father now gone, with her all the way on the other side of the continent, and with Dimitri just a few hours away from his departure, I have no one. But Kalli and I shared a childhood. She was a part of as many of my memories of Dimitri as our brother Tor was, so I know that she's asking about him, and rather than bristling the second we start our interaction, I rein myself in long enough to answer her.

"Dimitri's still at home. He offered to come, but I asked him not to. This seemed like a family matter." Crossing the room so that I'm not just speaking to the official, silver insignia on her purple cape, when I'm finally facing her, she is as unreadable as ever. Never before has she looked more like our mother in that way. But before I can follow that thought to the pain it leads to, I add hurriedly, "He did, however, extend an invitation for you to join us for supper once we're done here. I don't know if you've heard but—"

"Let me guess?" she asks. "The Shadow Crusade?"

With a frown, I tilt my head.

Kalli exhales a single curt breath through her nose. "I thought he was better than that. All the Shadow Crusade has ever done is wasted men on the wrong fight."

Rage, unrelenting and wild, boils inside me. She speaks as if he's some common fool. She speaks as if every Crusader hasn't fought for the people of Arcathain and sacrificed their lives just to save others. If it weren't for the Shadow Crusade who rushed to our aid during the demon scourge here, I'd likely be dead.

"Why?" I snap, casting all notions aside of having a civil conversation anymore. "Because Uncle Esmond says it's the wrong fight?"

"It's *Magistrate*, Halira. I know you've been living with Father all these years, but do not let yourself inherit his treasonous tongue."

My fingers tighten into fists at her proper speech. She never used to call him *Father*, nor our mother *Mother*. Not until she took such a high and prestigious position in the Capital.

"Don't call Pa a traitor," I growl, inching closer, my nails digging into my frozen palms.

Kalli's lips part, but before anything comes out, she presses them back into a hard line. She closes her eyes long enough to regain her composure, and I'm envious of how quickly she can return to her neutral state, even if there is always a displeased angle to her features.

"I'm not calling him a traitor. Our father was a good man, but he had his flaws."

"And the *Magistrate* doesn't?" I sass. "As far as I can tell, the Crusaders are the only ones doing anything to protect us. They patrol the borders of the Shadowthorn night and day. They defend the people when we fall under attack. Maybe they'd be more effective if the *Magistrate* brought the rest of his army here to aid us in their cause?"

Kalli's eyes widen, but where I expect to find rage, fear softens their usually hard edges instead. "*Us?* Halira, please don't tell me you have enlisted?"

My cheeks burn at the suggestion. It had been a slip of phrase, obviously. I only said *us* because of the recent attack and how personal all of this had become. But now that she's brought it up, I do feel the pull of it. As a child, becoming a

Crusader had always been a dream of mine and Tor's, but when my brother lost his life to the Shadowthorn, when his death shattered my mother and father, I abandoned that dream. Suddenly, I was afraid of what I could lose, and of what being lost could do to those I love.

But now, what's stopping me? After we finish our parents' pyres and send their souls off into the next plane, Kalli will return to the coast, Dimitri leaving soon after her, and the parents I'd stayed behind to protect are gone now.

"Halira. Tell me you haven't enlisted in the Shadow Crusade."

"No, I haven't," I say finally. "But maybe I should."

Rage flickers behind her cold eyes, but her exterior remains unchanged: hardened, unflinching. "The Shadow Crusade? The only ones who join that dying cause are those eager to die themselves. You're not actually selfish and pathetic enough to want to take your own life just because our parents are dead now, are you? Many have lost far more than their parents, Halira."

Fury spins me around and I bang my fists against the nearest thing. The table shakes with fervor. "I'm not doing this because I want to die! These people need protection, and the *Magistrate* isn't giving it to them!"

"That's because the real fight is overseas on Illashore with the mages. If you want to fight so badly, if you truly want to protect our people and these lands, join the Magistrate's Legion. Avenge our ancestors, and restore the soil that is right-fully ours, once and for all, before Qaeus has spread its reach too far to reverse."

Shaking my head, I lean into my hands where they're still pressed into the wood. Kalli left before the Blight reached us, so she's never seen a demon; she can't know the danger that she's suggesting I leave the people on the borders to; she didn't see our neighbors mauled, that child eviscerated, our parents feasted upon.

"The mages don't care about us anymore," I say through gritted teeth. "They fled the danger and now they're living their lives as if we're already dead. And if it's war they want, they'll overpower us anyway. We don't have magic to fight them—"

"The Magistrate has a plan for that. He's an intelligent man—"

My lip curls back at the sound of her loyalty, and I spin around to stare into the eyes of what I think a true traitor might look like. My sister, as firm in her stance as she is in her principles, glares back.

"It's nice to see who's side you're really on," I sneer.

Kalli looks away. To anyone who doesn't know her, they might think they've struck a nerve, but I know better than most that glaciers, like my sister, have no nerve endings. She has always been able to separate emotion from logic, and it's why she likely makes such an astute Senator, someone who's always able to calculate the risks versus the benefits and make the decision that is likely to have the most profitable outcome.

"The only side I'm on is that of Arcathain," she says, right on cue.

Now it's me who turns away, rolling my eyes before inadvertently letting my gaze fall to the place where the demon had been decapitated. Dimitri and I have since disposed of the body and set it on fire, but the inky blood still remains, and every time I lay eyes on it, all I can think about is the other demon who'd killed it.

And every time I think about that creature, the demon who looked part-man, I become confounded all over again. It must've been some kind of spell that the demon placed over me to make me think it looked human. I've heard fiends can do such things. I believe it's why the Crusaders wear those strange markings on their faces, to protect themselves from the influences of the tricksters. But I didn't realize fiends were able to leave the Shadowthorn. I thought they stayed inside the black lines and preyed on those senseless enough to enter. Come to think of it though, that would leave for slim pickings considering no one dares enter the Shadowthorn but the Crusaders.

Still, I'm astounded by how believable the trick had been. In that moment, I could've sworn that I was looking at a human, someone with a demon arm, sure, but someone with their humanity intact all the same. His eyes had reflected that, pain as well as rage—human emotions that don't belong in a demon's countenance—but I suppose that's exactly what it wanted me to see. What better way to kill a human than to trick them into coming to you?

I suppose it wasn't that great of a trick, if the creature couldn't entirely glamour its demon side away.

"I didn't come here to fight with you, Halira," my sister says into the quiet, empty home. "If you are so intent on joining the Shadow Crusade, then by all means, who am I to stand in the way of the one thing you've ever felt passionate about? I'm here today to put our parents' souls to rest before I return to my business with the Mayor tomorrow. Can we do that peaceably, like two, mature siblings who have better things to do than bicker?"

I'm so busy bristling over her jab at my lack of drive, and then at the insinuation that *I'm* the one who started this squabble, that I nearly miss the truce she's offering. The grieving, angry, ready-to-fight-anything side of me wants to yell back at her that I've been passionate about plenty, but then I remember that, for a woman who grew up impoverished and has secured herself a seat in the Senate, all by the young age of twenty-seven, my brief obsession with rock-collecting when I was ten won't compare to the level of ambition she embodies.

Besides, I've spent enough of the past few days in this state of half-cocked. I'm exhausted. I'm depleted. And I don't even know what I'd be arguing about anyway.

"Sure," I say quietly. "Follow me and I'll take you to their pyres. Dimitri and I finished building them earlier this afternoon."

FADE INTO THE PAST
MURWOOD HILL, GRAVENBURG, ARCATHAIN

*B*ack before the Shadowthorn swallowed the forest behind my home, there was a clearing in those woods where we would arrange to deliver our dead to the beyond by burning their flesh. But the Blight has claimed that clearing, and so the citizens of Gravenburg are forced to say their farewells to their dearly departed in a new location on the other side of town.

I lead Kalli to Murwood Hill, a place I'd never really visited much until the past few days, but now I feel quite familiar with it. It's far enough out of the reach from the Shadowthorn, and high enough into the atmosphere, that we can see through the black clouds to the bluish sky beyond. If I had known such a place existed so close to home, I might've found myself here more often, sitting on the grass with my knees bent, head tilted back to gaze into the forever above.

But as we crest the snowy hilltop, my gaze wanders no farther than to the two mounds of carefully stacked logs, branches, and kindling before us. Our mother and father, forever frozen in time, never to see another passing day.

Although I'm panting from the steep hike, Kalli looks as if

she has hardly even exerted herself. Not a single strand of alabaster hair is out of place amid her dense locks. At least her nose has finally tinged itself pink, despite the thick and expensive wool jacket she's encased herself in.

With her hands clasped before her, she wades through the snow to stand before each of the pyres. Both of the structures are tall enough to deter most animals were they to stumble upon these heaps before we were able to light them, but not so tall that we can't see over them, can't glimpse our parents' pale faces.

Kalli looks upon our father first. I watch her cold eyes rove over him, searching for the signs of death that one would expect from a demon attack, but even this close, she won't find any. I couldn't stand looking at him the way he was, his chest cracked open like an egg, his heart and lungs absent from the cavity. Once we removed his clothes, Dimitri and I filled his chest with sawdust and pine needles before we redressed him for the funeral. Not only did it make my father appear a little less disturbing, but the added kindling will help his body burn quicker, his soul find rest faster.

A silent nod is all the farewell my father receives from my sister before she turns and steps toward our mother.

The two of them had always been closer. Growing up, it was not uncommon for Tor and me to tease Kalli about how similar she was to our mother, even though now, looking back, I'm not sure that was a bad thing. Like Kalli, our mother had fierce drive. Whereas my sister devoted herself to politics and the well-being of all of Arcathain, our mother held that same level of commitment toward raising her children and caring for her bees. She would rise before the sun and not settle for the eve until long after the three of us had gone to sleep.

They shared convictions about the Shadow Crusade, about treating the Magistrate with respect regardless of his and Father's tumultuous past. When there was an argument within the household, you could bet that it was our father, Tor, and myself against Kalli and our mother. They even shared likeness for things the rest of us disdained, such as the earthy flavor of rye bread, the ear-shattering song of a barn owl late at night, and the stringent smell of onions.

Kalli reaches up to cup our mother's cheek, but the second their skin touches, she yanks her hand away with a small yelp. It's such an unusual show of emotion from her, that I actually look away, unsure of how else to react. Instead of glancing to me out of embarrassment, Kalli just hangs her head. I've never seen her so sad before, at least not visibly so.

The moment passes quickly. From the corner of my eye, I see Kalli wipe her cheeks and turn back around to approach me.

"Do you have the flint and steel?" she asks, already so easily composed again. It's like her voice is a winter storm, harsh and unyielding.

"Here," I say, holding up the flint in one hand and drawing our brother's dagger with the other.

She scans the blade without any show of the grief I feel whenever I see it, but there is a flash of knowing that passes through her eyes.

Then, she simply pivots to face our parents once more. "You'll take Father and I'll take Mother."

There is no question about it. She is not asking me for my preference. It is simply the way this will be, and frankly, I don't care enough to debate it. I loved our parents equally, but it's been obvious for years who Kalli favored.

I give one swift nod, though it's not until afterward that I realize she's already stormed ahead. Again, it's not like she had any reason to wait. The divvying of our tasks was already a decision that had been made in her eyes.

Flint and dagger in hand, I approach our father's pyre. I've spent the past few days saying my goodbyes, and so I do not hesitate. My parents have waited for release long enough. I strike the shadowsteel against the rough stone in my palm until sparks fly. The kindling around the base of the pyre catches first, a crackle of embers sparkling against the shavings like bursting stars.

They burn like that for a while, a dormant kind of heat waiting to be unleashed, and then they flicker into flames. The flames climb the branches, they catch on the logs, and within only a few moments, my father is completely surrounded by a fence of searing fire.

I hand the flint and dagger to Kalli before finding a safer distance to watch. Once our mother's pyre has been ignited, my sister joins me.

We stand, side by side, utterly silent. There's a moment where I think to reach for her hand, where I convince myself that there might be some comfort found there, but then I remember who's beside me. Not the brother who had been my idol. Not the mother and father who had supported me even in my insolence. Not the friend who had sheltered and fed me during the hardest days of my life. But Kalli. Cold, unfeeling, too-good-for-any-of-us Kalli.

Instead, I find comfort from my hand balled into a fist. It's only been days, but it feels like years since they were taken, and in that forever stretch of time, grief has latched itself upon me. It's left me rotted and lost. But underneath it all, it's also left me enraged. My parents didn't have to die. Before the Shadowthorn was at our doorstep, they led a peaceful, contented life, and would've done so for years to come, if given the chance.

I will not be cowed by my sorrow any longer. Rage is the only tool I need, and I let it fester inside me until there is only one thing I am certain of: Qaeus is going to die for the pain it has caused me and so many others, and I will be the one to sink my blade into its gut.

Together, Kalli and I watch for hours as the red flames give birth to black smoke, as the lumber starts to break down and collapse, as flesh becomes nothing more than ash.

Neither of us speak until our parents have finally found the peace they deserve.

"I better be going," Kalli says. The sun having long since set, from the dim glow of the fading embers I can just barely see the fog that her words ride out on.

"Yeah, I better—" Realizing her meaning, I cut myself off. "What do you mean, you better be going? I thought you were coming to visit us, even before they…"

Unlike with Dimitri, my words don't hang heavy in Kalli's company. She continues on with the conversation like I was talking about plucking an apple from a tree, rather than our parents' untimely deaths.

"I was coming for a visit, but it was to be brief. This was meant to be a business trip. Gravenburg is on the edge of the Shadowthorn. The citizens here expect a statement from the Magistrate and—"

"So you're his puppet, then?" I snap, bristling again. Before she can respond, I roll my eyes. "It doesn't matter. I told Dimitri you'd think yourself too important to deign him a visit anyway, so I doubt he was expecting anything less from you…"

But it's then, in the middle of my petulant tirade, that I realize the horizon is tinged pink. It's been dark far too long for the sun to have just set, which means it can only be on the rise. It took Kalli and I hours to reach Murwood Hill, and hours still for the pyres to finish burning. I completely lost track of time. If it's almost morning, Dimitri will be preparing to leave soon. The Shadow Crusade will be departing, and with it, my chance at retribution.

"Piss on a mage! I have to go."

I don't wait for a response. I simply run. But Murwood Hill is unmarked by trees, and so the snowfall there has been clean, no branches to catch the flakes before they drift down to the bed of white. The deep snow makes my journey all the more arduous and time-consuming. I can't run at full speed when each step I take has my foot sinking to my knees in snow. All the while I battle the tundra, I watch the sun on the horizon. The skyline fades from pink, to orange, to yellow, and I am frantic about my dwindling time.

What will I do if I'm too late? Where will I go? Will I have to wait for the next recruiters to come to town? To try to make the journey to the Castle of Nigh on my own would be suicide. The Blight has stretched so far now, that I'd have to cross through the Shadowthorn to get there.

Once I reach the bottom of the hill, the dense canopy of the pine trees has sheltered this area from much of the snowfall and so my pace hastens. My cloak tears on a low-hanging branch, my socks have long-since soaked through, but still I bolt. And as I'm racing, I realize I've never wanted something more in my life. This is my chance to prove that my life has meaning, that my sister is wrong about me, and that my parents could have relied on me. I *need* this, more than anything right now, and rising sun be damned, I won't be stopped.

Panting, hair plastered to my forehead from sweat and melted snow, I race through the town and into the square. It's still early enough that most of the citizens are still in their homes, preparing for their days, but the streets are peppered with a few. Mostly, I realize, hopeful Crusaders. Dozens of them huddle around the stage where Dimitri and I saw the recruiter speaking. I shove through them all until, at last, I find the familiar clean-cut, golden head of my one and only friend.

"There you are!" Dimitri exclaims when he sees me. "I thought I was going to miss you—"

At full speed, I crash into him, arms spread wide. The air leaves his lungs like an echo in a cave, but I squeeze tighter.

"I—" I say, my breaths ragged—"I thought I…was going to miss you too."

Dimitri pulls me away from him, eyes burrowing into mine. "What happened?"

I shake my head. "Nothing. I just lost track of time, but there's something I have to tell you."

"What is it?" he asks with bright-eyed hopefulness. The way he watches me, the way he practically holds his breath waiting for my response, it's like he's been waiting for this very moment all his life. Of course, it's more likely that he's only recently truly started considering it these past few days. Now that my parents are gone, maybe he knew before I did that it would come to this. Or perhaps this look is something more, something I still haven't allowed myself to consider.

"I'm coming with you," I say, mirroring the smile that lights his face. "I'm enlisting in the Shadow Crusade."

A FAMILY SO CRUEL

TOWN SQUARE, GRAVENBURG, ARCATHAIN

"Of course not!" the recruiter exclaims theatrically when I ask him if it's too late to enlist. "The Shadow Crusade is always open to new recruits." He slides the parchment across the jagged table and indicates to the quill and ink at the edge. "Just remember, once you write your name, you belong to Arcathain—in life, as well as in death."

A few days ago, that might've scared me. Even though I had little to nothing to live for beyond a candle making business that I never wanted to inherit, a few days ago I still wanted to live and even the mere mention of death would've alarmed me. Now it doesn't seem to matter. To live or die, to be no one or someone, to be my own person or to belong to my country, none of it matters if Qaeus survives.

The recruiter before me is doing his best to make sure that I'm well informed of the occupational hazards involved in the demon slaying business, but he doesn't realize he's telling someone who is already acutely, intimately aware of the dangers. As a Crusader, you train, you get deployed, and you either defeat Qaeus—which has yet to be done—or you die.

Death has already befallen too many of us. If the last Primordial isn't stopped, then soon we will all perish.

The only difference between those of us standing outside waiting to begin our training at the Castle of Nigh, and those still waking up inside their homes, is that they're clinging onto a way of life that is pointless as long as Qaeus still stands. And I understand that now. We, on the other hand, have already realized that none of us have the luxury of fearing death anymore. The last living Primordial must die, or we're all doomed, and it's going to take every last Arcathainian to do it.

"You think there is a less ominous way for them to tell us our lives are forfeit once we enlist?" Dimitri mutters over his shoulder.

I elbow him in the ribs.

"Oh definitely. Of course," someone says speedily behind us, drawing both of our disturbed gazes to a scrawny, overly enthusiastic boy standing awkwardly close. "They could probably omit that part entirely—it's common enough knowledge already, and a bit of a morale depleter, and if you look among us, there's already not much morale to syphon so you'd think that—"

"I'm sorry," I blurt. "Who are you?"

"Oh." He chuckles, his smile coming thin and small rather than widening. "My name's Maxwell Gregor Tiberius. Of course, you can just call me Maxwell. The rest would be a bit of a mouthful, considering we're about to spend so much time together training and preparing for the Shadowthorn."

My eyes bulge at the hyper young man in the rudest fashion, but I can't control them. He barely looks like he'd be able to hold Tor's dagger, let alone endure the thrashing fear that consumes someone facing a demon. His body is too tall for the thickness of him, his neck permanently slouched from having to duck beneath one too many doorways.

"What do you think the Castle of Nigh is going to be like?

Do you think it will be teeming with Crusaders or have they all been dispensed to the border towns? Do you think they have demons caged for us to practice on? I've heard it's the biggest castle in all of Arcathain, so I imagine they have dozens upon dozens of rooms and resources to ensure our preparation, though I admittedly wasn't able to find much about it in any of the library's books. The place is practically an enigma, and it's not like you can just walk up to any Crusader and ask—"

"Okay," I say, turning abruptly. "Nice to meet you, Maxwell, but some of are still trying to enlist."

"Oh." He laughs. "Sorry. I-I-I guess I'll leave you to it. We'll be spending plenty of time together soon anyways."

Dimitri and I share a peculiar look before I give the recruiter a sickeningly sweet smile and finally scrawl my name below the short list of others.

"Of one country, of one blood!" the recruiter shouts, thudding his closed fist against his chest.

Awkwardly, I mirror the gesture back at him, and ask, "Any idea when we leave?"

"Supposedly, at first light," Dimitri grumbles.

A tightly wound smile appears between the recruiter's cheeks. "Soon, I imagine. We're awaiting General Alphonse to make his appearance."

The familiar name seizes the muscles in my stomach. "Did you just say…General Alphonse, as in—"

"The Magistrate's bastard son?" a raspy, nasally voice retorts from somewhere off to the side of the recruiter's stand. She snorts. "The one and only. Well, as far as any of us are concerned."

Shifting my attention to the caged cart beside us, I find a red-haired woman leaning through the wooden bars, her nose crusted with blood, and possibly broken from the strangled sound of her voice. It doesn't take me long to recognize her as the girl we saw in the square the other day—bright locks like hers don't go unnoticed for long in a dreary place like this. She'd been arrested for theft, which is likely why her face is battered and bloodied.

The recruiter bangs his fist against the side of the cage. "Oi! You're not a free woman until you arrive at Nigh. Until then, hold your tongue or I'll cut it out for you. Do I make myself clear?"

The young woman's lips part in a crooked grin, a flare of mischief dancing in her predatorial blue eyes. She doesn't utter a word. She simply raises her hands, backs away from the bars, and plops onto the cart floor with the other prisoners.

If she's here, it's because she was given a choice: to be sentenced for thieving—the punishment for which could range anywhere from paying fines, losing a hand, or even meeting the guillotine—or she could *volunteer* to join the Shadow Crusade. If she chose the latter, she's either as fed up as the rest of us, or she's been caught one too many times to have been charged with a fine again.

Not that I worry about her for very long. At the same moment I remember who our general will be, Dimitri tugs on my arm.

"Look! I think that's him."

The murmurs of my fellow initiates dwindle as my cousin, General Alphonse, strides up the black stone road on his white steed. His leather armor is black and inky, just like the Crusaders who flank him and every Crusader behind them.

Alphonse carries himself like he is the most important man in all of Arcathain. He holds his reins with one hand, his pointed nose lifted so that his conceited gaze can remain forward.

But despite the show, his ego's too great not to look out among us to make sure we're impressed, and when he does, instead of finding an initiate who's awestruck by his show of magnificence and bravado, he finds me.

He stops, horse towering before us. To my surprise, his face is bare of the ink I've seen most of the Crusaders wearing. Truth be told, part of me wondered if they were tattoos, a physical marker imposed on each Crusader to prove their loyalty or something, so it would make sense that someone high up in the ranks, someone who was born of prestige and wealth, wouldn't have marred his skin with them. But Alphonse isn't the only one without the markings. Only two among their collective that I can see have them.

"Look what the scourge dragged in," he sneers down at me. "Had nothing better to do with your languid life than join this maggot-infested bunch of scum?"

I don't think he knows that my parents have died yet, not that he'd be any nicer about it if he did, and therefore I find no reason to tell him. It would likely just be added to the arsenal of weapons he has to use against me, a non-bastard now turned orphan.

I tap my chin and feign getting lost in a perplexing thought. *"Maggot-infested scum?* Hmm. What's it say about the laughable aspiration of the man leading said clan of maggots?"

Dimitri chokes on his breath. "Halira! That's your superior you're talking to. Don't you see the sigil on his chest?"

My eyes fall to the shield shaped patch sewn against his black leather. Every member of the Shadow Crusade—every member of the Magistrate's Legion, for that matter—wears the white, crowned phoenix. But unlike the other members of Alphonse's party, who's sigil are set in royal purple, the general's bird flies in a black backdrop, two rays of purple crossing behind it.

But I don't give a damn about sigils or rankings when it came to Alphonse.

"He's my cousin," I growl, glaring up at him from under my hard brow.

Dimitri just shakes his head, so appalled by my outburst

that he's apparently been stunned into silence. Sometimes I forget how by-the-book he can be. Somehow, I managed to surround myself with people who have the strongest of convictions, despite having few of my own.

Kalli's is doing what's necessary for the greater good.

My father and her held similar life mottos, though their implementation varied. Whereas Kalli enacted herself through logic, our father was one who followed his heart. His conviction had been to do what was right by the people, no matter the personal cost to him. He always granted discounts on arrows when his customers couldn't afford them; he was even sheltering and feeding the refugees who fled to our town.

Dimitri's conviction is order and hierarchy. He believes in following the rules even when they don't make sense. He believes that the people in power should be listened to without question or hesitation.

Truthfully, I've always hated that part of him, but I'm sure it will serve him well in the Shadow Crusade.

General Alphonse grunts his approval at Dimitri before narrowing his serpent eyes back on me. "Listen to your friend, *cousin*. You might all be maggots, ants even, but I am the one leading the ant colony, and you are the mindless drone at my disposal."

"Aren't ant colonies led by queens?" I say, unable to stop my tongue, nor the twist of my grin. "So, you're saying you're the queen in this scenario?"

Alphonse's lips purse together in a thin, white line. He quakes from the bellows of rage pumping within him like a small forge that's been filled with too many coals.

Lip pulled back in a snarl, Alphonse hisses, "It would do you well to show some respect, *initiate*. Only *I* decide who is worthy of becoming a Crusader, and don't think for one second that I just allow any worthless, mangy mutt among my ranks."

Dimitri yanks on my arm, pulling me hard so that I stumble behind him.

"My apologies, General. My friend here has just lost her parents. She lashes out only because she is in pain."

Alphonse straightens, a devious look crossing over him like a cat who's just learned a new way to play with the mouse it's been toying with. But he fixes the expression with false empathy quickly enough that I doubt anyone saw the initial flicker of nefarious delight.

"That is a tragedy, indeed, to have lost Uncle Oddo. My condolences for him. I wish I could say the same for your heathen mother."

Before I can lunge for him and claw his tongue out for speaking of my mum with such hate, Alphonse flicks his wrists, the reins snap, and the white stallion trots ahead. Dimitri holds me back as the other Crusaders follow after Alphonse.

"Let me go," I grit out, struggling futilely against his pull. "He can't talk about her like that!"

He jerks me around to face him. "He can talk about anyone however he wants. He's not your cousin here, Halira. He's our general, and you can't attack him like he's some snot-nosed runt you grew up with. You heard the recruiter. You belong to Arcathain now, and Arcathain has put you in the hands of that man"—he points ahead to Alphonse—"to be trained and dispersed to the Shadowthorn. To attack him would mean imprisonment. It would make you an enemy of the country. It could mean your death."

It's that thought that finally gets me to still in his grip. The whole reason I joined the Crusade was to fight to *live*. If death *is* to be an option, it should come in the Shadowthorn while I am avenging my parents and protecting the borders of Arcathain, *not* at the hands of my spoiled, cruel cousin.

"He called my mum a heathen," I say quietly.

Dimitri bends down to grab his packs. He swings one over

his shoulder and takes the remaining two in each hand before shrugging. "You know how some people feel about those who escaped the Forgotten Forest of Eyve when the wall fell. There's nothing you can do to change his mind."

As the horses pass, the rest of the initiates start to chase after them, and Dimitri falls close behind. But it takes me a moment to stop clenching my fists. My mother and so many others lived in the Forgotten Forest of Eyve with the Primordial for decades. They escaped the terror of their lives and came to Arcathain in search of a new beginning. If we think the Shadowthorn was bad, I can't even imagine what it was like living over there trapped with Qaeus and nowhere to run, and my mother would never talk about it.

If she is a heathen simply because the mages and the humans trapped her ancestors on the wrong side of the wall, then so be it. It'll be a *heathen's* daughter who saves Arcathain then.

Fortunately, I don't have much in the way of packed bags, and by *much*, I mean anything. Unlike the rest of the initiates, I didn't have the time to pack away my belongings or prepare myself for a week-long journey north to a new life, so it takes me exactly two seconds to catch up with the rest of the initiates.

My lack of baggage makes for an easier trek, but I also worry what it means for my home. What will happen to my mother's bees? To my father's shop? To the few belongings we had?

Hopefully, the Castle of Nigh has ravens because I'll need to send one to Kalli once we arrive, to make sure she arranges for our family cottage to be cared for, or at least to have some of my belongings transported on my behalf.

Just as we leave the city, a screech sounds from the sky. Every head looks up. A single raven circles overhead, before diving for us. Alphonse and the rest of the Crusaders keep moving, unperturbed by a meaningless bird, and so we try to keep up. However, the raven seems to grow infatuated with us. It circles the group, just under the tree line, like it's searching for something, someone.

The black bird narrows in on me. It swoops through the air and cuts over the group to land softly on my shoulder.

Perhaps Kalli beat me to it. It wouldn't surprise me. Ensuring our parents' belongings are in order is exactly the kind of thing that she is inclined to do.

I reach for the raven's claw, finding it bare.

"Huh," I mutter.

"What is it?" Dimitri asks. "Word from your sister so soon?"

"No, at least, I don't think so. There's no note."

He does his best to shrug, though the three bags he's carrying make the movement small. "So she didn't have paper."

"It's unlike her to send her raven without a note. What if it didn't find me? Or, better yet, what if it did but I have no clue what she wants me to do with it?"

The bird kicks its leg out of my hand, squawks in my face, and then leaps into the sky again.

I watch it as long as I'm able, neck craned, eyes squinting into the grey sky. It's not leaving. It just keeps circling overhead like it's following us.

Dimitri shoves me forward to keep me moving. "She probably just wanted you to take it to Nigh so that you two could keep in touch while you trained."

I level him a flat stare. "They have their own ravens there."

"Yeah, but you know how she is about *her* raven." We both chuckle at that. "Or, who knows. I suppose it could just be some wild bird. Gods know animals have always acted strange around you."

As our steady pace continues, I glance up toward the clouds less and less, and instead think about the new life I'm embarking on. I wonder what my parents would say if they were still here. Of course, my mother would call me foolish and likely busy herself with tidying up sections of the house that weren't even in need of tidying, but that would just be her fear getting ahold of her. They had been proud of Tor for joining the Shadow Crusade, for defending the border of Arcathain. Buried deep beneath all that trepidation, surely, if my parents were still alive, they'd be proud of me too.

Of course, if they were, I wouldn't be on the road with Dimitri. I would've been left in my less than fulfilling existence back in the Wallows, with only my mother's and father's trades to inherit, and a healthy dose of terror as the Blight swallowed everything we owned.

"I'm glad you decided to join me," Dimitri says quietly, eyes cast forward. From this angle, I notice the fine stubble growing along his chin. It dawns on me that, the past few days, he didn't leave my side once. He stayed nearby when I slept, was always with me for meals, and not once did he leave me to shave.

He wears relief the same way most wear pain. It's like not even he can accept a good thing when he has it, but that's just because he's grown accustomed to losing everything good in his life. With relief comes hope, and with hope brings the possibility of disappointment, heartbreak.

He might be relieved that I've come with him, but we both know the peril that lies ahead. Neither of us are safe, but there is a small comfort in facing these dangers together.

TO CROSS THE SHADOWTHORN

COUNTRYSIDE, ARCATHAIN

Never have I walked so far in my life.

Even when my family and I would visit my father's homeland on Drayfil Shore, or the one time we went to the Capital to witness Kalli's swearing-in to the Senate, it wasn't our legs that bore the burden of our journey. We rode on horseback, traveled by carriage and cart.

The Castle of Nigh is nowhere near as far as either of those places, and yet this journey feels like the longest I've ever been on. The endless snowscape makes it as such. Stinging pain burns through the soles of my feet with every step. My legs ache; the muscles in my back are so taut that I fear I might snap like a tree branch and collapse right here and now.

But one glance to the other initiates tells me that I am nowhere near as miserable as they are. For days now, we've been at this, and while my back is bare, the others lug their entire lives behind them.

"We'll rest here to feed and water the horses. Be ready to move again in fifteen."

The Crusader doesn't have to tell us twice. The entire congregation of recruits practically collapses to the snow. They rub their throbbing limbs and aching backs. Some of them even start discarding their belongings, casting them aside in the snow and freeing themselves of the unnecessary weight of sentimental value.

Dimitri begins shoveling out half of his bag to get rid of items that I'm sure at one point he deemed essential to bring with him. Some of his tools, a few tunics and other garments, and even a handcrafted pair of leather shoes that his master had made him when he'd first taken him under his wing. They're worn and tattered now, but the fact that's he's held onto them still, tells me just how much they mean to him.

I snatch them from the snow. "How could you part with such a thing?"

His response is a series of stiffly made motions and shakes of his head and shoulders. More than once he opens his mouth to respond, but nothing finds its way past his lips. It doesn't need to. I already understand. Where we're going, we have no need for sentimentality. A tattered pair of shoes isn't going to protect us once we're in the Shadowthorn, and no one's going to mourn us when we die, and therefore no one will have need of our personal belongings anyway. They are simply dead weight at this point.

Maxwell's chipper voice grates through the silence. "If you don't want that anymore, can I have it?"

The recruit he's hovering over, a disheveled man with a glint in his eyes, tosses the lump at him. "Have at it, kid."

Maxwell fumbles with the artisanal thing, a small wooden totem just a little bigger than his uncoordinated hand. He finally manages to clasp it between his pinky and third finger. Judging from how the thing dangles from its long tail, the carving could be equine in nature, a mule or perhaps a stallion, but from this distance I can't say for certain.

"I can't believe you'd just get rid of this," Maxwell says, tracing a finger over the smooth grain of the wood. "It's not like it takes up much space, nor contributes to the weight on your back—and the craftmanship! I don't know enough about wood to know the source it was made from but—"

"Birch," the other recruit answers, his voice heavy.

Maxwell doesn't seem to notice and keeps rambling instead. "It really is a fine piece of work. Look at the details of the horse's eyes. If a painter took to this with their oils, I'd swear this creature was alive. Where did you get this? The master artisans are a dwindling breed. Art stems from creativity, and creativity is hard to muster when you're facing fear every day, you know?"

"Maxwell, was it?" the man slurs, making me realize that the swigs he's been taking from his buckskin canteen are likely full of ale, not water. "Do us all a favor and kindly shut the fuck up."

Maxwell's mouth clamps shut. An apologetic smile quirks up the side of his face and he shoves the totem into a rawhide pouch hanging from his side.

If I wasn't so exhausted and numb to my core, and if I hadn't been thinking the same thing, I might've stood up for the awkward young man. He didn't seem the kind of person who handled such harshness very well. Then again, he was a recruit for the Shadow Crusade now. He'd have to learn to toughen up if he was going to survive the Shadowthorn, and me standing up for him would only make him soft, get him killed.

The Crusaders finish tending to General Alphonse's horse and we move out again, my joints already stiff and frozen from the break. Before we leave, I notice someone has discarded an entire bag. I might not have many belongings of my own now, but once our training is complete, we'll be sent to a border town and be charged with its defense; I may need a bag of my own for any items I might accrue between then and now.

Hastily, I empty out its contents—uninterested in dealing

with an argument from anyone down the line about how I'd stolen their sentimental items—and lug the empty sack over my shoulder before catching up with the rest of the group.

The short reprieve has livened some among us. The light-hearted conversation of strangers getting to know one another returns, met with the boisterous and squirrelly nature of those walking dangerously close to the Shadowthorn's edge.

"It's jokes you want, eh?" bellows one of the recruits. "Have you heard the one about the brave mage who fought valiantly for his country?"

"No," a few of the others muse.

The first recruit taps his chin thoughtfully. "Oh right, that's because there are none!"

Laughter trickles throughout the group, not the rich and hearty kind that often fills the dining halls of post-battle feasts, but the slight amusement of people warming up to the idea of laughing. It's hard to laugh for too long when we're all shuffling through the miserable snow.

While what little mirth we possess is still fresh, another recruit opens her mouth. "How do you tell the difference between a mage and a demon?" When the brief silence is filled with only the chittering of our teeth, the woman finishes. "One of them is pure evil, and the other is the spawn of Qaeus."

A rumble slips past my curved lips, carrying out through the wind with the others.

"A demon, a mage, and a Crusader walk into the Shadowthorn..." the next recruit starts. "Oh wait. There's no blighted way a mage would quit pissing himself long enough to venture across the dark border!"

More laughter dances around us, robust and corpulent. One after another, the recruits share their unflattering puns and witticism, discovering a bond over a common hatred for the magic-users who abandoned our people so long ago. The laughter becomes so infectious that even some of the Crusaders, perched atop their horses, join in.

"What's a mage's favorite pastime?" one of them calls.

Many among us offer their answers.

"Tucking their tails between their legs."

"Leaving millions of people to die."

"Pissin' themselves!"

The uproar becomes so loud that the Crusader can't even finish his joke. Instead, we find solace in the warmth we find in comedy, if we can find none from the brutal winter environment.

"I've got one!" Maxwell sticks his finger in the air in declaration. "What do you call an ageless mage?" A brief interlude of silence passes, his eager eyes scanning us all. When none know the answer, and he can contain himself no longer, he shouts, "He's just called *M*!"

The recruits and Crusaders groan. The one nearest Maxwell, a big blond fella who looks as if he could swallow the young man whole and his stomach would *still* growl afterward, gives Maxwell a hefty shove in the shoulder.

He staggers sideways, bumping into the horse flanking him, before staggering backward and bumping into me.

"S-sorry," he mutters.

My logic and reasoning still stands. Babying him might be a comfort in the moment, but in the long term, it can only mean his death.

And yet... I still find myself grabbing his elbow to steady him. "It's all right. The joke was..."

He ducks his head, embarrassed. "It was pretty bad. I know. I was never really any good with jokes. People tend to be more likely to laugh *at* me, rather than with me."

Dimitri slaps his shoulder heartily. "Don't worry. Spend enough time with this lot, and something tells me you'll be cracking jokes as good as any of them by the time we're through."

"You really think so?"

Dimitri turns toward me so that Maxwell can't see him and winks. "Sure! I don't see why not."

It doesn't take long for the solemn, wearied hush to reclaim the group once again. If anyone had known that transportation wouldn't have been provided, I'm sure most of the others would've brought horses and mules with them, if not to ride themselves, to at least bear the brunt of hauling the lives they packed into their bags.

It seems cruel to force us to wear out the soles of our shoes while the actual Crusaders sit atop their steeds. They could've easily brought a carriage, and I'm sure they have horses at the castle that they could've spared. It's like they're doing this just to torture us, like hiking through this grueling weather is supposed to do anything but piss us off.

Not that I needed any more reasons to scowl at Alphonse's backside; I have a lifetime of childhood memories to choose from:

Alphonse shoving me down to the ground and rubbing my head into mud to see if he could "wash away the tainted white" of my hair.

Alphonse claiming that when my parents die, he will inherit everything they own because me and my siblings are heathens and no heathen can own Arcathainian property.

Alphonse telling me I should go back to where I came from, even though I was born and raised in Arcathain, not the Forgotten Forest of Eyve.

Alphonse spitting in my face.

Alphonse spitting in my food.

Alphonse—

"You better watch the tone of your eyes." Dimitri's warning startles me back into the present.

I shift my scowl to him only to meet his glare and rise to the challenge he's laid out for me.

"You don't know what he's like," I argue, sounding petulant even to myself.

"Not this again." Dimitri throws his head back with a throaty groan. "I already told you, Halira. It doesn't matter what he *was* like, or what he *is* like, what he *did* or *didn't* do. Arcathain is full of assholes, and sometimes those assholes have more power over you. It doesn't matter how much we hate them or want to see them suffer for the way they've made us suffer. There are rules and we must abide by them."

Without even needing to mention the specifics, I know exactly who he's talking about, the rules he's thinking of, and once more do I feel the pang in my chest for his losses. When his mother died, he and his sister both decided to enlist in the Shadow Crusade together to avenge her. But unbeknownst to them, the Magistrate had recently set a new age requirement for recruits, after seeing one too many young souls be lost to the Shadowthorn.

Since Dimitri was still only fourteen at the time, he was denied signing his name on the log, but his sister had already written hers down. To this day, he still blames himself for her death most of all, if not his entire family's.

He'd wanted to enlist with her, even then, but the rules stated he needed to be nineteen first, and so he waited, long after his mother's death, long after his sister's, and a few more years after his father's, until he was finally of age and the Shadow Crusade recruits were paying another overdue visit to Gravenburg.

"Stand alive!" Alphonse calls over his black, gleaming shoulder plate, startling every last one of us to stillness.

If the hairs on the back of my neck could stand any more on end, they'd fall right from my skin, but the snow froze them days ago. My heart still pulses with warmth though, and so it has no problem leaping into my throat, pounding so fervently that I can't even swallow, can barely breathe.

"We are approaching the Shadowthorn," Alphonse informs us. "The Blight continues to spread; it blocks the path up ahead. We have to cross through if we are to reach the Castle of Nigh as planned."

"Can't we just go around it?" I blurt out, not even thinking twice. I know my cousin outranks me and that I should thereby heed his every command, but to me, he's still just the family I never cared for.

Dimitri's glare is like a hot iron to my face.

It's almost imperceptible, but even from this distance I can still see Alphonse's nostrils flare. "If you are so spine-lessness that you would rather add two weeks to your journey, skirting the edge of the Shadowthorn where demons can leap out at any point, rather than simply walking through it to reach the castle in two days' time, then by all means, *initiate*, take the scenic route. And while you're at it, perhaps you should reflect on your decision to join the Crusade, a legion of the bravest warriors, not cowards."

Cheeks burning, eyes raging, I bury my head as far down as it will go. If I had known the journey was that much longer, I wouldn't have suggested it.

"No? No smart retort? Are you quite sure?" Alphonse taunts, though he's not confident enough to give me too much time to respond. "Very well. Then, as I was saying, we go through the Shadowthorn. It is a short enough stretch of land, and the demons haven't yet noticed that the Blight has swallowed our path. They do not yet watch it like they do the border towns."

Alphonse motions for his men with a sweep of his arm. The horses that were leading us disperse. Two trot ahead, while the others circle back, two taking to the rear, and a few on either side until the new recruits and myself have at least one Crusader nearby for protection.

I watch the man next to me, large and bulbous, with unruly hair atop his head and chin. He's the one that joined in on our jokes. He's also one of the ones who didn't have the markings on his face, but now I watch him reach up to a vial hanging from his neck. His hands are so large that they look like they'd break the glass if they tried opening it, but somehow, he manages to pop the lid off. A brush comes out with the lid, coated in inky black, and he presses it to his forehead.

Twisting from where I stand, I watch the other Crusaders do the same. They mark their faces with a cross on their forehead, a trail resembling tears beneath each eye, and a single line down their chins.

"As long as you keep up, you will be flanked by a Crusader on every side and therefore safe. But I do suggest you keep up. We need to be swift. There's no reason to meander through the Shadowthorn and accidentally draw the suspicions of any nearby shadowcreatures."

Alphonse flicks his reins. His horse whinnies helplessly, clearly distressed about venturing so close to the Shadowthorn. But Alphonse ignores him, as do the other Crusaders, and they press forward, across the black stain that marks the stolen, blighted earth.

Since Dimitri and I are near the rear of the group, we get to watch as one by one our future comrades step into the shadowed land, until all that's left to do is follow.

I practically tiptoe across, tentatively sliding my foot into shadowcreature domain. My boots reach the black soil, and I swear it's colder here, quieter. I'd heard that the Blight took everything in its path—squirrels, ferns, every flower imaginable—but I never realized just what that meant. How could I? From the outside, the Blighted land doesn't look very different, aside from the darkness. The trees still stand, the grass still sways in the spring. From the outside, it almost just looks like a fire blazed through, but even that isn't fully accurate. Fire destroys. The Shadowthorn takes what is there and turns it into darkness, toxin, death.

Unaware I'm doing it, I hold my breath. Others do the same, and I realize in a fit of injustice that this is wrong. No one enters the Shadowthorn without ink on their faces, and none of these Crusaders even offered us any.

"You can stop holding your breath," Alphonse calls softly over his shoulder. His voice has lost its bravado. There's no show left in him here, only survival. "The Shadowthorn isn't poisonous to breathing. Just be wary of any fiends you might see. Believe nothing you see or hear."

We continue to creep along the trail, black trees arched overhead, black rocks beneath our shoes, black grass bedded along the forest floor. It feels like walking through a dream, a nightmare, like I've forgotten how to see color.

When I glance to Dimitri beside me, his sage-green eyes are the only indicator that I'm wrong. All of this is real. I know because the same fear is reflected in them, and I trust his judgment better than my own.

My heart thrums louder against my chest, and I worry that it is a pounding drum that will signal the demons for dinner. I didn't expect to be entering the Shadowthorn so soon. We haven't even had a day of training yet, haven't even picked out our shadowsteel weapons.

My hand grasps for my brother's dagger and holds tight. If I learned anything from the night my parents were killed, it's that I don't have any idea of how to fight, but feeling the leather hilt in my hand is reassuring enough. It beats being completely defenseless. If any demon strikes, at least I will go down swinging, slicing through as many as I can before I take my final breath.

"We'll be all right," Dimitri whispers, his voice harsh and

low. "They wouldn't bring us through here if it wasn't safe. We're more important."

I have half a mind to argue the opposite, that we are utterly dispensable, but even my argumentative self can realize that now is not the time, and it's definitely not the place.

Up ahead, Alphonse stretches his arm out. There are too many bodies between me and him, and I'm too short to see over any of them anyway, but I think he's pointing at our exit.

Salvation is just ahead. We only need to make it a little farther.

Really, this hasn't been too bad. I expected my first trip through the Shadowthorn to be filled with a brutal battle with bloodthirsty demons whose teeth were as sharp as splintered bones and eyes as red as blood. Maybe that's why Alphonse brought us this way. Maybe the whole point is to embolden us and show us that there is nothing to fear from—

A scream pierces the cold, dense air. We halt as one, every single member of our party.

An unsettling silence settles once more, denser, stiller. It's so quiet that even from this distance, I can make out the conversation being exchanged in whispers between Alphonse and one of the Crusaders.

"Could be one of our own."

"This far from Nigh?" Alphonse hisses. "Doubtful."

"Could be a local," the Crusader suggests. "Sometimes they wander back into the Blight to return to their homes, even when they know they shouldn't."

"If they are such incredible fools, then they deserve to perish." Alphonse spits to the black earth. "Besides, it's likely just those *heathens* from the Forgotten Forest of Eyve again, come to attempt another robbery on the catacombs for our ink."

He glances to me when he says the word *heathens*, and I feel heat rise to my cheeks, almost steaming against the cold chill of the air.

Beneath him, his horse's feet dance like the poor creature thinks it's standing atop flame. Alphonse jerks the reins hard, turns his back to the screams that continue to sound in the distance, and repositions the both of them to facing north, in the direction of Nigh.

"Let them rot," he sneers before ushering his steed forward.

As we follow in tow, my gaze trails off into the distance, and I wonder what I'd find there deep inside the Shadowthorn. I think about the *heathens* being attacked, the ones I feel more kinship toward than the cousin I've known my whole life. I wonder what their lives have been like, living in the Forgotten Forest of Eyve, or if, like my mother, they lived elsewhere in Arcathain when the Blight came. I wonder what their last moments will be like, surrounded by fiends who toy with their minds and demons who feast upon their flesh.

Then I wonder if they'll be deceived as I was, by a demon mysteriously guising itself as a man. Will they cry out to him for help before he sinks his teeth into the meat of their necks?

And the longer I stare into the shadowed forest, through the black branches and grey leaves, the more I start to see *him* everywhere, the more I start to see my parents' bleeding corpses.

If Dimitri hadn't come when he did, it's very likely that the shadowcreature I'd encountered would've done more than simply make me see it as partially human. I could've been lured into the Shadowthorn and been fed on for days. Worse, I could've become a blood offering for Qaeus.

Blinking, I spin back around, and fix my attention to the backs of the heads of my fellow initiates. A shiver runs down my spine when the last shriek is cut short, like the night air has been cleaved in two. I let fear fill the space, absorb it like it is the oxygen I need to breathe and the food I need to survive.

There are only three things I know for certain:

One: whoever was being attacked—whether Arcathainian, Eyvi, mage, raven, or whatever—they are dead now.

Two: they were killed by demons, or whatever other creatures lurk deep in the Shadowthorn.

And three: all demons are evil and deserve to die.

ARRIVAL

CASTLE OF NIGH, ARCATHAIN

The sun hangs red in the black sky, pierced only by the sharp, gothic spires of the castle.

It is a fortress of tall, pointed towers of the darkest shades of the ocean. The black slits of windows seem to bleed shadow and gloom, proof that this place has stood and weathered the tests of time. But it is unlike any castle I've ever seen. I'm used to the small chapel back in Gravenburg, the one that couldn't even fit all of the residents of the Wallows inside, it was so small. But this place…it's not just a castle—it's an entire city. There must be a hundred rooms spanning dozens of acres. There's an entire section that's already been consumed by the Shadowthorn. The black shingles of the rooftop are caved in there, that section of the building exceptionally darker than the rest, looking as if it has sunk to the bottom of an ocean.

Perhaps more than anything else I've seen this close to the Shadowthorn, the Castle of Nigh looks like death awaits us here.

Stone gargoyles perch on the long balustrade leading up to the gates, but I'm not sure what they're meant to be guarding. The small stone residence that crumbled to ruins behind them?

The barren land that cracks beneath our feet, despite the Blight not having reached this area yet? The Crusaders who dwell inside who will likely be dead within the year?

As we march closer, the tall spires loom overhead like they're passing judgment and I'm not sure I'll be allowed to enter. Who am I but a fletcher's daughter, a beekeeper in training? My only experience with fighting or anything close to it was reaching for my brother's dagger when my parents were attacked.

Then again, I look to my company; to Maxwell, the frail-seeming young man who never stops talking; to the drunk who never once shared his name or much of anything about his past, drowning it instead in the booze he smuggled for the journey; to the red-haired thief and the other prisoners who are only here because they had no other option. My guess is that this place gave up on passing judgment a long time ago. It accepts the sorry souls it can take. Even the orphaned daughters and sons of fletchers and butchers.

Alphonse hops off his horse, handing the reins to a Crusader of lower status at the gate. The others in our company do the same, though many of them accompany their own steeds into the crumbled stables that I'd mistaken for ruins earlier. One of the Crusaders sees to the prisoners who've traveled all this way in a dingy cart beside us. Their new life, their new *freedom*, is about to begin.

The initiates don't falter in keeping up with our general. Being so close to our destination—to actually sleeping on a bed instead of in tents less than a few yards away from danger—has invigorated all of us. They hasten their paces to keep up with Alphonse, Dimitri and I following close behind.

Alphonse pushes the tall, wooden doors wide and enters.

Inside, I'm even more convinced of this place's magnitude. We do not enter into a cramped hovel like the homes I'm accustomed to entering, but instead into an expansive foyer with a dozen options for where to go next: stairways and door-ways, hallways and nooks. Despite my lethargy, I want to explore them all. If given the opportunity, I imagine it would take days just to see the south quarter of this castle, at least a week to explore the rest of the place that hasn't been taken by the Blight yet.

"The men will follow me," Alphonse says, hands clasped at his lower back, never once deigning us a glance. "The women will head through the west wing. Follow the runner and it'll lead you to your dormitory. Anyone uncomfortable with either of those options can feel free to sleep outside for all I care."

He's moving again, heading up the stairs without even ensuring the male recruits are following after him. Dimitri and I only have half a second to glance at each other before he, too, is scurrying up the stairs. It's the first time I've realized how much I don't want to be left alone, and the first time I've admitted to myself that it might've attributed to why I left Gravenburg.

I don't like that realization though, nor do I much appre-ciate it coming to me now. It makes me feel weak and aimless, like some pathetic puppy who has no real sense of self or purpose beyond what she projects onto others. It would mean that everything Kalli said about me is true, that I never had any drive of my own, no vision or goals. No passion.

That changes now. If ever there was a motivation, it is avenging my fallen family.

Twisting away from the wide staircase that splits in two directions, I focus instead on the west wing. None of the other female recruits have moved toward it yet, giving me the perfect opportunity to prove to myself that I am more than just someone who followed Dimitri blindly into this thing. I *want* to be here. I *want* to be a Crusader. And most above all: right now, I really want to find my bed.

I walk through the archway and into the west wing. It's

nearly pitch-black in here, like I imagine it is in all of the rooms currently not in use. Fortunately, given what little light comes in through the foyer and the single gated window, I find an oil lamp on the table and light it.

By the time I spin back around to locate the crimson runner Alphonse had mentioned, the rest of the female recruits are standing behind me, expectant, silent. The entire journey here, not a single one of them ever struck me as the kind to feel fear. The thief acted like her predicament was almost comical; the tall, mysterious woman with raven hair carries herself like she's seen more suffering than can even faze her anymore; even a girl who seems far too young to be here has never cowed, never broken into sobbing tears because of the life that's led her here. There are others too, a half dozen or so, who carried themselves through the snowstorm like they were shards of ice themselves.

But now, standing in the candlelit room, shadows dancing on each of their faces, I can see it as clear as the skies uninhibited by the Shadowthorn's darkness. The regret. The terror. None of us would've chosen to be here if we didn't think we had to be.

And yet, here we find ourselves.

A silent understanding crosses over the room, one that is the start of what I hope will be a long sense of comradery.

"Let's see what we've got ourselves into," I say to them all, warranting a few chuckles before going into the next corridor.

Alphonse was right. The runner he instructed us to follow stops directly before a door at the end of the next hallway. Part of me is a little uneasy to know that there is a direct path marked on the floor from the front entrance leading to our rooms, but I can't afford to let that unnerve show now.

I twist the iron doorknob and push the door wide. It opens to a room with more doors. I step into the center, looking for the rug but finding that it will provide no more guidance. It ends at the door of the cold, eerily silent room. The others trickle in to stand beside me.

My confusion must be obvious because the raven-haired woman steps forward first and looks to me, something that is both thrilling and terrifying, to know that I have already gained such trust and respect.

"This is a dormitory," she says, her voice like liquid fire. "Some of these rooms will have open beds. Others won't. Hopefully it's obvious which are which."

The red-haired thief is first to open any of them, but her curiosity emboldens some of the others. We split into smaller groups. I follow the thief, feeling a sort of connection toward her for how sharply she spoke of my cousin. The raven-haired woman follows behind us.

"Holy Blight!" the thief exclaims, walking through the room lined with beds on either side. "This room's almost entirely empty. I mean, right? I don't see bags, or shoes, or anything."

Nodding, I glance around the room. My eyes rove over the dozens of empty cots, the ones with unruffled bedsheets and pillows without head imprints. I wonder if these rooms have ever been full, if the recruits die too swiftly to keep them stocked, or if they've simply been promoted and moved on to guard one of the border towns.

Behind me, the raven-haired woman sits rim-rod straight on the first bed just inside the doorway. She stares at the wall, utterly silent, just as she has been for most of the journey here. From this angle, though I can only see the dark hair spilling down her back, for days now I've recognized the ghost of memories haunting her. She's been like this ever since we left Gravenburg, and though I can't say for certain, I believe she might've been one of the few survivors of Ashenvale, come searching for refuge.

I turn back around to the sound of the thief plopping onto a bed with a leap and a sigh. She lays down, arms crossed behind her fiery hair. There are at least another twenty beds available, and I could easily take one at the end of the room and put great distance between me and either of them, but the last thing I want right now is to be alone.

"Mind if I take this one?" I ask her, pointing to the bed diagonal from hers.

"Go for it," she says. "If you don't mind sleeping close to a pickpocket, then I don't mind sleeping close to a girl from the Wallows."

Such a thing could be an insult coming from certain people's lips, but on hers it sounds more playful than anything.

"I don't think a thief would have much interest in me anyway. I didn't bring anything with me."

She props her elbows beneath her and watches me as I, too, sit on my cot. Something glints from the loose neckline of her tunic, but I avert my eyes when she readjusts her collar to conceal whatever she has hidden there. "I *had* noticed that. From my *cage*. Everyone else packed their entire lives, but you only had that ragged cloak. I thought maybe that guy you were walking with was carrying all of your stuff."

"Dimitri? No." I laugh. "He had enough baggage to carry for himself."

She chortles too. "Yeah, for someone leaving the Wallows, he had quite a bit with him. Where did he think he was going? On holiday?"

I shrug and give her a rueful smile. "When you have little to nothing left, I guess it's hard to leave any of it behind."

She becomes reflective, her nod knowing and all too telling of the circumstances that led her to a life of petty theft.

"My name is Foxlynn," she says abruptly. "But you can call me Fox."

I nod by way of greeting. "I'm Halira."

"Nice to meet you." She throws herself back against her

pillow with another long sigh. "Tell me, Halira, did you always want to join the glorious Shadow Crusade?"

I scoot back along my cot until I'm pressed against the pillow and the headboard. To lie down fully would feel too… comfortable for a place I still don't recognize as my new home.

"Not really," I tell her. "When I was younger, I guess I pretended I did. But then, you grow up. You realize it's not the heroic, valiant cause that you fantasized it being, and you decide that—"

"You decide that you'd rather live a life of running away from danger than one of running toward it," she finishes for me. Staring into the rafters, she laughs, a small, sad sound. "I always told myself that if it ever came down to the choice between my freedom or my life, I'd choose to die a free woman. But, when the Crusaders told me it was either I lose my hands or I join them…I guess I wasn't as fearless as I thought I was."

Nodding, I look across the room to the other woman. She hasn't moved since we got here, hasn't shrugged off her cloak or leaned back into the warmth her bed might provide.

"What about you?" I ask her. "What brings you here?"

Her head twitches toward the sound of my voice, almost imperceptibly, but her breathing, she has no control over. It hastens almost instantly.

Fox lifts herself back onto her elbows and tries a softer approach. "You don't have to tell us your life story. What's your name?"

Still, the woman says nothing. Silence settles over us like a heavy blanket, one that could suffocate if twisted the wrong way. In the rooms on either side of us, I listen to the other girls getting settled. They choose their cots just like we did, talk about their hopes shrouded in fear, share their names, the places they came from.

"Come on," Fox says, this time sitting all the way up. "If

we're going to be sharing a room together, the least you could do is—"

"Silver," the woman says, her voice as smooth as her name. Abruptly she stands, back still to us, and makes for the door.

"Where are you going?" Fox calls after her. "The general told us to go to our dorms. Don't you think we should—"

Silver looks over her shoulder, most of her face still shrouded by her hood. "Someone has come to retrieve us. We are to head to the dining hall."

Fox and I exchange a brief, worrying glance. There are rumors that mages and other mystical beings still exist among us. Without knowing any personally, my knowledge of what they're capable of is limited, but I imagine it could include things like foresight and premonition. But I've never heard of any mages being so open about their magic. Arcathainians hate two things with equal fervor: demons and the bastards who let us rot here when they fled with half of the continent.

At the same moment Fox and I both open our mouths, Silver adds, "I overheard them while you two were settling. They're at the next room over. They'll be here any—"

A Crusader, clad in black leather, appears in the doorway on cue.

"You are expected in the dining hall at high noon," he says. "I am to take you there. If you miss your escort, you won't be fed until next meal, so I suggest you get a move on things in here."

He exits, Silver following right behind him, and as I look to Fox, we both shrug, before scurrying after them.

DARK CORRIDOR

CASTLE OF NIGH, ARCATHAIN

It would be all too easy to get lost in these halls. The Castle of Nigh turns out to be quite the labyrinth inside, with enough winding corridors and dimly lit rooms that I feel like a rat set loose in an experiment.

I hear the dining hall before we arrive.

A raucous booming sound of commotion propels us farther down each darkened hallway, each corner, and through every door. It is the only remnant of life that I've seen here yet, the only telling that those of us who've found themselves desperate enough to come here still have a chance at survival.

The doors are propped wide by the time we arrive, and so the Crusader simply leads us into the dining hall. It's not as massive as I expected. Endlessly long tables are lined in mostly neat rows and crammed side by side in the small, stout room. The people sitting at them—what seems to easily be a hundred Crusaders—can barely stand up or sit down, or grab their forks without knocking elbows and backing into each other. Half of the riotous sounds we heard on our way down here seem to have been squabbles over who hit who, the other half-crass jokes and immature diversions.

Truth be told, I didn't expect to see so many Crusaders here. I thought once they finished their training, they were sent to guard the Shadowthorn border, or sent into the Blighted lands to search for Qaeus' whereabouts. But I suppose this place *is* rather sprawling. It likely takes most of them just to maintain the upkeep, let alone the ones who would need to guard the borders and ensure the safety of the initiates as they train.

We continue following the Crusader as he makes his way to the front of the hall to the display of food. It's no banquet fit for the Magistrate, but it's a far cry from the scraps my family was accustomed to eating. The table is loaded with too many foods to count, too many scents that I've never dared think about for fear of torturing myself. A steaming pot of peasant stew, another of beef. In the center, there's a cascading mound of freshly baked dinner rolls that have tumbled halfway across the table because someone grabbed one too greedily from the pile and upset the delicate balance at play. My eyes rove over the peaches and pears and grapes. My mouth waters at the fried cheese and roasted lamb.

"Dig in," the Crusader says, gesturing us forward. Then he points to the back corner of the room, to an empty section of the table. "When you've gathered what's to your liking, new recruits sit back there."

Fox practically shoves me aside and stumbles forward, grasping for one of the stacked plates. Some of the others with us join her, far too exhausted and hungry to care about anything as seemingly useless as manners right now.

But my eyes are trained on the back table. I see no signs of Dimitri, nor of any of the male recruits Alphonse took with him, and I feel the slick, greasy feeling of fear taking hold in my gut. I try convincing myself I have nothing to worry about. If Alphonse was going to do something awful to anyone, it would've been to me. But the longer I stare at the empty table, and then to the open doors where there is an absent of newcomers flowing into the hall, the more I start to worry.

"Eat," says a silken voice behind me.

I turn around to find Silver, two plates in hand. She extends one of them toward me.

"Don't worry about your friend. The male dormitory is farther than the female's."

Sensing the opportunity to connect with her better than I had in our own room, I summon a grateful smile and grab the plate from her. "How do you know that? Have you been here before?"

She shakes her head. "It is a simple deduction. When we arrived, it was mostly the women Crusaders sitting at the tables, while the men still clambered about for their seats. The women had been here longer because it took them less time to arrive."

Scooping some herbed potatoes onto my plate, I look up at her. "You have a keen eye, don't you?"

She reaches for a roll, the first thing she's grabbed so far, and what appears to be the only thing she plans on taking. I hear her words without her even having to say them. Whatever her past, whatever horrible heartache that brought her to this very place, she learned the value of staying alert at all times.

As I finish loading my plate with every mouthwatering, savory starch and meat I can fit, Silver walks quietly to the table in the back and takes a seat. The others and I join her, just as another group enter the dining hall. Spying Dimitri's muddied face among the others is enough to settle my stomach long enough to dig in.

"Scoot," Dimitri says after he's piled enough potatoes and pigeon on his plate that the thing looks too heavy to carry.

I smile at his wobbling hand. "Thanks for bringing me seconds. Now I don't have to get back up—"

When I reach for a roll, he swats my hand away. "Not for a mage's dying wish," he chastises. "Go get your own."

Rolling my eyes, I return to my food. The other male recruits squeeze their way down the line between the tightly packed tables and join us one by one.

"So, what are your rooms like?" I ask Dimitri.

He waits until he's done chewing to answer me, not noticing the dribble of soup that's hanging from the scruff on his chin. "Packed, as you'd expect seeing the dining hall."

I glance out over the sea of black leather. Most of the conversations have dwindled as the Crusaders have turned their hungry attention to their plates, but where they continue, they're still loud and animated. Though there are some women among them, it's difficult not to notice that we are obviously in the minority. I think most young girls grow up still longing for marriage, to start families of their own, so I imagine when given the choice, many decide to try their luck at outrunning the Blight rather than fighting inside it.

"You?" Dimitri asks.

I take another bite of my roll and shrug. "More spacious than your accommodations, from the sounds of it. It's just me, Fox, and Silver in our room." I indicate to the women sitting at our end of the table.

Fox waves with her pigeon leg bone.

Silver acts as if she doesn't even hear us.

"You're that thief we saw in the square." Dimitri juts his chin at her before turning protectively back to me. "You better watch your back, Halira. She's only here because she was too cowardly to face the consequences of her own actions."

"Dimitri!" I quietly hiss. I'm too shocked by his rudeness too say much else, too embarrassed that the new friend I was trying to make has almost definitely overheard him.

Fox doesn't appear to have the same problem with being struck speechless. She slams her hands against the table, drawing silence throughout the room. Judging from the curious glances cast her way, I'm guessing it's not unusual for spats and squabbles to take place here, but instead it's seen as one of the limited sources of entertainment. The other Crusaders watch with mouths full of food, glee sparking in their eyes.

As she stands, already the flare of rage in her has simmered into something more mocking, more challenging. It's exactly the kind of thing that I know gets under Dimitri's skin.

"Call me a coward all you like," she says coolly. "But might I remind you that fear is what brought all of us here. So to call me a coward is to call every Crusader and initiate one, including your arrogant self, so don't act like you're better than me or any of us."

A vein pulses on Dimitri's temple and he, too, springs up, half-cocked. "Don't fool yourself into thinking you're anyone's equal here. I worked for everything I owned. You stole the hard-earned goods and wares from people like me. I'm here for duty, to protect Arcathain from evil. You're here for your own selfish exoneration."

"Dimitri, stop," I say, tugging on his arm. He shrugs it out of my grasp.

"You really oughta listen to your girl," calls a man from across the table. He's sitting a few seats down from Fox, and I recognize the slur that parts his lips as he hovers over a chalice, his lips stained red. "Is arguing over the value of our past lives really worth more than eating a warm meal in peace, right now, of all nights?"

Dimitri's nostrils flare. It's been a long and grueling journey. We're all testier than we would be under normal circumstances.

The large man beside him reaches his sausage-like fingers up, grasps Dimitir's tense shoulder, and shoves him down hard enough to rock the entire bench.

"Sit. Eat," the large man says, a thick accent making his words sound barbaric.

Begrudgingly, Dimitri does as he's told, finally peeling his malicious gaze away from Fox.

"Roommates of yours?" I ask, indicating to the large man and the drunk.

He glowers at me. "Better than yours."

"She doesn't seem that bad," I tell him. "It wasn't too long ago you were in a position where you had to rely on quick hands to make ends meet."

He scoffs. "I labored for every piece of bread or apple anyone ever gave me. It wasn't stealing. It was an exchange. They needed the orchards tended, the dough meaded. I worked for my share." There's more venom in his voice for the last part as he glares across the table to Fox.

I lean my face into view to block his gaze. "Can we not do this right now? You don't see me antagonizing your roommates."

He snorts a laugh. "That's because you couldn't even if you tried. Güthric here," he says, patting the large man's shoulder beside him, "joined the Shadow Crusade for the same reasons we did."

"We fight!" Güthric growls, spitting a mouthful of half-chewed food across the table as he bangs his fist against the dark oak.

It's the first thing that has caught Silver's attention, who looks over at him with a scowl of disgust. I can't tell if it's the fact that shredded bits of lamb are now dangling from his yellow beard, or if she's irritated that the chalice beside her was rocked so thoroughly by his hammering that it splashed her and tinged her hand pink.

Whatever the reason, she scoots out from the bench at the end of the table. "Excuse me," she says, addressing us all. "It's been a long journey, and I'd like to rest since I have no more appetite."

Out of the corner of my eye, I think I see Güthric flinch, deflating like a scolded child.

"I'll be in the room should anyone need me."

"Yeah," Fox adds. "This has been fun and all, but I think I've had my fill too. We'll see you later, Halira, that is, assuming you're still willing to share a room with a cold-blooded apple thief."

She winks at me before turning her back to us.

Dimitri tenses at the jab, and I grab his arm again.

"I don't like you sleeping in the same room with her," he says through gritted teeth.

"It's really not that bad. She's nice, Dimitri. I like her."

He scoffs, a noise that has the habit of grating beneath my skin.

I roll my eyes, but still try to maintain my calm. "Besides, it's not like I brought anything of value with me for her to steal."

He looks to my waist and the most valuable possession I have that's tucked under the table. "What about your shadow-steel? That dagger could go for a fortune on the black market."

Heat rises up my neck at the thought, at the mere suggestion that anyone would dare take away the only thing left of my brother. But I can't afford to allow my rage to grow. When Dimitri and I both become volatile, things aren't good.

I swallow hard, the muscle in my jaw so tight that the motion is difficult to make. "That wouldn't happen. I carry it with me, always. And I'll sleep with it as well. If anyone even tries, I'll…"

The end of that sentence feels alarmingly brutal compared to the conversations I was having only a few weeks ago, about the honey harvest, repairing my family's cloaks for the winter, how much grain we could purchase the next time we went to the market. But I suppose this is my life now, one of ruthless killing without a second thought, and I'd better get used to it. Doubt might be the end of me once we're inside the Shadowthorn.

When I finally muster the courage to finish what I was saying, I turn to Dimitri, expecting to find him still full of conviction and hatred. Instead, he's shaking his head.

"No…you're right," he says, shocking me thoroughly. He closes his sage-green eyes, his fist tightening where it lay atop the table. "I don't have to like her, but she is an initiate, a potential Crusader, and therefore, I have to tolerate her. We are here to put an end to the Primordial and its demon spawn, not the pick fights with other Crusaders. Of one country, of one blood."

I have to suppress the urge to roll my eyes, especially seeing as how Dimitri has finally resettled. Seeing such disrespect toward the Shadow Crusade's mantra will only reawaken his rage.

"I should probably turn in as well. It's been a long week."

I expect him to be more suspicious, more judgmental. After all, it's still midday, and the way we were raised, I shouldn't be hitting my bed until well after dark. But without having any explicit commands from anyone, it appears that I can do with my day what I like, and after the grueling trek north, there is nothing more I'd like than to lay beneath the warm blankets of a bed. And apparently, Dimitri understands my inclination enough to simply nod his farewell.

Like my dormmates before me, I clear out of the dining hall to put some distance between the two of us. It's not rare for us to have spats like these. It seems to come with the territory of being lifelong friends who both have their tempers. But the days—the *weeks*—have been too long. I don't have the patience to deal with him and the many topics we disagree on tonight.

Instead, I spend the next few hours trying to find my dorm.

Admittedly, I should've asked for an escort or something before I'd left the hall, considering I knew even when we arrived that I wouldn't be able to find my way back on my own.

My home had been a small, cozy, three-roomed cottage consisting of only the living space, my parents' bedroom, and the room I slept in with Tor and Kalli before they grew of age and set out on their own.

But the Castle of Nigh is endless. The tight corridors and dark staircases run under and over each other like they are a tangled spool of the cords my mother used to use to make the wicks of her candles. They are an ever-dizzying maze that feels impossible to make sense of, but also too alluring to turn away from.

I work my way deeper into my hopeless lostness and into the castle, forgetting all notions of whatever turmoil I'd walked away from in the dining hall and instead giving myself over to the opportunity for exploration. The same thrill that used to overcome me as a child as I roamed the forests invigorates me now as well. I discover rooms stacked high with leatherbound books, atriums where flora blooms despite the darkness that surrounds the exotic flowers.

When I find the classrooms where I assume we will do our studies, I try to take a mental note of its location, but without my bearings of the sun, it's no use. I need to find a window so I can see the shadows on the ground outside and figure out if I'm facing north, east, south, or west. Only then will I be able to find my way back.

The farther I explore, the more deserted the hallways and lounges become. Even though lunch had been served, when I was still within the proximity of the dining hall, a few Crusaders had still roamed the hallways on duty or were performing their respective tasks: carrying armor to the launders, sweeping the hallways. It didn't go past me that we would be spending our days here doing much the same. How else would such an expansive place be taken care of?

But as the sounds of the dining hall faded, as the candlelight flooded the deeper halls less and less, I've become keenly aware of my isolation.

The corridor I turn down next is draftier than the others. Not a single torch is lit on either wall, so I hold the lantern I'd taken from one of the lounges up higher.

The darkness breathes against me, making the flame flicker and the hairs on my arms stand on end.

My stomach fills with fluttering moths. I tell myself I should turn around, but the more sensible side of my inner voice tells me I'm being ridiculous. I already know what lays behind me and it isn't my dormitory. If I'm ever to find it, I need to keep exploring, keep pressing on.

I suck in a breath and start walking down the black hall. My lantern flickers, casting shadows all around me and making it seem almost as if the hallway is twisting right out from underneath me.

Unlike the other corridors, the doors in this section are closed, making the hall appear even longer and narrower than it really is. Something tells me not to open any of the doors here, but I also know I can't just stand here and hope for the dormitory to appear out of nowhere. Any of these doors could lead to the corridor that will finally lead me back to my warm cot, and so, I have no choice but to try them all.

The first iron doorknob doesn't budge.

Frowning, I got to the next one to find that it, too, is locked.

I hold my lantern out to see farther down the hallway. Now more than ever I want to turn back. Now more than ever every sense of my being is telling me that something is wrong. I'm somewhere I shouldn't be and that could end very badly if the wrong person found me.

But my light catches on something up ahead that I can't pull away from, a vague mass that I can't quite make out.

I tell myself that I'm just going to go as far as the vague mass ahead and then turn back, just far enough to see what it is that's drawing me forward, and then I'll return to the dining hall and ask for help if I have to—if I can find my way back there.

I take a shaking step forward, the lantern trembling in my grip. My boots echo through the eerily quiet with each cautious step.

Finally, I find what I've been staring at.

Cherrywood chairs are stacked on top of one another. Not in the organized fashion of someone who had wanted to store them for the next large banquet, but in a manner that looks more like they were thrown down the corridor to be used as the base of a bonfire. Dozens of them, cast aside to create a feeble wall that separates this part of the complex from the next. Almost as if someone was trying to build a wall out of them.

Only, it's not a perfect seal…

Some of the chairs have been torn away, blown apart until all that was left are shattered chair legs and splinters.

Dread thunders in my chest.

I hold the lantern up higher. Blackness touches everything on the other side of the barricade. The flowers in the tall vases have withered where they stand, if they still stand at all. Glass from the mirror on one wall is shattered over the runner carpeting this corridor, the color of which I can't tell, even with the light. There's too much darkness. Farther still, the floor has caved in, the wallpaper tearing and curling like it's been singed off the walls in a great fire. But the air does not smell charred here. No, the air smells cold and earthy.

Worst of all, I swear I hear the hissing whispers of the fiends who are sure to be lurking in the darkness.

I realize with sinking horror that I've stumbled onto the Blighted section of the castle, the one I'd spotted earlier as we were approaching the gates.

I take a stumbling, hasty step backward, lantern still extended high. I keep moving, keep walking backward with my eyes trained on the dark, gaping holes between the chairs, not daring to glance away, but wanting to leave this dreadful place as quickly as I can.

For the first time, I realize my boots are crunching beneath me like the rug is crisp, not soft as a rug should be, and it's all too obvious that I have inadvertently stumbled into the Shadowthorn itself.

The Blight must've crept farther since whoever fortified this section of the castle. I wonder if anyone knows yet about the gaping hole in their barricade.

Suddenly, my back slams into something solid. I stiffen, my heart hammering its way up into my throat.

I can't swallow; I can't breathe. Fear has sunk its claws too deeply, rooting me to the floor.

Like a hawk diving through the sky, my hand darts for my dagger. My fingers grip around the hilt and tear it free, but just as I'm about to spin around and drive my blade into the fleshy mass behind me, someone gasps.

"Whoa, hold on there," the young woman says as I snap around to face her, the dagger gleaming in the space between us while I hoist my lantern overhead. "I-I didn't mean to scare you. I just thought you might need some help finding your way back."

I don't recognize her voice, but I don't need to for warm relief to flood through me. Human. She is human, all the way from the roots of the dark, coarse hair that cascades in waves down her back, to the caramel tips of her fingers, to the black leather boots that match the rest of her Crusader armor.

Her smile is pleasant and warm. "You looked lost," she says, smiling sympathetically. "My name is Eparah. You're one of the new recruits who arrived today, right?"

I don't respond. The dagger in my hand refuses to return to its hilt and instead remains pointed at the seemingly harmless woman before me. But the image of that demon-man comes to mind. Though he hadn't been able to disguise himself completely, I could no longer say with certainty that such a thing was impossible.

My skeptical gaze wanders up and down the woman who called herself Eparah. I take note of the sigil on her chest, purple like most of the Crusaders I've seen, but with a black mountain peak standing stark behind the white phoenix. If she is real, it would make her a captain, another member of the Shadow Crusade who outranks me and someone whom I should therefore *not* be pointing a blade at.

Just as I'm about to lower my weapon, I notice the shadow-steel sword she's rested atop her shoulder. It's no longer in an offensive position, but it's still accessible should she decide to use it, and I am the only person nearby to strike.

She notices my distressing stare upon it. "Oh, sorry." Eparah chuckles, lowering the sword to rest the tip of it on the runner beneath our feet instead. "Can't be too careful on this side of the castle. The Blight—well, I'm sure you've already noticed that it's taken over this part of the compound."

Looking down the dark hallway again, I position myself so that my back isn't turned to the abyss anymore. "It doesn't look like that barricade held. And the Blight has surpassed it."

"I know. *We* know. It's why there are some of us who still patrol this area."

Finally feeling a little more at ease, I sheath my dagger. We're quiet for a moment, the two of us watching the darkness as if it might strike back. It's far too quiet to be teeming with demons right now.

"The breach occurred about a month ago," Eparah says

solemnly. "The baths are near here. If you would've turned left instead of going this way, you would've reached them. When the demons flooded this section of the castle, it was right after sparring, while the female initiates were allotted their usual time to bathe. I'm sure you've noticed that your dorm was nearly completely empty upon arrival."

I turn back to her, my eyebrows a hard line as I listen to her answer the questions I hadn't even bothered to ask, hadn't even once truly considered. I listen now, horror-struck and confused.

"It's not always like that," she continues. "We get recruits from all over Arcathain. They arrive at varying times, enter various stages of training, and become initiated into the Crusade as units. There should've been others here when you all arrived, but instead, they were unfortunate enough to be caught indisposed when the demon scourge happened." She clears her throat. "We've since moved the baths to another room, on the other side of the castle. There aren't many who wander down this way anymore, unless they're on patrol, but even then, most of the patrolling Crusaders are kept outside."

She stops when she notices I'm shaking my head.

"I don't understand," I tell her. "If the Blight has taken over the castle, why are you still here? Why isn't this corridor guarded or cemented with brick and mortar?"

She opens her mouth to answer me, but snaps it closed instead. "Come on. We should get out of here. It's not forbidden, exactly, but it would be frowned upon for a recruit to be found this deep in the castle without explicit orders to be here."

She starts walking away, waving for me to follow. I have half a mind to argue and demand answers, but another breeze blows through the corridor, ushering me to follow after her instead.

Once the darkness is behind us and we find ourselves in a new hallway with ample torchlight, I ask my question again.

"Why doesn't the Crusade move elsewhere? It's just a matter of time before the entire castle is consumed. If demons can get inside, then we're in grave danger—"

"There is no danger here," she reassures me. "Or at least, none more than there is anywhere else along the border of the Shadowthorn."

I scoff, stopping in the middle of the hallway.

She halts only a step after me, shoulders tense as she watches me, assesses my stubbornness. "Try not to think about it. It's as I said, there are Crusaders posted on the outside perimeter of the castle, where the demons entered the first time. They protect anything from getting through—"

"They should cement that corridor shut," I growl.

"They have." She sighs, a melodic noise that's stretched and pretty rather than the annoyance I would've expected her to show me. She is a captain, after all. By no means does she have to listen to my suggestions. "But, you know how the Shadowthorn works. It keeps crawling. It takes time and resources to block every single corridor that it consumes, just for the demons to get through and the blackness to creep deeper into the castle anyway."

"Then we should leave," I say again.

Her voice becomes firm. "We can't."

"Why not?"

She shakes her head, her eyes flitting up and down the corridor on either side of us. "I've already said too much. We should get you back to—"

"Why can't we leave?"

Eparah groans and throws her head back. It's a rather immature expression, one that alludes to her younger nature, but is also odd to see on a commanding officer. She watches me for a moment, assessing whether or not I'll drop this, before peering down the hallway and yanking me closer.

"Because this is the final stand for the Shadow Crusade."

I can feel her warm breath on my ear and concern turns my expression rigid. "What do you mean? Our final stand as in—"

"As in, if we can't defeat the Primordial Qaeus from our most sacred landmark, we will be the laughingstock among the Magistrate's Legion. Not to mention, all of Arcathain will be lost because we'd have nowhere else to go, nowhere to train from. This is our last stance. Once the Castle of Nigh falls the Shadow Crusade is over."

Slowly, I straighten, mulling it all over. I've heard rumors about my uncle—*The Magistrate,* I mean—and his disdain for the Shadow Crusade. He inherited their oversight when he accepted his role as sovereign half a decade ago, but I think the only reason he's kept them in action is because they've been a beacon of hope for all of Arcathain for generations. However, with the Shadowthorn approaching the Castle of Nigh, it would be the perfect excuse to disband the Crusaders.

Eparah watches me with curious, dark eyes as I consider it all.

"Then," I say after what feels like a fortnight, "I guess we better take care of Qaeus."

A smile quirks up the side of her face. "I guess so. Come on. Let me show you the way back to your dorm."

As we make our way back through the drafty corridors and candlelit chambers, I take note of the rooms that are closest to the east quarter and make sure that I never wind up there again.

LET THE BEATING BEGIN

CASTLE OF NIGH, ARCATHAIN

My foot creaks on the floorboard as I enter the cottage. I can tell something's different the moment I enter, the way the air inside is stagnant and smells of something sick and syrupy. It doesn't take me long to find my parents' corpses, a raven sitting atop them. It squawks at me like it thinks *I'm* the one invading *its* territory.

"This is *my* home," I snarl, kicking at it with my foot. "Get off them!"

The raven does as it's told and blusters into the air, but it doesn't go far. When I take a knee to cradle my mother's head in my lap, I notice that the bird has perched itself atop the shelf by my head.

It screeches again—once, twice, incessantly—the grating sound reverberating through me and rattling my skull. Its cry is more than just the usual nuisance of an obnoxious bird. It leaves my ears ringing, blood seeming to pool inside them, and the pain becomes unbearable. I curl up into a ball beside my parents, and no matter how I rock myself, nor how firmly I place my hands over my ears, nothing seems to drown out the raven's ceaseless squawking.

Then abruptly, the raven stops.

Something heavier than silence befalls the small cottage, making my ears ring for entirely new reasons. Thoroughly exhausted from the pain, I rest there, my forehead pressed against the cold, slick floorboards.

At the same moment I realize the reason for their wetness, the blood I must be laying in, the floorboards rumble against my forehead with the slow rhythmic beat of footsteps.

I jerk upright, daring to look to see what horror is approaching me, but my eyes meet the demon man's, our noses almost grazing each other. He is exactly as I remember him: a human face with darkness creeping up the side of him.

I fumble for my dagger, finding the hilt empty. When I glance back up to him, he's grinning, sharp teeth stained with the blood of my parents.

The creature's mouth unhinges, and just as he sinks his teeth into my collarbone and tears me apart…

My eyes burst wide. Fox stands over me, her hands pushing against my collarbone to wake me.

"Come on. We're being summoned," she says, scowling at me with concern. "Gods, I thought you might be dead. You're impossible to wake, you know that?"

Bleary-eyed, I rub my face and try to sit up. There is a bundle of black leathers at the edge of my bed.

"Courtesy of the Shadow Crusade," Fox says, indicating to her own dark garb. "What do you think?"

Yawning, I nod. Bells toll somewhere in the distance and I wonder if they are to thank for the awful raven in my dream, as much as Fox's hands are to thank for the pressure still sinking into my chest.

Eager to break my cold sweat, I throw the blanket over the edge of the bed and swing my legs over. Silver is already gone from the room, her bedsheets tucked neatly under the mattress. Meanwhile, Fox hobbles down the center of the room, trying to squeeze her foot into her last boot.

"Come on! We're going to be late."

"Late for what?" I ask, still feeling groggy and disoriented from my fitful rest.

The dream had felt so real, and I wonder how many more will follow now that I've entered this line of work. Will I be plagued by every demon I encounter, or just the ones who wear human faces?

"For the first day of training, now come on. I can't be arriving without you. Who knows what that demented friend of yours would do?"

It takes me a moment to remember who she's talking about, the memory of my night with Crusader Eparah in the Blighted corridor too fresh in my mind. But slowly I'm able to drag the memories back up to the surface. "You mean Dimitri? He wouldn't hurt a fly."

She levels me a look that says she highly doubts that. "Wasn't he a butcher?"

I wince. "Well, he wouldn't hurt a *Crusader*, anyway."

"Let's not find out," she says.

Fox marches back to my bed, grabs the clothes laid out for me, and shoves them into my arms. I make quick work of slipping into them, cramming my feet into my boots as soon as she hands them to me. My shoes aren't even tied, and my cloak is only half on when she drags me out of the room.

"What time is it?" I ask as another yawn vacates me. "And where are we going?"

"I already told you. Those bells? That's the sound of the start of the rest of our pitiful lives. Everyone in the compound —be it Crusader, initiate, or even a Senator who's come to visit —that bell is a call to congregate."

"How do you know all this?" I ask, barely keeping up with her. My feet catch on a section of the rug where it's bunched up, but fortunately her grip tightens, catching me before I fall entirely.

She shrugs, smiling over her shoulder. "Because some of us were awake for breakfast when we were told what the day would look like."

"I missed breakfast?"

She nods.

"What else did I miss? What did they say? What will we be doing today?"

"Today we start our training as Crusaders," Fox says as we round the next corner.

She collides into someone's broad back. Even as I crash into her the moment after, even as my face is buried in her hair, it would be impossible to mistake Güthric for anyone but himself. He barely budges, hardly even seems to notice the two of us as we peel ourselves off him, joining the others who have bottlenecked at the door ahead as they try to file out of the castle.

While we wait, I start to recognize my surroundings, the wide staircase, the colorful painted windows that cast vibrant clouds of color onto the wooden planks beneath us, the vaulted ceiling of the foyer where I last saw my cousin Alphonse. Upon arriving, I haven't had much time to think about him. After shuffling to our rooms and then to lunch, and then stumbling onto the Blighted corridors, once I made it back to my room yesterday afternoon I didn't have the energy to do anything but sleep.

But now I think about him. If today is to be the start of our training, I have no doubt who will be present to ensure the experience is as miserable as possible for us all, but me especially. Alphonse has always been fond of making me feel like the measliest worm in the lowest, deepest earth.

Then again, I suppose I should've known this was coming. The moment I saw him in the town square, I should've been preparing for what it would be like to be under his command. And yet, still I falter.

As the crowded hallway depletes, the denizens of Nigh flooding into the courtyard, I stand utterly immobile. I stare through the great doors even after Güthric and Fox have gone through, long after the stragglers dart out into the open air. I can't help but wonder if I can really do this.

"You're not mageing-out on me, are you?"

Dimitri's gruff voice echoes down the stairs like molasses drizzled over bread. It soothes me instantly, calms every last one of my quaking, uncertain nerves.

I turn around to watch him descend, and prepare a retort that will continue to lighten the mood, but the words fall silent on my lips at the sight of him. My heart starts skittering erratically again.

It's only been a day—only been a few *hours* since I last saw him, and somehow, something in him has changed. It's not the butcher's ward, orphaned and powerless, who walks down the steps to come to my side, but a new man, one of intent and purpose. His green eyes cling to mine like ivy to trees. His gaze wraps around me until I am completely enveloped in his newfound confidence and rendered speechless.

A small quirk of a smile plays at his freshly shaven lips. "What?" he asks.

I balk at him. "Look at you! You're completely...you've changed."

Up this close, I can finally see that it's not just an internal transformation, but a physical one as well. The thick, golden brown mat of hair that usually rests flat upon his head has been washed, brushed, and even trimmed. The sides of his head have been shaved, leaving only the top of his scalp covered. On most people, it might've looked ridiculous or even juvenile, but on Dimitri it made him look all the more militant and assertive.

"You cut your hair," I say, my eyes still bulging and adjusting to him. "Like, a lot of it!" I reach up for his chin, pulling him close to the inspection of my eye before whining. "Aww, still refusing to let your chiny-chin-chin hairs grow out?"

He shoves my hand away with a scowl before stroking the smooth skin proudly. "Never. I'm filthy enough without a food trap dangling from my face, thank you."

I chuckle, shaking my head, but I can't take my eyes off him. The transformation is so subtle and yet so striking. I suppose it should be. If ever there were a time for reinventing oneself, now would be it, when we've left our entire lives behind to embark on something new.

"What?" he asks, lowering his head with a coy smile. "Did they take too much off? I warned Güthric not to get too creative with it. I knew I shouldn't have trusted that big oaf—"

When he reaches up to rub his head self-consciously, I snatch his hand away. "No! I-It's just going to take some getting used to it"

"Yeah, I know what you mean. It wasn't my plan, but one too many of the guys kept confusing me with Saimenimus, so I figured…" Catching my blank stare, he interrupts himself. "Saimenimus? You know, the slouched fellow who reeks of wine or beer or whatever else he can get his hands on?"

"Ah, him," I say emphatically. "I wouldn't want to be confused for him either."

We both laugh, but as the sound dwindles, I catch myself staring up at my friend. Light filters in through the open doors from outside, beaming against his face and making him look all the more radiant in their glow.

"So?" he asks.

My eyes narrow. "So what?"

"What do you think about the new look?"

I raise one eyebrow at him, trying to hide the flame rushing to my cheeks. Telling him anything other than a lie would only implode his ego. Not to mention I'd never hear the end of it if I even hinted that I thought he looked handsome this way. He'd tease me relentlessly.

I shrug indifferently instead. "I think Saimenimus got the better end of the deal."

Hiding the smirk on my face, I turn on my heels and head out the door to catch up with the others.

There are at least a hundred Crusaders gathered in the snowy courtyard outside the bell tower. You'd think after trekking through the cold for a week, I'd be used to the biting chill, but apparently one night of sleeping inside has already thawed my bones. I wrap my arms around myself as Dimitri and I shuffle nearer.

We are the last to arrive, but fortunately, most are too enthralled by the speaker's announcement to notice or chastise us. We nestle in among the other initiates—grateful for the warmth of being among other warm bodies—and try catching ourselves up on what we've missed so far.

"...someone strolling through the eastern quarters of the castle last night. Captain Eparah wasn't able to identify this wanderer, but I needn't remind you all that the eastern quarters are forbidden. The Shadowthorn has overtaken that particular section of the castle. Should you require something from one of the rooms over there, you should seek out your general for assistance."

Murmurs ripple among the new initiates, but they quiet fairly quickly when the other heads in the crowd turn to us. Either that the real Crusaders around us have already had this conversation and have no interest in having it again, or they already know how futile asking our questions would be. Of course, after my run-in with Eparah, I'm fairly certain I already know the answers, but even though the others don't, scrutiny from the Crusaders does its job in silencing us.

"...tests today are conducted by your unit general. Crusaders, head to your unit. New initiates, you returned with General Alphonse and therefore you will be training with him as your captain. Please report to the training grounds to commence day one of your Shadow Crusade training."

"I wonder what they'll train us on?" I whisper to Dimitri, but he doesn't even glance at me. Whenever we're in the presence of the other Crusaders, or of anyone with any authority, he gets like this. Focused. Attentive. It's like he can't tear himself away.

Fortunately, I find Fox standing beside me and lean over and ask her the same question.

"Oh, probably everything," she says. "How to fight with shadowsteel and without it, how to put your fellow Crusaders out of their misery should they be struck by a demon, how to tell the various shadowcreatures apart, navigating the Shadowthorn, and anything else that might help us survive just a little longer."

"Wow, it sounds kind of…"

"Intense?" she asks, raising an eyebrow at me. "What did you think you were getting yourself into?"

I shake my head, and Fox and I fall behind the other initiates as they shuffle to the next meeting area.

"I didn't think it would be rainbows and butterflies, but…"

"You didn't know what you were signing up for," she says. Fox looks over at me with pain in her eyes, and though she tries to bury it with a crooked grin, I see the pity she holds, for herself and for me. "Well, too late now. The only choice we have is to excel in our training and try to survive."

The training grounds aren't too far from the bell tower. Tucked in an alcove on the western side of the Castle of Nigh, nestled between the tall spires and stone walls, and shielded from much of the blistering winds, is a gated field. The rest of the compound is covered in sheets of luscious white, but inside the fence the snow is thinner, more of a sprinkling than a dumping.

General Alphonse awaits us like one of the gargoyles looming over the entryway. The sharp angles of his face seem to be sculpted from the harshest stone in Arcathain. He watches the twenty of us—*his* unit—approach, but there's a hard line set in his expression that makes me feel like we've somehow already failed him. I mean, I know how *I* have, and I came here today with no ill-conceived notions that I might be able to impress my impossible cousin, but the others he barely knows. He hasn't seen any of us in action yet to know whether we are worthy of his praise or not.

Beside him, I recognize Crusader Eparah. She is the softness to his edge, the warmth to his cold. Where his skin is pale and rough, hers is dark and smooth. He stands like a rigid, frightening statue, whereas she leans lazily on one hip, an inviting smile tucked gently into her lips.

We file into the training grounds and stand before the two of them.

With his arms tucked behind his lower back, Alphonse takes a single step forward to address us.

"Greetings, recruits. I trust you rested well yestereve." There's no pause for us to respond because he clearly doesn't care whether we did or not. "Allow me to introduce you all to Captain Eparah. Should you be initiated as Crusaders, she will be your primary captain out in the Shadowthorn. Until then, the two of us will oversee your training during your stay here in Nigh."

Eparah inches forward to stand beside him. "Hello, everyone. It's great meeting you all. I'm looking forward to—"

With a flick of his hand, Alphonse cuts her off, scowl deepening. "Yes, yes. We haven't gathered you here for pleasantries. Surely, most of you are aware that the life of a Crusader is anything but. So rather than waste each other's time, let's get to it, shall we?"

"Of course," Eparah says apologetically. She recovers her smile quickly and is staring back out over us within her next breath. I swear when she sees me, her smile grows even warmer. "You will spend the next few months training here, but before we begin, we need to know where your skill is already. Each of you will be tested in combat, mental fortitude, resiliency, and resourcefulness, as well as in your knowledge of the Shadowthorn. These tests will allow us to place you in the sessions that will be most likely to enhance your skills; but rest assured that you *are* a cohesive unit. Though you might be placed in different classes, you will train in combat as a team. The greatest asset you have in the Shadowthorn is each other. Never forget that.

"Any questions?"

Maxwell's hand shoots into the air and the recruits heave a collective sigh.

Fortunately, I don't hear what his incessant droning is about because Fox leans over to me and whispers, "I have a question. Who's that tall drink of water and will he be joining us when we spar?"

Disgust creeps into my expression. "That's my cousin,"

I might've spoke too loudly. The recruit in front of me glances back at us. The one beside me—Dimitri—shushes me. Worried that I might've drawn Alphonse's attention as well, I painstakingly bring my attention forward. To my relief, he and Eparah are doing their best to answer whatever concern or dilemma Maxwell has posed, but I can see the irritated tick of a muscle twitching beside Alphonse's eye.

"Cousins?" Fox recoils, glancing between the two of us

rapidly. Her nose is pink, complimenting the brightness of her rosy hair. "You two look nothing alike."

"Thank you," I say, until I realize that she's just insulted me within the same breath, for if she finds Alphonse handsome and she believes we look nothing alike, then what does that say about me?

I smack her in the gut, careful to keep the motion low so that neither Alphonse nor Eparah can see it over the pool of recruits before them. "Besides, what do you mean *who is that*? He traveled all the way from Gravenburg with us. Didn't you see him?"

She shrugs. "Yeah, I guess so. Hard to see much from the cage they kept us in."

"Oh," I say, sobering. "Right. Well, he's an asshole. And anyways, you're far superior to him, so—"

"Superiors need love too," she argues, and despite the playful trill of her tone, it burns my ears.

"That is revolting. No, stop."

Dimitri's elbow bumps into my ribs. I glare at him, though his head remains fixated forward.

"Relax," Fox whisper beside me. "I'm only giving you a hard time. Like someone like me would ever willingly seek out the company of someone like him. He practically reeks of law-abiding, stick-up-his-ass boringness."

This makes me snort out a laugh, one that I know immediately I should've suppressed. My eyes are fixed on Güthric's back, but I feel Alphonse's attention all the same. He and Eparah fall silent, except for the soft padding of his feet as he walks closer. When the footfalls cease, Güthric steps aside at Alphonse's behest, bearing me to my general.

"Something funny about the deaths of the Crusaders who came before you, Halira?"

I sneak a glare to Fox and find her pleading, remorseful eyes locked with mine.

"No, sir," I bite out, the words tasting like earth and worms on my tongue. But they're not enough.

"No, please. I insist. Enlighten your unit as to what you find so humorous about the Crusaders who fell defending Ashenvale, the ones whose boots you are here, quite literally, to fill."

My gaze falls to the boots I shoved on today, to the leathers keeping me warm. I hadn't even wondered where they'd come from, but I should've known. Crusaders live hard and die fast. There wouldn't be enough materials in all of Arcathain to make that much armor so rapidly.

My head shakes in small, hurried motions. "We weren't laughing at—"

"We?" he asks.

His eyes dart to Dimitri now, who's standing erect and tall, jaw clenched, eyes forward. If he knew Dimitri, he'd understand that I'd never in a millennia convince Dimitri to share in a side conversation while someone *important* was talking. But maybe he can tell that about him too because his gaze doesn't linger on him long before turning to Fox at my side.

"And you are?"

Rather than cowering beneath the weight of his fierce rage, or glaring at me for inadvertently outing us both, Fox strides forward, a smirk curving her lips. "The name's Fox."

He scowls. "I don't remember you traveling with us. Are you in the right place? This is the unit of new recruits we brought in from Gravenburg."

"Oh, I'm exactly where I should be," she says, either oblivious to his flaring nostrils or exceptionally good at ignoring them. But when he continues staring, waiting for further explanation, she finally refreshes his memory. "I was brought here as a prisoner, in the cart?"

Nodding, he looks her up and down until recognition finally washes over him. "And your crime?"

"Sticky fingers."

His snort of a laugh surprises me, even if it is riddled with contempt.

"Tell me, can you fight?" he asks her.

"Not really. I was hoping you'd teach me."

I know she's still toying with me, but hearing the flirtatious lull of her voice, watching her inch closer and closer to him, is something I can't stand. It's like watching someone flirt with feces. My stomach churns. It's impossible to even fathom that *anyone* could *ever* find Alphonse anything but repulsive. Even as a joke.

After another long scrutinizing gaze, Alphonse finally says, "Pity, but unsurprising. You're more of a scrounger, aren't you? Someone who survives in the shadows, not in a brawl in the middle of the streets."

Proudly, she nods.

Finally, he backs away. The only relief I find is realizing he's seemingly forgotten about me for the moment. I lean over to Fox and punch her in the arm. She laughs silently and rubs it.

Alphonse turns back around. He eyes every one of the recruits before him. "Hmm... You," he finally says, finger extended at Güthric. "You look like someone who was born in a bullpen."

Güthric frowns, looking to the rest of us for assurance. He pounds a fist to his chest when we have no answers for him. "Güthric fights," he answers, his voice low and gravelly.

"Perfect. Then I think we've found our first sparring match. Halira," he calls out to me, fingers flicking as one in his upturned palm. "Since you apparently think you're worthy already of filling the shoes of the fallen Crusaders, let's see what skills in strength you possess."

My jaw practically falls off my face.

"General," Eparah says, concern edging her tone. "That seems like an unwise match—"

He cuts her off with a single seething glare. Though Eparah

is our captain and someone we will one day take our direct commands from, here, he outranks her.

"She's right," I scoff, throwing my hands out at my sides. "I don't know how fight. If I did, don't you think I would've beaten your ass when we were younger?"

Dimitri chokes on the air he breathes. The drunk—Saimenimus, I think Dimitri had called him—snickers on the other end of the field. Fox, too, is smiling, though it's a smile that says I'm walking myself into a mound of trouble that will be far too entertaining for her to tear her eyes away from.

Dimitri takes a heaping stride forward. "I can take him. Let me fight Güthric. Let me show you how capable I am."

I gape at my friend. I'm not sure he's aware he's done it, but he's either inadvertently or purposefully moved in front of me, blocking me from Alphonse, and challenging a direct order.

Dimitri continues. "I have experience with hunting, tackling boars, and skinning deer." He sends a lofty smile to Güthric. "It would be fun to see who'd win between us."

Güthric pounds his chest again, a hungry, toothy grin curling his lips. "I win."

"Let's find out." Dimitri cracks his neck and rolls his shoulders.

And just when I think his ruse has worked, just when my nerves have finally started to calm, Alphonse throws his hand in the air. "I think not. I have no interest in seeing you *gut* one of our initiates."

"I wasn't going to—"

Alphonse silences Dimitri's protests again by raising his hand higher and glaring at him like he can melt him with his eyes alone. Only once Dimitri has stopped talking and the murmurs are hushed throughout the group, does Alphonse summon me forward.

"Halira, Güthric, come. We don't want to keep everyone here all day. Your match begins now and ends when one of you yields. The victor will earn an afternoon of freedom and lounging. The loser earns a night in the catacombs."

Frowning, I stride forward, arms splayed at my sides. "This is absurd. I don't know how to—"

"Begin!" Alphonse shouts.

At the pounding sound of footsteps, I glance over my shoulder to see Güthric already advancing. He swings a heavy arm and I barely have time to dodge it. But I have no coordination. I'm not the skilled warrior the Shadow Crusade needs. I'm a beekeeper's daughter, a girl whose only experience with fighting is cowering long enough for my bullies to lose interest.

I trip over a rock and stumble to the frozen ground.

"Yield?" I say up at Güthric who pauses mid-swing to glance over his back to Alphonse. The man's so large I can't even see past him to see my cousin's response, but when Güthric begins advancing again, that's answer enough.

"Wait," I beg, scooting along the dirt. "Wait!"

Güthric reaches his thick fingers down for me and hoists me up by my collar. He holds me high, feet dangling, unable to reach the ground no matter how much I kick and stretch. He cocks his arm back, fist clenched and solid as a brick.

"Come on, Halira! Imagine he's a demon!" Fox yells from the sidelines. "Better yet, imagine he's one of the mages who fled with half of our country. He's the one who condemned all Arcathainians to misery when he created Illashore. He's the reason you lost your loved ones!"

And just like that, determination and rage are triggered. I start swinging, wildly, at Güthric's rigid arm, trying to break his hold, trying to break *anything*. But wanting something and having the skill to do it are two different things. For all my efforts, my strength is outmatched. I can't break out of Güthric's hold, no matter how hard I thrash.

His fist flies forward and I watch it like time has slowed around us. At the last second, I pull my gaze away and whimper just as his bones collide with my cheek. Blinding light throbs my skull. My cheek shrieks, ringing in my ears like the boiling water of a kettle.

The force sends me flying through the air and back to the snow-drift ground where I land with a hearty gush of wind that bursts from my lungs. Head spinning, I try to make sense of where I am—*who* I am. I try moving my jaw, but another searing poker of agony twists inside my face and I stop.

Blinking, I start to push myself onto my hands, but something solid drives up into my ribs. I lose my breath again as I'm flung to my back. My head cracks against the frozen dirt, but the pain is nothing compared to the throbbing of my torso.

A shadow crosses over me. I can make just enough sense out of the moment to open my eyes. Güthric stands over me, a foot on either side. He reaches down and takes my breastplate into his hand again. When he pulls me up, my head lulls back, eyes flickering.

"Sorry," he says, and I think I really do detect an ounce of remorse in his tone before he puts it out like a flame pinched between his thick fingers. "But I fight."

He cracks me in the face again, just above my cheekbone. Pain seers through me, hot and liquid. I feel it trickling down my face, down my chin, and I realize I must be bleeding somewhere.

"Stop!" someone shouts. "She's had enough. She yields."

I recognize Dimitri's voice, the concern lying in wait beneath his calm exterior. But even in my delirium, I'm surprised to hear him speak up for me, for outright disobeying his superior *twice*.

My head rolls heavy on the ground, and because I don't know what's good for me, I still try to sit up. I'm mostly unsuccessful and just wind up slamming back against the dirt. Everything rings; everything is on fire.

"I'll say when she's had enough," Alphonse sneers. "And she seems fine to me. Güthric, continue."

"No," Dimitri shouts.

A second later, the man towering over me is knocked over. He's too burly to fall like a tree. Instead, he staggers away from me, Dimitri leaping over me to lunge again. I can barely open my eyes to watch, but I hear the blows they exchange. The cracking of knuckles on chins, the solid thumping of shoulders to guts. I hear them panting, feel the rhythm of their footwork on the ground, and wonder if they're close enough to trip over me or worse.

"That's enough!" Alphonse yells out. His footsteps come quick and resolute. I manage to get my eye open wide enough to see him pull Dimitri off Güthric, who he'd apparently managed to pin to the ground. "You will do well to remember your place, *initiate*. I will not tolerate disobedience. In the Shadowthorn, the only voice you adhere to is your commanding officer. Not yours. Not your friends. Not anyone's but..."

"You okay?" Fox whispers in my ear.

As she cradles my head into her lap, the chain around her neck falls free, a thin, silver ring looped through it. It pendulums above me, making my head spin and throb all the more until I have to close my eyes.

"I don't know. Do I look okay?"

There's a pause before she answers, "You don't look great, but I've seen worse."

Beyond us, Alphonse continues his lecture. "For your disobedience, today will be treated as *your* loss. After training, you will take Halira's place in the catacombs this evening. You are not to aid with the bloodletting; your duty will be disposing of any of the bodies the Spirit Keep asks you to. And I expect that, from here forth, you shall never cross me again. Do I make myself clear?"

"Yes, sir," Dimitri growls through his self-loathing.

"Well, in case I haven't, let me be explicit. Should something like this happen again, your initiation as a Crusader won't simply be postponed. I won't return you to Gravenburg like discarded pig lard from a slaughter. I will send you to the Capital to be tried for insubordination and mutiny."

If I could breathe, I might've gasped at such a threat, but my chest still aches from one of Güthric's blows. I want to run to my friend and thank him for stepping in when he did, but the grey quiet of my mind pulls me under, and as Fox drags me out from the training grounds, the last thing I hear before succumbing completely is Alphonse saying:

"Now, who might we pair next?"

THE DEAD

INFIRMARY, CASTLE OF NIGH, ARCATHAIN

*D*espite the hours of rest I seemed to have secured for myself due to my unplanned incapacitation, I wake up feeling just as horrid as I did when I blacked out. My head doesn't even feel like a head, but rather a gourd that's been hammered into nothing more than a great heaping pile of pulp.

Foolishly, I sit up too quickly, forgetting that my head isn't the only tender part of me. My ribs scream their disagreement. I'm all but certain that my moving has splintered them further, and that any second now, one will puncture some vital organ inside me.

Exhaling through my teeth, I lower myself back onto the cot.

"You should rest," a woman says from somewhere in the room. "You almost broke your ribs today."

I lift my hands from my abdomen to take a look, as if I could see them beneath my skin, let alone from this supine angle. All I see is the hump of black leather covering my breasts.

Judging from my failed attempt to move, it seems the obvious thing to do would be to lie here and allow my body to heal. I hate being this incapacitated though, especially while in the company of a stranger.

Ignoring the pain welling in my rib cage, I lift my head up enough to see who she is.

Eparah's warm smile watches over me from the foot of the bed.

Relieved for her company, I muster the energy to smile through my wincing. "Only *almost* broken?"

Her smile falters, saddening as if she was watching my earlier match unfold before her eyes all over again. But that warm demeanor of hers never seems to be too far out of reach, and she musters it again. "You're very lucky your friend stepped in when he did. You could've fared far worse."

"Dimitri…" I breathe the word, remembering him and what he'd done for me. It had gone against every rule of command that I knew of, but he'd stood up for me.

And he'd been punished for it.

I push myself upright, agony ripping from my belly to my chest, cleaving me in two as I sit at the edge of the cot. "Where is he?"

"He's all right," she reassures me, coming to my side to gently push my shoulders back. "His punishment could've been worse, as well, but the general only gave him your duties at the catacombs for the night."

I resist her shoving. "The catacombs?"

My brow furrows. I feel like I've searched this place high and low but apparently not low enough because in all my exploration last night I never came upon such a deathly place. I didn't even know people still had need for burial grounds such as catacombs. I thought it was forbidden to do anything with bodies but to burn them.

Eparah brings a wet washcloth to my forehead. "You should lie back down. When you didn't wake, the general had no choice but to pardon you from training for the day, but now that you have roused, he likely won't be so generous tomorrow. You won't be given another opportunity to rest, so I suggest you take it."

Her words seem to dissipate like smoke in the air before they can reach me. I'm too fixated on what little I remember about my spar with Güthric. The only thing I can recall with any real clarity is the first moment his fist crashed into the side of my face. Everything else is just cracking sound and searing pain and blurring motion.

I owe Dimitri my thanks, as well as an apology.

I scan the dimly lit room for the door. "Where are the catacombs?" I wince again as I try standing on my wobbly legs.

Eparah gasps, hands steadying me before I can topple over. "You're hardly in any state to—"

With one hand clutching my side, I wave her fussing off with the other. "Fine. If you don't want to tell me where the catacombs are, so be it. I'll find my way to them on my own."

Hurt wilts her expression. It carves into her face like a knife and her steady grip loosens. She doesn't let go though, not completely. Instead, she twists her head toward the door like she's afraid someone will be listening. It's the same thing she did when we met in the Blighted hallway, as if she knows that these walls have ears. It's something I'll need to keep in mind.

When she finds the doorway empty, Eparah returns her attention to me.

"It's not far from here, but you'll have to go outside. The catacombs are in a separate building. Exit left out this room, take the stairway at the end of the hall—the one *all* the way at the end, not the first one. The first one leads to Alphonse's quarters and I'm guessing you wouldn't like to run into him."

"Stairway at the end of the hall. Got it."

"It should lead you back to the main floor and to a door that will take you outside to the back of the castle. Be careful though. The Shadowthorn draws nearer every day. Demons do slip through the border from time to time."

I'm about to ask why she doesn't come with me if she's so concerned about my protection, but then I remember her skittish glances, and know that I'd be asking too much.

Instead, I start to move for the door, but she clutches my arms tighter.

"It's not forbidden or anything for you to go there. The initiates are often sent to assist with burning the exsanguinated bodies and aiding in the bloodletting but..."

That word sounds familiar. It reminds me of something I think I heard before I blacked out, but I'm not sure what it means. I mean, I *know* what bloodletting is, but I have no idea why new recruits would be asked to help with it—or rather why Dimitri was asked *not* to—and who they'd be *letting* the blood from, and why this takes place in the catacombs of all places.

But before I can ask her to explain, Eparah rubs my shoulders, a rueful smile playing at her lips. "I fear you've attracted too much negative attention from General Alphonse already. He will not like to hear that you have gone to visit your friend in the catacombs, but I can tell your loyalties toward each other are mutual. So if you are intent on going down there, I implore you to try not to draw any more attention to yourself. Go unseen, if you are able."

I nod once, resolute, and suddenly feeling like time is of the essence, I leave without another word.

Her instructions are dizzying for someone who's head still throbs, but I do my best to follow them. This time, I am smart enough to take note of the infirmary in relation to the corridor, so should I need to return, I know my way back. Otherwise, I take the corridor to the left and ignore everything in it until I reach the staircase at the end.

She didn't say how far down to go, but considering I need

to reach the main floor, I'm hopeful this staircase doesn't lead anywhere below ground.

It winds up only being one flight, and the door leading outside is close and unguarded, allowing me to leave the compound without being seen.

A gust of bitter wind greets me on the other side. In my daze, I'd forgotten it was still winter. The black Crusader leather is a far cry warmer than the rags I wore on my journey here, but fur pelts would still be better. I tug my cape around me and press out into the white abyss.

Snow flurries in the courtyard, making it difficult to see much farther than my own nose. At least demons are black; at least I'd be able to spot them easily in so much brightness, not that I'd be able to fend any demon off in this state.

Fortunately, I don't have to worry about that for long. Just up ahead, a grey structure comes into view through the haze. Gothic spires pierce through the winter storm. The cathedral before me is much smaller than the castle behind me, but it's still far larger than where I anticipated the catacombs would to be.

But that's when I notice the smaller, stone building to the side of it. Even from out here, the grim structure looks like a beacon for death. If I hadn't been assured that these buildings were safe to enter, I'd turn back around and march back to the safety that the castle has to offer.

But I have a friend to thank, so instead, I swing the iron door ajar and enter. I don't spend too much time in the main entrance. These are the catacombs I'm searching for, and everyone knows that catacombs are underground.

Down I go, an impenetrable darkness taking over after only a few steps. Mildew and iron clings to the air, heavy and pungent. It feels like I am deep, deep underground, even though I am only a few rungs in.

On the last step, I expect to come upon a door rather than

to enter straight into the catacombs, but here we are. Before me is a hallway of human remains, unlike anything I have ever seen. Each wall is sectioned with four shelves, the shelves decorated with human skulls and bones.

My boots echo as I walk down the thin passage, my hand sweeping through the cobwebs that entomb one shelf after another.

"May I help you?" croaks someone from the shadows up ahead. Their hunched figure steps into view, long and wiry hair framing what appears to be a frail and mangled female face.

I jump. My back slams into the wall behind me, and a neatly stacked collection of bones jostles before falling to the ground and shattering. The jolt to my ribs almost folds me in half, my arms clutching my side as I try to regain my stability. But I feel the person's gaze on me, sense them walking closer.

I try straightening, though my hand won't leave my throbbing side. "I was just—I didn't mean to—"

Suddenly I remember Eparah's warning about making sure that Alphonse doesn't discover my visit here, and I realize that I've already failed in this simple task. I have two choices: make things worse or accept this failure and wait to see Dimitri until tomorrow. As much as I want to see him, part of me starts to worry that I won't be the only one in trouble if Alphonse discovers I've left the infirmary. For Eparah's sake, maybe it's best I return.

"I'm sorry. I was just…leaving."

"Halira?" Dimitri's voice calls from around the corner. His head pops into view a moment later, and when he sees the state I'm in, there's no hiding his concern, or more palpably, his disapproval.

He addresses the shadow-lurker. "It's all right. She's a friend, come to check on me. I'll just be a second."

The hooded woman gives a shallow bow. "The bodies will

be waiting for you," she says ominously, before shambling down another hallway and leaving us alone.

"What are you doing here? Look at you! You can barely stand."

"You try fighting a boulder," I say as he helps me over to some steps and sets me gently on the bottom rung.

"I did." A cocky grin flashes from his mouth. "And I won."

I try to kick him, but the motion sends another sharp pain up my side again and I suck in a breath.

He rolls his eyes. "You should still be in bed."

"I had to come see you," I say, nursing my screaming ribs. My voice becomes heavy then as I recall the unfolding of the morning's events. "I had to thank you and apologize that you got stuck doing…" I glance up to him, noticing the strange rubbery apron he's wearing that matches his gloves. "What does Alphonse have you doing down here anyway?"

"Ah. It's like I never even left the butchery. You'd love it," he says sarcastically. "You see, there's all these corpses over there that have been drained of their blood and it's my job to drag them into the fire—"

Revulsion racks through me, churning and gnarling my already sensitive stomach. "Eww. Why are they drained of blood—" Then, thinking better of it, I shake my head. "Never mind. I don't want to know any more of the details. I can barely stomach the stench down here enough as it is."

He snorts a laugh, seemingly pleased with himself. I swallow hard though, remembering the reason I've come down here to see him isn't to learn about the bloodletting—I'm sure that'll come the next time Alphonse wants to punish me.

"It's not fair that you're down here," I say to Dimitri. "While I'm up there lounging in bed like a queen."

With a sigh and a tilt of his head, Dimitri takes a seat beside me. The warmth of him makes me realize just how cold it is down here and I find myself unintentionally leaning closer toward him.

"Yeah, well," he says, eyes slanting over his shoulder to meet mine. "It wasn't fair for him to make you fight Güthric. The general knew you two weren't a good match."

I shrug my good shoulder, careful not to disturb the left side of my body. "That's Alphonse for you. He's always been the cruel bastard—"

Dimitri jumps to his feet, nostrils flared and jaw clenched. "You're so quick to cast the blame back onto him. Have you learned nothing from this? Yes, none of it is fair, but you are hardly blameless. Are you so incapable of taking accountability for your own actions?"

I'm slower to stand, but I grab the railing and pull myself up. I won't be chastised and looked down upon like a child. "I'm here, aren't I?"

He scoffs, turning away from me. "Well, if you've come to besmirch our superior after *you* were caught laughing behind his back, in front of the entire unit, then maybe you should just leave. Some of us actually want to be here."

I quirk an eyebrow, my anger already dissipated. "You want to be here in the catacombs?"

"You know what I mean. The Shadow Crusade."

He starts to turn away from me, but I catch his arm.

"I want to be here, just as much as you do."

"Oh yeah? Prove it. Leave your past in the past and actually act like you want to succeed at this. Forget whatever squabbles you had with *your cousin* and instead treat this like an opportunity to impress your *general*. Because I can't stand here and watch you half-ass it."

"I'm not half-assing—"

"You are though!" he bellows over me. "You mock our general in front of everyone. You disappear for hours yesterday and no one knew where you were. You're late to the meeting this morning and miss all of your training the rest of the day."

There's no stopping him now that he's started. It's like he's been holding on to all of this since the moment we arrived, and now that he's released it, it pours out of him like a torrential storm blustering between the two of us.

I cross my arms. "Some of the things you're mentioning were hardly my fault. I got lost yesterday. And yeah, I was late to the gathering this morning, but so were you. And how can you blame me for missing the rest of training today? Need I remind you that I was incapacitated."

"Yeah, you were, because rather than learning to conform and do your duty, you'd rather goof around and piss everyone off. Rather than standing alert and learning what you can about combat—something you clearly know nothing about, and will need to if you're ever going to be a Crusader—you get yourself in trouble. You almost got yourself killed today. You know that? If I hadn't..."

His words trail off with an exasperated sigh. I follow them though, the ones he leaves unspoken yet speak so loudly down here in the catacombs. And now I finally understand where all of this frustration is coming from.

It was one thing for him to join the Shadow Crusade knowing that his own life was on the line, but now I'm here too, one more person who he has to worry about, one more person who could be taken from him.

"I'm sorry," I say quietly, uncrossing my arms. "I didn't mean to..."

Even as I stare at the damp stone floor, I can see him shaking his head and I can all but hear him accusing me of making excuses again. Maybe he's right. Maybe I do make too many excuses instead of just owning up to my mistakes.

"I *am* sorry. I know what you did for me, Dimitri. I know what my actions forced you to do and...I just wanted to find you to tell you that I appreciate what you did. I'm sorry you had to step in and challenge Alphonse's orders in that way—I know how difficult that must've been for you—and although I'm really glad you did it, I promise, I won't put you in that position again."

The hard lines of his face soften. He seems thoughtful for a moment, hesitant to accept my apology, but with a begrudging roll of his eyes, a smile tugs at the corners of his lips. "You better not."

With a smile of my own, I shove him away. He pushes me back, and I instantly suck in a breath between my teeth.

"Shit," he says, lunging for me. One of his hands steadies my arm, his other grips my waist.

His proximity forces me to swallow, hard. I can barely even notice the pain when I do it. I'm not even sure my ribs are still hurting; all I can feel is the warmth of his hand on my hip, his fingers laced around my lower back.

I look up into his eyes, suddenly aware of our closeness. Not just in this moment, but in all that we share. Outside of my sister, Kalli, I've known no one longer than I've known Dimitri. We share our childhoods, our adolescence, and now our path into adulthood as well. We've been with each other through every hardship and loss, through every challenge and triumph. No one understands me quite like he does, the good and the bad, the irrational and the destructive. I was there for him when he lost his parents, and he is here for me now that I've lost mine.

When our eyes meet, Dimitri releases me, abruptly. He backs away, glancing over at one of the bone-filled shelves.

"I should probably get back to it," he says quickly.

"Right, yeah, no." Suddenly there is nothing more important than the stone floor, and my eyes narrow in on every crack. "I just wanted to thank you. Sorry you're on catacomb duty on my behalf."

I see him shrug out of the corner of my avoidant eyes. "It's really not that bad. I mean, for me. It's like I spent the past few years preparing for this chore. I can't tell you how many dead deer and bears and boars I had to lug around before I could prepare their meat. I bet most of the recruits they send down here hurl their guts up the first few times. You," he says on a breathy laugh, "you definitely will."

If he were closer, I'd shove him again. "I love how you find me being squeamish around blood hilarious, and yet we never talk about how comfortable you are around it. Not sure I'm the weird one here."

"I'm just saying, my lack of discomfort around blood has paid off. I imagine we'll be seeing a lot more of it before this is over. You might try getting used to it."

Biting my lip, I try to avert my attention to more pleasant thoughts, but my gaze falls to the skeletons surrounding us and I know there's no hope of that while I remain down here.

"Well, I guess that's my cue," I tell him. "I'll see you tomorrow then."

Nodding, he waves and then heads back down the dark corridor. But as I watch him disappear around the corner, I can't stop thinking about how strange it is that, despite being surrounded by death—quite literally, with the empty eyes of the dead watching us from the skulls on the shelves—that I've never found myself more drawn to him, more...enticed.

I can't turn back toward the staircase until he's completely out of sight, and even when I do, it's like walking through the depths of the ocean trying to pull myself away from the boy I've known my whole life, and the captivating man he's becoming.

DUSTY SHELVES

CASTLE OF NIGH, ARCATHAIN

With my head propped on my hand, and my elbow up on my desk, my eyes flutter as the elderly scholar Amon Cornelius drones on in the background. Fortunately, I'm not alone. Almost every single one of my classmates seems to be struggling to stay awake with me. Well, almost everyone. Maxwell is the only one among us who's answered any of the scholar's questions in over an hour. Dimitri is doing his best to stay focused, but even he has to strain to keep his eyes open every time they become heavy. There's just something so hands-off and anticlimactic about listening to someone teach you about the Shadowthorn, rather than actually learning from going into it yourself.

If I've learned anything this past week at Nigh though, it's that training as a Crusader has been exactly the opposite of what I expected. I always thought they were so desperate for bodies that they basically took recruits, armored them up, and shipped them out across the Shadowthorn border with little to no training. But this?

Night and day, our preparations never end. We spar in the morning as a unit before breakfast, then break for classes.

Since Dimitri and I were declared the losers of our match with Güthric, we were placed in this Basics of the Shadowthorn class, along with Maxwell and Silver, who had been bested by Fox and Saimenimus. They keep us separated in cohorts for our more scholarly lessons before and after lunch—even though from what I can glean from Fox in the evenings, we're covering very similar content—but then it's back to sparring in the evening.

Scholar Amon waggles his ancient finger in the air. "Mmm, yes. Very good, Maxwell. The Blight is a well of toxicity. It mangles everything in its path—trees, flowers, grass."

Maxwell beams awkwardly, a thin and proud smile that says this is likely the first time in his entire life that he's ever been praised. Poor kid. I actually feel sorry for him.

"Some of you might be wondering," the scholar continues. "Why humans are not marred in its presence, why the Shadow Crusade can send its soldiers into the vile land, day in and day out, and still they return untainted."

Maxwell's hand flies up, but it's only there a moment before Scholar Amon points to him. "The Blight only affects the soil. Legends say that the Primordial Qaeus grew weary of hunting down the humans who'd condemned him to the Forgotten Forest of Eyve, so after years of roaming Arcathain, he decided he wanted the help of his friends, and he reached his hand down into the soil, released his shadows into the earth, and rebirthed the demons and fiends back into Arcathain."

"Ah-ah," the scholar says, his thin, wispy beard waggling in time with his finger. "Not just demons and fiends. There are other creatures, far more terrifying and ferocious than those."

It's at this point in the conversation that I finally perk up. I knew it. There had to be different kinds of shadowcreatures because otherwise there was no explanation for the *thing* I'd seen in my cottage.

"Before last week, most of you were simple commonfolk.

You lived in the villages and towns that were on the edge of the Shadowthorn, but few of you have likely seen it from the inside."

"I have." Silver's voice rings in the air like a sword drawn before battle.

Scholar Amon watches her with eager eyes, hungry to hear from someone who has been so quiet. All eyes turn to her, but she doesn't utter another word. It's like she's no longer even here. Whatever distant memories of Ashenvale's fall have resurfaced in her mind, they've pulled her back there thoroughly.

"Yes, very well. As I was saying, it's not just demons and fiends to fear in the Shadowthorn. There are other unimaginable and horrific creatures that dwell there. There are blind worms and ravagers, arachnids the size of houses and nevermores that would sweep you into the air and terrorize you with a plummeting fall to your death before finally commencing their feast. We will discuss the variety of shadow-creatures you will encounter at another time. For now, we review the basics.

"Who can tell me about fiends?"

The demon-man's face glares at me through my mind's eye again. My fingers curl. I try blinking him away, I try refocusing, but he won't disappear. For two weeks or more, his existence has haunted me, but I've been too afraid to mention him to anyone. I wasn't sure anyone would believe me. I'm not even sure *I* believe me.

Maxwell's hand shoots into the air. This time, he doesn't wait to be called on before gushing, "Fiends are more like pests than they are wicked. I mean, they're still evil incarnate—obviously, Qaeus created them, so they have to be—but they aren't as outright dangerous as demons. Fiends will toy with you. They'll steal your voice and use it to lure others away from the group. They'll make you think you're seeing something that isn't there, like a bridge across a lake, but then when you walk forward, there's no bridge, only the sirens awaiting you."

"Good. Yes. Anybody else?"

The silence tempts me, coaxing me to ask what I've been dying to ask.

Before I can, Saimenimus speaks, his voice sounding bored, and his eyes squinting from the hangover he's still nursing. "Fiends mostly appear as animals?"

"Excellent. That is correct. Small animals, especially. They take on the appearance of rats, snakes, owls, anything that is small and will allow them to lurk without being seen until they are ready to make their move. Fiends are not as brutal as demons. They won't rip your heart from your chest. Mostly, they seem to simply enjoy playing their tricks. Sometimes, those tricks lead Crusaders and other citizens to their deaths, so be vigilant."

The longer I listen, the greater my irritation grows. I've wondered what that demon-man was for weeks now, I've wondered how he could do such a thing as cloak himself as one of us. I don't want to learn about the basics of fiends. I want answers. For my parents' deaths, but also to prepare me for what is to come when we are finally sent into the Shadowthorn.

I raise my hand.

"Yes, Ms. Devonshire," the scholar calls on me.

When the rest of the initiates twist around in their seats to watch me, heat pricks my chest and cheeks. I know better than to ask such a bold question, to even suggest that a thing could be possible. It will make me look strange, and strangeness is often associated with mages, and mages are burned or hung.

Still, before class today, I hadn't been sure that shadowcreatures other than demons and fiends existed, so maybe there really is something to learn about that demon-man.

"Can any demons or fiends look…human?"

Scholar Amon adjusts his spectacles. "Well, I suppose a fiend could make someone *believe* that it looked human. But I imagine such a ruse would be difficult to perform and would be easily disrupted by the slightest movement or sound."

"Not a fiend," I blurt. After all, it's common knowledge that fiends cannot leave the Blighted lands, and this demon-man definitely had. He'd crossed clear across the border, entered my home, and tore another demon to pieces. "Could something other than a fiend make themselves look human?"

Scholar Amon frowns behind his cobweb beard. "Hmm, none that I'm aware of. But I suppose there is still much to be learned about the Shadowthorn and its creatures."

Defeated and even more perplexed than before, I crumple into my chair and gnaw on the inside of my lip. If he wasn't a fiend and no other shadowcreature can do what he was able to do…then what was he?

Maxwell raises his hand enthusiastically to respond to the scholar's rhetorical question. "Like where the Primordials came from."

The classroom awakens with grumbles and retorts, but with Saimenimus sitting right in front of me, his is the only one I hear.

"Everyone knows it was those bastard mages. They made the Primordials to kill the humans, but then the creatures revolted against them, and they left us to pick up the scraps."

Scholar Amon holds up his knobby finger. "Your information is hearsay. The origin of the Primordials has long been lost. Some speculate that those who possessed such knowledge were lost during the Great Rift."

"Besides," another student argues. "If they wanted the Primordials to kill us, why'd they make shadowsteel?"

The class becomes a boisterous cacophony of shouts competing against one another.

"Settle, students, settle. You have the rest of your lives to blame the mages for their sins, but such a discussion should be saved for your political classes. Here, we discuss the beings you will slaughter, and how to do it right."

As the scholar turns the conversation to our next topic of discussion, the ways in which demons manifest and slaughter, my mind still reels. I know I should just drop it; I should do as Dimitri said and let my past stay in my past. But no matter how hard I've tried to distract myself from that horrific night, it always resurfaces.

If I faced such a creature once, I could come upon one again. Worst, a demon like that could almost certainly walk among the people unnoticed. Given a heavy cloak and a cane, no one would look twice at a hunched man hobbling down the uneven streets of the Wallows, nor any of the other border towns.

And if I know myself, I won't be able to focus on anything until I know.

"Precisely," Scholar Amon says to Maxwell upon answering another question. "A demon's bite *is* lethal, but so is a scratch. One nick, and their toxin seeps in through the bloodstream. Once it reaches the heart, there is no saving the poor soul. It is a death known to most of our fallen Crusaders. I say this, not to scare you, but so that you are informed and aware of the dangers of allowing a demon too near. Always wear your leather. Keep as much of your skin as possible covered at all times."

"Of course," slurs Saimenimus from the back row. "No one wants to run into the Shadowthorn half-naked. That's like waving a juicy steak before a lion."

I haven't seen him drinking today, but the man doesn't seem to need booze in order to seem inebriated. Liquor must course through his veins or something because he is constantly staggering, constantly slurring his words and hiccupping. I can't help but wonder what's led him to be this way. Dimitri and I have suffered great loss, just as I'm sure everyone here has, but there's something more dire about his past that I can't put my finger on.

"Fair point, Master Saimenimus, even if it was articulated in poor taste." The scholar looks down past his spectacles, glaring at him to make his point. "Demons appear to serve but one purpose: they are Qaeus' minions, sent to massacre humans. They feast upon us, alive or dead." He waggles his finger when a thought strikes him. "In fact, another lesson for you today: demons are especially drawn to the dead."

"Glad I'm not the Spirit Keep then," Saimenimus adds under his breath.

Those of us nearest to him chuckle.

Scholar Amon is so hard of hearing that he doesn't notice. "We believe this is why they often attack places of poverty, where the dead are likely to have accumulated. They've even been known to attempt to infiltrate the catacombs at times."

Saimenimus holds up his arms as if expecting a round of applause.

"Here?" Dimitri asks, straightening in his seat. His eyes dart to the dagger at my waist like he's ready to grab it and march down there to defend it himself. "They've attacked the catacombs here at Nigh?"

I want to remind him two things: first, if he so much as even tries to take my dagger, I'll jam it clean through his hand; and second, the scholar can hardly be talking about any other catacombs considering the rest of Arcathain burns their bodies on pyres.

But I keep quiet. In the week since my match with Güthric, I've tried upholding my promise to Dimitri to try and stay out of trouble, even if my mouth sometimes wants to have a mind of its own.

"Yes, even here," Scholar Amon answers. "Their attacks have

become more frequent in past months as the Blight has impinged on our lands."

Now it's Saimenimus who straightens, an alertness sobering his eyes more than I've ever seen. "Then why do we remain here? Shouldn't we high-tail it out of here and go to another training ground?"

The scholar looks out over us, calculating and determining. "Ahh," he says at last. "You haven't had your lessons on the necro-ink yet, I see. Well, suffice it to say that when the mages abandoned Arcathain, some of the allies among them were unwilling to abandon the humans all together. They blessed the land—*this* land that the Castle of Nigh sits upon. This is the only place in all of Arcathain where necro-ink can be created."

If no one else will say it, I will. "Necro-ink?" I turn to Maxwell, prepared for his helpful rants of useful knowledge.

He shakes his head though.

"Surely you've seen the Crusaders," the scholar says. He brings a finger up to his eye and drags it down his cheek as if he's marking it. "The paint they use—that's necro-ink. It protects them while they're in the Shadowthorn."

"Protects them how?" Saimenimus asks.

But before the scholar can answer us, a brass bell tolls in the distance.

"I'm afraid that lesson will come in time. Until the 'morrow, my dear students, farewell. And please, remember to read your chapters tonight and come prepared for another riveting discussion about the creatures that lurk in the Shadowthorn."

My classmates stand from their desks, some of them struggling more than others as these seats seem to have been made with teenagers in mind. I can't imagine Güthric fitting into any of them. Even Saimenimus, who is as lanky as a birch tree, groans as he slides out from his.

Dimitri waits for me to stand, clutching a bag over his shoulder. "Where to?" he asks. "Are we studying in the library or are we headed to the courtyard for some midday shenanigans? I hear some of the other recruits will be borrowing some turnips and seeing who can carve the most accurate depiction of Scholar Amon."

My eyes narrow on him. "You never want to partake in midday shenanigans. You're testing me."

His mouth falls wide in mock offense. "Who me? I'd never test you."

With a roll of my eyes, I shove him aside and make for the door. "Wherever *I'm* going, I don't need *your* annoying company to join me."

"Ouch." He laughs, jogging up beside me with a huge, cocky grin. When he finally catches up, matching my strides down the dark and dimly lit halls, he grows serious. "Really, it's no test. We've been working hard this week, and as important as it is to read the chapters we've been assigned, I know you're going stir crazy."

"I am not," I say innocently, turning down the next corridor. "I *love* spending my afternoons in the library. Who wouldn't take the dusty, stuffy air of the packed bookshelves over the wide, open space and crisp coolness of being outside?"

He snorts but doesn't prod me further. I know the last thing he wants to do is goof around for the afternoon, especially not if it means defacing turnips to mock one of our more pleasant instructors, let alone any of them, but more than wanting to pass Dimitri's test, today I actually *do* find myself eager to go to the library. If Scholar Amon can't give me the answers I seek, then I'll have to find them on my own.

Three red oak doors line the wall before us, closed as they always are to ensure the utmost silence is maintained once inside the library. The doors, pointed to a tip and stained rust red, always remind me of bloodied claws reaching up through the floor, like they belong to some mystical book-loving creature who won't let anyone enter who would otherwise be harmful to the ancient and precious tomes inside.

I hold my breath as we throw open the center door and enter.

Before coming to Nigh, I had seen a total of two books in my entire life. The first was the Tome of Earth and Magic belonging to the bishop at the cathedral in Gravenburg. It contained the teachings of right and wrong, of the wickedness of magic, and documented in great detail the age-old war between the mages and the humans. The other was less a book and more a pamphlet with information about the Shadow Crusade. I found it drifting down a stream of sewage while playing in the streets of the Wallows with Tor. At first, he grabbed it just to chase me around with it, holding it out and threatening to make me eat it, despite being soaked in waste. But upon closer inspection, from that pamphlet, his calling grew.

For almost two decades, I'd only laid eyes on two books. Now, I have seen thousands.

The library at Nigh is a scaffolding of history and knowledge, each distinct from the last. From the center of the room, one can see all the way up to the rafters at the top of the vaulted ceilings, past level after level of books. To the best of my knowledge, this place has been here since the dawn of time, and over the centuries they've stacked the shelves from the top down, so that the most archaic and obscure reside on the top floor, and more recent developments on the bottom.

Tens of thousands of books are illuminated by the skylight windows and the arched panes on every wall of the tower. Come nightfall, this place will be cast in darkness, but fortunately it sits on the west side of the compound, and therefore we still have a few hours before that happens.

We ascend the winding staircase in the center of it all. Since the only entrance to get into the library is through the main floor, we have a ways to climb until we reach the seventh floor, where our textbooks are kept.

But as Dimitri steps off the stairs and onto the seventh level, my neck cranes back. If I am to find the answers I need, something tells me I'll need to go up even higher, perhaps even to the forbidden thirteenth floor. Those "texts" were written back when we only had the means of etching messages into stones, when we used pictures to depict meaning. If my answers are up there, I wouldn't be able to decipher them, even if I did manage to find them. But perhaps the levels between here and there, the ones where we first began inking words into sheep hide, back when our language had more of a distinctive melody to it and more complex spellings. I might be able to decipher those.

"I don't know how you can stand being on that old thing," Dimitri says, drawing my attention back to the seventh floor. He nods to the staircase. "It looks like it's going to collapse any moment." His gaze trails upward. "What were you looking at?"

I shake my head. "Nothing. I just...I was thinking about trying to dig a little deeper into some of the Primordial stuff. I'll meet you at our table in a moment?"

His brow darkens with disappointment. "Really, Halira? If you just came here to sneak onto the forbidden floor—"

"I didn't!" I protest. "For your information, I came here to learn. It's not my fault my appetite for knowledge can't be satiated by the beginner textbooks they have us reading. We already know about fiends and demons, Dimitri. We have first-hand knowledge of how horrific they are and what they're capable of. None of this stuff is going to prepare us for what we'll find in the Shadowthorn."

He shakes his head, back turned toward me. "Whatever. If you get caught, I want no part in this. Good luck finding what you're looking for. You know where I'll be."

I'm left standing there, jaw slack and skewed as the offense seeps in. For once, I actually *am* trying to understand what we're up against, and of course he still thinks I'm up to no good. What is it with my friends and family always assuming I don't care? Just because I've spent most of my adolescent years with no real compulsion to do anything, doesn't mean I actually *wanted* to waste my life away, and it certainly doesn't mean I'm always trying to goof off.

With a low, irritated growl, I try casting my frustrations with Dimitri and everyone else out of my mind. If I'm going to find anything on these shelves, I'll need to keep a clear head.

I spin on my heels and head to the next floor. Then the next. There's no real rhyme or reason why I think the answers I seek will be buried in the older documents—it's quite possible they're on the floor Dimitri and I study on, or even at the very bottom of the library where more recent history is stored—but there's a tingling in my gut that tells me otherwise. I just have this feeling that the information I'm looking for has been buried away for some reason, as if someone long ago thought it was too disturbing for the people of Arcathain to know. Kind of like how the innerworkings of the necro-ink seems to be kept from civilians—there are just some things that regular, defenseless people don't need to know.

But I refuse to be one of the defenseless any longer.

I reach the eleventh floor, tempted to try my hand at sneaking into the twelfth, but ultimately deciding my pride couldn't handle proving Dimitri right tonight. If it comes down to it, if after I've searched this library high and low and I still can't find anything about the creature I encountered in my home, then *maybe* I'll risk breaking into the top floor of the library.

Until then, I'll just work my way down from here, floor by floor.

I find my way to one of the corners of this floor—a level dedicated to the books, tomes, and artifacts gathered during the Shadow Massacre era, back when Crusaders were revered, and their numbers were unfathomable. It seems as good as any place to begin, so I start pulling out the scrolls and tomes tucked away on the shelves.

I come across legers with hundreds of names, the Crusaders who faced and slaughtered the other Primordials until there was only one remaining. I find the temporary treaty, signed and dated by the mages and the humans who were in power at the time. It grants humans the right to wield weapons, to possess items of magic like necro-ink and shadowsteel, and explicitly states that once the last Primordial falls, the humans will lose all of those privileges once more. There are drafts for how the mages made the shadowsteel weapons, blueprints for curating necro-ink. I find spells for healing and destruction, tools and ingredients that have lost their structure over time, but still stand like a testament to their contribution to the progress we've made.

There's one tome in particular that sucks me in. It's a detailed recounting of how each of the Primordials fell: Khaymus with a spear to the heart; Khunas, beheaded by a double-bladed axe; Qhistus blown to pieces by an explosive device created with scraps of shadowsteel and magic. I'm surprised to hear the mages referenced in these histories, even if it is infrequently. All my life, we've been led to believe that the mages abandoned us, but it would appear that even then we had some allies. For a time.

I skim through dozens of books, some of them boring, others enthralling, and some terrifying. One, in particular, a journal kept by a Crusader named Kier who lived within my parents' lifetimes, documents his many encounters with the demons he came across.

"They outnumbered us four to one, and we saw no better alternative than to run, if we were to survive. We fought until they had slain enough of us that they lost interest in the living and descended upon

the dead. I shall never forget their gurgling maws as they sank their razored teeth into my fellow Crusaders.

"But we couldn't look back. We ran as the demons tore the others to pieces, and for a time, we thought we were safe.

"But they found us. Despite our best efforts to cover our tracks, they scented our trail..."

It's there that I stop reading, horrified by the information I've just gleaned. I'd never heard that demons could do such a thing. I knew they were drawn to blood, and after today I am also privy to their taste for deceased flesh particularly, but I'd never heard that they could scent and track us.

It's valuable, life-saving information, but it's still not what I came here to find.

I put the tattered journal back on the shelf and keep perusing.

By the time I reach the end of the first bookshelf, the room is already cast in soft shadows of twilight. The sun is setting, and I am nowhere closer to the answers I seek. None of the histories transcribed on the pages I skimmed told of anything even remotely similar to a demon posing as a human, or any other shadowcreature for that matter.

I glance around the dusty bookcase to the hundreds of remaining rows on this floor alone. I'm getting nowhere fast. At this rate, I won't even make it through all the books on this floor before our official initiation. I'll be shipped out to some dangerous border town before ever learning what it was I had laid eyes on. If only there was some way to narrow down my search. Perhaps if I figured out the right, pointed questions to ask the other scholars, maybe they could help guide me in the right direction.

Something squeaks, drawing my attention back toward the corner from where I began. The sun has sunk so low now that no light graces the floor near the wall anymore, and therefore I almost miss the mouse scurrying past the bookshelf. I breathe a sigh of relief. At first, I'd thought it was a floorboard creaking, someone who had caught me in my independent studies and would expect answers.

I start to turn back around, intent on rejoining Dimitri before our study time is over, but just as I begin to drag my gaze away, I catch another flicker in the shadows. My eyes strain at the second mouselike shape that scurries along the dusty floorboards.

When a third and fourth one scampers by, I can no longer contain my curiosity. Either I'm losing my mind—in which case, I need to verify that these mice are only figments of my imagination so that I can report myself to the medical ward for further testing and aid—or...or I'm about to witness something strange and extraordinary.

Slinking between the bookshelves, I tuck my long hair away and out of my face, so as not to impede my eyesight further, and walk toward the end of the shelves. As I advance, mice continue to pour from the corner of the room, squeaking on the ground along the back wall. They practically march in single file, further proof that I am, in fact, losing my mind. Güthric must've hit my skull harder than I thought...

I reach the end of the bookcases. At my feet, the mice still march, twenty or more, and I swear, every one of them looks my way—looks me directly in the eyes—before they pass.

I look around me, confirm that I am not standing in Blighted territory and therefore this is not a trick of a fiend. That would almost be better than going mad...but something tells me that's not what this is.

I need proof, something to show me that what I'm seeing is really happening. Slowly, I squat to the ground, steadying my hand as I reach out to graze the soft fur atop one of the mice's heads.

The contact, though expected, makes me jerk back. Real, then; the mice are real.

"What in the Eyve is happening…" I gasp, cradling my hand to my chest like it's just been burned.

My eyes skirt the edge of the bookshelf, looking to see where the mice are headed. Part of me wishes Dimitri were here. If he were, surely, he'd have enough common sense to convince me to find mine, to encourage us to turn back, flee the library, and find the first Crusader we can to report this bizarre occurrence.

But I know these animals mean me no harm. If anything, dare I think that they're actually trying to help me.

The marching mice continue down, row after row, and I have no choice but to follow them. I have to see where they're going, have to know where all of this leads.

I take a wide step over them so as not to frighten any of them and then walk along the back wall beside them. At first, I walk slow, caution holding me back as I consider just how unusual this all is. But soon, my steps become wide, until I am practically bounding beside my new furry friends without a single hesitation in the world. My entire life, I've felt drawn to the animals around me, like I am connected to them in some deep and profound way.

I feel that same draw with these mice, like they are here solely for me, like they want to help me.

Up ahead, there's a tapping. I can tell before I even reach it that it's coming from the window, a small sound, hollow and clean. Uneasy, I slow my pace, shifting back to the other side of the mice so as to put some distance between me and whatever I will find on the other side of that window.

I slink closer, heart thumping in my chest in time with each tapping sound.

Tap-tap-thump-thump.

Tap-tap-thump-thump.

Tap-tap-thump-thump.

Finally, the old window comes into view. It's one of those

paned windows that can't actually open, the ones typically found in cathedrals and is more decorative than purposeful.

A bird presses itself on the ledge just outside. Every few moments, it looks away from the window, back out over the hills, and then it returns with a sharp snap of its head and two rapid taps.

Tap-tap-thump-thump.

Not just any bird, I realize. Its feathers are as dark and glistening as ink, even in the fading sunlight. Its beak is made from onyx, curved slightly near the end, but otherwise impeccably smooth and straight. Its eyes are like someone trapped the midnight sky into the two smallest, blinking holes they could find, where it could never escape.

A raven.

Dimly, I wonder if it's the same one that followed us all the way from Gravenburg here, but then I shake the notion from my mind. I may be ready to follow mysterious mice to what I hope are the answers I've been searching for, but I'm not ready to accept that a raven has for some reason become undyingly loyal to me. It's probably one of the castle's messenger birds, or perhaps it's wild, and when it saw the mice inside, it wanted to hunt them for itself.

I turn my back to the window—to the raven—and follow the mice down the aisle.

But the floor seems to plummet beneath me when I find the mice huddled in a bundle of skittering limbs and wiry tails, at the base of one of the bookshelves. A few of them stand on their hind legs, reaching up the dust jackets and vellum, while the rest of the little army scurries around them.

My gait slows again, like I'm suddenly afraid I might disturb them and make them scatter. They've brought me here for a reason, I just know they have, and I have every intention of finding out why.

I inch closer on the softest parts of my shoes, as light as I can make myself become, until I'm standing before the book-shelf, before the place where they have congregated. I scan the spines of the books, searching for a title or phrase or word that will stand out to me. *The Primordials: A Complete History, Magic Is the Land, The Development of Shadowsteel, Enslaved: How Arcathainians Reclaimed History*. But nothing seems to even hint at human impersonation, complex illusions, or anything I could be searching for.

Then my eyes skim another title: *The Druids of Arcathain.*

There is no reason this book should stand out more than any of the others. It bears the same tattered, leather spine and faded ink inscription as all of the others, but when I see it, it's like I suddenly can see nothing else. I lean closer, hand reaching out toward it. I've never heard the term *druid* before, which strikes me as odd, since the title clearly seems to imply that a *druid* is also Arcathainian.

But just as my fingers touch the top of the spine, just before I can pull the book out and hungrily devour its pages, a gasp sounds from the end of the bookshelf.

SECRETS

LIBRARY, CASTLE OF NIGH, ARCATHAIN

I jump so far back that my back slams into the bookshelf behind me. The sturdy thing is so heavy with volumes that it barely even wobbles. The mice at my feet are just as skittish. The moment they notice someone else is among us, they scatter, clambering between some of the loosely packed books, skittering into the holes beneath the shelves, and rushing back the way we came from along the west-facing wall.

I'm so terrified of who I will have to face that my mouth has all but dried up. Even if I needed to explain myself, I don't know I'd be able to; there is no saliva left on my tongue, no air in my lungs.

Quick as a whip, I snap my attention toward the gasp, toward the center of the library.

A whoosh of air escapes me when I see Fox's red hair and wide eyes.

"Piss on a mage!" she exclaims, trying to whisper. "Did you see that? Those mice! They just—they were all together, like —like—"

141

In my head, I tell her not to say the word she's thinking, the word I've tried not associating with myself my whole life.

"Like magic," she says, breathless and mystified.

Worry releases its hold on my tight chest, a moment of relief wrapping itself around me that even she could not bring herself to say *it*. The moment passes quickly though.

I shake my head, hands stretched out toward her as I rush to her side. "No. It's not like that. I'm not a—"

To my surprise she doesn't recoil. Instead, she wraps her hands around my own, her wide eyes peering into mine.

"It's okay. I'm not going to tell anyone."

"There's nothing for you to tell," I insist. "I'm not a mage."

She looses a short breath of a laugh. "What do you think just happened then? You think regular humans can command a rat army at their disposal?"

"They were mice," I say, voice becoming shrill. "And I *am* human. I'm Arcathainian, through and through."

Fox shakes her head, eyes rolling when she releases my hands. "It's whatever. I don't care what you are or what you call yourself. That—what just happened—*that* was magic. Like, real, enchanting, punishable-by-death magic. You can't be walking around doing…*that*." She flicks her wrist behind us to where the mice had been. "Especially here. The Shadow Crusade stands against all magic, be it Primordial, demon, or mage—"

"I'm not a mage," I growl.

"How did you do it? Like, do you have to chant some spell or something? I've always wondered about that. Mages get their magic from the elements, everyone knows that, but for something like commanding mice, do you like have to draw from the earth first or—"

"I'm *not* a mage." This time, my words are more emphatic, my embarrassment and rage like a whetstone to my voice, turning it sharp and dangerous.

Fox sighs, arms flung in the air. She falls silent for a

while, staring at me expectantly, but I'm too busy holding my breath to say anything. I know I'm not a mage. My parents hated them far too much for me to have some secret mage lineage. It has to be something else. Maybe it's because of the magic in this place already, the same magic that helps us create the necro-ink—maybe it's what commanded the mice.

"Look," she says after a long while. "I'll say it again: I don't care *what* you are. As far as I'm concerned, you didn't judge me when we first met, so I'm not about to not return that favor. Besides, if you're here, it means your ancestors were one of the ones who tried helping humans, not one of the ones who split the continent and hightailed it out of here."

"How did you know about that?" I ask, concern suddenly piquing. "About the mages who allied themselves with the humans."

She indicates to the shelves on either side of us. "It's referenced in most of the history books up here."

Nodding, I avert my eyes.

"But I'm right then? Your family was allied with us—with the humans?"

Another scowl scrunches my face, although this time it's not so much from rage as it is confusion and caution. The easiest way to convince her I'm not a mage is by telling her that my mom grew up in the Forgotten Forest of Eyve, but that's not necessarily any better in most people's eyes.

Finally, I say, "The mages are the reason my Pa's parents died. They lived in Drayfil Shore during the Great Rift. I promise you, I'm not a descendant of mages."

"Then what do you call all that?" she asks, flailing her hand out toward the floor. "Mice don't *do* that, not without magic involved."

I shake my head and fall silent. I wish I knew. For a few years now, strange, inexplicable things have happened around me, but until now, I've been able to ignore them since I've been the only person to witness them.

My attention fixes on the empty floor where only moments ago dozens of mice were crawling over each other to congregate at the base of this shelf. I look to the window next, only to find the raven gone as well.

I allow myself to consider something I've never wanted to believe: maybe there's a reason some people were trapped over the wall with the Primordial Qaeus, one that could explain the…instances that have occurred around me.

I face my friend again. She stares at me expectantly, defiantly, a hard crook in her brow as if to say that neither of us are leaving this spot until she gets answers. I wish I could give her any, but I can't. I don't even know them myself, but if I did, it wouldn't be worth it. Information like this not only puts me at risk, but her as well for associating with me.

But then it strikes me. There is one iota of information I have to offer.

"If it *is* magic, it's not me. But we learned in our Intro to Shadowthorn seminar earlier that the Castle of Nigh rests upon enchanted soil."

She scowls. "Well, yeah. That's how they make the necro-ink."

Skirting right past why we are separated into different classes if we're covering exactly the same information, I try to elaborate. "And you think that's all that the magic does? The mages could've done anything to this land. They could have left behind a trap that would ensure the death of all humans were we to break the terms of our treaty or something."

"That ship has sailed," she snorts. "Okay, but how does that have anything to do with those mice?"

"I don't know!" I say, growing desperate. I need to get her to stop asking questions that I can't answer. "Maybe it's some spell on the library that helps people find the books they're looking for."

Her brow raises in a skeptical arch. "Right. Okay, let's try then." Her voice becomes ethereal then, mocking. "Oh, great mage spirits. My heart flutters, my nethers tingle whenever I'm in the presence of my general, Alphonse."

"Eww," I say, shoving her.

Laughing, she continues as if she's trying to summon the dead. "Please, help me find a book that will help me woo him like no other woman ever has. Show me your best novel—nay, encyclopedia—on love and sexual desire."

I roll my eyes, crossing my arms before my chest.

Fox holds her ear up, listening for whatever whispers the make-believe magical library will send her way. After a moment, she frowns, drawing her gaze down to the floor in a mock search for the mice we saw earlier.

"Huh, that's odd," she says. "Doesn't seem to have worked for me. Then again, I'm not a ma—"

"There you are!" Dimitri stands at the end of the book-shelves, arms propped on his hips. Disgusts pulls back his lip when he notices Fox beside me. "Oh, and I see you've found…company."

"Hello to you too, Dimitri." She throws her arm around my shoulder, leans her red locks against my white ones. "Sorry to *steal* your girl away, but you know how I am, a thief through and through."

"She's not my—" Dimitri exhales through his nose, catching himself before she can get too much of a rise out of him. Instead, he saves most of his ire for me. "If you had other plans, Halira, you could've just told me."

My hands shove at Fox's side until I'm finally able to break away from her grip. I stare at her a moment, trying to assess whether or not she's going to say something about the mice to Dimitri. But her innocent blinking seems to suggest otherwise.

This isn't where I wanted our conversation to end. The last thing I need is someone thinking I'm a mage, but I also have nothing else to say to convince her otherwise. I don't know what just happened. It wasn't even helpful to me and the questions I had, so I can't even understand it.

I walk toward Dimitri. "I didn't have other plans. I came here to find a book, but I can't find it. Are you ready to go study?"

"Study?" He jerks his neck back, looking down at me like I'm crazy. "The sun's setting. We've already lost daylight. The only reason I came up here was to tell you I was heading down to dinner, but I can see you're *busy* so I'll leave you to it."

"Dimitri, wait."

I reach out for him, but he pulls away so quickly that my fingers graze the air he had been occupying, a lingering warmth filling the void of his presence. He walks away with his head down, feet thudding with more fervor than his usual gait, and I can't bring myself to do anything but watch him go.

I feel Fox come up beside me. "You two ever, uh, you know?"

Heat rises to my cheeks, and slowly I cock my head toward her so she can see the full magnitude of my glare.

She throws her hands up. "Just a question. And I know you didn't ask, but I think it could do you both some good, relieve some of that sexual tension between the two of you."

"There is no sexual tension between the two of us," I growl, a little louder than I mean to. Afraid that Dimitri might still be within earshot, I tug Fox closer, lowering my voice. "We're just friends. We've known each other since we were kids."

"I know. And growing up, neither of you were ever interested because, why would you be? Life was too hard in the Wallows of Gravenburg to ever think about those kinds of things. But you can't tell me that the last few years, once you finally became an adult and started having *adult* thoughts, that you haven't ever once considered..."

My cheeks feel as if they're being held up to a fire. The accusation reminds me of the last time I saw Dimitri without his shirt on, or the moment we shared in the catacombs, so close to each other that I swear I could taste his warm breath, or any of the dozens of times our hands have grazed, and I've wondered what it would feel like to actually close my fingers around his.

"No!" I growl, spinning on my heels and heading for the staircase. "Now drop it. Dimitri's right. We should get to the dining hall before they stop serving. I don't want to go all evening without food."

She jogs beside me. "You really have a problem with opening up, don't you? First the magic stuff, now this."

Already descending the narrow, winding staircase, I throw a glare over my shoulder.

"Why do you deny what's so obviously true? It's like a beggar denying themselves the option of begging—they want food, they need food, but they prevent themselves from asking. It's madness."

"It's called pride," I counter, passing the tenth floor.

"So you're too proud to admit that you're a mage?"

"I'm not a—"

"Too proud to admit that you have feelings for a boy you grew up with, one who already seems to show you undying loyalty and love? Tell me why pride prevents you from admitting you want him." Then she adds with a small smile audible in her voice. "Is it the clean-shaven jaw? Because, honestly, I agree. A little bit of facial hair could do that man some good."

The corners of my lips tug despite my best efforts to hold them down. "No! It's not that—"

"Ah-ha!" she exclaims as we pass the ninth floor. "So you do admit it! You like him. I knew it!"

I curse under my breath, only now realizing my slip. My chest constricts, but I don't let it show. I don't know why I don't want to admit it to her. I guess I just like some things in my life to remain private.

"Piss on a mage," I groan. "Why do you care so much about who I might or might not like? It's not like people like us have a chance at love. We signed our lives away to the Shadow Crusade. If we make it to initiation in a few months, most of us will be dead before the next winter. Complications of the heart don't matter for us."

"Don't you see? That's exactly why this type of stuff *does* matter. At most, we have a year left before we become demon food. I don't know about you, but I want to make these last months count." She grabs my arm and spins me around to face her before we reach the seventh floor. "Look, I'm not proud of my life before this. The way I had to live, to survive, it meant not having time for things like friends and crushes because everyone had things that I needed and didn't have. If I had allowed any of those people close, they'd just become targets for cons. Don't get me wrong, I'm not thrilled about being here —the last thing I wanted was to be forced into servitude to a cause that would certainly mean my death—but it's nice having things like a roof over my head, warm food on my plate three times a day, fresh clothes, a place to bathe…"

I watch her closely, paying careful attention to the way her eyes become misty, to the way she clears her throat when her voice starts to become brittle. With her usual sly smile and wise-cracking comments, sometimes Fox makes it easy to forget that each of us came here with a dark cloud hovering over us, even her—*especially* her.

"All I'm saying is," she continues. "This is the first time in… as long as I can remember that I'm in a position where the people around me aren't just marks. I get to allow myself to actually care about their lives."

"But…" I frown, rubbing my arms even though there's not a single draft in the library. "Wouldn't it be easier not to care? You said it yourself, we're all going to die. It's likely that some of us will even witness each other's deaths. Wouldn't it be easier to, I don't know, keep living the way you did?"

With a condescending but harmless smile, she pats my shoulder. "Oh, Halira, you have it all wrong. If you only have a few months left to live, rather than pretending your cold and dead inside, wouldn't you rather spend them truly living?"

THE WILL TO LIVE

CASTLE OF NIGH, ARCATHAIN

The next few weeks are nothing so extravagant that they'll be recorded in any future history books. We fall into a routine, the recruits and I, one of early morning sparring, late-night studying, and inevitably the forming of bonds with one another. It was difficult not to after that night with Fox in the library. Something about what she said struck me unlike anything had since I left Gravenburg. After my parents had died, it felt as if I had been left with no one.

But it didn't *have* to be that way. I could create a new family, one possibly even stronger and closer than the one I'd been raised with. After all, these were the people I'd be in the Shadowthorn with, standing back-to-back, shadowsteel blades raised as we are surrounded by an army of demons.

And I suppose that reason, above anything purely social, is why I let myself get close to them. I need to be able to rely on them once we're in the field, and they need to know they can rely on me.

I sought out Güthric first, to make amends and to ensure he knew I held no grudges over what happened between us; I made small conversation with Silver whenever she was feeling generous enough to share more than three words about herself; and I extended an invitation to Maxwell to join Dimitri and me in the library during our studies, though I'm fairly certain we needed his wealth of knowledge more than he needed to spend time studying with us.

And tonight, after a month of shutting down her persistent pestering, I finally caved and agreed to meet up with Fox, Saimenimus, and Güthric for a few ales after dinner.

"You won't regret it," Fox assures me, leading me down the dark corridors with a lantern stretched out ahead of her. "But whatever you do, don't try to keep up with them. They'll drink you under the table, no doubt about it."

I snort a laugh so hard that the flame of her lantern flickers. "Like I had it in my head that I was going to out-drink Saimenimus. I'm pretty sure alcohol has replaced the blood in his veins."

Fox tugs me sharply into an open door to our left, a fireplace already lit inside the long, dim room. We find Saimenimus lounging in an armchair, his legs dangling carelessly over the armrest, a bottle of something amber hanging loosely from his hand.

He raises an eyebrow at me in feigned delight, apparently having caught our conversation. "You think that's really possible? I've never thought to try, but it sure would save me the hassle of plucking these from the kitchen every night." He raises the bottle to me before pressing it to his lips and tossing it back. He finishes with a gasp that sounds like he's trying to put the fire out in his throat, then says, "And how many times do I have to tell you? It's Sai. Saimenimus was the poor, aristocratic bloke my parents thought I'd become, not the charming winner you see before you today."

"Sorry," I say sheepishly. "Sai."

"Don't let him bully you," Fox says, shoving me gently to walk farther into the room.

As she moves toward the fireplace, to where Sai sits in one of the two chairs—upholstered in forest green and gilded in gold—my eyes devour everything else in room. From where I stand in the doorway, it's like looking into a box with only a match to illuminate what's inside. The farthest corners of the room are too dark to discern any details, but the glow from the fire casts everything else in a deep orange hue. It makes the dark wood table appear burned, the walls distorted by flickering shadows.

Other than the furniture, the room is largely empty, which is odd considering most of the compounds are busy with decor. There is a small bookshelf, but it can hardly be called such considering there are so few books stacked on its shelves. Only one painting hangs on the wall above the fireplace, a portrait of some impactful Crusader, no doubt, that no one alive still remembers.

I venture a step into the room, closer toward my friends.

Fox grabs the bottle from Sai, eager to begin the night. She brings the bottle with her to take a seat at the table, and seeing she's taken his booze, Sai stands as well, swaying a little during the short walk. He pulls out the chair at the head of the table, the legs grinding against the uncarpeted flooring until he's created enough space to plop into it with much the same casual grace with which he had in his former chair.

"What is this place?" I ask them.

By way of answering, Fox pats the table across from her.

I'm not standing my ground in the doorway or anything, and seeing as I've already come all this way, I do as she asks and sit.

"A solar, of sorts," Sai says, eyeing me like he knows exactly why I asked. "If you're worried about being here, don't be. The men's dorms are right through there—" He points a languid, crooked finger to another arched doorway behind him before gesturing to the rest of the room with his arms out wide. "It's meant to be a place where we can relax, read, and most importantly, enjoy the company of others."

My attention snaps to Fox. "Do we have one of these?"

"Yep." She nods. "It's just nowhere near as elegant as this one." She takes another swig from the bottle.

My confused scowl brings out an uproar of laughter from them both, and Fox nearly sprays me with the mouthful of fluid; she is laughing too hard to swallow.

Instead, she offers me the bottle. I'm tempted to decline. We have an early morning tomorrow, as we do most days, and I'm sure that whatever is sloshing around in that jar will only cause me a headache. But, listening to Fox goad and tease me about being just as uptight as Dimitri is also migraine-inducing, so I grab the bottle and pour the amber fluid down my throat.

It burns—Holy Blight does it burn! It's no wonder Sai's cheeks are often scorched red. This stuff must be curated from the sun itself.

"I thought you said we were drinking ale," I sputter between rasping coughs.

Fox becomes nearly hysterical.

Sai grabs the bottle. "What kind of ale do you drink from a bottle?"

"I—" I'm about to argue that I typically *don't* drink ale; I don't drink anything. But, watching the two of them smirk and chortle, feeling the warmth of the spirit slither down into my belly and settle there like a sleeping cobra, I decide to let it go and join in the laughter.

Once she's settled, Fox begins shuffling a stack of cards I hadn't even noticed she was holding. Though she keeps the face of them pointed down at the table, I glimpse the detailed sketches every now and then. Most are a varying assortment of medallions, but a few have depictions of people: a squire, a knight, a regal woman in an extravagant gown of velvet and dazzled with jewelry.

"I didn't know you had playing cards," I say, staring at Fox's hands with wonderment as they work.

She raises a mischievous brow at me. "I have everything. You'd be surprised what you can nab when people are distracted by flattery or spirits…or both."

"Is that why you've invited me here?" I tease. "Still convinced I have something worth pocketing?"

Sai leans over the table. There's a challenge in his posture, in the way he plants his elbows and keeps his hands clasped close to his chest. "Truth be told, I was the one who suggested you come."

"And why's that?" I ask, a slight flutter of nerves in my belly wrestling with and losing to the cobra wrapped inside there. I become all too suddenly aware that Fox is the only one who knows that something is off about me. She could've told Sai and lured me here under false pretenses, though I don't know what the two of them would do to me. I've heard stories of mages being dismembered, of villagers feeding their bodies to blazing fires while they are still alive and conscious.

Nervously, my eyes flicker to the fire now, the crackle of the logs suddenly as loud as cannon fire in my ears.

Sai settles back into his seat. "Because I thought you deserved a rematch, maybe something that's a little more up your alley."

"A rematch?" I ask, confused.

He answers me only with a raise of his eyebrows and an indication toward the doorway.

It's only then that I hear the slow, booming footsteps approaching from the hallway. I twist in my chair to look over my shoulder, even though I know it can be none other than Güthric who is joining us. In the time that we've been here, I've seen no one else equal in his size, not even any of the other Crusaders.

His hulking figure appears in the doorway now, a brutish, simple grin plastered between his roughly shaved cheeks.

He pumps his fist into the air, two bottles of wine clenched between his thick fingers, and bellows out a hearty laugh at the sight of us. "We drink!"

A smile breaks out on my own face. Though we've settled things between us, I'll admit that it would be nice having some form of retribution for the beating he gave me. My experience with card games is limited, but surely I'll pick it up quicker than our simple Güthric will.

But as the man enters, leaving the doorway visible behind him, I spy someone in his shadow. Silver stands like a statue in mourning. She carries herself with ethereal grace as she enters the room, and though I find myself perplexed by her presence, I don't dare ask her why she's come, lest risk giving her any option to leave. It's rare that she joins us for any social activities, but I'm always grateful when she does. There's something comforting about her presence, something motherly despite her cold exterior.

But in Silver's wake, Eparah appears next, clad in the black leathers that the Crusaders never seem to take off, and the purple crest with the black mountains and white phoenix on her chest that marks her as our superior.

I stiffen in her arrival. Only my eyes dare to move, flicking to Fox to find that she is too focused on shuffling the cards to have noticed. Güthric has Sai enveloped in a rowdy embrace, so I can't tell if he's seen our captain either, and Silver enters the room as if not a single one of us are present.

With no other choice, I return my wide gaze to greet our captain.

"Relax, Halira," Eparah says smoothly. She filters into the room, smooth and swaying, like a steady brook. "There's no need to look so alarmed. I'm off duty."

"Like that's a thing," Sai snorts.

I'm still frozen in place as Güthric takes the seat beside me, Silver the one beside him, and Eparah across from Güthric. She detaches her captain sigil from her leather and sets it on the table.

It's not like we've been told not to convene like this, men mingling with the women over spirits and hearty laughs, but there's something about having our captain among us that makes me rigid.

That is, until she says, "Now, if I had been General Alphonse, well, that'd be a different story."

Sai bellows a hearty laugh. "Remember when he nearly caught us playing Chicken at the border? We scattered like a dropped bag of marbles, and big ol' Güthric here"—he leans across the table, shaking the man's shoulder—"thought his best bet for hiding was behind the thinnest birch tree in the yard."

"It work," Güthric grunts, grinning. "He not see me."

"Only because he thinks you're a strange man who would find enjoyment in things like spending your evenings with your face pressed against a tree trunk," Sai says, throwing himself back into his chair in a fit of laughter with tears running down his cheeks.

Eparah joins in, her laughter bright and brassy compared to Güthric's baritone and Sai's cackle. Even Silver smiles at the memory. And it must be the rye warming me and melting away my inhibitions, because I feel the snicker crawling up my throat as well, and suddenly it no longer matters what Eparah's rank is, only that we are all together.

The only person we're missing to make this family feel complete is Dimitri. They'd stopped inviting him to these gatherings days ago. Most of the time, he'd declined anyway, insisting that he had more productive things to do. I'd been told that on the rare occasion he did show, he'd spend most of the time telling the others all the ways in which they were breaking the rules or wasting their time or other varying castings of judgment.

But tonight, I'd finally decided to come. For myself. I'd been training hard, studying even harder, and I was in desperate need of a break.

Fox gives the playing cards a final shuffle before slamming the deck in the center of the table. "We ready to play?"

"What's the game tonight?" Eparah asks. "You lot prepared to lose at Basetta again?"

"As I recall, it was I who walked away the victor from that game," Sai says.

"No Basetta tonight," Fox tells us. "I thought we'd start with some Primero instead. Everyone know the rules?"

"No," I admit.

Fox swiftly starts going through the rules, but I just as quickly tune her out when I notice the interaction between two of our comrades. Güthric uses his teeth to uncork one of his bottles of wine. He hands it to Silver, who eyes it warily. But with a wide, toothy grin, Güthric pulls out a glass from who-knows-where and sets it on the table before them. Silver's smile is nearly imperceptible, demure and satisfied with a hint of appreciation, and she inclines her head for him to fill her glass.

"Understood?"

It takes me a moment to realize someone's talking to me. As Güthric passes the bottle to Eparah, I shake my head, returning my attention to Fox. "Sorry…I missed that. What were you saying?"

She throws her head back with a groan.

Sai reaches across the table for the deck of cards. "It's all right. You can join the next match. It's just as easy to learn by watching. Besides, I appear to have a bone to pick with our captain here."

From behind the tipped back wine bottle, Eparah wriggles her eyebrows at him.

"In," Güthric says.

"Fox, you want to do the honors?" Sai asks.

"My pleasure."

"Halira, you mind? I'll trade you," Eparah says, pressing the bottle against my chest and standing.

It doesn't take long to figure out what she's suggesting, so I grab the bottle and give her my seat so that the four contenders can be closer to one another.

The bottles continue to be passed around a few times each, but I mostly avoid Sai's. If I'm going to drink, I at least want it to be a remotely enjoyable experience, and the wine Güthric brought is sweetened with hawthorn berries and honey, reminding me a little of the forest behind my home and the beehives my mother and I would tend.

The game itself is intriguing to watch, but even though I have a visible view of Eparah's hand, it's not so easy to understand. Fox deals them two cards a piece and asks if each of them will be bidding. Everyone declines, and she deals out two more.

"We play with a hand of four cards," she explains to me, but judging from the way her eyes seem to hyperfocus on her hand, I don't think I'll be receiving much more instruction from her.

Güthric begins. He announces, "Numerus twenty," and puts the other unopened bottle of wine on the table beside the remaining cards.

Sai sighs. "You don't have to bid if you don't have a good hand yet."

Güthric frowns, looking to his cards with mounting approval. "I has good hand."

"A numerus isn't a—never mind. Eparah, you're up."

On Eparah's turn she says she'll pass, discarding two cards of high suit to draw two more. When she adds the six of clubs to her existing hand of an ace of clubs and a four of hearts, she winks at me. I pretend to be excited for her, even though I have no idea how that will be of use to her. Her second card is a king of hearts, which I understand to typically be a high-ranking card, but she seems disinterested in it.

At the start of Sai's turn, he exclaims, "Numerus forty-two," and tosses a silver coin onto the table.

"You really want to bet on a numerus?" Eparah asks.

"Maybe it's a numerus, maybe it isn't," he says cryptically, only fortifying my confusion.

"Well, if you're bidding, I hardly think a silver coin matches the bid already on the table."

Sai's mouth falls wide. He extends his arms out toward the bottle. "We both know he didn't spend a single silver on this bottle, so I think it's a remarkably fair bid."

Güthric's smile is wicked.

Eparah snickers.

"Right," Sai continues. "Now that that's settled, let me see what you have."

He reaches out an upturned palm, and Güthric hands him his cards. Sai snorts when he peeks at them, rolls his eyes, and hands them back.

"Make that two silver," he says, tossing in another coin.

"All right my turn," Fox says, winking at me. "Primero ten, and I'll match your bid, *Saimenimus*."

The play continues for three rounds. I keep expecting to catch on to something, to figure out what the numbers mean, or why each of them seem to be calling out different words, but nothing sticks. Every time I think I understand, something new is mentioned, or Eparah becomes excited about a card I didn't expect her to. All I know is she is extremely confident when she calls a *maximus forty-six*, and utterly devastated when the game ends and Sai reveals *chorus eighty-four*.

"You expect me to believe you actually won with the best

hand you can possibly get in this game?" Eparah exclaims. She's holding on to the tops of his hands, preventing him from grabbing his bounty.

His glare is playful. "Unless I'm more intoxicated than I realize, and my eyes are no longer reliable, it would appear so. This is a hand of four sevens, correct? One of each suit?"

She growls, releasing him with a huff as she sinks back into her seat. "I demand a rematch."

Sai drags his winnings across the table, the bottle rocking but his eyes fixed on it and ready to catch it should it fall. Of course, it doesn't.

"So sorry," he says. "I believe your turn is over. Fox's maximus forty-nine beats your maximus forty-six. And, Güthric…better luck next time, friend. It looks like the two of you are out, and Halira and Silver are in."

"Oh," I say, blanching. My arms fly up in defense. "I don't think I could."

"Nonsense," Sai says. "Besides, you need to warm up before your match with Güthric. As you can see, he's not much of an opponent, but still. I wouldn't want to throw you in with the wolves blind, even if that particular wolf is more like a sheep."

As Eparah frees her chair, a swagger to her step that hadn't been there the first time we switched seats, I am overcome by a warmth that I can't place, one different from the heat radiating from the fire, or the blanket of intoxication and relaxation that has wrapped itself around me. No, this is something else, something more profound.

For the first time in the month since my parents' deaths, I actually remember what having a family feels like. Whatever void had been created when their deaths tore my heart apart, I realize for the first time in weeks that it has been slowly filling. With Eparah's friendly smile, Fox's wry humor, the way Güthric lumbers like an ox but has as a heart as gentle as a butterfly. These people—the strangers I traveled from Gravenburg to Nigh with, nearly losing our toes to the frost, losing everything else before then—they are my family now.

And I realize now, in the glow of the firelight, that there is nothing I am more grateful for than having them.

"All right, all right," I say, scooting my chair out from under me. My legs, too, are unstable beneath me. I've lost track of how many drinks I've taken—seven, eight?—and so when I sidestep to the seat beside me, I crash into the arm and nearly fall to the ground. Warm laughter fills the hall, and Sai is surprisingly quick to offer me a hand up.

With his help, I settle into my chair. My silver hair hangs before my eyes, tussled from the fall. I blow the strands away from my face and point a challenging finger at Fox.

"Fine. I'll play your game. But you'll need to walk me through it better than last time. I could hardly keep up—"

Bing-bong.

I'm cut short by the brassy, hollow clang of the bell tower's toll. Güthric jolts out of his chair, sobered in an instant. Sai, Fox, Silver, and I are a bit more delayed, but we spring to our feet before the second toll, looking over our shoulders toward the direction of the tower as if we'll be able to see through these walls and the corridors between here and there.

"Two rings," Eparah says, still standing behind me. "They want everyone in the courtyard."

Sai scoffs. "Seems a little late in the evening for a—"

Bing-bong.

Everyone stills, becoming as rigid and silent as death itself.

Three tolls mean the arrival of the Magistrate; it's the same throughout all of Arcathain since the number three is revered as a number of great power. There were three sides during the Great Rift: the mages, the Primordials, and the humans. There are three lands now: Illashore, the Shadowthorn, and Arcathain. Three is believed to be the perfect balance of all things, thereby being a number of great power, a number perfect for announcing the Magistrate, the most powerful man in all of Arcathain.

Only, each of us already knows how unlikely an impromptu visit from the Magistrate is, which can only mean—

Bing-bong.

The fourth toll.

"Demon scourge," breathes Silver, a shudder in her breath.

But when the bell rings a fifth time, Eparah gasps. In almost one motion, she slams the bottle down and rips her silver insignia from the table, pinning it back in her black leather.

"Get to your rooms!" she shouts over her shoulder, already racing toward the door. "They're inside the castle."

"They're w-what?" Sai stammers.

Güthric clamps a fist to his chest. "I help."

"No!" Eparah roars, spinning back around to face us. All traces of her usually friendly expression have vanished behind the hard lines of her face. "Inducted Crusaders only. I won't have any more of my recruits dying tonight."

"What's going on?" someone asks as they rush into the room.

I turn to see that it's not just one *someone*, but many. A dozen or more of the male recruits have come out of their dorm to see what the excitement is about. My heart flutters when I spy Dimitri among them.

"Dimitri!" I blurt, stumbling to his side. I crash into his arms, and I'm grateful he catches me.

Thoughts of the scourge in Gravenburg are too fresh, too painfully seared in my mind to think of anything else. My friends. My neighbors. The refugees from Ashenvale who we'd been sheltering. My parents. Dozens of lives were claimed that night by the foul creatures that preyed on us, but Dimitri and I had survived. Dimitri *protected* me. If I'm to survive tonight, I know it will be at his side, so I cling to him like he is a cliff's ledge and I am dangling over it.

"You can't just expect us to hide out while the rest of you defend the fort," Fox says, stepping forward. "If they're inside, we should join the fight!"

"That's enough!" Eparah roars. She looks every vision of a lion roaring at her pride, and she stares each and every one of us down. "You *will* return to your rooms, and you will stay there until you are sent for."

"But—"

"That's an order!"

We're given no other chance to argue. Eparah ducks out of the room and into the dim halls without another glance back. Most of the recruits who joined us head back toward their dorms. The rest of us gawk at each other, ears straining for the guttural, screeching sounds of impending danger that could be anywhere inside these stone walls. But I hear none. Wherever the demons are, they're not in this wing.

I remember then, the night I met Eparah in the east wing. She'd told me that the demons infiltrated the castle through the Blighted corridors. She insisted that they now had Crusaders posted but, thinking about it now, how often do Crusaders fall in the Shadowthorn? How many demons would it take to get past the—what two? Three? Four Crusaders, maximum, who are placed at the eastern wing?

When Dimitri releases me, the cold takes his place. It wraps its arms around me, digs its nails into my skin, and the sensation is so jarring, so counter to everything I wanted that I stagger back.

"You should go," he says, matter of fact and to the point.

"Go?" Sai snorts. "They should stay. Their dorms are halfway across the castle. They'd be safer if they stayed here for the night."

"That's not what the captain said," Dimitri growls, a muscle feathering along his jaw.

"Piss on a mage! Are you daft, boy?" Sai shouts, a disbelieving smile plastered on his face. "We can't send them out there. We don't even know where the demons are!"

"Well, they can't stay here either. There's a reason there's a male dorm and female dorm. They don't want us commingling like that. It's against the rules—"

"Rules be Blighted!" Sai becomes hysterical. He marches across the room, pushing past me so that he's right in Dimitri's face. "Maybe you're too young to have figured this out yet, but rules are subjective. They're created to apply to general scenarios in the interest of keeping people in line. But let me tell you something: this is not a general scenario. This is one of those instances where the rules are meant to be broken. Or would you rather send our friends out to their possible deaths?"

"Hey," Fox bristles. "We can handle ourselves."

"Not helping," Sai sings out the corner of his mouth. He turns back to Dimitri, examining him like a child would look down into a pond in hopes of spying a fish or something to prove that their trek through the woods hadn't been for nothing.

Dimitri only looks away, nostrils flaring.

"Tell you what," Sai says. "Should we survive the night— should General Alphonse and our oh-so-uptight captain—I promise I'll take the blame for insisting the ladies stay."

The two of them are silent for a moment. I keep looking over my shoulder like we are losing time, but the truth is, I have no way of knowing. I'm not sure how bad the infiltration is, how many demons have broken into the castle, how many Crusaders are fighting, how many have already died, but I know I'd feel immensely better if I was in a room that had a door, especially one that locked, instead of standing out here in the open.

"Get out of my face," Dimitri growls at long last.

"Gladly," Sai sings, bowing his head. Then he turns around

and extends an arm out toward us. "Come on, girls, you're sleeping with us tonight. My cot's plenty big enough for two, maybe even all three of you."

"In your dreams," Fox says, equally as singsong. She comes up beside me and takes my hand into hers, soft and warm and steadying. "Are there even any empty beds in the men's dorm? I heard you guys were crowded."

"I has beds," Güthric announces, but though his response is to Fox, he's staring only at Silver. "I protect."

The raven-haired woman gives a vigorous, nearly imperceptible nod, but I'm surprised she's even registered what he's said. Her eyes have gone wild, her body trembling.

Güthric holds out his hand, as large as a dinner plate, and Silver slides hers atop of his. He leads her toward the male dorms, glancing to Fox and I only once to tell us to follow. I have no intention of moving, not without Dimitri. We survived Gravenburg together, and we'll survive this scourge together too.

But Fox's grip is unbreakable. I stumble along with them, trying desperately to seek out Dimitri's gaze, but he won't look at me. He just stares at the fireplace, fire drawn to fire. And eventually, I stop fighting. I'm too uncoordinated right now to protest anyway, and the jarring tugging makes me queasy, so instead, I let Fox and Güthric lead us into one of the dorms and shut the door behind us.

IN THE NIGHT

MALE DORMS, CASTLE OF NIGH, ARCATHAIN

I awaken with a jolt to the snarling rumble of a demon about to devour its meal. Or at least, that's how I make sense of the noise I hear in the pitch darkness. But as I bolt upright on my cot, the sound becomes rhythmic, a slow, steady, grumbling inhale followed by a short, airy exhale.

The rigidity of my bones relaxes when I remember, groggily, that we're not in our usual rooms, and that I'm only hearing Güthric snoring a few beds down.

My eyes adjust to the moonlight offered from the skylight overhead, and I peek down the row of cots blearily. Silver rests like a peaceful princess frozen in snow, while Fox looks like someone threw her on the bed, all crooked and splayed limbs, and then haplessly flung a blanket over her, though it only reached her legs. And Güthric, he looks like he could use four of these small cots pushed together in order to sleep comfortably. Then again, it doesn't seem to bother him that his head is pressed against the wall, his feet and arms dangling over the edge of the bed. He sleeps on, as do the half dozen other recruits in the room with us.

Vaguely, I remember falling asleep. I crashed onto the bed,

the room spinning around me and certain I wouldn't be able to sleep until we heard that the threat had been dealt with, and then, I was out.

But now that a few hours have passed, and the coaxing effects of the alcohol have worn off—aside from the lingering pounding in my head—I can think of nothing but the attack on the castle.

For all I know, the fight could still be going. Or, worse yet, maybe it finished and we are the only ones left as the demons work their way through the corridors, killing everyone they come across.

I swing my legs over the side of the bed, hop to the cold floor, and take a moment to steady myself. Almost by instinct, my hand finds Tor's shadowsteel dagger at my hip. Even though I'm still learning to use it in any matter that could be described as useful, it always makes me feel safer knowing it's nearby, like my brother himself was walking beside me.

On the soft pads of my feet, I tiptoe toward the door. When I crack it to glance out into the adjoining corridor of bedrooms, something heavy leaning on the other side makes the door swing wide.

A soft gasp escapes my lips, and it's not until the startle passes that I realize how utterly useless such a response is—I wasn't even loud enough to alert anyone else in the room.

A body crashes at my feet, and despite the darkness, I understand the implications all too well. Someone's dead, which means a demon can't be far.

But as the body falls, as I jump back, the silhouette grunts.

"Dimitri?" I whisper, and then falling to his side on my knees, add, "Are you all right? What happened?"

He pushes himself up onto his elbow, rubbing his head with his other arm. "Ow," he whispers. "What are you doing awake?"

Confused by the seemingly normal tone in his voice and his

question, and still too groggy to counter, I simply answer, "I—I couldn't sleep."

I look out into the hallway, sniff the air. Blood has a distinct scent. It's heavy and metallic and, most of all, sickening. I know this because of my best friend's former profession. But the hallway smells of none of these things. All I can smell is the burning coals of the dying fire, the crisp winter air that's seeped into these halls, and the musky, warmth of Dimitri as he closes the door behind us and sits up, inching closer.

"What are you doing out here?" I ask, eyeing him carefully.

"I couldn't sleep either," he admits.

There isn't much light in here, only the outskirts of what's left from the fire's glow in the other room, but I can feel his eyes on mine, feel the warmth of his breath against my cheek.

I lean back on my heels and put some distance between us. The cold settles into me like I've just landed in snow, but it's the crisp kind of reawakening I need to realize where we are, where Dimitri has seemingly been all night.

"Were you…guarding the door?"

He doesn't respond, and in the darkness, his silence only serves to confirm my suspicions.

Eventually, he clears his throat, the short laugh that follows doing its best to conceal it. "Someone had to. We all know just how abysmal you are at fighting—"

"Hey!" I snap.

He continues. "And that's when you're sober. You were piss drunk last night."

I swing at him, hoping to slam my fist into his shoulder and reveling in the thought that if I hit his jaw by accident instead, I can just blame the pitch darkness. But Dimitri's fingers grasp my wrist with the swiftness of a hawk diving from the sky. He uses the momentum to shove my arm aside, and I fall forward, stumbling and twisting, my shoulder slamming into his chest.

If I had any plans of insisting I was actually coordinated or could ever hold my own ground in a fight, I'd just lost it. And perhaps it's the alcohol, the lack of sleep, or just the sheer exhaustion of training relentlessly for the past month and finally catching a moment's reprieve, but the both of us explode with laughter.

We spend the next few moments shushing each other so that we don't disturb any of the other recruits from their slumber, and then laughing all the harder at how unbelievable it is that any of them are still sleeping.

It's only when I realize, with sobering clarity, that I'm resting my head back on Dimitri's shoulder, that his arm has slid its way around my waist to wrap me protectively against him, that my laughter turns into something else.

Quick breaths.

A fluttering of wings in my stomach.

Dimitri's laughter fades at the same moment mine does. His fingers stiffen against my hip like he's unsure if he should release me or pull me closer, and I'm not sure either. We've been friends for so long now; he means more to me than anyone else alive, but I know neither of us are headed anywhere. The only future that lies ahead for the both of us is death.

And perhaps it's for this reason that I twist around in his arms, careful not to break away from his comforting embrace. Over my shoulder, I search for his eyes in the dark and only recognize them by the glint of the firelight reflected there.

My heart quickens. We've experienced so much together, but this is unchartered territory.

He swallows, his voice shaky and hoarse. "I can still smell the wine on your breath."

"Shut up," I say, a small laugh trickling through my words, but my voice sounds just as weak as his, my words soft and frightful as I continue to inch closer and closer until his lips are so close to mine that they almost brush against each other. "Just, shut up."

Dimitri stops speaking, stops moving. Even where I'm pressed against his chest, I can't even feel his lungs moving. Time itself seems to have joined in the winter's freezing, as if all of Arcathain is holding its breath just for this moment.

For us.

With a shaky inhale, I close the last sliver of space between us and press my lips against his. His kiss is sweet and soft at first, a cautious toe dipped into the pool of uncertainty. A first kiss, dainty and unsure, awkward and frightening.

Though the moment feels suspended, my lips pressed against his, my mind is anything but still. Doubt and fear and confusion rage inside me. I worry about what he's thinking, what I'm feeling; I worry that this might've been a mistake and that I've just changed things between us forever. I can't live without him; he's all I have from home.

Suddenly, I'm overcome by an even greater dread. What if Dimitri discovers what I am? What if he finds out that I have… something far too similar to magic? I'd lose him forever then. If anyone was convicted in their hate of the mages, it's Dimitri.

My lips break apart from his at the flash of possibility. With my eyes still shut, I can see the disdainful way he'd look at me. It cracks my heart in two.

But when I open my eyes, it's not hatred I find staring back at me through his firelit eyes, but untethered longing.

"I've wanted to do that for so long," he admits, cautiously bringing his hand up to hook around the back of my neck. "Please tell me that won't be the last time."

Just like that, the fear that had me frozen melts away as a flare of fire lights in my core.

I shake my head, too breathless to speak, and Dimitri drags me to him again.

A surge of heat ignites my skin as our lips find each other

again. This time he's less cautious, less careful. Like a bear awakened, Dimitri's hand flexes where it's been stationed on my hip, becoming more explorative and dangerous. The hand crooked around my neck, desperate and greedy, draws me deeper into him still, pressing me so close that I gasp.

But he's not ready for air yet, and truthfully, neither am I.

The two of us crash into each other again, and a wave of euphoria, charged and urgent, rolls over me. I sigh against his mouth as he opens it to mine. Time loses all meaning here. I can't tell if I've been kissing him for seconds or days, but however long, it's still not enough. I'm afraid for it to stop, afraid we'll break away and he'll see me as he used to: a bratty child uninterested in following the rules.

But he keeps kissing me, his lips warm and silken against my own. His hands don't seem to know what to do —neither do mine—but I savor their clumsy hold. They clutch onto each other so tightly, as if we're both afraid of what will happen when we let go. But the longer we stay here, the more I submerge my tongue into his delicious taste, the less worried I become. Something about him feels so comfortable, so natural, that in no time at all I convince myself that we've done this before. This isn't our first kiss, but one of many that we were inevitably bound to share.

And I revel in every one of them.

The small brushes of our lips as we break for air.

The hungry, deep drinks we take of each other.

The playful nips and licks and pecks.

The kisses he plants on my forehead and cheeks; the ones I leave trailing along his jaw.

For the life of me, I can't figure out why it's never come to this before. Though, the longer it goes on, the more I realize that it's probably best it hadn't; now that I know what it feels like to be pressed up against him, now that I know what he tastes like, what he sounds like when I kiss just the right spot on his neck, I don't ever want to stop.

But after hours of clinging to each other like our lives depend on it, as the sunlight slowly begins to shine through the skylight above and when we hear our fellow recruits waking and readying for the day, we finally, begrudgingly, pull ourselves apart.

Which is just as well, because not a moment sooner, the bell strikes twice. The bedroom doors swing wide, and recruits start shuffling out of their quarters with tossed hair and drool still crusted on their chins.

Dimitri and I have already shot to our feet and are standing at an awkwardly safe distance apart when the door to the dorm I'd been sleeping in opens wide. Güthric's lumbering form staggers out first, followed by Silver's graceful, elegant strides. All of the other recruits we'd been bunking with exit before Fox finally emerges, bleary-eyed and hair tussled.

"There you are. I was wondering where you'd run off to—" She stops short, spying Dimitri a safe, but obviously self-conscious distance away from me. She glances between the two of us, her lips twisting with the most obnoxious of grins before she winks at me. "I should've known you'd find a way to keep warm last night."

My cheeks ignite with prickling embarrassment. My mouth unhinges, prepared to defend myself and my intentions, but it's of no use. A smile sneaks its way to the edge of my lips and I've given myself away, as if it hadn't been obvious before.

Fox chuckles as she walks by me to join the others.

"Come on," Dimitri says stiffly. "I don't want to miss the announcement."

He doesn't wait to see if I'm following behind him, and I don't know why I think he should. He's always been this way: duty first, everything else second. And I know I shouldn't lament over it, now of all times. Just because we kissed doesn't mean anything else has changed. He's still *him* and I'm still *me*.

But I find myself gazing back to the place on the floor where we'd spent the past few hours enveloped in each other, wishing the sun had never risen.

Caught up in my midnight romance, I'd almost forgotten what this announcement would be about until I enter the congested courtyard. The Castle of Nigh had been infiltrated—my captain among those sent into battle. If the crowd of Crusaders congregated at the bell tower was any thinner than the last time we convened, if our numbers are fewer since the night's events, it's difficult to tell. Though every single one of us does *seem* different, changed. Darkness has made a home beneath most of our eyes. Some have arrived still dripping in the demons' black blood, still out of breath as if the battle only just ended.

Or perhaps is still ongoing.

When General Alphonse addresses his legion, I can't help but notice that one captain in particular is missing from his flank.

Out of everyone here, he seems the most well-rested. His porcelain skin is taut and flawless. His dark hair isn't matted by demon blood, but instead combed down his back to silken perfection. But there's no mistaking the changes in his armor. Leathers are typically worn by the Crusaders. They allow us to be more agile than steel would, and they're mostly just as effective considering the demons only wield their claws, not blades.

However, today Alphonse has added some silver plating to his armor. His chest is bulkier with an additional breastplate, his shoulders heavy with spiked metal pads. He's so bulked out that it would be easy to mistake him for someone else—*anyone* with the body of a warrior instead of a feeble, spoiled brat. His thighs, his calves, even his feet have been fitted with a steel layer of protection, just in case things become too dire here.

I doubt he'll remain here that long though. His father might've given him this assignment to make him prove his worth, but he's still the Magistrate's son. If Alphonse decides he needs to flee to save himself, I have no doubt that my uncle wouldn't accept him with welcome arms and leave the rest of us here to die.

Standing at the front of the crowd, Alphonse raises his arms. Silence follows, slow and steady, until all eyes are fixed forward.

"Crusaders of Arcathain," he begins, bowing his head in consternation. Dark hair cascades over his shoulders, casting all but his pointed nose in shadow. "As I'm sure you are aware, the Crusaders stationed at the eastern wing of the castle were ambushed yestereve, the compound infiltrated. Throughout the night, our warriors fought to secure these walls and defend the east wing from another onslaught, and they were successful. However, the Blight continues to spread over the castle, and now that the demons are aware of us, I'm afraid now more than ever that the east wing will serve as a beacon to all that is Blighted.

"I have sent word to the Senate for aid in closing off the east wing, once and for all, but in the meantime, I have tripled those we have stationed there. Crusaders, your first order of business is to report to your captains. They have your new assignments, and washing linens or emptying piss pots is no longer among them. Recruits, we shall convene, as usual, at the training grounds.

"A final word before you go," he says. Slowly, he stares out among the crowd, frightening in his resolve and conviction.

"Man has fought demon for centuries, and we are still standing while their numbers dwindle. We will *always* be standing. Just like the day always extinguishes the night, we will *always* extinguish the demons who come into our land. They are scum. They are filth. They are the pathetic scabs of the nearly extinct Primordials, and soon they will be extinct too. This is our home, our land, and we are the Shadow Crusade!"

He pumps his fist in the air. "Of one country!"

And the Crusaders roar back, the air abuzz. "Of one blood!"

ANCIENT SHADOWSTEEL

TRAINING GROUNDS, CASTLE OF NIGH, ARCATHAIN

"Where is Captain Eparah?" Silver is first to ask. "Has she survived?"

Alphonse tries placating us. "Your captain is alive and unharmed. However, I'm afraid we lost some of our other senior ranking officials, and therefore she has been temporarily reassigned to oversee the security of the east wing. As I mentioned, we have declared a state of emergency and requested aid from the Senate. Hopefully, they will provide additional Crusaders, as well as resources, to help cement the corridors closed. In the meantime, we've sent word to some of our neighboring border towns to have some of our Crusaders return along with a few others, at least until we can retrieve some of our dispatched Crusaders—"

"Forgive me, but," Maxwell says, his squeaky voice fraught with reason. "I'm afraid I'm not comprehending our stationary position. The Shadow Crusade exists across Arcathain—primarily along the border, sure, but throughout, nonetheless. If the Blight has already reached the castle, perhaps it is time to relocate. The velocity at which the Shadowthorn expands seems to suggest that within two years' time or less, the castle would be confiscated anyway."

"Silence, recruit!" Alphonse bellows.

"B-but, surely, there is no purpose to remain here." Maxwell turns his pleading eyes to his peers, to us, searching for any signs of support. He finds none. General Alphonse has made it clear what happens to those of us who challenge his word or talk back. Even I have learned to hold my tongue in his presence. "The castle will fall. It is inevitable. And until then, the demons have unrestricted access to—"

"I am warning you, recruit," Alphonse snarls, lip twitching from the restraint it takes him to temper his rage. "Speak out again, and you will be sent before the Senate and tried for treason."

Maxwell's typically vibrant amber complexion goes ashen. He staggers back, either consciously or unconsciously tucking himself deeper within the group until he's amid those in the back row, mostly hidden from our general.

"Besides, the Castle of Nigh will not fall, because we will not fail in our mission. Just this morning, a unit returned from the Shadowthorn having narrowed in on Qaeus' position. Soon the Primordial will be slain, the Blight destroyed, and the castle salvaged." Alphonse clasps his hands behind his back, a vision of arrogance and aristocracy. "Any other questions before we begin?"

I've pushed my way to the front of the group before I've even realized my feet are moving. "Let us help," I say. "Last night…we were treated like we were useless, but we could help. Either defending the east wing or by going into the Shadowthorn. Let us fight."

"As much as I'd love to send you, especially, to an early death, it would be negligent to assign recruits to two of the most crucial Crusader stations. The castle must remain defended by the most experienced among us, lest it fall, and only Crusaders are assigned shadowsteel and necro-ink in order to enter the Blighted zone.

"However, due to our heightened need for actual trained Crusaders, and given that the Magistrate himself has taken an interest in the recent scourges here, your training will be accelerated. Starting today, recruits will be expected for physical training thrice daily: before breakfast, before lunch, and before dinner. No exceptions."

Quiet groans rise from the group. Training twice daily has already pushed our bodies to our limits. I wake up sore, I stumble through my day sore, and I plummet to my cot sore. I'm tempted to tell him that he's demanding too much, but the hard line of his eyes suggests that if anyone should disagree, he will cut them down where they stand.

Lest he see the disagreement in my eyes, I avert my gaze to the dirt.

"There is good news yet, though," he continues. "In addition to an accelerated training protocol, the commanders and myself have decided to commence your training with shadowsteel."

I look back up as he takes a wide sidestep, revealing a rack of glistening silver weapons behind him. The shiniest silver I've ever seen gleams, even from the dark shadows cast over us from the tall castle. Blades that are curved, blades that are straight, blades that are short and long, and even some that aren't blades at all. An arsenal of pikes, halberds, longswords, claymores, rapiers, and every other type of weapon imaginable are presented to us like a feast.

Everyone is antsy on their toes, but no one is brave enough to approach the selection without explicit instruction.

"Güthric," Alphonse calls out. "You may come select your weapon."

The large man grunts, a devious smile splitting his face as

he pushes through the recruits to make his way to the collection. I don't think anyone is surprised when he pulls out the largest, heaviest mace I've ever seen.

Turning to face us, he grips the wooden handle and swings the spiked shadowsteel ball overhead to slam it into the ground with a thunderous crack. He pulls it back up, eyes it approvingly, and rests his new weapon over his shoulder before returning to the group.

One by one, Alphonse calls his recruits up and they select a weapon. Dimitri is called shortly after Güthric and selects a broadsword for himself, a blade that complements his sturdy stature and dependable personality and seems to suggest he should've been wielding one all his life.

Silver's called a few recruits after him, pulling from the pile a long pole with a scythe-like blade that curves at the end, sharp enough to eviscerate any of the monstrosities we may face in the Shadowthorn.

Fox and Sai both select shortswords, though where Sai's is straight and heavy, Fox's has a slight curve to it, a sleekness that suits her beautifully. Maxwell grabs a lance, jabbing the air with the pointed end like he's trying to clear cobwebs.

My hands ball into fists at my sides, as one by one everyone goes up, except me.

"I guess that just leaves you," Alphonse says when I'm the last one left. He examines his own shadowsteel sword, a light and thin blade that is nearly invisible until it catches the light, and gestures to the remaining collection of weapons. "Hopefully, you'll find something of interest among the scraps."

Hatred bubbles inside me, hot and full of rancor. I'm so tired of his mistreatment, so tired of him acting like he's better than me when he's not. I'd rather crack him in his jaw than go up and grab my weapon. Thanks to my brother, I already have shadowsteel anyway, so it's not like I need another.

Then again, a dagger is hardly a great weapon to hold when

facing a demon scourge. Its best asset is that it can be used in a tight space, if I've been tackled and pinned by a demon, and have no other range of motion but to slip my hand to my waist and rip my blade out.

But if I were facing multiple demons—dozens, even—I'd want more than a dagger to defend myself with. I'd wanted more than a dagger the day I faced the demon that'd killed my parents. I'd wanted every shadowsteel weapon known to mankind at my disposal.

Dimitri nudges my ribs, pulling me away from my hateful memories.

"Go on," he mutters out the side of his mouth.

I do as he suggests and step forward. The wooden apparatus that had just moments earlier been overflowing with weapons is now sparse. My options are limited. A half-dozen daggers remain, and it's no wonder considering we are only given one shadowsteel weapon, and as I've already said, a dagger is only handy in a few, specific instances. I need something more than a dagger at my disposal, something with range.

I glance over the remaining broadsword twice my size, aware just by looking at it that I wouldn't even be able to lift it, let alone wield it in a fight. A spear remains, a weapon that would be light to carry, but one with limited applications in a fight. Stab or throw. Stabbing is limited to only those I'd be facing head-on, and throwing anything that I could use in a fight seems absolutely reckless and counterproductive.

The thick, shining club tempts me little, as well. Without an actual blade to slice into the demons, the only way I'd kill one with a blunted weapon would be to bludgeon them to death. I'm not sure I have the muscle, nor the stomach, for such a strategy.

But my eyes fix on one of the weapons I haven't even noticed until now. A battle-axe leans against the back of the container, a few broad swords resting on top of it and blocking most of it from view. The only reason I even notice it is because of the black skull, stark against the rest of the silver, pressed beside the blade of the axe. It is truly demonic by nature, a carving from bone then singed in fire until it blackened. There is nothing but hatred and malice in the carving's hollow eyes. Four horns stem from the top of its skull, and two more curve down like tusks.

I recognize the depiction immediately as the fallen Primordial Khunas. I might not have even recognized it if it weren't for my trip to the library, the day I stumbled onto the tome of the deaths of the Primordials. The book had said Khunas was beheaded by a double-blade axe, and my recollection sends a thrilling chill down my spine, one that has me shoving the other swords aside so that I can pull the axe out and bring it closer.

Whereas the other recruits took their time in examining the ancient Arcathainian etchings of their blades, running a finger over them to test their sharpness, and looking for any chinks in the shadowsteel, I glance over the axe quickly.

Instead I stare at the black skull, my thumb tracing idly over the horns. When I pull my finger back, I find no sign of soot or ashes there and confirm what I already suspected was true: the bone was not singed by fire; it was already black to its very core.

The Primordial Khunas' skull.

Within the blink of an eye, I've already reasoned how it could be so small. The same mages who were able to relocate an entire section of the continent, no doubt had enough magic to shrink down the size of a Primordial skull.

Eyes widening with understanding, I twist the axe so that the blade is facing away from me as I search the opposite side. At first glance, I find nothing, just the pole for which the axe has been fastened to. But I run my fingers over it just as I did the skull, and I feel not only a rough indent that seems to be big enough for another axe head, but also the slightest tingle of residual magic.

Whenever a Crusader falls, his weapon is returned to the Shadow Crusade, with almost no exception. The only reason I have Tor's shadowsteel dagger is because my uncle just so happens to be the Magistrate, and with the Blight encroaching on our home, he found an ounce of compassion in his heart for his brother's family, and he sent us the dagger once Tor's body had been retrieved.

That being said, to my knowledge, every other shadowsteel weapon is returned to the Crusade, so that it may aid the future generation of Crusaders in our multi-generation battle to end the Primordials.

Over time, I'm sure this battle-axe and the spear that killed the Primordial Khaymus have been passed through hundreds of Crusaders' hands. This fight has lasted so long that I doubt most even know which weapons have accomplished what. It wasn't until I'd read the books from the eleventh floor in the library that I'd ever heard the Primordials' individual deaths referenced. I had never even considered where those weapons might be, or what became of them.

A soft, airy laugh escapes me. I turn to face my friends, my colleagues, with a sense of wonderment rippling through me like moonlight shining from my very core. I am holding one of the most powerful weapons in all of Arcathainian history, and none of them even realize it. Not only do they not realize it, they themselves could've been in this very position, but they all chose a different weapon.

As I return to my place among them, it's easier than it should be to ignore Dimitri's worried gaze.

"Are you sure that's the right weapon for you?" he whispers

to me. "With your build and skill set, a smaller blade would've been—"

"I'm sure," I tell him, my eyes fixed on the etched shadow-steel steel, to the incantations that made it possible for this axe to tear down a Primordial. "I am absolutely sure."

BRUISES

TRAINING GROUNDS, CASTLE OF NIGH, ARCATHAIN

If I thought our physical training had been grueling before, I was sorely mistaken. Now that we're using weapons, it has left me far more exerted than I've ever been in my entire life. It uses more strength to heave our shadowsteel around, takes more effort to free our blades from the wooden dummies, and forces our minds to remain alert and ready to dodge at a second's notice.

"Again!" Alphonse roars, cracking his thin sword against my already bloodied knuckles.

Weeks ago, the impact would've made me lose my grip, but thankfully my hands are so calloused by now that I almost —*almost*—can ignore it.

I tighten my hold on the black leather grip and find my stance again. What I wouldn't give to be able to bury this axe into his shoulder, to cut out his wretched tongue so he might never speak ill of me again. Of course, to do that, I'd have to best him in a match, and last I counted, he'd still bested me a hundred times out of a hundred. To this day, the only recruits I've managed to win against are Maxwell, on more than one occasion, and Sai—though, I think he'd come to training inebriated that afternoon, which isn't an advantage I'll get once I'm in Blighted territory.

Before I can hoist my axe into its readied position over my shoulder, Alphonse lunges. His needle-thin sword thrusts at my gut, and I only barely scuffle back in time to avoid getting a new bellybutton. But that wasn't his goal. No, of course it wasn't. Like he's done with nearly every one of our matches, his only intent is to throw me off-guard before the fight even has a chance to begin.

And it's working.

I jerk back so fast that my axe falls forward. If I was a true Crusader, I might be skillful enough to use the momentum to my advantage and swing it in dancing motions before delivering a counter blow. But the axe is too heavy for my unaccustomed limbs. It plummets forward, jerking me with it, and before Alphonse can slice at my exposed throat, I have no choice but to abandon my weapon and leap backward again.

I thud to the dirt. Alphonse stands over me not a moment later, his grin smug as he aims his sword carelessly at my throat.

"Yield?" he asks, the tip of his blade pressing against the hollow at the base of my neck.

I'm forced to hold my breath for fear he may spill my blood yet, but there's another reason too. I can't allow myself to speak because I wouldn't be able to give him the answer he seeks, the one I know is the only reasonable answer someone in my position should give if they want to walk away with their life intact. Call it stubbornness or pride, but I'm done yielding to him. He has shoved me to the ground too many times to count. I have cowered at his feet more times than I care to remember. Maybe I won't ever best him in a physical match, but the yielding ends here, now.

He is not better than me. He does not deserve my submission. If anything, *he* should be afraid of *me*, not the other way around, because after all these years of loathing each other, I would not hesitate to end him were our positions reversed. I would revel in punishing him for his gratuitous cruelty, for the untold bruises and scars he left on and beneath my skin, for the years of torment and ridicule, for the way he spoke ill of my mother just days after her death.

If I could, I would return every ounce of suffering he bestowed upon me.

"Yield?" he asks again, his tone as sharp as the sword he presses harder against my throat.

I inhale deeper, but my eyes are set. I will utter no such thing.

Understanding flickers behind his eyes before churning into blazing indignation.

Before either of us can make our next move, a lone squawk tears through the silence that has settled over the training grounds.

Alphonse looks up. "What in the Eyve?"

The tip of his sword only remains pressed against my skin for another second before Alphonse starts screaming and flailing, a bird, black and large, curled around his face.

"Get it off me!" he cries, stumbling backward, my body freed. "Get it off me!"

I push myself upright and watch him stumble around the grounds with a massive raven clawed to his face, one that I dare wonder might be the same bird that followed me from Gravenburg to Nigh. The only trouble is that it's a preposterous thought. Ravens aren't exactly known for attacking people unceremoniously, nor are they known for seemingly following someone across the country just to stalk them and reappear in the worst moments, but I have no other logical explanation to grasp at. If what happened a few weeks ago at the library with the mice had been me somehow, then maybe

I'm doing something to this bird too, possessing it to hang around, to step in for me when I'm in danger.

The other recruits swarm our general, but none of them get too close to do much to aid him. They don't know what to do. Despite having shadowsteel blades in hand, Alphonse is flailing about so violently that even if they tried to avail him of the wild creature, they'd likely cut Alphonse down in the process too. With no other option, they yell at him to remain calm, to stand still, to stop running about, but Alphonse either can't hear them or is actively ignoring them, too frantic to do anything but rack his hands at the bird.

For a long while, I just stare at him, stunned. I don't understand my part in it, but I *know* I have one, and I'm grateful and terrified and confused.

"Nice going," Fox says in my ear as she helps me stand.

I startle, staring at her with my heart in my chest. "I didn't—"

"Don't even try that," she says.

I clamp my mouth closed, aware that there's no point in denying what we already know to be true, even if neither of us understand it. I don't know how it's possible, but maybe I really do need to start considering that I might actually have mage blood in me, and if that's true, I need to figure out how to get rid of it so it doesn't get me killed one of these days.

Finally, the bird flies away.

Alphonse turns his back to us, hunched and heaving. Anyone else who had been attacked like that might appear wounded or in need of aid. Not Alphonse. Everything in his posture seems rippled with rage and embarrassment. He's so rigid, it looks like his bones might snap from how tightly he's flexing his muscles.

No one dares approach him.

After a few short moments, smoothing his dark, oily hair

back, he finally starts to relax, to straighten his back and resume some of his composure.

"That's enough for today," he says quietly.

When he turns around to address us, his face is sliced and bloodied. Blood rains from a particularly bad gash in his eyebrow. Suddenly, I lose all the rage I held toward him just moments ago. I had forgotten the most important thing I'd always told myself: *he is not better than me*, or rather, I am better than him. I don't need to beat him down to feel better about myself. He is just as human as I am; he bleeds just as I bleed, and he deserves life, just as I do.

His eyes are still squirrely with fear, unable to look at any of us directly, when he says, "Go. Rest. Remember, tomorrow we will meet in the catacombs for our morning session."

We start to clear the field, but Alphonse catches my elbow when I walk past him.

"Don't let this interruption go to your head," he warns. "You are nothing. You cannot defeat me, and you will not last in the Shadowthorn."

I shrug my arm from his grasp. "Yeah? What's it say about you to be bested by a raven?"

His lip pulls back, dark rage folding around him. But he blinks it away almost as soon as it's come, a cool smile twisting his lips instead. "And what's it say about you that even a raven could find the upper hand?"

He adjusts his armor with the haughtiness of an eldest child who's just tricked their parents into punishing his younger sibling. Then, head held high on his narrow, irritating neck, he leaves. Long after he's out of sight, my gaze yearns to burn holes into him.

"Don't let him get to you," Fox says over my shoulder. "We both know that raven *was* you besting him." Catching the cross look I shoot her, she adds, "Besides, magic or not, you've improved leagues since we started."

Sai walks up behind us then. "You even know which end of the axe to hold."

His comment is too casual for me to have to worry whether he heard Fox mention my alleged magic, but I glare at her anyway. She should know better than to say such things aloud, out here in the open where any number of people could hear us and report me as a mage. They wouldn't need proof. If Fox wouldn't tell them willingly why she thought I had magic, they'd force it out of her, and she *would* cave. Even if she hadn't seen me with the mice, anyone caught under the iron of the Magistrate's Legion said whatever they needed to say to end their own torment.

Fox punches his shoulder, and he walks away, leaving us alone. Or so I thought.

"You need to practice more," Dimitri growls, coming up behind us. He's slicked with sweat from yet another grueling match with Güthric. The two of them are quite well-matched, with Güthric's brutish strength and Dimitri's agile swiftness. There isn't a single cut on him, nor bruise. "You need to learn how to use your assets."

I flush at the unintentional compliment, and eager to see him squirm too, I lower my lashes. "You think I have assets?"

His cheeks burst the most scarlet of reds, like a field of blooming poppies announcing the arrival of spring.

"Aaaand that's my cue to go," Fox says. She starts to walk away, but glances over her shoulder at me. "See you tonight? Or will you be in the library *studying*?"

She winks and I stiffen, burning all the brighter. I can't tell if she's implying that Dimitri and I use *studying* as an excuse to spend time together in a more intimate and private setting or if she's referring to me summoning another army of mice. One glance at Dimitri tells me he's interpreted it as the former, so I pretend to do the same.

Fox leaves, her throaty laugh mocking us even as she disappears around the castle walls.

"I don't understand why you humor her," Dimitri finally says.

"She's my friend."

"*I'm* your friend," he says, the protectiveness of his tone turning my heart to liquid. "What has she done for you but get you in trouble?"

I open my mouth to protest, but a sigh fills the space where my words should be. "Don't you ever tire of this conversation? I know I do."

I spin on my heels so fast that my silver hair whips through the wind sharp enough to cut. I'm tired of arguing with him. For once, I just wish we could enjoy a moment together and not be at odds with one another. But we've always been like this, two branches crafted from two different trees, different in more ways than we are alike. My mother used to say that was what drew us together. Opposites seek each other out because we all need balance, we need people in our lives to help us see things from other perspectives. It is simply the way of the world: long summers need long winters.

Truth be told, I always rolled my eyes at her for believing such a thing. It always seemed to me that things would be a lot easier if more of us shared the same beliefs and common ground. If Dimitri could just see the value I find in this friendship—

His hand, calloused and damp, catches my wrist. He tugs on me to turn me around, but I resist.

With a low groan, he says what's on his mind. "You're right." It's such a foreign statement on his lips that I can't help but look back at him. His head is lowered, jaw flexed as he considers his words. "I don't trust her, but...it's clear you have chosen to. I will...stop bringing it up."

My shoulders relax, expression softening.

"On one condition," he adds.

My scowl returns with a swiftness. I roll my eyes and begin to pull away from him again, but his grip is set, as are his eyes when he spins me back into him. The palm of my hand lands on his chest, taut and warm beneath his black leathers. I'm tempted to melt right into him, and I'm sure he sees my irritation waver, though he doesn't say it.

"What's your condition?" I ask, my voice uncertain.

Despite myself, I lean into him. He releases my wrist to brush a tress of my hair back behind my ear. His hand continues to trail down my cheek, along my jaw. When he pinches my chin, he licks his lips. Closer, and closer, I am pulled into him. I am ivy with no other purpose but to wrap myself around him.

Our lips are a breath away. Sweat glistens on his skin like morning dew on grass, and I just want to gaze at him, like this, forever.

"That you remember who it was who stepped in for you when Güthric was beating you bloody, while *your friend* was partially responsible for your punishment. That you remember who it was who you enlisted with, admirably, while *your friend* was behind bars for stealing from people like us. That you remember that, once we're in the Shadowthorn, I will do whatever is in my power to continue protecting you, but people like *your friend* will always, *always* choose to protect themselves."

My mouth is open, whether to protest or in welcome invitation, I cannot tell, but Dimitri heeds it none. He leans up to place a gentle kiss on my forehead, gazes into my eyes with something akin to sorrow, though I'm not sure for what exactly, and then leaves me alone with nothing but my thoughts.

BLOODLETTING & NECRO-INK

CATACOMBS, CASTLE OF NIGH, ARCATHAIN

A raven circles overhead as we make our way across the courtyard. I watch it from the corner of my eye, unable to convince myself that it's any ordinary bird. After what happened yesterday at the training grounds, and days before that in the library, and weeks before that as we were leaving Gravenburg, I'm not sure I'll ever look at another raven the same way again.

The other recruits and I march out the north exit of the castle and veer toward the Shadowthorn, making our way through the frosted grounds and to the catacombs. My breath is grey and gauzy, and I burrow as deep as I can beneath the folds of my cloak. It's never deep enough though. Winter has been harsher this far north, and my simple wool cloak is no match for the glacial winds that seem to sweep over the valley.

This morning falls more silently than usual. No matter how early we're forced to rise, the air almost always rings with the sounds of our lighthearted chatter, the hallways echoing with the myriad of ways we keep each other distracted. We have little time to enjoy each other's company, so it's often during these transitionary periods when we are at our utmost unruly and jovial.

But today, none can seem to shake the feeling of impending doom as we approach the catacombs of Nigh.

The last time I'd been here, I hadn't thought about the bodies stacked in the crypt walls, hadn't once considered who they'd been, or what that could mean to me. Oh, but it's had all night to sink in now. They are the fallen. They are the former Crusaders whose beds we lay in, whose leather armor we have inherited, and whose weapons we now wield. They are the reflection of the only path that lies ahead of us, and ever since Alphonse told us what we would be doing today, I have not been able to once stop thinking about them.

Dimitri's sharp elbow finds my ribs. "Chin up. The dead don't bite."

"Says you," I say with an unamused laugh. "The man who's never been uncomfortable around them."

"Not *never*," he counters with a considering tilt of his head. "But life makes stone of us all before we're turned to ashes. You have to harden to the elements you're presented with, lest they crush you."

Biting my lip, I think about how, despite knowing what he says is true, I still struggle to come to terms with certain things. I know I'll see death again once we're inducted to the Shadow Crusade as true Crusaders; I know I'll see my comrades eviscerated, decapitated, devoured, but no matter how much I try to numb myself to all that darkness, my chest rips apart every time I consider it.

The thought of watching Dimitri as a pack of demons rip apart his arms and tear into the soft flesh of his neck, churns my stomach every time and makes soup of my fragile heart.

Fox huffs beside me. "Maybe *you've* allowed yourself to be turned to stone, Dimitri, but some of us would prefer to hold onto our humanity, lest we become the very beasts we're meant to hunt."

Wedged between the two of them, I cringe at the hostility that hisses in the very air around us. If it's not Dimitri poking at all of her shortcomings, it's Fox doing the same to him. Their hatred toward each other grows stronger every day, and I can't wrap my head around it. We are fighting on the same side.

Dimitri, for what it's worth, crooks his head and glances down at me as if to say, *She's* your *friend,* and then he hastens his pace to catch up to Güthric, Silver, and Sai.

My shoulders tense and I turn to Fox, ready to chastise her with the same lecture I gave Dimitri. It worked with him, after all. Maybe it'll do her some good as well.

But Fox leaves me no opening. She leans over, her voice a low whisper. "Why do you think we're just now being brought here?"

I blink back my surprise at her new line of questioning. "W-what do you mean?"

"I mean—" She huddles even closer. When Fox lowers her hood, auburn hair shining like blood against the backdrop of snowy white, I notice the short length has been tied back in two sections that barely reach past her ears. "Why wouldn't they teach us about the necro-ink in the catacombs until today? Our very first day we were here, General Alphonse sent recruits to dispose of the bodies—in fact, by now, we've all been down there at least once. Why not tell us about the necro-ink before?"

A cold, sluggish sliver, like blood that's clumped in a body long dead, slips down my spine. Since our arrival a little over a month ago, I've had to assist with disposing the bloodless bodies in the catacombs at least a dozen times. It was one of Alphonse's favorite ways to punish me, knowing just how much I hated to be in their presence. To be fair, it seemed his favorite punishment for everyone. That is, everyone except Maxwell and Fox.

To the best of my knowledge, they'd only been sent to the catacombs once each, enough to have seen the process for themselves and sooted their hands, but after that, their punishments always varied. Emptying Alphonse's chamber pot, dusting his personal study, emptying the ash from his private fireplace, changing the linens on his bed—it was like Alphonse was grooming them to become his personal assistants once they were initiated into the Shadow Crusade.

It was easy to see why he'd give such tasks to Maxwell, who hardly seemed capable of a life outside of Nigh once he was initiated, but Fox was a different story. She'd done well in every physical match she'd had. She even managed to stay standing the few times she'd been paired with Güthric.

The only rational explanation I could think of was that Alphonse was doing it to punish her and I both.

Giving her these tasks meant she had less time for socializing, which meant he was taking her away from me, something I was sure he reveled in. But it was more than that. On more than one occasion, Fox would be summoned during our lessons, missing out on crucial information about our survival in the Shadowthorn and making her all the more vulnerable once we stepped foot across the border.

Fox had been a criminal. Coming here was meant to exonerate her, but she was still being treated as if her life was meaningless. The same treatment wasn't given to all those who'd been caged alongside her on their journey here. He saved his scathing remarks and trivial tasks for her, and I knew without a doubt it was because she was someone I called friend.

Regardless of any guilt I might feel toward Fox's predicament, I was still relieved he saved those special tasks for her. Far worse than having to drag dead Crusaders into a blistering forge was having to spend any additional time with Alphonse, especially time waiting on his every whim.

Fox continues, growing more animated as she speaks. "Why have they waited all this time to tell us what that place is for, why the dead bodies are returned there, and why we keep burning them?"

My nose scrunches involuntarily at the mention of the burning bodies. Every time I'm sent to the catacombs, it takes me days to remove the acrid stench from my nostrils, and then I'm sent right back for another evening of disposal.

Her questions don't surprise me though. I've often wondered about them myself. But there's an air of secrecy about the catacombs that made it obvious we were never meant to ask.

"I don't know," I say at last.

"Please-please-*please* tell me we're not about to uncover some disturbing truth about the Shadow Crusade?"

A few of the recruits walking ahead of us glance back at her theatrical cries, but it's Dimitri's disapproving glare that has me clearing my throat, and with it, the carefree smile I'd let slip into my expression. I'm grateful our *general* isn't with us right now. Such an outburst might've earned us both a night of chamber-pot cleaning.

Clearing my throat, I straighten and resume my march forward. "I guess we'll soon find out."

Alphonse is already waiting for us when we enter the cramped foyer. Without a word, he motions for us to follow him and he leads us down below. We lose the morning sun in the dark, winding corridor, and have nothing to guide us but the torch he grabs from the wall. From our place near the back of the group, I only have the faint shadows on the wall to guide me, the vague outlines of the people before me flickering over the stone like dancing ghosts.

Once we reach the bottom and filter into the catacombs, the torchlight becomes ample, if not still dim. Dozens of them are sconced on the walls, equally spaced between the shelves of skulls.

As the recruits and I funnel into the cramped entryway, Alphonse stands with his back to us and places his torch in an empty bracket on the wall. He mutters something, and it's only when I prop myself to the tips of my toes to see over the recruits in front of me that I notice the Spirit Keep standing beside him. She looks…well, as grim and ancient as ever, but there's a liveliness behind her grey eyes that sparkles more than it ever has when I've been down here, as if she's been looking forward to whatever is about to happen here.

"Very well," Alphonse says to the Spirit Keep, before returning his upturned nose to the group. "We'll break into groups for the tour."

Tour?

Every troublesome impulse in my bones urges me to remind my incompetent cousin that we've all been down here before—some of us numerous times—and that if he's dragged us all the way down here just to learn the lay of the land then he's wasting everyone's time.

But I catch the warning flicker in Dimitri's side-eye, and so I clamp my mouth shut.

Fortunately, I'm not the only one who finds this ludicrous.

"Sir?" Maxwell's arm shoots up like a bean pole.

Alphonse notes it with an exasperated roll of his eyes. "Yes, Initiate Maxwell?"

"Um," the recruit says, head lowering self-consciously. "Forgive my boldness, General Alphonse, but have we not all visited the catacombs of Nigh by now? Would our time not be better spent training in the courtyard or studying with our scholars or—"

Pinching the bridge of his nose, Alphonse sighs, a low,

grumbling sound that makes Maxwell's breath hitch as if he were addressing a demon.

"I am well aware that I have sent each one of my recruits to the catacombs. But you were sent here with one purpose: to dispose of the dead before their bodies could rot. Nothing is more tantalizing to a demon's appetite than rotting flesh, and as such, it's imperative we dispose of the bodies quickly, and who better to carry out the less than preferable task than recruits who still have to prove themselves, hmm?"

Maxwell, still staring at the ground and the feet of the recruits before him, nods his head vigorously.

Alphonse continues. "You have seen the parts of the catacombs that were meant for you to see, but the channels down here are vast, and there is still much for you to uncover about the innerworkings of what occurs here.

"But first—" he raises a dark, slender eyebrow as he assesses us all—"A tour."

No asks any other questions. They're all either too afraid to risk being seen as challenging his authority, or they, like me, are too enthralled about what we're about to learn. If it's taken them this long to tell us—weeks after our arrival and the start of our training—it must be something intriguing.

We're split into two groups, half of the recruits heading with Alphonse while the rest of us are left with the Spirit Keep. When I notice Dimitri has been left as well, I blush. I'm still unaccustomed of how to *be* around him now. Truthfully, for the most part, nothing has changed. After the night we shared our first kiss, we have mostly gone back to being just friends… friends who, on occasion, kiss each other good night. But it hasn't gone past that. I may be new to the idea of romantic involvement, but I expected us to grow closer, to share more stolen moments together, and for the life of me, I can't tell which one of us is getting in the way of that. Maybe I'm too nervous to let things be as they are or should be, or maybe it's him. Maybe he regrets the night of the siege and how we spent those late hours tangled in each other's arms, barely even parting for air.

As I glance up at him now, his gaze remains forward, dutifully following the Spirit Keep's every word as she guides us through the narrow, dingy halls. It shouldn't sting as badly as it does. We are recruits, he and I, training for the Shadow Crusade. We have better, more important things to think about than when we'll get to melt into one another's embrace or inhale the musky scent of him or feel his breath on my neck—

Before that longing can awaken and heat my core with a delicious ache, I blink back to reality. Right now, Dimitri's attention is exactly where it should be: on the Spirit Keep. However, knowing that doesn't make me feel much better. Suppose we *are* able to find and slay Qaeus. Our lives would be our own again. We could have a future beyond dying in the Shadowthorn, and I know it's frightening to dream about, but I guess I just wish I knew if he thought about it too, what our lives will become if we are to succeed.

Sighing to myself, I follow Dimitri's lead and give the Spirit Keep my undivided attention.

With a bucket in one hand and a thin, stiletto knife in the other, she hobbles through the corridors, guiding us to a variety of nooks and crannies throughout the dismal place. She shows us where the oldest of bones are kept and where she's been stacking the new ones. She shows us one hallway that has shelves upon shelves of vials. I recognize the shape as something I've seen many of the Crusaders wearing, though we have yet to discover why.

At long last, after spending the better part of two hours down here, she finally leads us somewhere new. An open room with a high ceiling, lit by two large windows that look outside. Between the two windows, a ramp leads to a door that must lead outside.

Rust stains the stones, unsettling my stomach and making my knees weak. I've smelled this odor before. It's lingered over us every time we've set foot into the catacombs, but it's stronger here.

It reeks of death in this room. Not just the saccharine decay of flesh or the earthen scent of brittle bones, but of bloodshed. Of carnage.

In the farthest corner, beneath one of the painfully bright windows, stands a table that's tilted at an awkward, impossibly sharp angle.

I stifle a gasp when I notice the lump atop it is a body. A young man. His arms and legs are strapped down. His skin has taken on a chalky pallor. His lips are purple. But it's the small, black hole in the side of his neck that forces me to stare with bulging eyes.

Something dark and malevolent oozes from his wound, like a slug born straight from the Shadowthorn. It's thick and slow as gravity pulls it out from the man's body and plops into the bucket stationed beneath his head.

Looking around the room, I suddenly take note that there is no shortage of cadavers here, and I realize what it is we're about to be asked to do.

"The time has come for you to learn the art of bloodletting." The Spirit Keep's rasping, ethereal voice makes her sound as if she belongs among the dead herself.

She takes two final, painful strides to a table much closer to the door we entered. Though its surface lies flat rather than jutted up in a harsh angle as the other, the lumpy shape beneath the black fabric leaves no room for wondering what she is about to reveal underneath.

With the swiftness of a bird spreading its wings, the Spirit Keep flings the cloth away, revealing milky skin and the two glazed, half-lidded eyes of a young woman.

Silver's breath hitches, recognition crossing her usually

poised features. I watch her strain to look away from the body displayed before us, the one she so obviously recognizes. I'd wondered where these bodies had come from, the ones we'd been asked to dispose of. Glancing over at the other man on the table, black goop still leaking into the bucket beneath him, I recognize him. He was one of my neighbors, one of the ones I saw gutted as I raced to my cottage to find my parents.

Understanding settles over me now. These bodies, they're gathered from the fallen towns. Ashenvale. Gravenburg. It's likely there are bones in these walls from every single village the Shadowthorn has claimed.

"It is time you learned where necro-ink comes from."

For someone so decrepit, her next few moves are done with the swift lethality of shadowsteel. The Spirit Keep pulls a knife from somewhere inside her billowing robes and strikes the young woman's neck on the slab.

The stony walls seem to waver and quake. They crush in on me like a tomb as my breathing hastens, alarm seizing my chest.

But just as I fear I'm about to collapse, Dimitri appears at my side. His arm wraps around my waist to steady me and he shifts, taking on some of my weight. He is always here when I need him. Always.

On shaky breaths, I inhale the musty air like it is fresh and rejuvenating, only to instead smell more blood. I look up at him with pleading eyes, practically begging him to take me out the door nestled between the two windows, the one that surely leads outside to fresh air. But he doesn't meet my gaze. He holds his focus on the impaled woman, even as his eyes twitch with the slightest show of unease.

Something about seeing this small show of weakness and his fortitude to push through it, emboldens me to do the same. If I can't look upon dead bodies now, while within the safe limits of Arcathain, doing so in the Shadowthorn will only prove more impossible and more life-threatening. Once we're inside Qaeus' dark domain, I won't be able to afford such hesitations.

I swallow the bile rising up in my throat, and once my head has anchored itself back onto my shoulders, once the dizziness begins to fade, I force myself to look upon the dead woman again.

"Once a demon's venom enters the bloodstream," the Spirit Keep says, continuing her instruction. "The blood can be harvested, but only once the body is brought here."

With another burst of striking alacrity, the Spirit Keep jerks her knife from the child's neck. She is utterly insensitive to the very notion that she is disfiguring our loved ones, our friends, people we grew up with and, if not cherished, and least valued as fellow Arcathainians. She stabbed this young woman as if she was nothing more than a poached squirrel.

The squelch of flesh as the blade springs free will be seared into my mind for eternity, followed by the slow dribbling of the poor girl's blood as it clumps into the rusty bucket. I've been around dead animals enough to know how blood is supposed to look, how it's supposed to smell and move. Her blood is sludge from the forest floor after a torrential rainfall. It is as dark as demon skin, and reeks of fetid plums and lamb meat that's been left out in the sun too long. The only semblance it bears to normal blood is its sheen that manages to catch what little light is provided from the windows.

"Ashenvale fell over a month ago," Dimitri says, morose but thoughtful. "Gravenburg suffered a demon scourge not too long after. These bodies…they were torn apart by demons. There should be no more blood left in them to give."

"Ah, someone's been studying the dead." The Spirit Keep chuckles. She lifts one bony finger into the darkness. "But the dead differ from the Blighted. Those cut down by demons die with their venom in their veins. It curdles the blood, stills in the body, and will remain that way for quite some time, unless coaxed to come out."

She leans over the young woman's naked, grey body. She presses her palm between her breasts, places her other hand on top, and thrusts the weight of her down. Again and again she pumps. The dead woman's ribs crack beneath the pattern of her compressions.

"The bloodletting," she says between compressions, catching her breath with every few words as she goes. "It requires us to do the work the heart would normally."

The dead woman jerks every time the Spirit Keep presses against her chest. My stomach lurches, a horrific sickening squeezing my intestines. Of all the times I've been sent here to help, never have I seen this side of the process. If this had been the task that had awaited myself or any of the others the first time we were sent to the catacombs, I have no doubt that the Shadow Crusade would have triple the number of deserters that they have now.

Now that I'm watching her, it's easy to understand why such a thing would be kept from us. We were too new, still too unsavvy to the horrors of the Shadowthorn. Information like *this* isn't meant for regular people. They shouldn't have to know what happens to the retrieved bodies of their mothers, fathers, brothers, and sisters.

"It looks exhausting," a recruit mutters.

"It is," the Spirit Keep says simply. "That is why we warm the bodies and angle them. It makes our work easier."

"But," I hear myself breathe. "Why are we learning this now?"

"Ah," she says simply. "Another astute pupil. You are aware of the scourge that occurred the other night, yes?" She doesn't wait for me to respond, nor does she ever stop pounding away at the woman's chest, black sludge oozing down her neck in sickening pulses. "You are being taught bloodletting because it is imperative that the ritual never be lost, but as the Shadowthorn creeps nearer, it is only a matter of time before we lose Nigh. You may be the last unit of Crusaders to pass through these halls, to sleep in the cots in your dorms. Someday soon it will be *you* entering the Shadowthorn, and you will need to know where to find necro-ink and how to harvest it."

I have more questions. Judging from the looks of the others, so do they. But the sight of her pumping against this young woman's chest scares every word right out of me. I can't help but see Tor in this woman's place. Did his fellow Crusaders do this to him upon his death? Did the Shadow Crusade perform the bloodletting on Dimitri's mother and sister?

Once the last droplet of sticky darkness has been drained from the dead young woman on the slab, the Spirit Keep picks the bucket up by its squeaking handle and carries it back out the way we came. She doesn't instruct us to follow her, but our only other option is to stand here among the dead and exsanguinated. I'd rather be abandoned in the Shadowthorn than left down here, and apparently my fellow recruits agree because we all shuffle after her, never once looking back.

The bucket sloshes, the Spirit Keep swaying with the effort it takes to carry it, but even when Güthric or Dimitri offer to help, she snaps at them to remember their place.

"We each have a role," she croaks, the exertion surely pushing her to the brink of what must be her impending death.

She manages to survive the entire journey back to the place where the many corridors convene at the base of the stairs. I'm not surprised to find Alphonse and his group already awaiting us there. He grins like a smug child who thinks he's just bested us in a game.

Beside him, however, Maxwell grimaces, a heavy bucket clutched in his hand. I assume they spent their first hour practicing the bloodletting while we were wandering these dusty halls before the two groups switched. They had likely even been working on the man we saw when we first entered the morgue.

"There you are," Alphonse says, examining his cuticles. "We were starting to wonder if we should begin without you."

"No you weren't," says the Spirit Keep with a motherly wave of her hand. She lowers the bucket and summons us closer. "The bloodletting is how you obtain necro-ink, but the application of it is what really matters."

Leaning down over the bucket, the Spirit Keep dips her bony finger knuckle-deep into the tarry fluid. As she stands, she drags her finger down her forehead, black ink smearing in an uneven line between her eyes.

"No way," Sai blurts, shaking his head and backing away from the buckets set ominously before us. "I-I'm not going anywhere near that stuff, let alone putting it on my face. It's laced with demon toxin. She said so herself."

Alphonse sighs and pinches the bridge of his nose. "Whatever demonic qualities possessed the blood, once the body is brought to Nigh, for whatever reason, it is absolved of its harmful effects on humans."

"*For whatever reason?*" Sai throws his arms in the air. "Oh, okay. Well if it's just for *whatever reason*, then by that logic, I should—" His words become emphatic, pointed—"apply black blood directly to my skin."

Alphonse rolls his eyes. "If you must know, the Castle of Nigh once belonged to the mages, before they fled Arcathain and abandoned it. The Crusaders of that time believed this place to be crucial to efforts to find and slay the Primordial. Conclude from that what you will, but it's of little importance—"

"*It's of little importance?* Piss on a mage! I beg to differ," Sai wails. I've never seen him so hysterical, so attuned to what's being left unsaid. He's more likely to be found saturated in booze and heavy-lidded during any topic of conversation that it is rare for him to offer anything to the conversation other than a snide remark or roguish grin. "Not only do you want us to paint demon blood directly onto our skin, but now you're implying that said blood might be imbued with ancient magic?"

The other recruits start muttering to one another, paranoia strong among us Arcathainians. It begins soft, but their concerns become too big for them to carry quietly. An onslaught of questions and accusations are thrown at Alphonse. He staggers back with each one, utterly unprepared and increasingly more terrified. My guess is, as his back slams into a stone wall, he's asking himself whether this trip had still been too soon. If he had just pushed it off until—well, forever —we would've been all too eager to never think about the catacombs or the bloodletting again.

"That's enough!" Dimitri's voice bellows beside me as loud as the bell tower's toll.

The other recruits hush and turn to him. I'm almost too stunned to do the same, too fearful of seeing the disapproving way he's staring at them all because, even though I wasn't in an uproar with them, I wanted to be. Their hesitations are the same as mine.

Valid or not, I already know what Dimitri is going to say.

"It isn't our place to question the ways of the Shadow Crusade!" His jaw is a taut wire about to snap as he yells. He lets the echo of his scolding ripple down every chamber of the catacombs before speaking again. "We came to *learn* the ways of the Crusaders. We came here to *serve* our country."

Alphonse brightens, his ego thoroughly stroked. "Precisely, initiate. Well said. The rest of you would do well to heed your friend's advice. Need I remind you that we will face an ancient Primordial, a creature with such vile power that it continues to seep across the lands, consuming Arcathainian soil and ravages our people. It has cursed our neighbors, Blighted their lands, and sent demons to devour their flesh. The mages may have been despicable for their abandonment of this country and its inhabitants, but in their haste, they left us with certain advantages.

"Your shadowsteel, for instance. Those blades can only penetrate the demons' skin because of the magic infused with them. Would you prefer us to abandon every tool at our disposal and enter the Shadowthorn defenseless?"

Sai grumbles something as he lowers his head.

"What's that? I don't believe all of us could hear you."

"I said, no," he says through gritted teeth.

"Very good. It would be suicide to want such a thing. It would be the genocide of our people to believe that we could possibly defeat Qaeus without using every possible advantage at our disposal. Whatever means necessary." A muscle feathers in his jaw, and I get the impression that he's talking about something more than just shadowsteel and necro-ink. The moment passes, and he continues. "Now, either you can learn how to apply the necro-ink so that you may safely enter the Shadowthorn when the time comes, or for those of you who disagree with this philosophy, leave now. Crawl back to the dung heaps and cesspools we found you in, embrace a life of squalor and persecution, and live out the rest of your pathetic lives as deserters, knowing that you gave up on saving our country."

With his arm extended toward the stairway, we all fall silent. Something drips from down one of the bone-lined corridors. I tell myself it's likely just a leak, that places as old as this one often suffer from structural decay, but my mind knows better. It thinks of the young woman, of the black sludge that slithered from her veins.

After a painfully long moment, Alphonse finally lowers his arm. He turns to the Spirit Keep who's hunched over one of the dark buckets and dipping vials inside the putrid waste until they fill.

Alphonse bows his head to her. "I believe they're yours then."

She gives no indication she's heard him. She just keeps dipping her vials. Once each one is full, she twists a small cap on top to seal it before wiping the thing clean with one of the loose-hanging cloths draped over her billowing, tattered gown. We watch her so intently that when she finally stands, at least a dozen vials in hand, we all jump.

"This is your personal vial of necro-ink," the Spirit Keep says, handing each of us one of the containers. She sets the glass into my palm, the leather cord that's attached to the cap dangling past my fingers. "Do not misplace it. Do not break it. Do not misuse it."

I hold the vial up between my thumb and index and examine the dark contents inside. These are the same vials I saw the other Crusaders wearing when we journeyed from Gravenburg to Nigh, the same vials that they wear even while we're in the secured confines of the castle.

Once each of the recruits has their own vial, the Spirit Keep hobbles to the center of the circle so that she's visible to us all. She opens the cap on the vial around her neck to reveal a small brush is attached beneath it. I check mine impulsively and am surprised to find I have one too. I didn't see it while she was securing the caps, but then again, my thoughts had been more focused on the contents and not the vial itself.

"What did I say?" she shrieks.

I jolt upright and slam the lid back into place. Thankfully, she's not talking to me, though she might as well be. She's turned to another recruit, to Maxwell who has also opened his vial. He clumsily twists the lid back on, and only once the vial is dangling safely from his neck again does the Spirit Keep whack him upside the head.

"What part of caution was unclear to you? Do not misuse your necro-ink. Do not misplace it. Do not break it. Do not open it unless you need to or are otherwise instructed."

Maxwell nods vigorously, blinking with each bob of his head.

The Spirit Keep glares at the rest of us, her face pale and layered in the brittle wrinkles of age. Only once we've all conveyed our understanding does she begin her demonstration again. She takes the wand, already lathered in necro-ink, and brings it to her forehead.

"With the necro-ink," she says, black ink pressed to the base of her forehead. "We guard our minds from the demons that would try to inhabit us."

Aware that we are being trained on something few Arcathainians ever learn, I try paying attention to the skill with which she uses the brush. She draws one small vertical line that almost reaches the brim of her nose. Once it's placed, she marks an even smaller line horizontal across it to form a cross. I've seen the marking before, on too many Crusaders to count, but I'd never known the exact purpose for it. I had no idea it served to protect our minds.

Across the way, some of the other recruits mimic the action with their fingers. I decide to do the same, even if I'm not sure how helpful it is.

"With the necro-ink," she begins again. This time, she moves the brush to a spot beneath her eye, just under her lashes. "We open our eyes so that we may not be deceived by any of the fiends that may cross our paths."

This marking is just as simple as the first, a single line that falls from either eye. On anyone else, it might accent her cheekbone, but age has already hollowed her face too much.

Now she brings the brush to her bottom lip. She drags it down in one heavy stroke, all the way down her chin.

"With the necro-ink, we protect our voices so that no creature of the Shadowthorn may take ours from us and use it against anyone else."

I marvel at all of the perfectly straight lines, at the finesse with which she drew them, even as she spoke, even as her brush ran over one wrinkle or another.

"Today, you practice the necro-ink symbols on each other. The placement can be challenging on oneself, the shapes even more difficult to master, so select a partner. Practice on each other and examine your handiwork."

I twist beside me to eye Dimitri and ask him, without words, to be my partner, but as I do, Güthric heaves his arm across his shoulders. I shift my gaze to the ground, trying to hide my disappointment. I suppose Dimitri is probably one of the only people here tall enough to reach Güthric's face, so I shouldn't take it too personally. To soften the blow, I catch Dimitri's sympathetic gaze as Güthric spins him around.

I turn to the other side of me and find Silver, clutching her vial to her chest like a long-lost heirloom.

"Partners?" I say.

She inclines her head. "Of course."

The Spirit Keep walks around the room as everyone pairs up. "Remember, these symbols will not protect you from death in the Shadowthorn, but they are of great use, and you will come to rely on them, so take great care with your application. Keep your lines clean. Place them with accuracy. And when you've finished, examine each line with great care."

I hear Sai mutter beside us, "May bravery fill my heart and protect my soul," as his partner begins to paint the necro-ink onto his face.

Grimacing, I look down to the vial dangling around my neck. "Do you want me—"

"I can go first," Silver says. When I look up at her, she's already opened her vial, the brush sodden with curdled, black blood.

"O-okay. Are you sure, you don't—"

She presses the brush to my forehead. I don't know why I expect it to be warm, but I recoil at the frigid touch, a chill running down my spine.

"Hold still," she says simply, face completely impassive.

I can't help but frown as I wonder how she can be so calm about all of this. We just watched the Spirit Keep pump the blood out of a dead woman—someone who apparently came from Ashenvale—until there was nothing left inside her but shriveled veins. We saw the bodies that have been retrieved from Gravenburg, Ashenvale, and the other surrounding towns that the Blight has impacted.

But as I marvel, my brow bunched, Silver glares over her work at me as if to ask if she really needs to repeat herself. I force my face to relax.

She continues painting the markings on my face with finesse equal to that of the Spirit Keep. The other recruits, they struggle to hold the vial in one hand while the other paints, they struggle to keep their lines straight as the skin pulls with the stickiness of the brush. Not Silver. She has the steady, slender hands of someone who knows their way around this level of detailed painting.

"You're good at this," I say when she dips the brush back into the vial for more ink.

Her hands still, her posture becoming rigid. With great care, she pulls the brush back out and says stiffly, "I've...had practice."

"You've done this before?" I whisper.

As she leans in to grab my jaw, her eyes flit to mine. It's all the answer she gives and it's one that speaks volumes.

"But...how is that possible?" The question tramples out of me like a wild horse stampeding through a field. I have no control of it, and now that it's free, there's no reining it back inside, no containing what's already been spoken. What's worse, the longer I wait for an answer, the more my own mind tries making sense of the impossible, but none of the possibilities make sense. I finally have no option but to voice one of them, any of them, before my mind spirals out of control. "Were you…have you been a Crusader before?"

"No…" she says softly. "My…husband was."

Grief swells inside me, a cold blanket of darkness that wraps around my barely beating heart. Ever since our arrival, hurt has shone in Silver's eyes. I always knew tragedy was the story she had to tell, but I always reasoned that was the truth for us all. Loss and heartache didn't make us special; it united us.

But I've never known the loss of losing a husband, a companion, the person you'd sworn to spend the rest of your years with.

As she lowers her dark eyes, I see her in a new light now: the wife of a Crusader, a woman who married a man whom she knew would die young and ghastly. Perhaps they lived in Ashenvale before, or maybe they relocated there once he'd been stationed on the Shadowthorn border, but I can see her now, painting the necro-ink onto his skin every morning before a mission into the Shadowthorn, and wondering for days at a time if he was coming home.

"Before you ask," she says, as quiet as a petal falling onto a bed of flowers. "Yes, he died as most Crusaders do, tucked far away in the Shadowthorn. We never saw him again."

I jerk my eyes to meet hers. She said *we*. Her eyes widen when she realizes her accidental reveal. Her lips part, as if she could inhale and take it all back, but what's said has been said.

She wasn't just a wife, I realize. She was also a mother.

Silver clears her throat and takes my chin back into her hand. "That was a few years ago now." She angles my face upward. "Are you ready for the last symbol?"

It takes me a moment to recover and realize what she's

talking about, but she holds the necro-ink brush up and I grimace. Dryly, she raises an eyebrow at me, and I shake away all signs of my disgust. At least it's out of my system now, as long as I can focus on anything but *what* is about to be placed on my lip.

I tilt my head up, press my teeth against my bottom lip to smooth out the hump as best as I can for her, and inhale. "Do it. I'm ready."

I hold my breath when she presses the slick brush to my lip. I continue holding my mouth steady as she drags the brush lower, the cold, slick blood leaving me sticky. If I think hard enough, I can imagine it's just the honey I used to sneak from our harvest. My mother would find me with dribbles of it down my chin on a daily basis during the harvest. She'd always laugh, a warm, chittering sound, and say to me, "Well, it's a good thing you're not in charge yet."

Only, no matter how I try focusing on the memory, it's not good enough to convince me otherwise. There is a sweet scent to the necro-ink, like there was with my mother's honey, but something putrid lingers just beneath it, and no matter how much I refrain from inhaling, the odor still drifts up my nostrils.

With my help, Silver finishes the final line on my chin and closes her vial. I'm silent as I apply her symbols, half distracted by the sudden surge of familial memories flooding my thoughts, while also trying to focus on the precision of my brushstrokes.

The cross I draw on her forehead seems too tall, and it sits in the center of her forehead instead of near her nose like the Spirit Keep's. No matter how many times I go over the marks under her eyes, they're always uneven, one of them drooping lower than the other, and the second more curved than the first.

Finally, I have to admit to myself that this is precisely why we're practicing. I'm not the only recruit who is struggling with this. Despite the steady hands that most of the other recruits have when wielding their weapons, their hands quake with the weight of the necro-ink and the life it once contained.

Since there's no point in trying to make the markings perfect, I move onto the final line. Using my thumb, I pull her lip to the side to make it taut.

But just when I press the black ink to her lip, someone comes bumbling down the stairs. They take them two—three— at a time, panting and heaving, calling out for the general. The man crashes to his knees when he reaches the bottom of the landing, his black leathers glistening. I hadn't heard any rain, but I guess this far down, we wouldn't.

An acrid smell swarms the room after him, and I realize that's not rain on his shoulders. It's demon blood.

Panting, bent over with his hands on his knees, he utters, "Demons."

A HORRIFIC STAND

CATACOMBS, CASTLE OF NIGH, ARCATHAIN

*A*lphonse leaps over the crumpled man, bounding for the stairway, black cape rippling behind him. He stops on the first step, twists around, and points at us. "Defend the necro-ink! Go!"

While most of us are left dumbfounded and frightened, the sounds of screams carry down from the carnage above and Alphonse bounds up the stairs after them. If there is a tug on my heart for him, it is too faint for me to tell. Right now, I'm more worried about the rest of us. With the massacre happening right above us, we are trapped down here with no way of escape. Our only hope is that the Crusaders above will rise victorious. Or, if not, that the demons won't bother coming down here.

But then something that Scholar Amon said during one of his lessons on demons whispers in my thoughts. *"They feast on human flesh. They especially love the flesh of the dead."*

What better place to find the dead than in the catacombs?

The Spirit Keep gathers her robes off the cold stone floor and skitters down the corridor. "This way, initiates."

I stare at the abandoned bucket of necro-ink, wondering if perhaps she didn't hear Alphonse's last command.

Fox finds her way over to me and shrugs, apparently noticing the same thing, but it's not like either of us are going to call after her, or lug the bucket of sloshing putrescence with us. As the Spirit Keep disappears around the bend, the other recruits hot on her heels, we have no choice but to follow. Perhaps the Spirit Keep knows of a place where we will be safe. Perhaps she's leading us there, necro-ink be damned.

But with every twist and turn down a new corridor, I can't help but think the path she takes us through is vaguely familiar. As familiar as anything can be down here, I suppose, when you're walking past shelf after shelf of yellowed bones and chipped skulls. With layers of earth between us and the sun, it's difficult to keep my bearings, harder still to tell in the darkness if the alcove of skeletons we passed was one of the ones I saw on my tour earlier.

I shove the thought aside and focus on keeping up with the others. Safety, that is the only place she can be taking us, the only place where recruits *should* be.

But as the acrid stench of blood thickens in the air, my dread builds. I know that smell.

The Spirit Keep turns a final corner and we find ourselves back in the morgue. The young woman's lifeless body still hangs limp from the slab, as does the man's.

I realize now that Alphonse wasn't asking us to protect the two buckets of necro-ink, but the entire harvest waiting back here.

I can tell by the way Silver assesses the room that she draws the same conclusion.

"We are useless without our shadowsteel," she says, her beauty severe in the face of death. "He can't mean for us to protect them when we can't even protect ourselves right now."

It's true. Because we had planned to spend the morning in

the catacombs instead of training, we left out shadowsteel weapons back in the dorm. Lugging around the long halberds and heavy maces seemed excessive at the time. Now I'm sure I'm not the only who wishes they had kept their blade ready.

Shadows flicker over the stained-glass window. The pane is deeply colored, and tightly designed, so that it's impossible to see anything happening on the hill just outside. But steel rings in the air, a sharp, whining sound that is only pierced by the guttural cries of the fallen and the hungry snarls of the demons.

We face the ramp and the door at the end, our rigid backs to the corridor we entered from. Even if the demons get into the catacombs from the other end of the floor, it'll take them time to find their way back here. But the demons outside, all it will take is for one of them to become curious about what's on the other side of these windows.

My hands tremble at my waist. They press into my black skirts until my knuckle brushes against something hard and cold there. My brother's dagger. It didn't save me the last time I faced a demon, but I remember the comfort it gave me, the hope.

Frantically, I unlatch the leather and pull the dagger from my belt. It quakes in my shaking hand as I hold it out, my arm stiff, my heart thrumming in my chest. If the demons get in, I won't be able to protect everyone on my own; I likely won't even be able to protect myself. But as expected, having the blade in my hand, my fear is stanched, if only a little. I feel like my brother is standing beside me, whispering in my ear like he did when we were children and the clouds were warring with the sky throughout the night. Tor would tell me that thunder was nothing more than noise, and noise couldn't do anything but bother our ears.

I was only four then, too young to yet realize that lightning accompanied the thunder, and lightning, very much so, could harm us. But I pretend the truth still holds, even now. The growling and shrieking outside, it is nothing more than noise. Just like the thunder, soon, it too will pass, and the skies will be golden and inviting again.

My shoulders relax. My hand steadies as my arm lowers to a more comfortable and natural position.

And just when I've convinced myself that there is nothing to fear, the stained-glass shatters, and a black, terrifying beast pops its head inside and roars.

The recruits scream. *I* scream. We jump back, stumbling over the bodies on the floor in a mad race to put as much distance between us and the demon as possible. But our backs slam against the stone wall, and our yelps serve only to alert the other demons that there is more food to be had down here.

The other window shatters. The door at the end of the ramp, secured by a thick wooden board, begins shaking furiously.

The demon in the window snarls again, its shoulder stuck but its eyes set. Drool glistens on its fangs as it claws its way through the small window, growling and howling every time another of its rotund limbs get stuck. Another demon appears in the other window, desperate to get inside as well.

I raise my arm again, my dagger the only thing standing between me and the demons.

A crunch catches my attention from the dark corridor, and fiery fear surges through me again. They're already inside. We are surrounded. We are doomed.

But it's only Dimitri who steps out from the shadows, a long femur bone in hand, splintered at the tip.

"Arm yourselves!" he shouts, pointing to the shelves of bones behind him.

"They're just bones," Fox counters. "They can't kill them."

A glare settles in his eyes. He doesn't take it off her as he reaches into the wall and rips out another bone, this one smaller and curved. He charges toward Fox, slamming the bone against her chest.

"They don't have to die, and neither do we. But we *do* have to fight."

With renewed hope and fearlessness, the other recruits charge into the corridor. They tear at the bones of the dead like the famished flock to a feast. Bones crack and snap. Dust fills the airs as the tombs are disturbed for the first time in years. One by one, our fellow recruits return with sharpened bones in hand, just in time for the first demon to crash to the floor.

With a chilling roar, Dimitri pumps his bone spear into the air and charges. A few other recruits join him in the attack, Güthric among them. He flanks Dimitri, a femur in one hand a skull in the other, and they collide with the creature just as it leaps to all fours.

The three of them slam into the wall below the broken window, more demons clawing through the opening above while Dimitri crams his bone into the demon's gut and Güthric slams the skull against its face. Dark blood, as black as the raven that's been stalking me, sprays with each impact. The skull shatters in Güthric's hand and he uses his fist instead, and Dimitri pulls his weapon out to impale the demon again in the neck.

The beast thrashes and wails, but all they seem to be doing is making it angrier, and the others too. For every wail that gurgles out of this demon's mouth, the demon who crashes down from the other window, and the one still wedged inside the other, become more vicious, more insidious as they claw their way through the openings.

Another demon plummets from the window and lands on Güthric. The two of them roll and slash, a tangle of dark and white. The demon pins Güthric down by his pummeling arms and shrieks a wet snarl in his face.

With two makeshift daggers at her sides, Silver sprints for

him. She slashes with the wild blindness of a tornado. More recruits join her, targeting the next demon to crawl its way through the other window. My colleagues are whirlwinds of jabs and kicks and strikes and stabs. Everything we've ever reviewed and practiced seems fresh in the forefronts of their minds as they take down the ravenous demons.

I, however, cannot move.

I am the only one with a real weapon that could kill the demons, and yet I am frozen by my terror. One swipe of their claws, one snag of their teeth, and any of us would become the next bodies lying here in the morgue.

I want to run.

I want to scream.

But I can't do either. It's like I'm standing in my cottage again, the dead bodies of my parents lying on the floor behind me, mauled and eviscerated, and I can't leave them, even if it means saving myself.

Something shatters as its thrown across the room. I turn to see the handful of bones scatter, ricocheting off the burly body of a new demon that's entered. His eyes are fixed on something in the corner of the room. I turn and see the Spirit Keep, pressed tightly into the corner, reaching for another handful of bones that are piled on that side of the room.

Just as she heaves another handful at the creature, the doors burst open. Darkness funnels in, swallowing every last remnant of hope we had.

Demons pour inside. They tackle the recruits on top of their fellow brethren. They sink their teeth into necks and lungs and guts.

I don't know why I can hear one roar over the others, but my head snaps around just as a demon lunges for the Spirit Keep. The next handful of bones she chucks at it smack the creature in the face, disorienting it only long enough for it to blink and jerk its head away, but in two bounding strides, it's upon her.

The Spirit Keep glares up at the mammoth creature. It stands on its hind legs, hunching because the ceiling is too low for it. It watches her like it enjoys seeing her fear, like that's just part of its hunt.

I'm racing toward them before I'm aware of it. My cry is muffled by the sounds of the fighting and dying around me, and the demon doesn't seem to know I'm coming for it. Unhinging its jaw, it leans back. I lunge, closing the gap between us with my dagger outstretched.

The blade sinks into the creature's bicep and it bellows. The black beast jerks its arm away, my dagger still inside it.

Faster than I can register, its thick, mangled hand is around my neck. It roars in my face, fangs just inches away from my skin. Its hot breath is fetid, but I can't smell it for long. It squeezes me, cutting off all of my air supply with one tight clutch.

I start banging on the demon's bristled arm. I claw at its tough skin. I kick my feet, but they can't get a good hold.

The ceiling swirls behind the demon's face. My blows soften, my grip on reality waning. No matter how hard I gasp, I can't find the air I so desperately need, and my eyes soon start to flutter.

Maybe it's best this way. At least if I'm unconscious, I won't have to watch everyone I care about die; I won't feel the demons as they consume me, limb by limb.

Just as my vision is about to fade, a large shadow swirls overhead. It collides with the demon, and the creature disappears, crashing somewhere out of sight, as I fall to the floor. My head strikes something soft, not stony like I expected, and I'm only faintly aware between my gasping breaths that the thing beneath me is a warm body.

I push myself up, lungs aching and hungry for air. I swallow it all, guzzling it in like I've never been thirstier in my life. Tears stream down my cheeks from the effort, but I can't stop. Nothing has ever tasted so good.

Bleary-eyed, I finally glance up. With the chaos still live around me, the only thing I can think of is finding my dagger, but just as I'm starting to make sense of the crumpled masses on the floor, someone grabs me.

I'm hoisted to my feet before my eyes have a chance to adjust fully. The shape is that of a man, a strapping one, at that, with unbelievably dark skin. He takes my hand, closes it around something light and familiar. I look down to find my brother's blade clutched in my grasp.

With each clearing blink, I bring my gaze up, my eyes roving over his inky chest and the ripples of muscle I find there. He could fight off an entire army of demons with his bare hands if he wanted to. In fact, as my eyes continue adjusting, and as I start noting the slickness that covers most of his body, I start to wonder if he hasn't already.

The acrid stench of demon blood wafts between us. I wince, drawing back just enough to slide my gaze back up to the thing standing before me, only to realize I've seen him before.

Dark eyes. Dark hair. A creature with a human face and body, but with demon attributes like wings, horns, and his demonic arm, still blackened and bristled. As for the rest of him...

Too stupefied to move, and too curious to do so anyway, I extend a shaky finger out and drag it down his chest. The black ink smears away, leaving only his pale skin to break through the demon blood he's painted on him. I drag another finger over his demon arm, pulling it back to find it still clean.

Shaking my head, I start to back away. How is he here? How did he find me?

One of the journals I'd read in the library answers for me: some demons can scent their prey.

But this demon is unlike any I've read about, still through all my studies. We haven't discussed demons who make themselves appear human in any of Scholar Amon's lessons, nor have there been mention of them in any of the discarded and forgotten books.

My brow twitches. I'm overcome with horror and bewilderment. "Who are you?"

His jaw tightens, as if he can actually understand me. It looks like he strains for the words, but I'm not even sure he knows the human language. The only sounds I've heard demons make are the vicious ones churning around us.

"Ry—" he begins, but the syllable is cut short by the ringing of shadowsteel before I can figure out if it's an actual language he was about to speak, or it was just a sound.

Out of the corner of my eye, I spy the Crusaders filing into the catacombs, their weapons drawn, their strikes true.

The partial demon before me snarls, twisting away without another word or growl. He slams into the wall, defying the pull of gravity as he walks across the stones as if it were the floor beneath my feet. He bounds for the window, clears it in one go, and is gone.

The Crusaders slash through the beasts that have cornered us inside. Within a matter of minutes, they've killed every last one of them.

I pull my thoughts away from the half-demon to search the carnage around me for my friends. I lost track of all of them during the fight. I'm not even sure if any of them made it.

With my heart in my throat, I push through the Crusaders toward the window. It's the last place I saw Dimitri standing. Before Güthric had been knocked back, the two of them seemed like they were winning. But what happened to the skull Güthric wielded could've happened to Dimitri's bone blade too, and once the other demons entered the catacombs, there's no telling how long he stood, or if he even lasted that long enough to…

I burst past the Crusaders and stumble over the heap of demons lying at their feet. My boots squelch in the dark blood, but I hardly notice. Every one of my senses are trained on Dimitri. His hand is pressed against the wall, his back hunched and breathing ragged. The moment I enter the clearing, he glances over his shoulder as if he can sense me. He pushes himself off the wall, his terrified gaze quivering as he takes me in, scans me for the same wounds I'm searching for on him.

He shakes his head, answering the question I'm too afraid to ask. A small smile twitches on my lips. I don't know how it's possible, how he's alive, how he's not even injured. He is drenched in blood, the black splatter of demon gore the most concentrated on his chest and the arm he was stabbing with. It reminds me of the way things used to be, how often I'd find him at the end of the day covered in bloodstains, wrist-deep in the intestines of a hog or a deer or some other woodland animal he'd hunted. I'd been afraid to touch him back then, too sickened by the blood and the thought of getting it on me.

I bound for him now and throw my arms around his neck. He wobbles with the weight of me, still exhausted from the fight, but he steadies quickly, his arms reaching around my waist and squeezing me close.

Hurried, panicked strides thump down the ramp. "Report. What damage has been done?"

Alphonse strides into the gloomy morgue with all the tact of an elephant. Under normal circumstances, I might begrudge him for it. He talks about the deaths of his Crusaders like they're just meaningless numbers. But his hair is frazzled, a few rogue strands dangling from the typically straightened mass. His face is covered in grime. It's only once he's in the center of the room, wildly looking around at all of us for answers, do I see the thick darkness coating his shadowsteel sword like a quill dipped in ink.

I suppose it's his job to tally the dead after encounters like this, and any of us would be just as tactless if we were in his shoes.

"Did they take any of the necro-ink?" he growls, enunciating his point.

He doesn't care about the dead. All he cares about are the resources that the dead provide.

I stifle a gasp as I watch him with horror. Since accepting the role of general to the Shadow Crusade, is he even human anymore? How can he walk in here after what we've just endured and speak so coldly about lost resources?

Dimitri clutches me tighter and I'm not sure if it's because he's afraid I'll do something stupid, or if he also needs something to hold onto to stop the world from spinning around him. I still haven't recovered from my near strangulation, and so, rather than calling Alphonse out for his callousness, I lean back into Dimitri and scan the crowd of those still standing.

Fox.

Güthric.

Silver.

Sai.

All of our friends have survived. Even Maxwell, despite all odds, is still standing.

But many are not. Bodies of the other recruits litter the ground, as do a few of the Crusaders who came in to defend us.

Not *us*, I realize. The necro-ink.

"Did they take any of it?" Alphonse bellows, a vein bulging down the side of his neck.

"I would have to check," the Spirit Keep says from the back of the room. She hobbles closer before she speaks again, the Crusaders clearing out of the way as she approaches. "It doesn't appear so, though. None from in here, anyway."

"They took two of the dead," one of the Crusaders informs him. "They retreated to the Shadowthorn before we could stop them."

With slow lethality, Alphonse turns to face the man, his teeth pressed tight together. "And did you not think to go after them?"

The Crusader stammers, "I—we were under attack, sir. I didn't think it wise to abandon—"

Our general curses in a terrifying rage. He presses his fists to his forehead as he paces the small place on the floor where bodies haven't amassed.

After a few moments, he flattens the stray, frayed tendrils of hair, moving them behind his ears, and addresses the recruits. "You will be escorted back to your wards. It is unsafe to have novices about. You're merely a distraction and you'll get yourselves killed. The rest of you, ready yourselves. We will retrieve our dead."

One of the Crusaders, a dopey-looking woman who seems more terrified than any of us, leads us back through the catacombs and to our rooms. Just before we reach the women's ward, something pierces my heart. A tinge of sorrow, of loss, of heartbreak, call it what you will, but I reach up to soothe the ache in my chest only to find that I touch nothing but my armor.

My necklace, the vial of necro-ink, it's gone.

HUNGER

FEMALE DORMITORY, CASTLE OF NIGH, ARCATHAIN

Silver undresses silently in the corner of the room. As she removes her blood-drenched layers, her gaze always wanders back to the door, like she's expecting someone to knock. Or hoping for them to.

I saw the way she came to Güthric's side. I've seen the way they are together. If she's found happiness with someone, even after all she's lost, I hope she knows to embrace it. I'm sure, like most of us though, she's too fearful to even admit it. It's a feeling I used to understand, but now I know life is too short, especially for us.

Fox throws herself atop one of the empty cots without even removing her dripping boots.

"What a morning," she says, arms folded behind her head. "Do you think they'll be all right?"

"Hmm?" I ask.

"The general and the Crusaders he's taking to chase down the demons who stole the necro-ink. What's that about anyway? Why steal ink? They're demons. They don't need it."

My hand floats to my chest, to the empty space where the vial should be.

Fox scoots up to her elbows. "No," she breathes, and then repeats herself, even more irate now, "what in the Eyve would demons want with necro-ink?"

Not just demons, I think, and I have to bite my lips before I accidentally say it out loud. The very idea of a half-demon is unheard of. To suggest it, I'd be considered mad, maybe even possessed by one of the demonic creatures themselves. Besides, Fox already believes I'm a mage. I don't need her thinking that I can also see half-demons too.

But it has me wondering…if such things as half-demons *do* exist, why would they travel with full demons? By most accounts, the man I saw seemed more human than shadow-creature. Surely, any demon would devour him before thinking twice about it.

"It is a reckless mission, one that will only cost more lives," Silver huffs, buttoning her nightgown. When she turns around, she stares only at her bed and then lies on top of it without bothering to get under the covers.

I remember then that it's still only morning, not even time for lunch yet. I wonder how long we'll be left in here, if we'd get in trouble for leaving—

"Reckless, sure," Fox replies. "But we can't let them win. We can't let them think they can just come here, kill us, and then steal our supply of necro-ink. They need to be taught a lesson."

If Silver hears her, she doesn't make it known. I can feel the tension in the room, see the collision of their perspectives as if they were storm clouds rolling above us.

I want to change the subject, but I can't think of what to say. My eyes, like Silver's, keep drifting to the door. I didn't have much of a chance to talk to Dimitri after the attack. I can at least take comfort in knowing he's all right, that he'll live—a precious gift known not to all of us today—but I still worry. I want to know how he's feeling, what he saw; I want to hear how he survived, and I want to tell him that I am so unbeliev-ably grateful that he survived.

"Go," Fox says, settling back onto the pillow. "None of us will stop you."

I screw my brow at her. "Go? What do you mean—"

She snorts. "Don't play that innocent game with me. It's obvious who you're thinking about, who you're worrying that pretty, silvery head of yours over. Just go. See if Dimitri's okay. It'll spare us from having to watch you moon over the door."

"I'm not mooning over the door," I argue, my voice higher in pitch than I mean for it to go. I swivel my lips, aware I've been caught. "But what about what Alphonse said? We're supposed to stay in our dorms until they've deemed the grounds safe."

"Don't be such a mage," she teases. "He's gone, remember? And he'll likely be gone for the rest of the day, so if you were going to go roaming the halls, now would be the time."

A smile curves my lips. I spring up from where I'm leaning on a bed across from her, but I stop short when I notice some-thing off about her. Her eyes, they're glistening.

I slow and take a step toward her. "Are you all right?"

Fox sniffles and rubs her face with the whole of her arm. "Me? You don't gotta worry about me. I'm good. I'm great."

She rolls onto her side, turning her back toward me and effectively preventing me from reading her face. Not that I need to. By now, I know her well enough to know when she's hiding something that's bothering her.

Before I can press her about it, she clears her throat. "Don't worry about me. Just go. Find that exasperating man of yours. I'll be here when you're done."

Doubt wiggles its way into me, and I am torn between staying and going. On the one hand, I don't believe a word she's saying. I've never seen her shed a single tear, which means if she's doing so now, something is *not* okay. But I also know her well enough by now to know that she views this as a show of weakness, and that she will now do everything in her power to deny she's hurting, even if I were to stay. The thing she wants most right now is to be left alone.

And so, I do as she suggests, and I leave our dorm to find Dimitri, my heart hammering beneath my ribs.

But as I swing our bedroom door open, I come face to face with the very man I was prepared to go searching for.

"Oh!"

"Oh, sorry," he utters. "I didn't mean to—"

"No, you're fine. It's all right. You just startled me, is all."

"My apologies. I just—were you headed somewhere?"

My cheeks prick with heat. "No, I…well, I guess I was."

He flushes too. He brings his awkward gaze to the ground and steps aside. "Right. Well, sorry. I'll let you go then—"

"No!" I reach out and grasp his shoulder.

He stills beneath my touch.

I clear my throat and lower my voice to a more normal, less embarrassing tone. "I was coming to see you."

His grin is boyish, familiar, the kind of smile that makes my stomach warm with memories of summers spent chasing each other through the woods.

I shove him backward with a wry smile of my own and close the door behind me.

Stumbling back, his smile only growing, becoming more arrogant and handsome, he licks his lips. "So, what was it that you were coming to see me about?"

I cross my arms. "I might ask you the same thing."

He opens his mouth as if to answer me, but instead simply shrugs. I roll my eyes and pretend to head back to my room.

"Wait," he says, the word drawn out and mournful.

By the time I turn back around to face him, all signs of flippant arrogance are gone. He watches me with the sad eyes of a forlorn pup. His arm is reaching for me, and without even realizing it, without taking my eyes away from the forest bed of his gaze, I grab his hand.

He pulls me closer, my feet pattering in small, shy steps. This is still too new for me to know what he's thinking, what he wants from this moment, from me.

"You…scared me today," he says quietly.

"*I* scared *you?*" I balk playfully. "You were the one who charged a demon with nothing but a splintered bone."

He bends his head and chuckles, our foreheads drawn to each other. His thumb draws idle circles on my hands and he breathes the scent of me in.

"You scared me when you drew your dagger," he confesses. "Before that moment, I thought maybe the Crusaders outside would protect us, that we wouldn't need to see battle. But then you drew your weapon, and I realized I had no way of protecting you if I needed to." He swallows, his neck bobbing with the weight of a plum. "I know the path we've chosen. I know it means danger and facing death every single day. And I know we don't have much time left together. But…I'm not ready to lose you. Demons will rue the day they take you from me because I'll…"

He's shaking, trembling in my grasp like the last leaf on a tree before winter.

I squeeze him tighter. "That's not going to happen. At least not for a long while."

His grin is crooked, unsettled. "I want to believe that, but we both know what this life is like."

He finally brings his gaze back to mine. He reaches up, tucks a strand of white hair behind my ear. Even the slightest caress of his fingers ignites a new spark, each one adding to the wildfire growing inside me.

I lean into his palm and close my eyes. He presses forward, the warmth of his chest like fire against mine. He hasn't bathed since the battle. Neither have I. We reek of blood and sweat and the vilest of decay, but he has never smelled more alluring to me.

My eyes pop open. The hunger has set deeper in his gaze, a craving that I want to answer.

Bringing myself to the tips of my toes, I draw near his mouth. "You're wrong," I say, licking my lips. "We know what our *deaths* will be, not our lives. The only way to know that is to *live* them."

His nod is imperceptible, his breath quickening.

I am desperate to hold something, to grasp something, to cling onto some part of the world that will make me feel as if I will be here forever. Not just another Crusader who dies in the catacombs, or is lost forever to the Blight, but *here*. Alive. Everlasting.

And there Dimitri is. Where he's always been. Here. With me.

We pull toward one another at the same time. Our lips collide. There is no more awkwardness as we crash into one another. No more fears of what this might mean for him, for me, none about the damage that pursuing this…this connection might or might not do to our friendship. There is only passion. Need. Desire.

I want him, now. It doesn't matter what our lives were like before, whether this attraction existed back then or not, and the bleakness that lies ahead of us doesn't matter. This moment, here, now, that's what matters. And the attraction between us is tangible, all-encompassing. It is a rope wrapping around our bodies and squeezing so tightly until I can hardly breathe, hardly press against him closer.

But, oh, do I try.

I arch my back as his rough hand cradles the back of my neck. I moan into his mouth, a plea for more. More of his lips. More of his caresses. More contact with his skin. More of everything. I want it all.

We slam into the wall beside the doorway. I'm faintly aware that my friends are on the other side, but only until Dimitri catches my bottom lip in his teeth. I sink into his bite, eyes fluttering with pleasure.

I know him well enough to sense the flicker of hesitation when he releases my lip. He is the kind of man who binds himself to duty and responsibility, to rules. We both should be in our rooms like we were instructed. I know he's wondering now if this has been a mistake, if he should go back now that he's made sure I'm all right.

But now that we've started, I don't want him to stop.

My nails dig into the backside of his leather armor and I press him against me, my muscles straining to prevent him from doing anything but continuing what he's started. His groan is regretful at first, but the low rumble turns ravenous when I nuzzle my face to his neck. Playfully, I draw a line of kisses with my mouth, following his pulsing vein up to his jawline, and making my way back to his lips.

I taste him again, raw desire plunging me into oblivion. I ignore the stinging chaffing of the scruff he keeps on his chin and upper lip as our mouths work against each other. It's all just part of it, isn't it? Part of him. And I realize with sudden desperation that I want it all.

We break away from the deep kiss, his body still pressed against mine where I'm back against the wall. Our gazes focus on one another. Trepidation lingers behind the green of his eyes, but it's overpowered by the desire that's consuming us both. Neither of us have to ask the question hanging in the air.

Instead, I grab his hand, pull him into one of the empty dorm rooms, and slam the door behind us.

THE FINAL TEST

FEMALE DORMITORY, CASTLE OF NIGH, ARCATHAIN

The snow has almost melted entirely, and winter will soon be a thing of the past. It very well could be my last one, and it's only today that I've realized it. So many things could be my last without me even knowing it: my last meal, my last laugh, the last time Dimitri and I spend sharing a bed.

In a few days' time, the Magistrate will arrive, and we will be pronounced Crusaders. We will also be given our assignments, and though we have trained as a unit, if either of us are selected for more domesticated work, we will be stripped from our team. Either one of us could wind up stuck in the Castle of Nigh, mopping floors and emptying bedpans, while the other risks their lives inside the Shadowthorn.

It's a thought I've had many times in the last few weeks, and one I promptly punch in the face every time it arrives. We will know soon enough what the future has in store for us. There's no point in spending what could be our last few days together worrying about it.

When I open my eyes, Dimitri is already gone, but I already knew that. All the heat in the room seems to leave with him when he returns to his dorm, and I might as well be left sleeping in a bed of snow.

I can hear the recruits in the other rooms getting ready for the day, and judging from the sun shining through the tall windows, I decide it's time for me to as well. It's almost second nature to dress myself in my black leathers now, my hand often feeling empty without my axe in my grasp. After the attack on the catacombs, we'd been instructed to carry our weapons everywhere: to meals, to classes, even when we bath.

I grab Tor's dagger last, sheath it in my belt, and meet my dorm mates out in the hallway. Despite our impending initiation into the Shadow Crusade, nothing in our schedules has changed. We still train thrice daily, perhaps even harder now that it has become so glaringly apparent that danger does not limit itself to the confines of the Shadowthorn.

And so, as we have done for months now, we head to the training grounds to meet our general.

My heart warms to find that he's not alone, but that Eparah, after nearly a month of guarding the eastern wing, is with him. I almost forget myself and run toward her, arms wide, but I hear Dimitri's voice in my head. He tells me that I need to stay focused on securing my spot on the unit. I've already offended Alphonse dozens of times, and so the chances of him using his authority simply to force me into a life as his personal servant is already likely. In all the times we've spoken about it, I've reminded Dimitri that Alphonse hates me enough to send me to an early death in the Shadowthorn, but every time I say it, my doubt grows stronger. If given the chance to give me a swift death or torment me for years, I can't say for certain that Alphonse would pass up the opportunity for the latter.

I still have a few more days to prove to him that I belong in the Shadowthorn, and so, I stifle my urge to smile too brightly, hold my eyes steady on our general instead of examining the other twenty or so Crusaders with them.

Güthric sniffs the air. "Food."

"Yes, big man," Alphonse replies, dipping his head. He gestures to a burlap sack on the ground. "Today, you will be missing your meals in the dining hall."

Curious glances are passed all around between the recruits and me.

Alphonse continues. "When preparing to face demons and shadowcreatures alike, there's only so much experience to be gained from behind the safety of these walls. I have done what I can to prepare you for the horrors you'll witness once you're inside the Shadowthorn. Now all that lies between you and your title as a Crusader is one final assessment." He paces the front of the group with his hands clasped gently behind his back, his chin tilted up. "Today you shall accompany one of our units on an expedition."

Murmurs break out among us.

"An expedition?"

"We're going into the Shadowthorn?"

"About time."

"What is our purpose?"

"Are you sure we're ready?"

The last voice belongs to Silver, but she says it so softly that I'm not sure if she's intended for anyone but the ghosts who haunt her to hear.

"Where is the expedition going?" Fox asks.

"Ashenvale," Alphonse says promptly. "A few of the dead remain there, and their carcasses are too valuable to leave behind."

I look to Silver who's shaking her head. Her skin has gone as grey as fog.

"No," she whispers. But panic rises within her, tumultuous and frantic, turning her voice into a storm. "I—I can't go back there."

All eyes whip to her, Alphonse's especially. His resolve is

iron hot as he takes slow, pointed strides through the gathering of recruits. They part for him the whole way back until he's standing over her.

Regaining her poised confidence, she meets his gaze.

Alphonse's glare deepens. He's always seen it as a threat when someone—especially a woman, especially someone of lower standing—isn't afraid to look him in the eyes.

"Did you come here to join the Shadow Crusade, or did you come to cower with fear like the rest of the peasants?" His lip twitches, venom dripping from his words.

"Hey!" I yell, the word leaping from my throat before the voice in my head which—is sounding increasingly more like Dimitri by the day—can warn me not to speak.

Alphonse crooks a displeased eyebrow at me. Seeing who the defiance has come from though, his expression contorts with sickening satisfaction. He's been waiting for this, for me to challenge him and give him the opportunity to yet again remind me who between us holds the power.

"Do you have something to say?"

My chest hitches. I turn my sorrowful gaze to Silver. I want to help her; I want Alphonse to leave her alone, but no matter what I say, he'll just do as he plans. The only thing I accomplish by challenging him is getting myself in trouble, maybe even securing my place as a servant to the Castle of Nigh for good.

My muscles creak as I force my head to lower, and I swear I can hear Alphonse's sickening smile as he turns back to Silver.

He looks her up and down before waving his hand through the air and returning to the front of the group. "Stay if you want, but I'll have you arrested for absconding your post. It's your choice. Imprisonment or Ashenvale."

My jaw unhinges. It's true that he's within his rights to threaten such a thing. After all, once we enlist, we belong to Arcathain and the Magistrate; we're supposed to follow every order we are given. But he's being unnecessarily cruel. If he knew anything about Silver, he wouldn't present her with such an unfair choice. I'm not even privy to her full story, but I know too much pain awaits her in Ashenvale, her wounds too fresh.

Then again, as I've already witnessed, Alphonse is heartless, hardly human at all.

A hand squeezes my arm. I look behind me to find Dimitri, pleading at me with his eyes. He knows me too well, knows that he is the only thing preventing me from telling Alphonse exactly what kind of vile monster I believe him to be. But he also knows that his grasp on my arm isn't strong enough to clamp my mouth at the same time. If I have something to say to Alphonse, I will say it.

But Dimitri clears his throat and steps around me so that he's in the line of sight of our general. "Might I ask," he begins. "Why are we going to Ashenvale now? The town fell months ago, and from what we saw in the catacombs, the dead have already been retrieved for the necro-ink inside them."

"Not all," Alphonse replies, utterly unperturbed by Dimitri's approach. "A few bodies remain. Some of our own fell during our last expedition there, leaving behind shadowsteel that cannot be abandoned."

This is absurd. The more who return there, the more likely it is that more will die there. It is a vicious cycle, one that will amount to an endless supply of necro-ink, and the continued rescue mission for shadowsteel weapons.

Dimitri doesn't say any of that though. No one does. He simply nods and steps back beside me.

"To be a Crusader is to follow orders," he whispers out the side of his mouth to me. "If you want to make the cut for the unit—"

"You know I do," I hiss.

"Then don't think about whatever has infested your mind. Just do as you're told."

A low growl escapes me, but fortunately it's only loud enough for Dimitri to hear.

"If that's all, before we set out, I'm told some of you lost your necro-ink in the catacombs. Now, I understand that those were…extenuating circumstance, but in the future, do be sure to hold on to your ink. It is a limited resource."

He holds up three necklaces with black vials attached, and me and two other recruits go to him. Alphonse hands the first two vials to the others with a pleasant nod, but when he loops mine over my head, he comes close to my ear.

"Don't lose it again," he growls, and a moment later, he's standing tall again, an air of importance about him as he addresses me and the recruits. "This is the true testament to your skills and training. Those who survive this mission will become Crusaders in a few days' time. Those who don't will become our next batch of necro-ink."

My stomach sours at his callousness, but it shouldn't surprise me. He doesn't care about us. All he wants is to impress his father when he arrives. He wants his catacomb rich with necro-ink and bodies to be harvested, he wants his arsenal stocked for the next generation of recruits. Since he still hasn't brought down the Primordial Qaeus, these are the only things he has to make himself feel important.

Alphonse twirls his hand in the air. "However, there is one more purpose. Those of you who return to Nigh bearing a gift for the Shadow Crusade—a discovered vial of necro-ink, a retrieved shadowsteel weapon—you will be selected as a member of a new unit of Crusaders, the very one to be led by Captain Eparah."

Dimitri and I exchange a look.

"So, be vigilant in your time in Ashenvale. It will define the rest of your service to Arcathain."

The necro-ink still feels wet where I placed it. Anything else would've dried by now and begun to crust away with the slightest change in my expression. But this stuff, sticky as tar, prevails in its liquid nature.

I shouldn't be thinking about it though. My mind should be void of anything other than the quiet shadows around us, the whispers of the trees as the wind blows through their blackened leaves, and the soft sounds of our feet as we slink through the devastated land of the Shadowthorn.

We spent all day yesterday walking through obliterated fields and demolished villages until we reached a burrow where the Crusaders rest for the evening.

Prior to our arrival in Nigh, I never even knew sleeping in the Shadowthorn was possible. I'd always imagined the place to be so heavily crawling with shadowcreatures, so wrought with danger, that it would be impossible to rest for so much as a drink of water, let alone to catch some sleep. But, in the weeks since we arrived, nearing two months now, we've been taught how to camp in the Shadowthorn safely. The prepping begins well before entering the Primordial's territory, and Alphonse came well prepared. One of the many useful items packed in his burlap sacks were jars of meat soaked in brine. The solution ensured that the meat wouldn't go bad, and the airtight jars concealed the scent so that none of the demons would smell the carcass.

At least, not until we wanted them to.

Sleeping in the Shadowthorn is apparently a simple feat as long as flanks of meat are rigged in varying locations a safe distance away from the real meal—us—and as long as an adequate shelter is built, one that relies on tree branches to conceal it underground. The Crusaders have made this trip so often that they already had one made.

The night passed relatively quiet, aside from the yowls we heard in the distance when one of the slabs of meat was found.

I slept as well as I could.

Today though, I woke up more unnerved than before. Every step we take deeper into the hazy darkness feels like we are walking straight into Qaeus' maw. I've never been this far into the Shadowthorn before, never thought I'd find myself this deep willingly. And still, we push farther. It goes against every natural instinct in my body to keep going. We know the dangers that lurk ahead, and we know that we're only putting more distance between us and the safety we had in Arcathain.

This is the life we chose. If I'm lucky, there will come a time when I feel more at home in the Shadowthorn than I do back at Nigh. I'll have lived through so many expeditions that I'll know this place as well as the Crusaders guiding us now do.

"It's just up ahead," Eparah calls over her shoulder.

I've never seen her like this before, so grave and vigilant. It's nothing like the warmth I'm used to feeling from her, and if my interest wasn't so suddenly piqued to see the state of Ashenvale, I might've wondered how the Shadowthorn will leave its mark on me, as well.

"Be alert," she continues. "The demons know we return here frequently. It's very likely they patrol this village regularly so remember to move quietly, and keep your eyes trained on the shadows."

My throat becomes the dusty parchment of the forgotten books in Nigh's ancient library. Sneaking a glance behind me, I spy Silver. Fear takes hold of her in more blatant displays. Her bottom lip trembles when we walk through the main gate of the town. I wonder if she's able to find any comfort in having Güthric by her side, or if she's too far away to even notice him standing beside her, watching her like his gentle, giant heart is breaking.

My frightful, skittish eyes rove over the derelict houses and buildings around us, the rafters collapsed and the doors thrown wide. Still, Ashenvale looks nowhere near as devastated as I expected it to. For reasons unknown to logic, I thought the place would be in flames, smoke still rising from where the shops had scorched during the scourge. I thought the streets would be littered with the decayed bodies of the forgotten, the poor souls who couldn't escape in time, and the ones the Shadow Crusade were trying to retrieve. At the very least, I expected to have to step over hundreds of scattered bones, the discarded remnants of whatever was left after the demons had their feast.

But the streets of Ashenvale are bare, the air crisp, if not a little earthy. This place is so vacant, it doesn't even look like anyone ever lived here. I see no stalls, no abandoned carts of fruit that have long since rotted, no shops full of linens to be purchased or bartered, and no horses in the corral.

Ashenvale has been thoroughly gutted, by demon and man alike. I can't imagine there's much left to be scavenged here.

Once we're a fair way inside the village, Alphonse slows, bringing the rest of us to a halt behind him.

"Here," he says, clearly speaking to the Crusaders among us. "Take two recruits each, scavenge what you can, and return here within the hour." They nod all around, but he tightens his voice. "Do I make myself clear? One hour. No more."

"Should you come across—" Eparah pauses like she can't quite find the right word from too many horrors to choose from. She eventually settles on, "Anything, call for aid. If you're too far out, send someone back and stand your ground until your brethren can find you."

Alphonse waves his hand lazily in the air. "Yes, yes. They are Crusaders. I'm sure they know what to do in case they come across any of the shadowcreatures." Abruptly, he turns to face the recruits. "Güthric, Dimitri, with me."

Watching Dimitri walk away feels like my stomach is made of knots and he is the cord pulling taut on my insides. I don't like this; I don't like this at all. How am I supposed to feel safe without my best friend at my side? How am I supposed to survive if anything happens while he's halfway across the village?

Silver appears beside me. She doesn't look my way. In fact, ever since we entered Ashenvale, her gaze has been trained forward like she can't risk looking anywhere else. Though the horror of what happened here has practically been wiped clean, it has stained her mind forever. But I know her closeness isn't by accident. She was a mother, I remind myself, and some days I think she's still a mother now, the way she watches after us.

As the Crusaders grab two recruits each as they were instructed, Eparah strides over to us.

"Are you two ready?" she asks, and there's such sincerity in her tone that I think if either of us said *no*, she'd actually wait here instead of forcing us to explore.

But to abandon this moment is to abandon all hope of either of us ever leaving Nigh. If we don't find something of value while we're here, Silver and I will live the rest of our days in the castle, bleeding corpses for necro-ink and cleaning chalk from the classroom walls.

"Yes," Silver says, resolute and unflinching.

I nod as well, and the three of us set out. We comb through the nearly empty buildings and prowl the vacant streets. On the side of the tavern, we find a box wagon tucked behind some opened and scavenged crates. Eparah drops to her knee, her bag dropping to the ground beside her with a dull clang. She pulls out a rusted tool of some sort and hooks it onto the front of the wheel.

"Is that necessary?" I ask, my voice a harsh whisper. I glance nervously to Silver who's scanning the area around us while we both kneel. "Shouldn't we be searching for bodies?"

"No, that's what you need to search for," Eparah says with a grunt as she lifts the cart up. She nods to me to help her, but I don't have the slightest clue what to do. She chuckles. "Okay, you lift."

We trade off, and she begins cranking at the wrench, spinning the wheel every once in a while as she goes. A knob that was holding the wheel in place comes off.

Eparah tosses it on top of her bag and grasps the spokes of the wheel. "Hold on tight."

I scoff, incredulous. I'm already holding on as tightly as I can. The base of the wagon cuts into my fingers, making them burn and strain. She gives the wheel a strong tug, and I'm sure my fingers are going to fall off, but the wheel comes off clean.

"Okay, you can put it down."

I'm all too eager to be done with the weight of it, but I'm cautious about making too much noise, so I ease it down gently. My arms go limp at my sides, and I throw my head back to catch my breath.

Eparah gathers her tools back into her bag, tossing in the iron knob she retrieved from the wheel.

"I don't understand," I say, my breaths easing back into their normal rhythm.

Eparah stands. She places her hand on the rim of the wheel at her hip and sighs. "*Your* job is to find shadowsteel and necro-ink, but Ashenvale has mostly been scavenged already. It's an impossible task that only those who went to the north side of town will be successful in. *My* job while we're here is to gather any materials that might prove useful to the Shadow Crusade. Wagon wheels break too often to pass this one up—"

"W-why did we go south then?" I balk. "Silver and I, if we

don't find any shadowsteel or necro-ink, our chances of becoming Crusaders—*true* Crusaders—are ruined."

Eparah shakes her head, eyes closing. "I'm sorry. It's an unfair test, one he never meant for you to complete. The last unit of Crusaders to come here for supplies was attacked. A few of them fell and the others fled before they could retrieve their belongings. Alphonse predetermined who would be taken north to the last battle site, and who would be led astray." Noticing the hurt in my expression, she adds, "It's not all bad, though. We can still do good here. We can find more items of value to bring back with us—"

I shake my head.

"Halira," she begs. "Please, you must understand. He is my general. I must do as he says. And he is yours, as well."

Slowly, I start backing away. The likeliness of me ever becoming a real Crusader has been rigged from the start. I never stood a chance, not with my hateful cousin in charge.

"Halira?" Worry edges Eparah's tone. "Whatever you're thinking…don't."

I frown at her, unsure of what it is she's cautioning me against doing. I'm not sure I was thinking anything other than how unfair this is. I've trained just as hard as everyone. I've lost just as much. I want to become a Crusader and avenge my family just as badly as all the others.

But the look in her eyes gives me an idea. Though the odds are stacked against me, it's not over yet.

I turn on my heels and run north.

My feet pound against the earth, as strong as the thundering heart in my chest. I don't know how long we'd been walking, but I know I've already lost precious time. Alphonse and the others might've already arrived to the battle site; it's likely the bodies of the fallen have already had their necro-ink vials and weapons lifted from them. But I have no other choice.

I have to try, even if it means directly disobeying Alphonse's order to stay with my Crusader, my captain.

A guttural shriek impales the crisp air.

My feet trip to a halt. I look east toward the cry, deeper into the village down a path that I think I saw Maxwell and his company head down, more poor fools who were never meant to complete the task.

I stare north again, toward my only chance at success. I should keep going. I'm not much of a fighter; I'd be of little to no use to Maxwell and would likely just put myself in harm's way. If they encountered demons, then surely the Crusader he's with can protect them. Besides, the most responsible, rational mode of action would be for me to find Alphonse and let him and the others know that some of our people are in danger.

"Help!" a different, shakier scream pierces my heart from down the street. It's Maxwell's, I know it is; I can tell by the adenoidal whine that strains on his sinuses. "Somebody, please!"

Biting my lip, I curse under my breath and dash down the street. This is stupid. This is reckless. This is precisely the kind of idiotic, heroic act that got my brother killed…but I have no choice. Maxwell's whimpering continues to echo across the ruins of Ashenvale, but I hear no others. I think he might be the only one left, and if that's true, he wouldn't survive me wasting another second.

Instead, I do the next best thing.

"Demons!" I yell, reaching over my back to pull out my battle-axe. Though its size makes it awkward for me to run, there's no way I'm running headfirst into battle without it drawn. "Demons! To the east!"

It's not much, but hopefully someone will have heard me. At least Eparah and Silver, they might be close enough to—

I skid around a corner, following the last cries I heard that seemed to be coming from this direction, but stop dead in my tracks when I see the shadowcreature hunched over a bloodied Crusader at the opposite end of the street.

Horror stories of demons are told to children to scare them into obedience. Though they can take many forms, they are mostly described as savage animals overcome by raw, concentrated evil. They resemble the most ferocious beasts that roam the land—bears, wolves, cougars—but their fur is stiff, not soft, and their skin is as black as hate. They fuel our nightmares and cripple us with fear.

But the creature before me puts them all to shame.

It has no face. No eyes, or nose, just a smooth, membranous skull with a crescent slit for a mouth. The teeth inside are as thin as fish bones and as green as seaweed. Even from here, I can smell its fetid breath, the sickening stench of blood from its recent kill.

When I notice the weapon in the Crusader's hand, a shadowsteel shortsword, I muffle a soft gasp. I'm looking at Sai's body.

The shadowcreature cocks its head, spying me down the road and grinning with deadly intent.

My knees quiver.

The beast screeches and takes one step toward me, his leg like a spider's as it juts from his torso and bends in odd, unsettling angles.

I shuffle backward, but I trip over the pole of my axe and stumble to my rear.

The shadowcreature's grin widens. Its bony, horrid limbs are as jagged as the barest branches of winter trees, and it moves like a predator on the prowl.

I am nothing more than a puddle of fear now as I scramble backward, scooting and crab-walking as fast as I can, unsure of where exactly I think I'm going. I can't outrun him—he's almost as tall as the two-story inn on my right, and as I stare at it, eyes wide with terror, I realize it has wings anyway—two large, membranous wings that are curved and as sharp as hooks.

Never in my life have I seen its equal. Even in our studies, the scholars never described a beast quite like it. They only ever eluded to there being more than just demons in the Shadowthorn, and that we didn't know of all of them yet.

Fear strangles me, my thrilling heart beating so violently in my throat that I can barely breathe. My hands won't scoot fast enough, while my feet suffer from shuffling too quickly.

The creature gains on me, even with its languid movements. It watches me with its eyeless face like it knows it, too, like it will take great pleasure in watching me suffer as it plucks the flesh from my bones.

My back slams into something—the outside wall of a building I think, but I don't dare pull my eyes away to confirm.

The creature stalks forward, a thin string of saliva dripping from its dark mouth and pointed chin.

Just when I think it's over for me, just as I begin to make peace with my life and hope I'll be reunited with my departed family, I catch a glint of shadowsteel behind the creature's gnarled legs.

Maxwell tiptoes out from a shed with his lance held stiffly before him. He nods at me too vigorously to convey confidence and too rapidly to convince me that whatever he has planned is going to work.

Before I can think of a way to tell him to stop without giving his position away to the stalking shadowcreature, Maxwell cries. He bolts into a run, knuckles white on the pole of his weapon, and leaps. He throws the weight of his entire body—which isn't much, but is better than nothing—into his jab and spears the shadowcreature in the calf.

The beast shrieks, a fluid sound like a bird drowning on its final squawk. It jerks around to face him.

Maxwell is already backing away, lance readied again, but

he's too close. The shadowcreature sees him now and the only thing it knows is how to kill.

He needs to run.

And he does, but, not the right way.

By the time I'm on my feet, Maxwell is charging the beast again.

"No!" I cry, racing toward them.

The shadowcreature swings his skeletal hand at Maxwell. The force of it sends him flying across the courtyard and crashing against a building. The wooden boards splinter and quake, but he doesn't break through the foundation entirely. He slumps into a limp heap of limbs, and I can't tell from this distance if he's alive or dead, but I know that if I don't do anything, soon the shadowcreature will finish him off.

The nightmarish beast seemingly casts all notions of me aside as it redirects its attention on Maxwell, moving on him with lethal intent.

With my axe raised, I charge. Deftly, I'm aware that this is the same thing Maxwell did and I know how poorly that ended for him. But what choice do I have? If I do nothing, Maxwell dies. If I do nothing, *I* might die.

As I race forward, I notice the well on the far side of the courtyard for the first time. The shadowcreature is about to pass it, but if I can get there before the beast moves too far away…

I push my muscles harder. They ache with every reverberating, thrashing step, but still, I dash. I run like the beast is chasing me, like there's an entire horde of demons and shadowcreatures slashing and snapping at my feet.

The well draws nearer, and I prepare for something that I'm fairly certain is never going to work. My plan is so reckless and dangerous and overly confident that I'm sure it can only fail. But the only alternative is repeating Maxwell's mistake and striking the creature in an innocuous place. My blow has to count. It has to kill.

With bounding strides, I leap onto the stone wall of the well. In the fraction of the second that it takes me to press my weight into the leg on the wall, I anticipate the rocks to wobble, for my foot to slip on the dampness of the stones, and for me to plummet down into the dark abyss. But my foothold is solid, strong. If this part of the plan is working, then the rest just might too.

Using the momentum of my run, I shove off the stone wall and spring into the air. I become weightless, timeless as my legs kick and the beast draws nearer. The axe is heavy over my shoulder, but my grip is tight. I swing hard, shadowsteel burying into the creature's skin to the hilt.

The beast shrieks wildly, back arching. It stumbles to the ground, twisting, and writhing, shoving itself back to its feet only to fall again, all the while its cries carry through air like a death toll. If the Crusaders didn't hear Maxwell or me earlier, I'm certain they hear this now. And if they can hear, so can every other creature in the Shadowthorn.

I run to Maxwell in the broken wood, keeping a cautious eye on the shadowcreature as it continues writhing. Its twitching has already begun to slow, its cries quieting behind its rasping breaths for air and life. I take comfort in knowing it'll die soon, but we can't stay here. Depending on how far away any demons are, this place will be crawling in no time.

"Maxwell," I say, giving him a shake.

A snarling howl rumbles somewhere behind the buildings, maybe a few streets over. We don't have much time.

"Maxwell, we have to go."

I glance over my shoulder to the giant creature and its stilled limbs. My axe is still buried in its heart through its back. I feel so naked without it now, the dagger at my hip doing little to nothing to soothe my nerves as the snarling seems to circle us. There must be a dozen demons in the area coming to the aid of their fallen monster.

Maxwell's eyes remain closed. I grab him by the arms and heave him over my shoulder. He's small enough that I can carry him, but he's still a full-grown man. The weight of him almost buckles my knees as I shuffle to the fallen beast. I drop Maxwell, leaning him against the creature's dead body while I wiggle my axe out from the beast's back.

Thump.

My spine goes rigid. Something heavy drops to the ground a distance behind me. The snarling is louder now, the throaty growl so close it sounds like it's right in my ears. The first demon has arrived.

SURVIVAL

ASHENVALE, SHADOWTHORN

I turn around to face the demon. Considering its back is to a building, I estimate that it jumped down from one of the rooftops. It turns its head, licking its muzzle as another demon appears from between two of the buildings to stand at its side. They're canine in form, which doesn't bode well, but I should've known considering the way in which they were circling. The scholar taught us that these kinds of demons travel in packs, and they attack much like wolves do. They fan out, surrounding their target, and when they see an opening, they lunge.

"Maxwell," I say pleadingly, kicking his boot.

Two more demons catch the corner of my eye. They enter from the road I came down, their snarling wild and vicious.

I keep my back to the fallen shadowcreature behind me, if not to serve as a reminder of what I am capable of, to at least offer me some protection. It's so large a creature that the demons will have no choice but to attack me from the front. That is, as long as no demons leap down from the roof behind me.

I tighten the grip on my axe and ready my stance. I'm not

sure if the blade of my shadowsteel is sharp enough to slice through them all if they lunged at once, but I suppose I have no choice. I will die fighting if I am to die at all.

Thump.

The sound comes from behind me.

No... If a demon has landed at my back, then I have no defense against it. If I turn and look now, the creatures in front of me will lunge, fangs glistening and eager to sink into my flesh. But if one *did* land behind the massive creature at my back, for all I know it could be climbing the fallen demon I'm huddled against; it could be standing over me in a matter of seconds; it could tear into me even quicker.

The large body of shadowcreature I'm backed up against rocks as if something is climbing up from the other side.

My breathing hastens. My gaze rotates between the two demons before me, the two beside me, and up toward my hairline, to check for dripping fangs. I want to scream for help again, but that's something else we've been warned against. The demons thrive off fear. Hearing terror sets them in a frenzy, and my cries for help would be devoured by their hungry jaws.

A shadow falls over me and my skin goes cold. The demon is standing directly above me then. Morbid curiosity forces my gaze upward to the thing standing tall on the dead creature. But it's not canine like the others though. In fact, the darkness covering its body only takes over its arm and neck. The rest of its body is pale flesh. Skin. Dare I say human.

The hulking figure bounds over me, hardly glancing in my direction at all, save for the briefest flicker of interest when its midair. It launches itself at the first demon I laid eyes on. The two of them collide, their rock-hard bodies crashing against each other with the rumbling sound of thunder. The other demons growl and bare their teeth, but they seem too confused to move. I am too. The only other time I've seen demons fighting each other, let alone one that had humanistic qualities was—

The first demon's head is ripped off its body, and the demon-man I've encountered now thrice rises from its crumpling corpse. His dark eyes meet mine, a humored look about them as recognition crosses his expression, as if he himself is just as surprised to find me here as I am. Or perhaps I'm misreading it. Perhaps the thrill of the hunt is what flashes through his dark eyes, his prey finally cornered.

Our eye contact is fleeting though when the demon beside him pounces. Its jaws snap, sharp teeth begging for a taste of his bared chest and arms, but he holds the creature at bay with his impressive muscles. The demon has strength too, and in its frenzy it writhes and wiggles, inching closer and closer until its teeth are so close that I'm sure they graze the demon-man's chest.

He brings his elbow down on the shadowcreature's snout before it can clamp shut on his exposed skin. The beast whines, sniffing the air and looking from the half-demon and back to me as if it doesn't quite understand why it's been prevented this hunt.

Truth be told, I didn't either at first, but then I recall the way this demon-man tore the head and limbs from the creature that killed my parents, just so he could have the beast's spoils. Unlike the canine shadowcreatures surrounding us, the demon-man doesn't belong to a pack. He hunts on his own, and considering how far he's followed me already, I fear he will stop at nothing to ensure my demise is brought about at his own hand.

But I can hardly think about that right now. My options are not looking too favorable. There are too many demons to outrun. Even if I tried, even if I managed to sneak away while the demon-man had them distracted, he'd still come for me.

For the time being though, we appear to be on the same side. He wants the creatures dead. So do I.

As he wrestles one of the demons, the other two grow impatient. Snarling, they prowl toward him, casting me a minimal glare before giving him their full attention. He's already killed one of their pack, and they likely don't want him to get away with killing another.

My arm shakes under the weight of my axe, but I dash across the courtyard to the demon-man's side, just as he draws a shortsword from a sheath I hadn't seen at his side, and buries into the demon's neck. There's a half second where I'm able to startle at such an act—no demon knows how to wield a sword. The beast whines, staggering away a few steps before collapsing and I become even more stunned.

It wasn't just any weapon the demon-man struck with, but one forged from shadowsteel.

The remaining demons become frenzied. Hackles raised, they howl and snap at the air, all of their rotten fangs showing in a menacing show of the weapons they will use to avenge their fallen brethren. Seeing two of their pack die at our hands has cemented our fates. They will tear us limb from limb.

The shadowcreatures pounce, invigorated and wild. The larger beast leaps for the demon-man, but the other comes for me.

There is no skill behind how wildly I swing my axe, but I swipe the air with the mad desperation of a cornered house cat. I remind myself that not moments ago, I took down a demon thrice its size. I should feel emboldened, confident, capable. But this desperation is different. I'm not doing what I must to protect a helpless friend. I'm fighting for my own life. You'd think that would be incentive enough to remember my train-ing, but it has the opposite, crippling effect. My life is on the line. One wrong move, one too-slow a parry or careless offensive strike, and the demon will have me. One prick of its fangs or claws, and I'm as good as dead.

The demon takes another snapping leap toward me and I dodge backward just before its teeth can sink into my leathers. It's toying with me, I realize. These creatures defy human prowess. They can leap impossible distances; they can run faster than any known animal can, and yet this one prowls intently, slowly.

It wants me to be afraid. Fear, above all else, is what satiates a demon's hunger. And so, this one continues lunging and snapping, and I continue swinging and backing away, until my back is pressed up against another building.

"Piss on a mage," I curse to myself, wishing I was more skillful and more keenly aware of my surroundings. But how can I focus on anything other than the beast in front of me and the weapon in my hand?

My back flush against the wall, I don't have the range I need to swing my axe with any lethality. If the demon lunges for me now, at best I can hope for is to shove it aside.

But the creature throws me off when it lunges instead for my weapon. Its jaws clench around the pole of my axe and it twists it from my grip, casting the blade aside with a jerk of its head.

Chest tight, I fumble for my dagger as the demon slowly returns its crimson gaze to me. Its eyes have been playful until now, the impish kind of mischief that has made it clear how this game will end. And the end is now. The play seeps out of its red eyes, leaving nothing but the cold darkness of death reflecting back at me.

My dagger finally comes free, and I clutch it in my sweating grip. I have nowhere to run, nowhere to dodge, and my weapon is too small to reach the demon until it'll be too late. This is where I'll die, I know that. The Crusaders will retrieve my mangled corpse and squeeze me dry of any necro-ink that might be lingering in my veins. They'll take my axe, Tor's dagger, and I know I should hold no remorse over it, that I should hope that the next to wield them will be far more skilled than I, but something sour tinges my heart. I'm not ready to give up. I wanted to do more, to avenge more of the fallen, my brother, my family.

My fingers tighten around the hilt of Tor's dagger. I'm not going down without a fight. If not for me, then for the people residing in the border towns, for the ones who fled Ashenvale and Gravenburg, and for all those who came before them. I will take this demon down with me if it is the last thing I do.

The demon's eyes flicker, its intent silent but I understand completely. *Now.*

My eyes focus on the creature's neck, to the place I need to strike, no matter what comes before or next or after.

The demon's legs bend as it readies itself for a massive leap. I do the same, sinking into my defensive pose and hoping that my blade will strike true.

But before the creature can clear the air, its black body is rammed aside by a blur of darkened limbs. The two demons and the demon-man crash to the ground together. I start to slide down the wall, to put some distance between me and death, but then my grip tightens on Tor's dagger.

Running would be too easy. Running is what all of Arcathain has done. Running is not what a Crusader does. I made a vow to kill these beasts, for my parents, for the future Crusaders, for all of Arcathain.

The larger demon flips to its feet and charges the demon-man again. Its claws tear at his chest, but my gaze is fixed on my match. My lips pull back in a vicious snarl, and I dive, dagger thrashing. The creature's chest is cold and damp, its body rigid as stone. It feels as cold as death already, but its evil has not yet been uncleansed. My shadowsteel blade punctures its skin effortlessly. Once, twice, a dozen times. I keep stabbing until the demon finally stills, and even long after.

I collapse against its stiff fur, only faintly aware of the black blood oozing from its wounds beneath me. Something grabs my shoulder, and I bolt around, dagger drawn again.

But I find myself staring up into the russet eyes of the demon-man. He's clutching his chest with his other hand, red streams trickling all the way down his stomach. Red, not black.

My dagger falters. "W-what are you?"

He releases my shoulder as if to say he means me no harm and begins backing away slowly. He indicates to the large demon he's slain, bowing ever so slightly before turning away.

My already spasming heart crashes against my ribs. He cannot go yet. There is so much I still don't understand. Besides, why would he leave? He's been hunting me for weeks, and here I am: alone, an easy target.

"You spoke last time I saw you," I call out across the grey expanse. In the quiet that follows, I can almost hear the fiends nearby awakening. They will soon descend upon this place if I'm not careful.

The demon-man halts in the middle of the road, his black wings twitching and tensing.

I continue before he thinks to take to the sky. "You said *Ry*. Is that what your kind are called?"

He sniffs. "My kind." And soon he's marching away again.

"O-okay, not *your kind*. I didn't mean to offend y—" Before I can finish, a flutter of laughter escapes me. "What am I doing? Am I apologizing to a demon?"

He whirls around, a dark shadow flickering over his expression. "I am no demon."

"Then what are you?"

It's like I've slapped the anger off his face. He staggers back, confusion racking through him. "You...you can understand me?"

An airy laugh bolts from my lungs. "Apparently I can. Should I not be able to…" I ask, but remembering our last encounter, I add, "Ry?"

It takes him a moment to recover his resolve, but when does, he finally says, "Ryven."

"Ryven then…" In truth, my question could end there. There is no greater mystery to me than *what* he is. In all the books I've scoured in the library of Nigh, none of them have mentioned creatures like him, demons with human attributes. But when I notice a muscle feather in his jawline and see the hurt flash across his face, I try to backpedal. "Why have you been following me? What's your game?"

A wry smile ticks up the side of his mouth. "Game? I might ask you the same. Do you have a death wish or are you just this unlucky?"

"I'll have you know, I was just fine until you came along," I snap, heat rushing to my face. It's a blatant lie, and a terrible one at that, but I don't appreciate what he's insinuating. I point to the fallen shadowcreature, the large beast I killed before his arrival. "I was able to take this creature down without your help, wasn't I?"

Footsteps pad softly from around the corner. I barely have time to worry about what might appear before a small group of people emerge, but instead of filling me with relief, concern thrashes through me again. They're not in Crusader leathers. Their garments are every color of autumn, though in the Shadowthorn, their brightness is muted.

"There he is," one of them cries, pointing to Ryven. "I thought we'd find you in the middle of trouble—" But his jaw falls slack before he can finish. His honeyed eyes mist as they cross over to me. "Halira?"

As the party draws closer now, I recognize the roguish man in the lead. "Uncle Adrien?"

He sheaths his drawn cutlass with a disbelieving chuckle and throws his arms wide. "Come here, you."

I fling myself into him.

In all my life, I've only met my Uncle Adrien a handful of times. My father, Oddo, and him were close when they were younger, but once Esmond became Magistrate, Adrien became shunned in a sense. He'd been no stranger to petty theft and tomfoolery, and had already been outlawed from more towns and villages than I could count. But being the Magistrate's brother, meant that his actions now reflected on Esmond as well. The Magistrate wasted no time in placing a bounty for Adrien's arrest so that Esmond could deal with him before the eyes of Arcathain and prove that not even family was above the law.

With nowhere else to go, my father said Adrien left years ago for the Forgotten Forest of Eyve, and we hadn't heard from him since.

Despite having little to no relationship with the man I call uncle, his embrace is just as familial and comforting as one from my own father. I sink into his arms, giving myself over to him fully. He smells of salt and leather and dirt. I pull back to look at him, and upon seeing the grime caked into his beard and covering the rest of him, I wonder if he's been wandering the Shadowthorn ever since the day he left.

"What are you doing here?" he asks, brushing my white hair aside to get a better look at the face that's matured since last we saw each other.

"I...I'm a Crusader now," I say, breathless, but pride seeps into my tone. It hasn't been made official yet, but being just a couple of days away now, and after having downed the large shadowcreature behind us, I think I can confidently say I've earned the title. "I joined the Shadow Crusade. I'm here to retrieve shadowsteel and..."

My teeth clamp down on the words. If I am to claim the

title of Crusader, then I should also uphold their secrets, and the Spirit Keep had made it clear that knowledge of the necro-ink did not belong among commonfolk.

To my chagrin, Adrien doesn't beam at me with pride at the mention of my accomplishments. Why should he? The life of a Crusader is brutal and quick. But it's more than that. He is a man who's made a life out of evading the Magistrate, his legion, and all the Crusaders under his command. If I am a Crusader, I am his enemy.

"I can't imagine your parents are too thrilled about that." His words twist in my belly like a knife.

I lower my gaze, unable to hold his, but his hand finds my shoulder, and I have no choice but to look at him.

"My brother…" he says cautiously. "Is he…has he…"

I purse my quivering lips together.

Adrien nods and sucks in a shaking breath. His hand drops from my shoulder, and he paces the courtyard, deep in thought. While he takes the time he needs to mourn in private, I use the opportunity to examine the people he's with more closely. There's six of them in total, including my uncle, and they're about as varied as anyone else in Arcathain. There's a woman who's tall and dark, and a man who's short and pale. Another among them has a scar stitched over his eye, and another wears thick black bands of tattoos like armor.

My gaze lingers the longest on Ryven, and he watches me right back. Even as he nods to whatever the group is discussing, his dark eyes always find their way back to mine.

Adrien finally returns to us. He makes his way over to me again, and as he stands, I realize his posture is nothing like the aristocratic stiffness of his brother's or his nephew's.

He crooks his thumbs into his belt, a lazy lean to his spine. "The Shadow Crusade, they're led by my brother's bastard son these days, so I hear?"

I nod.

He grows pensive and leans in closer, as if he doesn't want the others to hear him. I don't understand why he'd keep the company of people he doesn't trust, but then again, I've never been a fugitive.

"Be careful around those people," he whispers. It takes me a moment to realize *those people* he's talking about aren't the ones behind him, but my fellow Crusaders, my family. "Your cruel Uncle Esmond has always hated your family, and I wouldn't put it past him to bestow that hatred onto little Alphy as well."

I smirk at the childish nickname, knowing it's precisely the kind of thing *General Alphonse* would abhor. But Adrien isn't wrong. There isn't a bone in Alphonse's body that doesn't hate me.

But then my thoughts latch on the phrase *hate your family*.

"Alphonse and Esmond *are* my family, whether I like it or not," I argue. "They're the only family I have left, besides you and Kalli…"

Adrien's shoulders sink again at the insinuation of the family I've lost recently…his own brother.

"I'm sorry—"

"It's quite all right, Halira," he says, dipping his head. He looks up at me through lowered lashes, his roguish smile telling me that the last thing I need to worry about is hurting his feelings. "But I was talking about your mother's side. Come to think of it though, as I go down the line, there's really not anyone those two don't hate. Me, your father."

I chuckle. "Me, as well."

He dips his head again to hide his smirk. "Yes, well, Esmond has harbored a special hatred for your mother ever since she and Oddo met. You know how the Magistrate is about unwanted refugees from the Eyve."

Rolling my eyes, I stifle a growl, but being here with Adrien, with family, makes it impossible to hold on to my frustrations.

I still can't believe I ran into him, here of all places. Truth be told, I can't believe he's still alive.

I want to spend hours catching up with him. He has always been a wealth of endless stories, and I want to hear them all. His perilous adventures evading the law, the whirlwind romances that always end with him leaping from some duke's balcony as their wives discover their infidelity, or with him drifting out at sea with a pirate lord for months until he falls for one of his crewmen. My uncle knows no limit to the life he lives. Every moment is seized. Every story, captivating and riveting.

"They're coming." Ryven's voice is as low and ominous as a growl, jarring me from my whimsical dreams of this family reunion. "Tell them, the Crusaders are coming."

"Me? Why do I need to tell them anything. They're standing right here—"

Before I can finish, Ryven spreads his membranous wings and leaps into the sky.

"What did he say?" Adrien asks, urgency in his tone.

Gaping up to the dark sky, I can no longer see Ryven. He's disappeared somewhere behind the black clouds, but I still can't stop staring. There is still so much I don't understand about him, about why he was here, about any of this.

"What did he say?" my uncle asks again, more earnest this time.

I blink, pulling slowly on the words like they have sunk into honey. "He said the Crusaders are coming."

"Dark as shadows!" mutters the man with the scar. "They'll take our shadowsteel if they find us."

"And the necro-ink we've managed to syphon," adds one of the women.

Adrien runs his hand through his long, umber hair.

"We have to go," the woman says gently, though there's something frightened lingering beneath her tone.

"I know, I know," Adrien says quickly. He turns his sorrowful eyes on me. "This really isn't the reunion I had hoped for. Forgive me, but we must be on our way."

I can feel the sting of tears prickling to break from my eyes, but I do what I can to hold them back. The last thing he needs is to see me hurt and feel compelled to stay, thus risking being captured by the Crusaders who would most certainly turn him into the Magistrate. And although a life in the Shadowthorn sounds hard and cruel, it is at least one of freedom, a thing my uncle Adrien values above all.

"I-I understand."

He flashes me a rueful grin. "Be well, my niece. And remember, guard your secrets well. I know your mother is gone, but Imryll will protect you now."

My heart stutters. A cool wave of uncertainty and panic wraps around me until I am too strangled to even speak. What secrets is he talking about? Does he know of the strange occurrences that have been happening to me, of the mice and the ravens that I've been able to summon? And that word, *Imryll*, I've heard it somewhere before, but I can't remember where. I've stumbled across a few books in the library written in the archaic Arcathain languages, so I suppose it might be something from there. Who knows the kinds of beliefs my uncle has adapted since his life in the Shadowthorn or in Eyve—wherever he dwells.

But it's not until he and the rest of his crew disappear between the buildings and leave me standing alone in the courtyard that the word rings clear in my mind. It takes on a new voice though, not my uncle's, not mine.

My mother's.

Imryll, I remember, had been her last dying word.

And my uncle, a man who I may never see again, might've been the only person who could've told me what it meant.

OF ONE COUNTRY, OF ONE BLOOD

FEMALE DORMITORY, CASTLE OF NIGH, ARCATHAIN

*S*itting, hunched over the edge of my cot, I twirl the letter over in my hand and read it for the dozenth time since its arrival this morning.

Dearest Halira,

It is not customary for Senators to attend the induction of the Shadow Crusade's newest members, but seeing as you are family, the Magistrate has made an exception. By the time you receive this letter, I expect we'll be just a few days away.

Until then,

With love,
Senator Kalli Devonshire

By her standards, the letter is quite heartfelt. The fact that she would address me as *dearest* and sign it *with love* might speak to a certain emotional development since the last time we spoke. But I doubt it. I can't help but notice the clipped, formal tone, and the fact that she still signed her name with her professional title. And surname.

I scoff. My sister takes too much pride in her work. Although, I suppose soon I'll come to understand what that's like. After today, I will no longer be a mere recruit, I will no longer be the orphaned young woman who abandoned her late parents' professions on a whim that would've given her mother constant heartache. No, after this evening, I will be a true member of the Shadow Crusade, and I have Maxwell to thank for that.

Once the Crusaders found us, and once we were able to finally rouse him, Maxwell had insisted I keep Sai's shadow-steel sword for myself. Not only did he say he understood what was at stake—that Alphonse had rigged the day so that he and I both, as well as a few others, would never complete our task—but he also insisted that he was actually looking forward to his service at the castle.

"What's a few chores, if it means I have a roof over my head, and I never, *ever* have to step foot in the Shadowthorn again. Besides, think of how much I can learn from the scholars!" he'd said animatedly.

I didn't press him further. I didn't want to risk convincing him he was making a mistake. And though I mourned our friend Sai, there was no way I was letting grief prevent me from seizing my one chance at a place among the Crusaders. I would rather choose a life chasing demons through the Shadowthorn than being shackled to the castle, a place that will soon be swallowed by the Shadowthorn and overrun with demons anyway.

I'd presented the shadowsteel sword to Alphonse the moment he arrived. The look of disdain he gave me is still seared in my mind. I don't know why I thought that even *he* would be able to see past his hatred to approve of me just once in his life. After all, I'd saved one of his recruits; I'd slain the most terrifying, enormous demon I'd ever laid eyes on; and as far as Alphonse and the other Crusaders were concerned, I then took out four demons on my own, as well.

Few Crusaders begin their careers with such feats under their belts, but leave it to our *general* to give a careless wave of his hand and say smugly that he is still considering who will be nominated for the unit and who is better suited for the castle. There hadn't been time to argue. There hadn't even been time to gather Sai's lifeless body. Demons snarled from the surrounding trees, and we'd fled Ashenvale before there could be any more casualties.

But that was a couple of days ago now. I wouldn't have to guess for much longer who Alphonse would allow among his ranks.

Just as doubt starts to creep in of what my future might or might not entail, there's a knock at the door.

Dimitri peeks his head inside, a worried look scrunching his browline until he sees that I am the only one inside. He's likely already been to the dining hall, and upon discovering my absence, asked one of my roommates—likely Silver—where he could find me.

He's clad in the same black leathers we've worn every day for the last couple of months, but he's never looked more handsome than he does now. He's cleaned up the scruff on his chin and reshaven the sides of his head. The oils and wildflowers he must've bathed in this morning linger on his skin and waft all the way across the room to tantalize me. I don't think he's ever been this clean in his entire life. It suits him. Being a Crusader suits him. He already carries himself with the duty and commitment of one. All he's missing now is the Shadow Crusade sigil on his chest.

"You ready?" he asks, slowly walking into the room. He doesn't try hiding the way he's looking at me, how his eyes rove over my freshly brushed hair, his nostrils flaring at the scent of rose petals that wafts from my skin.

I keep my gaze lowered when I stand from the bed, playing coy as I meet him in the walkway.

"What do you think?"

He chokes on his tongue. "I—you—I think you look great."

I flush despite myself and meet his eyes. For years, his meadow gaze has comforted me, and I let myself fall into it now, giving myself over to the promise of warmth and comfort I find there.

"Can I confess that I'm worried?" I say into his shoulder.

He slides his arms around my lower back and squeezes. "You have nothing to fear. You fought a formidable shadow-creature and survived. You killed four more demons afterward. And because of you, Maxwell lives to see another day, and the Shadow Crusade gets to keep one more of their Crusaders. General Alphonse can do nothing *but* reward you with a position on the unit."

"You don't know that."

"I do." Dimitri grabs my shoulders and gently pushes me back so that he can look me in the eyes as he says, "I promise you. Nothing is more important to the Shadow Crusade than having worthy fighters out in the field. You proved yourself yesterday, Halira. Any petty childhood grudges he held toward you, they don't matter as much to him as ensuring we have the best chance at defeating Qaeus, and I don't know how you did it, but you proved that you are one of our best chances."

Guilt seizes my chest and makes me avert my gaze again. Dimitri mistakes it for yet another of my humble denials and kisses my cheek, but that's because he doesn't know the truth. No one does. Once the Crusaders arrived, I had no choice but to act as if I'd killed every shadowcreature by myself, lest risk blowing my uncle's cover. Alphonse would've delighted in hunting him down. What better prize could a boy eager to please his father deliver to him: the outcast, fugitive brother found wandering the Shadowthorn like he truly fits in among demons better than he does the rest of Arcathain.

And so, I told the lie that most of the Crusaders while walking up to me—covered in demon blood and quaking—already believed anyway. I had wanted to tell Dimitri the truth; I had. But I feared his unyielding sense of responsibility might cause him to confess that I'd been lying.

He grips my chin between his fingers, and I can barely look at him. I hate lying, especially to him. Once our places in the newest unit of Crusaders are solidified, I plan on telling him everything. He'll be disappointed, I know he will, but hopefully he'll find it in his heart to forgive me knowing that I only lied so that we could stay together.

Besides, the most impressive part of the entire story isn't even false. There are still times when I am utterly dumbfounded that I was able to kill that shadowcreature by myself. I've hardly been able to win any sparring matches since my arrival at Nigh, but I guess when one's life is truly on the line, the stakes are different.

"You worry too much, Halira," Dimitri says softly, his thumb tracing over my bottom lip. "After today, we're Crusaders, the most fearless warriors in all of Arcathain. Today is a special day. Indulge in it."

He leans forward and kisses my lips. I inhale the scent of him, fresh and flowery, so unlike the Dimitri I'm used to being around. But his current cleanliness feels like a symbol of this moment, of the grime of our pasts being washed away as our blank-slated futures unfold before us.

I push myself up to my toes and deepen the kiss. My hand slides along his jaw and cheek, relishing in the smooth warmth of his skin, a once in a lifetime experience to breathe him in with the scent of lavender still fresh on his skin, I'm sure.

His arms grip my shoulders.

"Halira," he begs when he finds an opening, but I press my mouth back against his.

He's trying to push me away, to insist that we go because we have a duty or an obligation or whatever form of responsibility he has enslaved himself to today, but I don't care. Right now, I want nothing more than *him*. His skin isn't stained with blood, his face is smooth to the touch, and despite his best efforts to act like he's disinterested, it's obvious from the bulge pressed against my thigh that he's never been more aroused in his life. I'm not foolish enough to think it's all because of me—though I have no doubt that the extra care I've taken to look presentable today is helping—but Dimitri finds satisfaction from honor and hard work. The thought of training every day for three months straight, of besting his classmates and rising to the top of our ranks as far as the good graces of the general, and finally amounting to something in his life that goes beyond the Wallows of Gravenburg has him thrumming with excitement.

"We have time," I moan against his mouth, nipping at his bottom lip with a gentle tug. My hands slide down to his chest, my fingers twirling around the topmost leather latch.

"No, we don't. The others were finishing their lunches when I left. They'll be heading to the cathedral soon."

I bite his lip, tugging on it gently as I pull away. I peek up at him from behind my heavy lashes and pout. "We can be quick."

He groans.

"I promise," I say, taking his lip back between my teeth and sucking.

A knock on the door startles us both.

Dimitri rips away from me and storms to the other side of the room. His chest is heaving, sheer horror having drained him of all his color by the time the door cracks open.

"Sorry to interrupt," Fox says, peering into the room with her hand over her eyes. "I just came to let you know everyone is transitioning to the cathedral. The ceremony will begin soon."

She disappears without another word. Dimitri storms by me, his chest puffed out and his cheeks red.

"I'll see you there," he grumbles, disappearing after Fox.

The cathedral is more crowded than I expected it would be, and not just with Crusaders either. Though many of the bodies filling the pews are clad in black leathers, there is a sprinkling of commonfolk among them, parents and spouses, brothers and sisters, proud family members who have come to witness their loved one's receiving their hard-earned title of Crusader.

The initiates and I stand in two rows at the dais in the front of the cathedral while the people filter in. It seems as if every candle in all of Nigh has been brought here. The place is illuminated with a hazy, ethereal glow that's mesmerizing and only serves to churn my insides more.

The anticipation has my stomach in knots. If I could forgo such a lavish commencement, I would, and gladly. I'd rather receive my orders in private, where I won't feel the eyes of everyone on me as I try to hold back my tears when Alphonse tells me I'm staying here.

The longer we wait, the more certain I become that there can be no other outcome. He's hated me for too long to let me have anything I want now. His entire life and all the torment he sent my way has been leading us to this final moment.

When the Magistrate enters the room, everyone hushes. The audience spins around in their seats to watch him walk up the walkway, and I bob onto the tips of my toes to see around Güthric.

My uncle Esmond is just as I remember him: intimidating in his nobility. Time has only served to darken the already sinister creases of his face. He takes languid but powerful strides down the walkway, each step echoing up the high ceiling cathedral and demanding the full attention of everyone in the room.

General Alphonse follows a short distance behind him, doing his best to mimic his father's confident, aristocratic posture. I'd never realized where he'd learned to clasp his hands behind his back, or just how similar his upturned nose is to his father's, but seeing them next to each other, one directly in front of the other, the resemblance is uncanny.

Alphonse's scowl is deeper than it usually is, and I can't tell if he's as disinterested in being here as I am, or if it just pains him that much to be in his father's shadow.

The Magistrate steps up onto the center of the dais. He scans us all with his dark eyes before turning sharply and taking his place at the edge of the platform. He is here today to witness, nothing more.

Alphonse steps up next, and as he turns around to begin the ceremony, I glimpse my sister coming in behind them. Kalli doesn't come up the platform—according to her letter, it's not customary for Senators to attend these ceremonies. Instead, she veers left at the end of the walkway, taking an empty seat in the first pew. We share a cordial smile before we both fix our attentions to Alphonse.

"Greetings citizens of Arcathain. You honor the Shadow Crusade and our initiates with your presence today." He gives a sweeping gesture to the rest of us behind him. "The mages abandoned us, expecting the demons to slaughter all of humankind. But what they did not know was that we are too brave to cower and die. We are the Shadow Crusade! For years, we have defended your borders from the demons that would terrorize you in the night. For generations, we have fought the

Primordials and aimed to rid the world of the evil that plagues us. To be a Crusader is to be a protector, to be fearless in the face of death. A Crusader not only fights for themselves, but for all of Arcathain. To a Crusader, there is no greater purpose than serving our country."

The Crusaders in the audience slap their chests and roar, "Of one country, of one blood," in a rumbling chant that startles most of the people in the room.

Alphonse smirks, but he holds his hands up. Once the room has quieted again, he signals to the rest of us. "Today, we gather to see a new generation of warriors join the Shadow Crusade. The initiates behind me are as cunning and committed as any others I've overseen in the past three years I've been general. They came here with one purpose: to serve their country and defend it from the bane of shadowcreatures infesting our lands."

The Crusaders in the audience holler and pump their fists into the air. The nave becomes a chorus of bravado and virility. Alphonse tries taming them with another raise of his hands, but they continue, the boisterous whooping too thrilling to ignore in such close proximity.

"That is enough!" the Magistrate bellows, the cathedral hall falling as silent as Ashenvale. "Is this a brothel or a commencement of honor? Alphonse, if you will."

The general bows deeply to his father, mostly to hide the pink tinge of his cheeks, I think. Once he's finally upright again, Alphonse turns his back to the crowd and finally assesses the recruits.

With his palm turned up, Alphonse signals for Dimitri. "Step forward, Initiate."

Together, they walk to a pedestal on the other end of the platform, opposite the Magistrate. A silver bowl rests atop the velvet pillow, but it's too tall for me to see what's inside. I suppose I'll find out soon enough.

"Dimitri Adams of Gravenburg. You heard the call of your people to defend your land to your dying breath. Their fears are yours; their survival is in your hands. Are you prepared to fight for them, every day for the rest of your life?"

Dimitri stands as solid as a statue. He doesn't even seem to be breathing when he answers, "Yes, General, I vow it."

Alphonse reaches for the pedestal and retrieves a tool resting on the plush pillow. From this distance, I can't see what it is right away, only that the rod he's holding matches the silver of the bowl, and the tip of the instrument is as black as night. He dips it into the basin and suddenly I understand why.

Alphonse brings the dripping brush to Dimitri's face and draws the necro-ink symbols upon his skin. When he's finished, he sets the brush into the bowl instead of on the pillow and grabs a scrap of fabric, one that bears the shape of a shield on the other side. His Crusader's sigil, the only mark of rank any of us will ever receive.

"I present you, Dimitri Adams, with the rank of Crusader. Take your sigil and accept your place among the Shadow Crusade."

Dimitri smacks one fist to his chest, reaching out with his other hand to retrieve the patch. "With honor," he says, and returns to stand in the row with the rest of us.

One by one, Alphonse summons each of the recruits up to the pedestal. He paints their necro-ink on for them and presents each of them with their patches, the white phoenix sigil amid a backdrop of royal purple.

A few aren't as lucky though.

Maxwell is the first to receive the rank of ward, a gold bird of less magnificence, its wings spread before a grey backdrop. Another girl who has shown little promise is also given the title. To my surprise, they both appear far more grateful for the *honor* than I would be.

Fox is summoned next. She is just a few people down from

me in the row, and my heart quickens all the faster as my time draws nearer. She clutches her collar bone and the token I know to be concealed beneath her leathers. When this is all said and done, when we are finally Crusaders and therefore as bound as family, as sisters, I will finally muster the courage to ask the significance of the silver ring she wears around her neck.

"Foxlynn Abigail of Gravenburg. You heard the call of your people to defend your land to your dying breath. Their fears are yours; their survival is in your hands. Are you prepared to fight for them, every day for the rest of your life?"

"Yes, General, I vow it," she replies.

Alphonse makes quick work with the necro-ink and pulls Fox's patch from the stack.

"I present you, Foxlynn Abigail, with the rank of ward. Take your sigil and accept your place among the Shadow Crusade."

Ward? Ice trickles through my veins. Fox can't stay here. She deserves to fight in the unit just like the rest of us. This is absurd. She's just as skilled in weaponry, knows just as much about the shadowcreatures as any of us.

But Fox doesn't falter. She dips her head and accepts the sigil with a polite, "With honor."

She meets my gaze on her way back to our row and shakes her head as if to tell me not to worry about it. I don't know how I can *not* worry. For whatever reason, he plans to keep her trapped here, to torment her as his personal slave, and she doesn't deserve it.

Sobering fear rolls over me. If he has decided she will remain here, then certainly he's decided the same fate for me.

The other recruits take their turns. I drown out their induction. My panicked thoughts are thundering inside my skull, a raucous whirlwind that's far too loud for me to hear anything else.

Someone clears their throat. "I said step forward, Initiate."

I blink the cathedral into view and find that all eyes are on me, including Alphonse's. They're full of fiery impatience and I stumble forward.

"Halira Devonshire of…Gravenburg," he says the word with disdain, likely wishing he could force me to claim my mother's homeland instead, despite the fact that I've never stepped foot in the Eyve. His eyes are cold on mine. "You heard the call of your people to defend your land to your dying breath. Their fears are yours; their survival is in your hands. Are you prepared to fight for them, every day for the rest of your life?"

My voice is brittle, but I muster the courage I need to speak the words that will end this quickly. "Yes, General, I vow it."

The necro-ink slides onto my skin as sickening as ever. I breathe through my mouth to avoid the smell, until he places the line on my bottom lip. When he's finished, he takes one of the last patches. The sigil side faces him so that all I can see is the same shield shape he's handed everyone.

Finally, he places the patch in his palm and shows it to me.

All of the patches resemble one another in most ways. The crest of the Shadow Crusade is a crowned phoenix with splayed wings. The backdrop is always a combination of black and purple, the variances of which determine rank.

My eyes blink repeatedly, unconvinced that what they're seeing is true.

"I present you, Halira Devonshire, with the rank of Crusader. Take your sigil and accept your place among the Shadow Crusade."

My hand floats to the patch as if I were in a dream. "W-with honor," I say, breathless.

Clutching the patch to my chest, I scuttle back to the rows of recruits before Alphonse can change his mind. I don't hear any more of the ceremony; I'm too busy staring down at my patch, my reward, the very thing I've worked relentlessly for.

When Alphonse concludes the ceremony, I catch my sister's

glittering gaze in the crowd as she stares up with something akin to pride. By the time I walk up to meet her, whatever glint had been there is gone. Perhaps it had just been the candlelight reflecting in her grey eyes.

"Care to walk with me?" she asks.

I bow at the hip and stretch my arm out. "Lead the way."

We take our time walking the grounds, a heavy fog settling at our feet that feels like it belongs more in the autumn months than now as we're departing from winter.

My sister is quiet, and if I know her at all, then I know her mind is at work. She keeps eyeing me when she thinks I'm not paying attention, but her penetrating gaze is difficult to ignore when it lances through me.

"What is it?" I finally ask.

But she simply shakes her head. "It's your ink. Your cross is crooked."

Reflexively, my hand comes to my forehead. Embarrassment overcomes me. How could I be so sloppy as to mark myself with a crooked cross during my swearing-in? But it's then I remember, I wasn't the one who applied my necro-ink today.

"Alphonse," I grumble.

The slightest of smirks appears on her lips. "What? He wasn't proud of his cousin's achievements today?"

I snort. "Not in a million years."

Her laugh is haughty and malicious. "He always was a pompous ass, wasn't he?" Sighing, she adds, "A small man with an ego made from glass. It says a lot about a person who's threatened by someone else's victories."

I can't argue with that. "If he'd have it his way, I would've been bleeding corpses in the catacombs for the rest of my life."

"Well, thank the Gods that you no longer have to worry about that." We fall silent, meandering toward the courtyard. We walk down the stone path, my eyes drifting to the collapsed gargoyles with new understanding. I wonder if the outside of the castle is so broken because of demon scourges like the one that occurred the other week, or if it had always been this dilapidated. I wonder just how longer this fortress can stand.

"So, tell me," she says, eyeing me with otherworldly grace. "How did you convince our rotten cousin to give you your Crusader sigil?"

Instantly, my tongue feels heavier. If I've struggled lying to the others, to Dimitri, lying to my sister will prove impossible. She knows me too well. She, of all people, has a keen eye for these sorts of things. It's one of the reasons she makes such a great Senator.

"I...killed some shadowcreatures," I admit, keeping it vague so that I'm not outright lying.

She arches a slender brow. "Demons? Multiple?"

My gaze shoots down to the fog. "I don't know what it was. We've learned about some of the other creatures that dwell in the Shadowthorn, but no one's been able to give this one a name." I turn toward her, the thrill of the fight sinking into me. "You should have seen it, Kalli. It was so big—I've never seen anything that size before." My brow furrows, pulling up the horrifying memory of it. "I-it didn't have a face. It was almost skeletal, aside from the thin, black skin stretched over its bones."

She watches me impassively. I try reading her, to see if she was already aware that such beasts exist, but she's always been like this. Kalli holds information close to her heart, even the innocuous kind, until she's certain the time has come to share it.

"And the others?" she asks.

I blanch, at once thinking she means Ryven, Uncle Adrien, and the others they were traveling with. My guilt is too palpable, too irrational. She can't know that. No one does.

I clear my throat and grip my fear. "W-what others?"

"You said *shadowcreatures*. Plural. As in, more than one. So tell me about these great monsters that my younger sister disposed of."

"Oh, yes, well, you see, the others were regular demons. The canine type."

Her arched eyebrow rises higher. "They hunt in packs, yes?"

I nod, relieved to hear her taking an interest in me for once, but also aware that this feels oddly like an interrogation. Like a nephila spider, Kalli has a knack for spinning a massive web, one that her prey doesn't even see coming until they're wrapped up tightly inside it.

"How many of them did you encounter?"

"Four," I answer promptly.

"And how is it that you killed four demons the first time you were in the Shadowthorn?"

And there it is. The question that I've been dreading ever since we left Ashenvale. The Crusaders had been all too eager to celebrate my momentous victory. The other recruits had asked, of course, but their questions were quickly followed by excited imagined tales of heroism and cunning, stories where I ripped spines from the demons' backs and used them to crack the other demons' heads clean off their bodies. Their stories only became more elaborate, and by the time they were finished, everyone had lost interest in hearing the real story because they knew the ones they'd told would be better.

Kalli is not the kind to be swept up in excitement. She's not the kind to miss important details like how a single person, a mostly inexperienced young woman, could kill four demons with nothing more than a battle-axe that is still, at times, too heavy for her to carry.

I'm desperate to change the subject, to keep walking and disappear into the fog and out from her piercing, calculating eyes. I try thinking of a story that might convince her, but even I have no imagination for it.

One thought does come to mind though, the same one I've had throughout the last couple of days:

Where was the raven when I needed it? If I have magic over the animals, why did none come to my aid when I was facing death?

All my fear settles to the back of my mind because I realize the story of those demons don't matter. If Adrien knew what Imryll was, maybe Kalli does too. Maybe he wasn't the only one with the information I needed. After all, no one was closer to our mother than my elder sister.

Blinking furiously, I summon the courage to gaze into her grey eyes. "Has anything…strange ever happened in your presence?"

Her forehead creases, the question taking her off-guard but enticing her inquiring mind. "Strange in what way?"

"Strange like…" I swallow hard. "Something that could almost be described as magic?"

Cool fury bursts behind her eyes. She glances around the courtyard and grabs my arm. She pulls me into the shadows of the castle wall, tucked behind one of the pillars miraculously still left intact.

"*Never* speak of such things," she hisses. "Never. To anyone."

"I—I know. I'm sorry. I just—"

"Do you know what they'd do to you if they thought you were an abhorrent mage? You'd be hanged, and that's if you're lucky. They've been sending alleged mages to the coast for months now, to use as bait to convince the Lords of Illashore to consider negotiations."

"Negotiations?" I scowl. "The Magistrate wouldn't want to negotiate with mages."

"That's beside the point, Halira. Are you even listening to me?" she snaps. "You are not a mage. Don't ever say that you are. You have no magic. Whatever you think happened to you, didn't. Ignore it."

Vigorously, I shake my head. I've never seen her so enraged before, but even I can tell the anger is just a mask. Deep down, she's frightened. Terrified. Which means her words mean nothing. She's covering something up.

My eyes widen with understanding. "What do you know?" I beg her. "Please, tell me. I—I need to know."

With an exasperated growl, Kalli peels away, her heavy white locks beating against her back. She paces the area, clutching the bridge of her pale nose, and I await whatever answer she is considering giving me.

But when she finally stops, her breaths grey in the cool, evening air, her words are more unexpected than anticipated.

"Congratulations on your accomplishment today, Halira. Our family would be proud."

She storms away, the ropes of her white hair smacking against her back as she disappears into the night.

*W*ith nothing left to do but stand outside and freeze, eventually I decide my sister isn't coming back. At least not tonight. Whatever she's warring with inside herself, the secret that frightens her so terribly, she'll probably want to think on it for the evening before we convene again. I can give her that, if I must. After all, I've already waited this long.

I head back inside the castle, unsure of where I'm headed. My feet wander aimlessly through the dim halls. It would make sense to seek out my friends, to celebrate our accomplishments today together, or at the very least to check in with Fox to see how she's doing with her rank as ward, but as I draw nearer to the chanting and hollering of celebrating Crusaders, my feet guide me down another hallway.

I wish I understood it all better. I wish I'd had time to ask my uncle proper questions that would've actually enlightened me instead of shrouding me further in darkness.

I'm in the deep northwestern wing of the castle when I hear a rasping, feathered sound coming from down the hall. I have every intention of changing course again. Whatever the sound is, it must mean people, and right now I'd rather put distance between me and others.

But then I realize the scratching noise is more than just that; it's a whispered conversation, one that's being had in the farthest reaches of the castle.

I know I should mind my own business, but my feet are in charge right now. I slink farther down the hallway and peer through the cracked door.

"When?" I recognize Alphonse's voice and see him a moment later as he stomps across the room.

I angle my head to get a better view to find him standing before his father.

"Soon," the Magistrate says, giving his glass a twirl. "Once my legion is whole again."

Alphonse smacks the drink out of his hand, the glass shattering on the hearth and the amber liquid sizzling into the fire.

Slowly, the Magistrate rises from his seat in the armchair, shadows stretching over his face and deepening his ferocity, but Alphonse doesn't back down.

"You can't expect me to just abandon this place!" Alphonse growls. He's no longer whispering. "You said I could have the Shadow Crusade. They're mine. You have your own warriors."

"Need I remind you, boy, the Shadow Crusade belongs to me, as does all of Arcathain. I'm merely loaning the Crusaders to you to appease your juvenile insecurities about whether you're important or not."

Alphonse's fists flex at his sides. "Father, please. I beg you, do not take the Crusaders. We're getting close. Just last month, a unit narrowed in on Qaeus' location. And with this new batch of Crusaders, we might stand a chance at going deep enough into the Shadowthorn to destroy him once and for all, and end the damn Blight. We wouldn't even need to bother with the mages then—"

"That's enough," Esmond says. He straightens his robes and

sucks in a deep breath. "You speak of the mages as if they are no longer a threat to us, but have you forgotten that they took our land? They severed it without a care for the Arcathainians who'd be injured in the process. Your grandparents died in the Great Rift, as did countless others. The mages have gone unchecked for too long, and the time to challenge them is now."

Alphonse lowers his head, the heat of his gaze singeing the carpeted floor.

"I *will* have my Crusaders returned to me, Alphonse. I gave you time here, but you have shown no progress."

"We just need another month—"

"Another month is far too long. In that time, your castle will become consumed completely. The Blight's growth is increasing. Arcathain doesn't have much time, and we can't rely on the weakness of men to rescue us. We need the mages."

Alphonse throws his hands in the air. "And how do you propose we convince them to help us? They abandoned us, Father. Centuries ago. If our people ever shared remorse and respect for each other, it would've been then, not now after so many years of separation and hatred. They will not come to our aid."

"I am not inviting them to," the Magistrate says cryptically.

Alphonse eyes him warily. He shakes his head. "I don't understand your plan. Attacking them will do nothing but provoke them. We don't want that kind of magic to be unleashed upon Arcathain."

Esmond strolls to the edge of the room where he finds a decanter and another glass. "That is why the attack comes second, son. First, we need leverage."

Following close behind him, Alphonse asks, "Do you really think you'll be able to abduct one of the Lords of Illashore? They're mages, Father. If they don't see you coming, they'll blast you with magic until you're dust."

From behind his glass, Esmond looks down at his son with a look of contempt. "I have told you, you are not to call me Father," he says when he's polished off the amber liquid. "I have a title. You will use it."

"Yes, Magistrate," Alphonse says through gritted teeth.

"As for the mages, you overestimate them. They are not all powerful, especially not like they were. Our spies tell us that ever since the Great Rift their magic has been waning. They stole away from the source of their power, and now they're paying the price. They'll be eager to negotiate with us if they believe we intend to give them back their power."

"I don't understand—" Alphonse starts to say, but he's cut off by the man who's even more pompous than he is.

"No, I don't expect that you do. But it's of no matter. Tomorrow, your Crusaders will assemble in the courtyard and receive their instructions to join me back to Arcathain Capital."

"Fa—Magistrate, please."

Esmond silences him with a single menacing look. "That is all, General. You may return to your men now."

Begrudgingly, Alphonse smacks his chest, but before he can turn around and start to stomp toward the door, I flee down the corridor. I overhear Esmond telling him to wait, that he has one other matter to discuss with him about one of the recruits he mentioned earlier, but I don't hear the rest of what's said. I don't risk it.

I duck into the nearest door I can find, press my back against the wall, and wait for Alphonse's thundering footsteps to pass. It takes longer than expected, their conversation carrying on for quite some time and making me wish I had stayed to hear it. But nothing could be more upsetting and terrifying than the news I've just overheard.

My mind reels from it. All this time we spent training to attack the demons in the Shadowthorn, only to be plucked from that very duty and taken to the Capital. That's not why I came here. It's not why Dimitri, or Silver, or any of the Crusaders are here. We came to avenge our fallen loved ones, to protect the citizens of Arcathain, the ones living in the border towns that are tormented by demons daily.

We came to fight and slay Qaeus.

The Magistrate can't do this.

I race down the hall, unsure of where I'm headed next, but urgency surges through my every stride. I follow the sounds of laughter and chanting, the stringent aroma of spilled wine and tankards of beer guiding me to the dining hall.

Frenzied, I barrel through the doors. It's so loud inside that few notice me. My friends at the nearest table do though, as my hip crashes against the edge where they are sitting.

The joy is leeched away from their faces when they see me. I must be quite the sight, eyes wide, mouth bobbing like a fish struggling for air. I can't find the words; I don't know where to start.

"We have to...we're not going to...they think they can just—"

Dimitri stands from the bench. He hooks an arm around my shoulder, tells our peers not to worry, and guides me back out of the room.

"Calm down," he says softly.

"I can't," I breathe. "You don't know what I've just overheard."

"No, I don't," he says, leaning back against the wall and crossing his arms. "That's exactly why you need to get a grip on yourself so you can tell me."

I'm shaking my head, but I know he's right. My lips pursed together, I force a deep inhale through and out my nose. It already helps gather my thoughts, and so I do it again.

Once my breathing has finally settled, Dimitri pushes himself off the wall. "So, what is it?"

"The Magistrate," I say quickly, louder than I intend. I

search the corridor around us, fearful to find Alphonse lurking nearby.

Dimitri's hand settles on my shoulder. "It's just you and me here. Everyone else is inside or in bed."

"Alphonse wasn't. He was with the Magistrate. They were talking about…a war."

"Which one?"

I roll my eyes. "Not a war from the past. Something Esmond—*the Magistrate* plans to begin."

Dimitri's eyes narrow. "An attack on the mages?"

I nod.

He snorts. "It's about time."

"No. You don't understand. He means for us to join him."

"*Us* who?" Dimitri asks, eyes narrowing farther. Concern edges his words like he's finally starting to understand the devastating impact of this realization.

"*Us*, the Crusaders," I tell him. "He told Alphonse that tomorrow morning we'll be asked to congregate in the courtyard, and the Magistrate will give the announcement that the Shadow Crusade is rejoining his ranks at the Capital."

Dimitri jerks his head back, eyes wide with surprise. He runs a hand over the nakedness of the back of his head and takes a few steps down the hall.

"Well," he says at last. "I guess this means we're going to the Capital then."

I balk. "That's it? You're just going to go?"

"Of course I am. What do you even mean? We are Crusaders now, Halira. We took an oath. We listen, we obey, and we go where we're told."

"I didn't sign up for this," I insist. "We came here to fight the demons who took our parents, not to threaten war on the mages."

"Whether you like it or not, you did," he says simply. "Look, we both knew the risks of coming here. The recruiter warned us when we enlisted."

A tear streams down my cheek as I recall the memory. The man had said that the Shadow Crusade was a branch of the Magistrate's Legion. At any time, we could be asked to reunite as a whole. But in all the years that the Shadow Crusade has existed, I never expected it to happen the very first day of our service.

As my vision blurs, Dimitri's arms find their way around me.

"It'll be okay," he says into the softness of my hair. "We'll still have each other. And I've heard that serving in the Capital isn't so bad. We might actually live to see our thirties."

I sniffle a laugh and bury my face against his chest. His new patch presses against my cheek, a physical reminder of just how bound to this decision we are, whether we agree or not.

I look up at him. "But…my parents…my brother…"

"I know," he says, brushing the tears from my face. "We will avenge them some day. If the Magistrate means to go to war with the mages, I'm sure he has a plan to end the last of the Primordials, and end the horde of demons that plagues our lands for good."

I shake my head, but no more words fall from my lips. Despite the truth of what Dimitri's saying on all accounts, I can't shake the feeling that all of this isn't going to turn out as planned.

EVIL SHALL BURN

COURTYARD, CASTLE OF NIGH, ARCATHAIN

We stand in the courtyard. The Crusaders are still lively with exuberance from the celebration of yesterday, but I haven't cracked a smile since before our ceremony. I worried that Fox would notice something was wrong with me, and she'd pester me until I finally cracked and told her—Dimitri had thought it best we keep this discovery to ourselves. But I never saw Fox. I tossed and turned most of the night, and she never appeared.

Even as we congregate now, I search for her with no avail. I wonder if perhaps she has a different assignment today already. Admittedly, I don't know much about the duties of the wards. I spent most of my time with the other recruits.

Alphonse stands beside his father on the bell tower steps in front of the crowd. When I notice Kalli's absence, my heart fissures a little. I had hoped she'd stick around long enough for us to talk again, but perhaps I miscalculated her conviction of silence on the matter. Perhaps rather than having to deal with my prodding again, she's simply removed herself from the equation.

Scanning the backs of heads before me, none of them share Kalli's white, knotted braids.

I'd foolishly hoped she'd come around after she had a chance to reflect; I'd hoped that she'd see my accomplishments here yesterday and deem me worthy of the information she's withholding. How imprudent I was though. I know my sister. If she deems something unnecessary or too risky, such as sharing with me a secret that I have asked to know, then nothing will stop her from being tight-lipped.

Without her knowledge, I'm left to ponder whether I should heed her warning or try to learn more about myself without her. The journey to the Capital will be long. I expect I'll have plenty of time to try to occupy myself and I doubt the library would miss a book or two...

"Good morning, Crusaders," Alphonse calls out over the crowd. "Today marks the first day of service for some of you, and for the rest, just another glorious day serving our country."

As Alphonse drones on, I have to turn away. I can't watch his performance. I can't stomach how easily he can make it seem like this decision was something he wanted too.

As my gaze wanders, I catch a glint of red hair down the row of Crusaders from me. Glancing to the bell tower, I slide down, trying to limit the attention I'm drawing to myself as best as I can. Fortunately, from the back of the crowd, this is mostly easy to do.

I finally sidle up beside Fox, and I'm surprised to find guilt in her eyes. I hope she knows she doesn't have to be ashamed of her rank around me. Of all people, I know the cruel ways in which Alphonse likes to toy with people's lives. He short-handed her. She deserved better.

"Where were you last night?" I whisper. "I was worried about you."

Her eyes flick to mine but only for a fraction of a second

before she shushes me and continues watching Alphonse speak.

I recoil like she's just backhanded me. I can understand her shame and frustration, but she has no reason to take it out on me. I wasn't the one who gave her the title of ward.

Still, I'm too stunned to respond. Instead, I turn to watch Alphonse deliver the rest of his speech, just in time as the audience goes wild. I missed the last thing he said, but I can deduce from the cries of outrage from the Crusaders that he's just told them we'll be heading to the Capital.

"Of one country!" he yells out over the hollering.

The Crusaders around me still, their enraged eyes glued to him, but they don't answer his call.

"Of one country!" He enunciates each syllable this time, spit flying from his lips as he screams across his legion.

The cry comes back, quiet, but dutiful: "Of one blood." I even hear the words uttered from my own lips.

Alphonse runs his hand back and over his black hair, a gesture that appears to calm him, if just enough so that he can continue delivering the information he's been instructed to share.

"I understand your objections and vexations," he begins. I think I'm the only person in the crowd who notices the scathing glance he shoots at his father. "But you took an oath to your country. We fight in the Shadowthorn for the good of Arcathain, but now Arcathain needs you elsewhere."

"What of the people in Amendell?" cries a Crusader.

"And Hogsmire," another adds.

A third Crusader weaves through the crowd, her shoulders drawn, her hair smooth. It's not until she speaks that I recognize that it's Silver who's standing before the group. "If we pull the Crusaders to the Capital, we leave the people in the border towns defenseless. When you took the Shadow Crusade out of Ashenvale, you sentenced those people to their deaths."

The Magistrate steps forward now, a frown permanently etched in his expression. "I issued an evacuation for Ashenvale months before the town succumbed to the Blight, just as I will issue one for the border towns now. If people remain behind and die, it is their own choice."

Silver's voice turns lethal. "It is not the choice of impoverished women and children to die. They remained because they had no place to go and no aid was provided. The refugees who fled weren't given shelter or food. Half of them died in the snow because they were promised safety and were given none."

The Magistrate breaks her gaze and looks out over the crowd. "I assure you; the people of the border towns will be provided for. But that should concern none of you. You have been given an opportunity to be part of something greater than yourselves, to end the Blight that causes our people so much suffering, once and for all.

"It is time we abandon Nigh, so that we may direct our efforts to more lucrative gains." He looks back down to Silver now. "How many more women and children would you like to see perish?"

A low murmur trickles over the Crusaders.

"N-none," Silver says.

"And you all?" Esmond asks, gesturing to the legion below him. "Do you share this hope for your fellow Arcathainians?"

Everyone nods or voices their agreement.

"Then it is for that precise reason that I ask you to join us in the Capital. Rest assured, that the well-being of all Arcathainians is my only intention for this modification to your station. There are plans in motion, none of which I am permitted to share with you all now, but with your help, we *will* defeat Qaeus and all of his little minions. First we just need to regroup."

He bows to Alphonse as if to say he's done his part and expects the rest to follow accordingly. I don't anticipate it won't. I can already see the impact his speech has had on the Crusaders. Silver has returned to her place back in the crowd, and some of the other Crusaders who looked ready to fight him have settled into more neutral postures. They are true Crusaders, loyal to their duty without fault. I wish I was more like them, that it came natural to me, but I have to fight my every impulse to run.

"The Magistrate leaves for the Capital later this evening," Alphonse informs us. "You will have until then to pack your belongings so that we may accompany him on his return journey." He waits for agreement before adding, "All this time, we've been fighting the demons, but they keep coming. Our resources are limited, the necro-ink, the shadowsteel, even Crusaders—our numbers keep dwindling. But our fight has never been with the demons directly."

"Yeah!" a few Crusaders shout from the crowd.

"Our conflict lies with the Primordial Qaeus. We've tried fighting through the Shadowthorn to reach him, but when have we succeeded? Hmm? In all the years we've launched our expeditions to search for him, we've come up short. We are nowhere closer to defeating him now than we were a decade ago."

Alphonse gives no indication that these words are like poison on his tongue. He recites the speech well, the writing of which I'm sure came directly from his father to help rile the Crusaders to his side. And it's working. All around the courtyard, my brethren are bobbing their heads. They stand with fearful scowls and malicious intent. The mere mention of Qaeus and his possible defeat have them ravenous.

"But I have news for you, Crusaders," Alphonse continues. "We could never defeat the Primordial alone. This was true centuries ago when the mages aided us in the first three kills, and it's truer now. The Primordial Qaeus has grown too strong. We need something just as powerful to defeat him, and we believe the mages—as filthy and treacherous as they may be —we believe they hold that power.

"In fact, we believe there's already one among us."

My skin prickles with fear, and I scan the Crusaders around me to see if any of them seem guilty of the accusation. But I've lived with these people for months now. Surely, I would've known if any of them were—

"Halira Devonshire." Alphonse's voice cuts through the air like a cracked whip.

The Crusaders part, not only stepping back to be farther from me, but simultaneously giving Alphonse a line of sight as he approaches. His smile is wicked, cruel. Its coldness permeates the courtyard until I feel like it's winter again.

Dimitri rushes to my side. He looks down, watching me from worried eyes. "It's not true," he says so quietly only I can hear him. "Tell me, it's not true. You can't be a—"

"Did you think we wouldn't find out?" Alphonse asks once he's close enough to reach out and grab me, even if he doesn't. "Did you think you, a novice fighter like yourself, could take down such a goliath shadowcreature without us beginning to wonder how you accomplished such a feat?"

I'm shaking my head. "No…I'm not a mage."

"She's not a mage," Dimitri argues on my behalf.

I stare out at the wide eyes of my peers. Panic seizes my heart. I should've just told everyone the truth about Ashenvale from the start. Instead, I let them paint this picture of me as some formidable, powerful mage.

"I didn't kill those demons," I blurt, hoping it's not too late to set things right. "I had help. It wasn't just me—"

"See?" Alphonse sings. He spins around slowly for the crowd, arms held out. "She admits it. She had help; she used her magic."

"That's not what I meant—" I plead, but I cut myself short when I see the pain and betrayal in Dimitri's eyes. I want to tell him that it's all lies, I want to reassure him that I'm not what Alphonse is making me out to be, but the truth of it is, that I don't know. Kalli wouldn't tell me; my mother and father never said a word about it.

"Arrest her." Alphonse waves his hands at two of the nearest Crusaders. "Take her to the dungeon until we're ready to leave."

"What are you going to do with her?" Dimitri demands as the Crusaders wrap their hulking grips around my biceps.

Sneering, Alphonse looks him up and down. "If anyone would like to join her, there's more room in the neighboring cells."

Dimitri stiffens and falls back into ranks.

The Crusaders drag me away. I have no fight left in me. Maybe if the accusations were wrong, but...as far as I know, they're not.

Just before they drag me out of the crowd, my gaze settles on Fox. She's another person I want to reassure, to comfort and tell her that I'll be all right, but I find no surprise in her expression, no concern.

She shrugs unapologetically, and the breath leaps from my lungs. She was the only one who knew about what happened in the library, the only one who seemed to notice that the raven who attacked Alphonse was somehow linked to me, and she was missing for hours last night.

I thought she was my friend. She told me that she wouldn't tell anyone.

But now I start to understand. The circumstances for how she came to the Shadow Crusade, the offhanded comments she'd make about our general's attractiveness, her rank as ward, her absence last night and this morning.

I can't piece it all together—I don't know if her intentions were malicious or out of self-preservation—but I have no doubt that I have her to thank for my predicament. Should I ever be released or see a day of freedom again though, I will find her, I will have my confession, and I will make her pay.

They drag me to the back side of the castle, into a drafty dungeon below. I'm stripped of my necro-ink. My shadowsteel battle-axe is taken from me. But it's the removal of Tor's dagger that is most heart wrenching. It was the only thing I had left from him, the only possession I'd taken from Gravenburg, and now it'll go to the next batch of recruits to walk these halls, if there is one.

The Crusaders throw me into a cell, the metal bars slamming shut behind me with a deafening metallic ring and leave to stand guard outside.

Once I've pulled myself off my knees, I slump to my rear on the cold ground, my back pressed against the wall.

"I warned you about telling anyone."

I bolt upright at the silvery sound of my sister's voice. "Kalli!"

I crawl to the bars and lean my head against them to try to look at the cell beside me. All I can see are her arms resting out from the bars. Her hands are clasped, her knuckles white beneath the crusted blood.

"What happened?" I ask her.

"How funny. That's the same question I've been wondering myself. Not more than an hour after I left you, they came for me."

Twisting around to face the darkness of my cell, I lower myself back to my rear and bow my head. "It was an accident. A friend saw something she shouldn't have…"

"A friend?"

I snort my own contempt, but my heart aches to believe that I can still call Fox that. Maybe she was threatened? Maybe someone else saw something? Or maybe Kalli's right. Maybe Fox never was my friend at all.

"I didn't know what I was doing," I tell her, since there's no point in keeping it all in. She can't run away from me now. "Why won't you just tell me what this is?"

"Because I don't know either." I can hear the grinding of her jaw, the pressure of her knuckles popping beneath her grip. "Mother said she would tell me the next time I saw her. She said it was time for me to know my lineage. But then…well, I didn't come home soon enough."

I heave a sigh and sink lower. "But…you *know*, don't you? The things that have happened to me, they've happened to you, as well?"

Kalli falls silent, and I can almost hear her mind at work.

But before she can answer me, the door leading into the dungeon creaks. I spin around and back away from the bars. The sound of footsteps echo down the corridor, and I brace myself for whatever scorn has come down to visit us—

"Dimitri?" I race back to the metal bars and reach for him. "What are you doing here?"

Hope blooms in my chest. He's comes to rescue us, of course he has. He wouldn't let Alphonse get away with something like this.

But that same hope bursts into flames when Dimitri flinches away from my grasp. He staggers a step back, and it's only then that I see the guarded look in his eyes, the distrust and fear.

My arms retract back inside my cell. "Why have you come?"

He glances to the cell beside me, sees my sister, and shakes his head. "So, it's true. You're both mages. Your whole family is. All this time we've known each other and you never thought to tell me? I mean I—" He cuts himself off with a heavy sigh and begins pacing the dungeon. He rakes his fingers over his face, through his hair, and back down his neck. "What in the Eyve, Halira? You're a mage!"

"No, I'm not…" I say feebly. "At least, I don't know that for certain."

He throws his arms up. "What does that even mean? I know *I'm* not a mage. I can say that with complete confidence. Every *human* can. Why can't you?"

"We're still human," my sister growls in the cell beside mine.

"Are you?" he asks, voice as harsh as the crack of a whip. "Because last time I checked, *humans* were humans, and the mages were just the heartless, tyrannical filth who abandoned us to be picked off the face of the earth by demons."

His chest is heaving by the time he's finished. I've never seen him so enraged before, not even after his sister died in the Shadowthorn, not even after his father was lost to it shortly thereafter.

But it's not his rage I'm concerned about—we've had many a spat and squabble that ended with one of us red in the face. No, this is something that stings deeper.

My eyes well with tears. "Is that really what you think of me? That I'm some tyrannical, heartless monster that would leave you to die?"

The flame leaves his eyes instantly, but my lip still quivers. I've lost him, the one person I had left to hang on to. He hangs his head low and buries his face in his hands. I don't know what to do. I want to reach out for him but I'm afraid of what he might do.

A moment later, he finally resurfaces, crossing the space between us with such vigor that it startles me.

"No, of course not," he says harshly, reaching through the bars.

Stupidly, I blink, my eyes alternating from his grasping hands back to his face. But I don't risk making him change his mind. I grab his hands.

"I'll talk to him," he says. "I'm sure this is all just a mistake."

I haven't the heart to tell him it's not. Whatever I may be, whatever they may call me, I *do* have magic. I've denied it long enough. But I'm too weak and afraid to admit it out loud, especially not now that he's willingly come closer.

We lean our heads together, the bars digging into our skulls, but I savor the contact of his forehead.

When suddenly, there's a commotion outside. The solid thumps of fists colliding with stomachs, the whooshing grunts of air being struck from lungs. A skirmish is happening, just beyond the dungeon door.

Demons is my first thought. Dimitri's too, for he draws his sword and stands ready to defend me from behind these bars.

But when the dungeon door swings open, it's not demons who enter.

Silver slinks down the steps, Güthric lumbering close behind her. She stares at Dimitri; he stares back.

"I assume you're here for the same reason we are," she says smoothly.

"And what reason is that?" he asks, planting his non-sword-hand on his hip.

Güthric claps his hands together, as if to remove the blood of a fight from them, and moves past Silver. He shoves Dimitri back and says in his gruff voice, "Break out."

Dimitri flushes bright red. "We—you can't. The Magistrate...he'll arrest you."

"I'd rather be arrested than be an accomplice to the abandonment of our people," Silver says.

Güthric nods his agreement.

"He'll only arrest you if you're caught," Kalli says from the cell next door. I can just barely make out her arms where she's rested them on the bars. "If you can free us, then you must. They won't just hang us for being accused of wielding magic. They'll use us to lure out the other mages. Or worse, to lure the demons."

I don't know what she's talking about, but it's obvious that she has some intel as to what Esmond is planning. Now's not the time for a discussion. Alphonse said the Shadow Crusade will leave midday, which can only be a few hours away from now. If we're breaking out, we need to do it, and fast, if we have any hope of putting some distance between us.

For a solid hour, Güthric hammers at the bars. He uses his mace to bang and whack at the hinges, but to no avail. These cells were forged from something even stronger than shadowsteel.

"It's no use, Güthric. You tried, but that's all you can do." My rueful glance slides over Silver to find Dimitri still slumped on the floor, his head buried in his hands. "You should leave before the Crusaders retrieve us."

He looks up. "I'm not leaving you. I don't…I don't know what I'm doing, but I'm staying here, with you, until Alphonse comes to retrieve you."

Silver exchanges a look with Güthric. "She won't be here when he arrives. If we intend to run, then we have to go now."

Dimitri guffaws, jumping to his feet. "You're deserting? You can't even get the door open. How do you think—"

Silver stares him down. "This isn't the job I enlisted for. I vowed to hunt Qaeus, not start a war with the mages."

He crosses his arms. "So you were planning on abandoning your post before Halira was accused of anything?"

"I planned on doing what I promised I'd do when Ashenvale fell. I will not let those people die in vain."

"Then you should go," I say through the bars, drawing their attention away from one another. I take a shaky breath, the truth of what I'm about to say settling in like a crisp winter wind in my lungs. "If you mean to leave, you should leave now."

"We can't leave without you—"

"It's no use. You've tried, but the bars won't budge or break. Kalli and I…we've met our fates. I appreciate you trying but, I won't let you stay here and be captured for trying to aid a mage —not that I am one, but…you know what I mean."

Silence descends, but neither of them move.

"Go," I say, harsher now. "You did what you could for us and I will never forget it, but there's still time for you to leave. Please, go."

Silver watches me with unwavering conviction. I've seen that look before. I recognize its stubbornness.

Realizing she's not budging, I do the next best thing. "Fine. Don't leave us. We can wait for the guards to return. They'll have the keys. Once they free us, you can ambush them and we'll go. But we can't flee this place with no weapons and a limited supply of necro-ink."

Güthric holds up his arm and stares at mace as if checking to make sure it's there and not just a figment of his imagination.

"We'll need more than the two weapons you possess. I'll need my axe, and Kalli will need…something sharp."

Silver's eyes narrow on me, and for a moment, I fear she might challenge my suggestion. But after she considers the options, her expression becomes thoughtful. "We can stock-up on necro-ink at the catacombs, and I believe I know where they've taken your weapon. If you're sure this will work—"

"You took out the other guards, didn't you?"

If I didn't know any better, I'd swear her cheeks tinged pink.

"Then go. You don't have much time, and you'll need to make it back before the Crusaders do."

"This is absurd," Dimitri bellows. "It's mutiny. We'll all be tried for treason!"

"You do not have to come," Silver tells him, and she says

nothing more. With a nod to Güthric, the two of them climb back up the stairs, leaving us for the time being. Part of me hopes they'll return too late and we'll already be gone. I hate the thought of them risking their necks for me. My life is already forfeit. There will be no escaping the Crusaders nor the Magistrate. Once they come for us, my death is all but written in the ashes.

I think about my mother and the secrets that died with her. I wonder what would've become of our lives if she had lived long enough to tell Kalli and I about ourselves. I wonder how our mage ancestors came to be in Arcathain, if they had stood against the Great Rift, or if they had been accidentally left behind. I wonder if I'll ever learn the significance of the word *Imryll*.

"Did Mum ever talk to you about Imryll?" I ask my sister, my back to the stone wall between our cells, but my hand extends through the bars of mine to hold Dimitri's.

I'm still shocked he's remained this long. I knew how much he meant to me, but I hadn't realized what I'd meant to him. I am his last family left. Even if he can't bring himself to go against every honorable bone in his body to try to find a way to break me out, he will not leave my side. I am all he has.

"Imryll?" my sister repeats.

"It was the last word Mum spoke. I thought it might be a spell or something."

Dimitri's grip tenses in mine, the mere implication of mages making his blood boil.

"Maybe it was then," Kalli says, a calculating note to her tone. I can hear her pacing in the cell beside me. "How did she say it?"

"What do you mean?" I ask, straightening.

"I mean, *how* did she speak that word? Was it said with a high pitch or low? Was it spoken from her throat or through her nose? Which part of the word was enunciated? I don't know much about magic, but spells are precise. The inflection, the tone, the enunciation—everything has to be recited perfectly. Do you remember how she said it?"

I take myself back to that day. My mother's death. The fear and pain she must've been in. She likely knew she was leaving her family behind, knew it would be the last time she saw one of her daughters and that she wouldn't get to say goodbye to the other.

Only once my heart has thoroughly shattered do I utter the word, "*Imryll.*"

A gust of wind blows the door into the dungeon open and a raven glides in on the breeze. It lands on the floor in front of my cell, Dimitri scooting as far away as he can and shrieking the word *magic* over and over again. But I just stare at the bird. I know it's the same one I've seen all along, and I get the feeling that my mother summoned it just to watch over me.

"Who are you?" I ask it.

Before our eyes, the raven shifts into a beautiful woman, with the same white hair as our mother. She stands before me, naked and graceful, and says, "I wondered when you'd ask."

MAGIC FORGOTTEN

CATACOMBS, CASTLE OF NIGH, ARCATHAIN

imitri shrugs off his leather tunic and shoves it toward my aunt. She takes her time slipping into it, as if she's thoroughly unphased by her naked flesh.

"Who are you?" my sister asks, her tone less bewildered and warm than my own.

The woman turns to face her, her lips twitching. "You must be Kalli. I am Imryll, your aunt."

I could've guessed as much. The woman is the spitting image of our mother. White hair. Hard set eyes. Sharp features.

"I didn't know we had an aunt," Kalli snaps.

"No, you wouldn't. When the Blight came for Harwood and your mother left, she decided to leave everything about her druid life behind, including me."

"*Druid* life?" I ask.

"Ah, my apologies. I forget how little you two know. Evelyne promised to tell you when you were of age, but I suppose she didn't get the chance. The druids are a well-kept secret, but they are the dwellers of the Forgotten Forest of Eyve. Long ago, the humans knew of them, but they were mostly left to their own devices. It's why it was so easy for the humans to shut us out and lock us away with the Primordial: they did not know us and so they did not care for us."

"You weren't…alive then, were you?"

My aunt laughs. "No, I'm afraid not. But the stories are passed down and I know them well. But this hardly seems like the time for me to educate my nieces on their upbringing. Shall we move?"

"We can't," I tell her. "The gates, they can't be broken."

Imryll tosses her hand in the air. "There is much for you two to learn."

She closes her eyes and aims her hands at the ground. The floor begins to quake, the stones cracking and breaking apart. The floor hitches, the iron bars cracking apart from the stone ground.

Kalli and I step outside our cells, me with wide eyes, Kalli with skepticism.

"The druids are mages?" Kalli asks.

Imryll laughs again. "I'm afraid not, but we'll talk more about that later. For now, we must run."

"But where are we going?" I ask her.

"To the Eyve, of course. Now that you both know who you are, and since you're being persecuted for it, where else would you go?"

I haven't thought about him in a while, but suddenly I say, "We could find our Uncle Adrien? I ran into him, when I was in Ashenvale."

"Of course. Adrien is already waiting for you in the Shadowthorn. He knows you summoned me, and he awaits us to find him."

"Uncle Adrien's alive?" Kalli asks.

"I-I can't just let you leave." Dimitri's voice cuts the conversation off at its knees. "I don't want you to die, Halira, but this…you can't ask me to do this."

Imryll raises her hand, an all-too-magical gust awakening in the room around us.

"Wait," I tell her, racing toward Dimitri. "Please. Just this once, when it is most important, don't think about the rules. My life depends on it. My sister's life. You of all people know what it's like to—"

"Don't." He jerks his hands away from me, but I reach for them again.

"I'm sorry, Dimitri. I know it hurts, and it seems like a low blow, but it's the truth. If you prevent us from leaving, then you're killing my sister. You're killing *me*."

A muscle ticks in his jaw and he hangs his head low.

"Please. Allow us to pass. We will leave and never return, but at least you'll know that it wasn't you who allowed us to die."

Dimitri's confliction only gnaws at him the more that I speak. His expression becomes as hard as stone as he watches me, considering our dwindling options. I know him well enough to know that his call to duty is too powerful, no matter how much he cares for me. Because the truth is, I'm no longer all that he has. I'd been wrong. After yesterday, he now has hundreds of brothers and sisters, an entire legion of Crusaders who would defend him and he would them. And regardless of what happens to me, he will need to live on, and the Shadow Crusade is his life now.

So when he takes my chin into his fingers, I flinch at the gentleness with which he raises my eyes to meet his.

"I will not let you die."

Tears prick my eyes again, but they have no time to fall. I give him an appreciative nod before returning to the others.

"We should do as Silver and Güthric did, and head to the catacombs to gather some necro-ink. We might even be quick enough to meet them there and take them with us."

No one argues my point. In fact, none of us utter another

word as we sneak through the grounds. Fortunately, the court-yard is sparse of any Crusaders. After Alphonse's orders to pack up, I imagine many of them are inside doing just that. It allows us to go undetected as we flank the west side of the castle and head north toward the catacombs.

Instead of going through the main entrance, we opt to go around the back to where we know we will find bodies, if not already drained necro-ink.

But from outside the recently repaired doors, the conversation occurring from inside reaches us.

"These are my catacombs and you'll take no necro-ink from them!" the Spirit Keep shrieks, shrill and defiant. "The dead will haunt you if you so much as steal a drop!"

Kalli, Dimitri, and I duck near the door, listening to Silver and Güthric barter. But the Spirit Keep won't give them any necro-ink, which means she likely won't give us any either.

"What are we going to do?" I ask my sister.

But as I turn to her, Imryll steps out from around the ramp, her arms outstretched and wind gusting at her back. It blows the doors wide open and she strides into the morgue, drawing the attention of all three of the people inside. With a flick of her wrist, she calls to the vines of ivy climbing the stone walls, and they slither inside along the floor like snakes. They reach for the Spirit Keep, and she scrambles back, but they take hold of her ankles, hold her in place as they climb the rest of her to restrain her torso and arms, and then secure her to a wall.

"Sorry," Imryll says. "We don't have time to negotiate. We will only take what we need. The vines will release you once we're gone. I hope you understand."

We fill our vials in a fresh bucket of black ink, then grab one more vial each and fill another. Silver hands me my battle-axe as well as Tor's dagger, and hands Kalli the shortsword that I think had belonged to Sai.

"Oh," my aunt says, drawing my attention away from the

dagger in my hand. She unbuttons Dimitri's tunic with slender fingers and eyes the Spirit Keep. "I'll be needing your garb as well."

When the Spirit Keep doesn't respond, Imryll has her vines remove the tattered thing from her themselves. The rest of us avert our eyes as both women are bared before us, and though I feel guilty leaving the older woman naked and restrained, we flee the catacombs not a moment after Imryll is clothed again and dash for the Shadowthorn, filling Silver and Güthric in about my strange aunt along the way.

But just as we reach the Shadowthorn border, the bell tower tolls.

SHADOWTHORN

The bell strikes four times, signaling a demon scourge. It's either the perfect distraction we need, or the exact complication that will wind up getting all of us killed.

"Run! To the Shadowthorn!" Imryll cries.

With nowhere else left to go, we heed her and bolt. Demons lurch out from the border and I ready the axe in my hand. Güthric, Dimitri, and Silver hold firm on their weapons as well. Kalli stays near the center of us all, but Imryll takes the lead. She uses the druid magic at her disposal to cause a landslide and windstorms, tossing away any demons that might be coming our way.

Once the Crusaders come, she gives them the same treatment.

I try not to look back. These were my friends, my colleagues, after all. But I know they'll be all right. She is holding back the full force of her power, and only using what is necessary to allow us to escape.

A cloud of darkness suddenly shrouds the bright sun overhead. Just when I think it's because of our proximity to the

Shadowthorn, thunder booms in the sky. Rain falls in sheets, making the grass slick as we race for the tree line.

"You have nothing to fear," Imryll yells at me over her shoulder. "We will make it."

I don't know what she means, why she is saying that only to me. Then I realize, the storm. It must be me. This has happened to me before. Sometimes in Gravenburg, during the harshest of winters, I'd curse the flurrying wind, and right before my eyes it would cease. When Tor died, I sobbed for days and the sky wallowed with me.

A new motivation makes my legs pump faster. Not only do I need to outrun the Crusaders, reach the Shadowthorn, and survive the demon attack, but I need to live long enough for Imryll to explain. I need to know who I am and what I am capable of.

Imryll gives a final quake of the earth. Demons are tossed into the air by the fissures, our path cleared.

She looks back over her shoulder. "You have a clear path now. I'll scout ahead and find Adrien. Keeping running."

I nod, despite the pounding of my heart telling me not to let her go.

But while we're still sprinting, she pulls the draped gown up and over her head, tosses it to me, and with a single leap, turns to feathers and takes to the sky.

My strides only falter for a moment as I watch the raven dive into the Blight ahead. I wonder if I'll be able to do the same someday, or if it's even something I want to try. But I don't linger on the daydream long. Another bout of demons emerges from the shadowy border, claws glistening, and teeth bared.

We charge harder and hold nothing back. Güthric swings his mace like a fatal pendulum of justice. His mighty swings clear the demons by the handful, and while he takes them on, the rest of us push forward. Dimitri's broadsword slices through two of the demons who flank us, and Silver's war scythe whistles as she swings it through the air.

A bear of a demon lumbers out from the Blight. It's red eyes lock onto mine, a promise of death snarling from its twisted maw.

With a ravenous roar, the creature bounds toward me, heavy paws pounding into the dirt and tearing it to shreds in its wake.

"Halira! Watch out!" my sister bellows, too far away and engaged in her own fight to help me.

I drop my aunt's tunic and yell back at the beast in return, unleashing every bit of pain and hate that's piled onto my shoulders today. The friend that betrayed me. The cousin that condemned me. The country that's forsaken me. The roar bolsters me, it becomes an additional layer of armor to shield me from all of the doubt and insecurities I had before. Ever since Ashenvale, I no longer have to worry. I know now that, in the face of death, I will overcome.

I swing my axe, heavy and true, and it buries into the demon's thick neck. The creature collapses, taking my axe and me down with it. Grimacing, I crash into the creature's side, my face pressed against its crunchy fur, its blood gushing around my cheek. I waste no time in jumping to my feet. My heart hammers in my chest as I struggle to pull the shadowsteel free.

"Come on! Let's go!" Dimitri yells, rushing to my side. He grabs my elbow, but I pull back.

"I can't leave it," I grunt, the weapon barely budging.

"You have your dagger!"

I heave harder. "I can't leave it!"

Behind me, Dimitri snarls as another demon engages him. I hear their struggle, hear every whoosh of air that leaves Dimitri's lungs when he's knocked back, and every growl when he strikes, but I keep my focus on freeing my weapon.

"Come on," I grit out, the handle pressed into my chest as I use the weight of my body. The demon its imbedded into rocks with the effort.

Out of the corner of my eye, another demon charges. It bounds on all fours across the field, licking its jowls like it can already taste me. Weaponless, I am an easy target, a quick meal.

"Come on," I say, heaving again.

The demon draws closer, its snarling audible now, even amidst the rest of the chaos on the field.

Finally, my axe hitches free. I raise it overhead. The creature bounds toward me and I heave my axe forward. It cracks into the demon's head with the sound of thunder and yet again I find myself struggling to free my weapon.

"We have to go!" Dimitri yells again.

Just as I'm about to scream back at him that I'm not running into the Shadowthorn without a proper weapon, Güthric lumbers toward me. He stomps his foot onto the back of the creature's neck, takes the handle of my axe into his mighty grip, and yanks the blade with one heave.

He hands it to me with a proud grin before bending to retrieve my aunt's robe.

We leave Nigh screaming behind us, with no way of knowing if our friends will survive, or how long it will take them to discover we've gone. I shouldn't care. The Shadow Crusade had all but condemned me to die, and my sister. I should be pleased if they were to perish. But I couldn't be. My thoughts wander to Maxwell, to the Spirit Keep, and to all the others who weren't quite able to make the cut for a Crusader unit. Hopefully, the captains like Eparah will be able to protect them.

That is, if the demons ever stop coming. I've never seen so many push through the border at the same time. The bell tower toll must've been like a summoning beacon to all the evil in the area. Even once we're inside the Shadowthorn, the creatures that dwell inside are still frenzied. Fiends leap overhead from the branches, trying to watch the spectacle through the tree line. They're so thoroughly excited that they don't even pay us any mind. Demons still charge through the shadowed underbrush. Most of them barrel right past us, their hunger trained on the meal awaiting them in Arcathain. We tear through the ones who veer course, and for every demon we kill, I tell myself that's one less friend I'm leaving behind who will die.

Only once we're deep into the Shadowthorn do the cries of the Crusaders fade, and with it, our sense of urgency. The forest becomes quiet, the kind of silence that unsettles the nerves and pricks the skin with the sensation that someone—or some*thing*—is on the watch.

When a raven swoops down from the sky, I finally exhale my fear. The moment her talons land in the black grass, they change to human feet, the rest of her limbs following close behind. Güthric is waiting beside her with her robe just as fast as she's finished her transformation.

"Well, niece, I hear you've got yourself in quite the trouble," my uncle says, emerging from the forest. "Missed me so much you decided to join me in my fugitive lifestyle?"

"Uncle Adrien!" I leap into his arms. He sweeps me off my feet and rocks me in the air until he lays eyes on my sister.

When I'm back on solid ground, I watch her approach him with cautious wonder. "I thought you were dead."

His mouth quirks to one side. "Now, why in the Blight would you think that?"

Her scowl makes me chuckle. Somewhere inside me, I know I shouldn't be able to feel such warmth so soon after just having abandoned everything I've ever known—*again*—but being with them, with *family*, makes it easy to forget for a moment, however fleeting it may be.

"Surprised to see you here, too, Kalli," Adrien finally admits, his tone turning somber. "And I'm sure it wasn't your choice."

Her jaw tightens when she looks away. "No, but I suspected it was bound to end up like this eventually."

The unanswered questions cling to the air, dangerous and unpredictable, like branches that have already broken from the tree but have yet to plummet to the ground. I can't turn away. This is the moment I've been waiting for. With Adrien and Imryll together, Kalli and I can finally have the answers we need.

But Adrien's expression softens. He tilts his head to something behind me with a gentle suggestion.

Begrudgingly, I turn around. Dimitri stands off away in the distance, his back turned to the rest of us. His arms are rigid at his sides, his hands balled into fists.

Looking back to my uncle, he reassures me without a single word that we will have time to talk later. So, I make my way over to Dimitri.

When I lace my hand into his, his fingers don't respond. They dangle around my hand like he isn't even aware I'm beside him.

"I'm worried about them too," I admit softly, hoping not to disturb him too much, but enough to let him know he's not alone. As long as I'm alive, he never will be alone. "But the Crusaders are strong. They will survive without us."

Dimitri yanks his hand from mine. His chin dips as he avoids my piercing gaze.

Unsure of what to do, I finally start to walk away.

"I'm going back."

His words are quiet, but they carry the resounding force of an earthquake, one that makes me unsteady on my feet.

"You're...what?"

He pivots to face me. "I saw you to your freedom, but I cannot abandon my vows, Halira."

Tears sting my eyes and I rush toward him. My hands claw at his chest. "You can't go back. Dimitri, I need you."

His calloused hands close over mine. "I can't be a fugitive. The whole point of this was to defend the land so that we could find peace and live a normal life again. I love my country. I plan to grow old, to have children, and to share with them the love of my land. But if I stay with you, even after Qaeus is defeated, we'd still be running. We'd never be allowed in Arcathain again, not without threat of hanging for the abandonment of our posts and evasion of the law."

My face twists with the onset of grief. It hasn't quite dug its claws into my heart yet, but then again, I'm still not convinced he's leaving. There's still a chance that I can persuade him to stay, for me, for us.

"But...I love you." I imagined the words having more power than they do in my throat, but they waver and warble as I drown in sorrow. I bite my lip, and hope that when I hear him utter them back to me it'll be all the bandaging my aching chest will need.

But he doesn't say a word.

Dimitri stares into my eyes with so much resolve that I whimper. The battle I was preparing to fight has already been lost, his mind already made up. He's choosing Arcathain over me.

"What will you tell them?" I ask him, my voice a trembling brook. They'll arrest you for helping me and my sister escape."

He nods, as if thinking to himself. "They think you're a mage. I'll tell them you used your magic and forced me to release you."

A sad smile twists my lips, another sob breaking loose. His response comes too swiftly for it to have been thought of in this moment. I wonder how long he's planned on leaving me. Did he decide as we crossed into the Shadowthorn and the gravity of his decisions began to sink in? Did he begin to wonder while we were fighting through the demons in the courtyard? Or has he known ever since he stepped foot into the dungeons?

"I'm sorry," he says, as if somehow confirming my suspicions.

I shove him away, hot anger coursing through me. "Is this because of what I am? A druid?"

He angles his head. "No, Halira. I…don't even know what a druid is."

"Exactly. And that terrifies you. When you thought I was a mage, you knew you could at least replace the way you felt for me with loathing. You could pretend I was one of the heartless creatures who fled and abandoned us all to our fates. You would've gladly blamed me and the part my heritage played in Qaeus' growing power, in the loss of your sister and mother and father."

"It's not like that."

"Isn't it, though? You were so eager to blame me, you were practically relieved to see me in that cell."

His hand comes to his forehead, and he massages it like I'm irritating him, but all I see is a man hiding his face, his shame.

"And now that I'm not a mage, but a descendent of druids who dwelled in the Forgotten Forest of Eyve, you want nothing to do with me."

"You're not just a fucking descendent, Halira! You are one of *them!*"

The disdain in his voice causes me to shrink back. I press my hands against my throbbing chest. *Now*, is when grief sinks its claws into me.

Dimitri sighs, rubbing his temples before looking back at me. "You told your sister you can summon animals—your aunt can even turn into one. She caused an earthquake just to free you from your chamber, and I'm not blind. I saw the way you started that storm. And now that I've had time to think about it, those things have always happened around you. The few times you came hunting with me, it was like the animals were warned before we even set foot in the forest. You'd part the clouds when you wanted to spend a day at the lake, your garden flourished the year everyone else's became diseased.

"So don't fool yourself, and don't lie to me. It's not just about you being a descendent. You have powerful magic, power that no one should possess, power that you can't even control."

I hang my head low, aware that we've drawn the gazes of our travel companions.

"Then you should leave," I say, my voice quiet and clipped.

Dimitri doesn't say anything for a long, excruciating moment. It lasts so long that I'm not even sure he's still there. But when I hear his soft, approaching footsteps, the ache in my chest eases for a moment. Maybe he's changed his mind. Maybe he's realized that I'm still the same person that's been his friend for years, the same girl he's spent the last few months entangled in.

He presses his soft lips to my forehead. For what I fear might be the last time, I relish the graze of his smooth chin on mine.

And just when I convince myself he's staying, he breaks away, turns his back to me, and jogs back toward Nigh. I close my eyes, tears trickling down my cheeks, and hope that the press of his lips will be embedded in my skin forever.

The tears are still clinging to my eyelashes when a rageful cry bellows from the trees.

"You thought you could run from me!?"

The fury in Alphonse's voice is more volatile than the snarl of any demon I've ever heard. He thunders out from the shadows atop his blindingly white stallion like a bolt of lightning sparking in the middle of night. When I look up, I'm surprised to see that Dimitri is still within sight, having started his trek back to Nigh, but not having made it very far. He watches Alphonse and a small crew of Crusaders barrel by, only glancing my way once they've past him.

Their horses whinny to a stop just a few paces away from me.

Dimitri jogs up to us.

Alphonse's dark hair is wind-tossed from the hard ride. He runs his hand over his dark locks, eyeing us all, and paying extra attention to my aunt, then my uncle.

Disgust gnarls his lips. "I should've known the type of company you'd keep, cousin. Fugitives and more mages? Predictable. Tell me, do your friends realize that you've doomed them?"

"I-I made them come. With my magic," I blurt, frantically having remembered Dimitri's plan. My eyes find his now, full of apology and sorrow, but I blink away before I can feel sorry for him. *He's* the one breaking my heart, I remind myself. "They are innocent," I tell Alphonse. "Whatever you have planned for me, just spare them."

He snorts. "You must think me a fool if you truly expected me to believe such a thing."

"It's true, General," Dimitri says, staggering closer to the man. "I tried fighting away her suggestions, but she was too powerful. Only once we made it in the Shadowthorn, once she stopped giving me commands, was I able to break away. I was trying to flee her presence in hopes that the distance might return to me my freewill."

"Is that so?" Alphonse raises an eyebrow at Silver and Güthric. "And you two? Why are you not fleeing?"

My mind scrambles for a rational excuse, but I know too little about magic to think up one.

Silver answers for me, her spine as straight as a rim rod. "We came of our own accord. We have no plans of joining you in the Capital."

"Kill Qaeus," Güthric replies in support.

A touch of wicked amusement plays at Alphonse's lips. "What? Just the five of you? An entire legion of Crusaders couldn't take him down, and you think because you have a mage with you that you'll be able to finish what the humans started?"

Imryll strides forward. "That is enough. I will hear no more talk of the mages. We are druids, you foolish boy, and we will be treated with the respect we deserve."

Alphonse braces himself with a mocking chortle that comes in one wave after another, the laughter deepening into his belly until he is rocking with it.

"Respect? For *you*?" He gestures to the grey burlap draping over her naked flesh, a robe that's even more unflattering on her than it was on the Spirit Keep. "Never in my life have I bowed to a peasant, and I don't intent to start now."

"Oh," Imryll says, wickedness laced in the silkiness of her voice. "That can be arranged."

She beckons to the underbrush of the Shadowthorn, to the tarnished leaves and the blackened branches. Vines creep along the forest floor like spider legs.

Alphonse shrieks with horror. His horse rears, tossing him to the ground. The other horses do the same, launching their riders before bolting back toward Nigh. The vines grab onto the Crusaders; they twist around Alphonse's ankles, his shrieks frantic and shrill. They wrap around his legs, dropping him to his knees with a thud. At the same time, more vines climb up his sides until they can reach his wrists. They lock him in a vise and tug his hands to the ground.

With the grace of a black swan, Imryll glides over to the kneeling Alphonse. Alphonse tries recoiling as she bends down to look him in the eyes.

Imryll smirks. "There, now you can say you've knelt before a druid."

He growls, a vicious, ugly thing.

Imryll straightens. When she speaks, she addresses the Crusaders as much as she does him. "The choice is simple. You will return to your castle and proclaim us dead. No one will come after us, and you will leave with your lives."

"You can't threaten to kill them!" Kalli interjects. "These are Arcathainian people. They're Crusaders. They will be treated with the same respect you demand."

Slow and lethal, Imryll pivots to watch her, a slender brow raised. "You will remember that I requested said respect and was denied. Therefore, respect is forfeit here." Her gaze pierces back to Alphonse. "If you do not agree to these terms, I will summon the roots from the earth, they will spear your hearts, and I will leave your bodies for the demons to pick apart. Do you understand?"

"You can't—" Kalli cries.

Adrien shushes her, reaching for her arm but she pulls it away.

"Just who do you think you are? I don't care if you're a druid; I don't care if I'm one. You will not kill the people of Arcathain senselessly."

"I will if I must."

Kalli balks. "You're just as bad as the demons!"

The two of them continue on like this, their voices carrying in the clearing. My ears twitch for any sign of danger, but it's difficult to hear anything over their bickering.

Finally, after my nails have started digging so deeply into my palms that they've started to draw blood, I turn to them both, a chastisement on my lips.

But a blanket of black folds over me, something heavy, amorphous, crushing my chest. My feet leave the ground as I'm thrown through the air, a ragdoll floating and gasping in a sea of black. I crash to the ground with a whooshing breath of wind. I strain for air, but I can't find it, not immediately anyway.

"Halira!"

The scream is too distorted, too buried beneath my confusion and pain, for me to recognize it for anything more than something being yelled in the chaos.

Finally, I gasp, the air returning to my lungs. The day returns too, or at least the grey hues of it that the Shadowthorn permits through the trees. But as the demon rises from my chest, releasing my arms so that I might grasp for a weapon—a rock, a stick, a handful of dirt to be thrown at the beast to distract it long enough to scramble away—the creature unhinges its fetid, dripping jaw and sinks its angry teeth into my side.

Pain lances through me, searing blades of bright red iron puncturing my stomach. White flashes before me, blinding and agonizing, and I arch. I scream.

Another demon barrels over me. It slams into the first one, the two of them crashing somewhere in the trees beside me, but I'm too busy writhing to see where they've landed. My gut screams, the demon's claws freshly ripped out of me, and allowing a new heat to pour into the wounds as hot as liquid metal.

As I arch anew, more demons leap over me from the shadows. I brace myself to be teared apart, but they bound beyond me.

"Demons! Attack!" someone cries, the voice of a true Crusader.

Adrien slides to my side as the ringing of drawn shadow-steel weapons echoes around us. He examines my stomach with a trained eye I never knew him to have and says to someone, "She should be all right. The claws didn't go deep enough to cause any real damage, and her druid blood should be able to combat the venom."

I tilt my head to see who he's talking to and find Ryven kneeling opposite him.

"Guard her," Adrien tells him. "And if things start to go bad, you leave us and take her back to camp."

Ryven nods, eyeing me as if to make the promise to the both of us.

My stomach bubbles with another bout of scalding pain. My jaw locks. I dig my fingers into the dirt to hold onto something—anything.

"What's…happening…to me?" I manage to grit out.

"It's the demon venom," Ryven says, his gravelly voice harsher than usual. "It'll burn through your bloodstream until it reaches your heart." He must see fear dilate my eyes because he adds hastily, his crooked smile warm and somehow reassuring, "You have nothing to fear, Halira. You have druid blood in you."

Although his mouth doesn't move, I swear I hear him utter the word *yet*.

I wonder what purpose he's serving by reminding me of my newfound heritage, and why he thinks that would assuage my fears. Once a demon has broken a human's skin, once their venom is in our veins, there is no saving us. I am a walking corpse, destined for a burning pyre, if I should be so lucky.

Before I can ask him how druid blood is supposed to calm me, Ryven's lips pull back in a sneer, his gaze ripping away from me to something behind me. I feel the pounding of the demon's legs through the earth beneath my head as it charges for us, but another scream of pain tears through me and I am ripped away from reality once more. My world flashes, white hot and cold black, the venom tossing me between life and death so rapidly, that I can't tell which one is which, if the fog from my lips is my breath or my departing soul.

When the Shadowthorn appears again, Ryven is gone. Feet scuffle near my head and I tilt back to see him locked, arms to shoulders, with a demon equal in his size and bulk. Still, I fear he will be outmatched. All Crusaders die by demons eventually. They lose one unlucky battle, forget to shift on their feet just right.

Mustering all the will I have left, I fling my writhing, aching body over to my side, then stomach. I push my chest off the ground. My entire body trembles with the effort, but I push through it. I push up onto my knees, and once I've caught my breath, I sink back onto my heels.

The demon snarls, heaving Ryven across the way with a single mighty swing of its corded arm. Ryven slams into the dirt, the impact of which makes me sway, but seeing the dazed look in his eyes, and the predatorial focus of the demon's, I stagger to my feet. The world shifts beneath me like the ground isn't solid at all, but water, a rocking ocean that's about to sweep me out to sea.

Ryven props himself up on his elbow and spits blood from his mouth as the demon approaches. He doesn't seem as frightened as I think he should be, not until he sees me hobbling toward him.

Dark eyes wide, his lips part. I already know what he's going to say: that I should lay back down and rest, that I'm in no condition to try to sneak up on this demon and help kill it.

So he surprises me instead when he shouts, "Behind you!"

My hand dives so instinctively for my dagger that I'm convinced Tor's ghost is with me. He spins me on my heels, the pain from the demon venom either overpowered by adrenaline or smothered by my big brother, and I am propelled forward. My shoulder crashes into the man in front of me, a Crusader, I realize, judging from the black leather armor. We stagger together until I slam his back against a tree.

When I look up, the fury of the fight revived in my twisted snarl, I'm not surprised to find my cousin, Alphonse, sneering back at me.

He spits in my face and I stagger back.

Wiping my face, I sneer up at him. All around us, the battle continues. Demons fighting Crusaders, Crusaders fighting fugitives, fugitives fighting only for their freedom, their lives. It shouldn't have come to this.

"I'm as good as dead now anyway," I say, the two of us walking in a circle, keeping our distance from one another. "Just leave us."

"And waste a potential source of necro-ink?"

I grimace, the sudden thought that they could do that to me churning my stomach.

A wicked grin blooms on his face. "Once the Spirit Keep is finished with your blood, I'll tear your spine out myself, and fashion it into a crown to wear to instill fear in all the other mages who see me because they'll know I've bested one of their own."

I'd remind him that I'm not a mage, but that simple fact can't seem to puncture his thick skull.

"And I'll do the same to your sister."

This part of his threat, above any other, snuffs out the rest of the light inside me. It is the howling wind that blows out a lantern on a midnight stroll, leaving everything in total darkness.

"You won't touch her." My growl is so low that I almost don't even recognize my voice myself.

"Oh," Alphonse titters. "But I will. And knowing now how much you'd despise it, I'd take great joy in dismantling her. Maybe, I'd even fashion pendants for my Crusaders, bones they could wear in honor of our kill."

Snarling, I lunge for him. My dagger nicks at the air, but Alphonse is swift. He dodges just at the last second, my dagger slamming into the black tree trunk instead. The reverberation sends another ripple of nauseating pain through me, but I try to swallow it down, to stay focused and present.

Pressed up against the tree, I catch a glimpse of the horrific fight happening around us, a blur of blood and black.

I spin away from the tree before I can tell who's winning or losing.

Alphonse swings his fencing sword in a swishing, looping motion before striking. I block him with my dagger, using the crook between the blade and the bottom of the hilt to catch his sword and shove it away.

He tries a different tactic, jabbing at me instead. I jump back to dodge being punctured by anything else today, but then dive for him with my dagger ready. He anticipates my desperate strike though, sidestepping me again so that I stumble off-balance. He thumps me in the shoulder and I nearly fall, but stagger to my feet and face him again.

As Alphonse and I dance the coranto of blades, our slashes and twirls perfectly mirroring and thwarting each other in a dizzying swirl of life and death, I'm able to spot my friends through the chaos around us in more detail.

Strike.

I see Dimitri and two other Crusaders. They're circled by a pack of demons, but their swords make quick work of slicing through them.

Parry.

Imryll flashes between bird and human, dodging the shadowcreatures and using her moments of reprieve to send a gale of wind to blow them off balance, vines to secure them to the earth, and sinkholes to hinder their lunges. Without a shadowsteel weapon though, I can't help but notice she isn't able to kill, only encumber.

Jab.

Adrien and his people switch between fighting demons and their other foe, the Crusaders, the Magistrate's army for whom my uncle has been outrunning for the better part of my life. His skill with a sword is flawless, bordering cocky, but the way he moves with it, I suppose he can afford to be swelled-headed about it.

Dodge.

I spy Silver and Güthric last. They fight back to back, Crusaders and demons closing in on them. Güthric uses his hulking body to shield Silver from the demons that would otherwise lunge at her. His mace is no match for their decaying bones.

But horror pierces through me when I watch one of the Crusaders heave his sword into Silver's leg. I yell out for her as she falls.

Güthric, no more than a yard away from her, turns around and sees it all. Before the Crusader can deliver a killing blow, Güthric charges the man. His mace pulverizes the man's weapon arm with a single blow, the thing dangling limp at his side like an uncooked loaf of bread. The man screams, he pleads, even as Güthric pummels his skull until there is nothing left of him.

My screams fill the space of his as Alphonse slices through my hand, the one clenched around my dagger. The blade drops, a pool of blood gushing atop it.

I cradle the flayed thing against my chest and as I shriek, I keep my eyes locked on Alphonse's. Only wickedness reflects there. He truly enjoys this. Seeing me suffer. If I ever had an ounce of empathy toward him, I lose it now. I have tolerated his hatred for long enough.

My lips bunch together, my nostrils flaring while rage consumes me. It is as black as the night, as wrathful as the depths of a demon's eyes. It knows only death.

Fury erupts from my lungs, a rageful scream calling to the sky. The Shadowthorn darkens, the clouds shifting far above us to do my bidding. A low rumble of thunder sounds in the air, and Alphonse blanches. He lowers his blade, realization setting in.

"Wait. Halira, please," he begs, becoming every inch the sniveling child that I had been back when he was the one who held the power.

With slow strides, I advance on him, each step causing him to stagger backward. He holds his hands out.

"Please. Don't. I'll—"

Nothing that can come from his lips next matters. The churning darkness of my mind becomes our very surroundings. The battle slows behind us, or perhaps is swept away from us so that only we remain. Alphonse and I. Years of sorrow and pain and misery. My moment to correct it all.

The darkness flashes. A sizzling bolt of revenge shoots down from the black sky and spikes through Alphonse's chest. The impact sends him flying, his body bright and crackling with the charge of a hundred lightning bolts. He seizes, only for a moment, before justice takes its hold on him, and his eyelids fall limp.

Like a strong wind blows overhead, the dark clouds part. The grey sunlight filters back into the Shadowthorn and illuminates the carnage all around us. The demons have all been slain. A few Crusaders have fallen, but most still stand, watching me with horror.

To my surprise and relief, I find that all of my friends are still breathing, but Silver is on the ground, her pained expression reminding me of the venom scorching through my veins and the lethargy ravaging my muscles.

The moment my awareness returns to my body, I crash to the ground beside my cousin.

"Halira!"

Dimitri's scream booms, colliding with the ringing of my ears in an off-putting cacophony of panic. My head thrums from my painful landing, but not as mightily as my heart. I've seen what happens to those who succumb to demon wounds. If the gash isn't deep enough to cause someone to bleed-out, the venom will finish what the demon started.

I can almost feel the sludge sliding through my veins as it curdles my blood to necro-ink, until I am nothing but a sepulchral body of waste and death.

Dimitri crashes to his knees beside me. He jerks me into his arm, his hand pressed to my abdomen. He knows as well as I do that it's no use. Staunching any of the blood is futile now.

The others draw toward one another, their hushed voices hurried with strategy. I feel their close presence, can sense their worried glances, but they keep their distance, giving me and Dimitri a moment to say our goodbyes.

He presses his forehead to mine, the pain in his expression shielded from everyone but me.

"I'm sorry," he sputters, the grip on his emotions slipping. "I shouldn't have helped bring you here."

"I would've come here if you'd helped me or not." Wincing through the dark pain coiling around my heart, I reach up to cup his smooth cheek. "At least this way, we get to say goodbye."

A crystal tear splashes on my cheek and I open my eyes to gaze up into his. In all the years we spent together, even as danger lurked around our homes and our families were taken away from us, even as we enlisted in the Shadow Crusade, a life we knew would be short and dangerous, I never actually believed it would end like this.

"It's not supposed to end this way," he says, as if he can hear my thoughts.

Behind us, I hear my sister ask if there's a cure, all the while maintaining her composure and the calculated way in which she approaches every problem.

"I know," I tell Dimitri, not wanting to hear my uncle break her heart. "But it is."

We stay like that, wrapped in each other's arms, simply breathing in the warmth of one another. Even with the bouts of pain that trample over me from time to time, I find peace. If I am to die, at least it will be in the arms of the man I love. It reminds me of my parents, and for the first time since their deaths, I'm able to be grateful that they died together, even if I wasn't able to be there with them.

"We have to go now," I overhear Adrien saying. "All of us."

When Dimitri looks up, I realize my uncle is hovering over us.

"I'm not leaving her alone," Dimitri growls.

"I'm not asking you to," Adrien says gently. "With the scent of fresh blood in the air, demons will flood the area. We must leave and put as much distance between us and here as we can."

My frightened eyes find my uncle's. The thought of being

left behind with the dead—even if I'm dying myself—is too terrifying to consider. I don't want to die alone. I don't want to die without Dimitri.

My uncle, understanding my hastened breathing, puts his hand on my shoulder. "We're not leaving you, niece. Your family will be with you."

He gestures behind him to my watchful sister and aunt, then narrows his eyes on Dimitri.

"If you'd prefer to return to your life in Arcathain, now is your chance. The Crusaders"—he bobs his head behind him—"they'll be leaving soon. You fought alongside them. They respect you, I can see it in their eyes. They'll vouch for you before the Magistrate. With his son gone…I doubt he had knowledge of your relationship with Halira, and therefore he'll have no reason to have doubts about you anyway."

Dimitri's expression hardens. "He could blame me for Alphonse's death."

Adrien inclines his head. "He might. But that is not the choice you face. Do you want to chance your life in the Shadowthorn with us, or in Arcathain with the Crusaders?"

Dimitri purses his lips together. He looks back behind Adrien to the three remaining Crusaders. I don't recognize them, but I see the familiar way in which they watch him, and I know that the male dormitory was a mixed bunk of recruits and Crusaders, so the chances of him knowing these burly fellows is at least not completely impossible.

They nod to him, a gesture that even I find reassuring. After the battle they've endured, after all they've lost, and seeing Dimitri fight alongside them, I think they're prepared to vouch for him.

Dimitri looks down to me, guilt thrashing through him and I do what I can to ease it. "This isn't what I wanted."

"I know," I say, wincing through the pain. "Believe it or not, it's not what I wanted either."

He hangs his head lower. "I don't want to leave you, but to stay would make me—"

"It's all right, Dimitri. I know. You have to go. I'll be…gone soon anyway. You weren't meant to live among fugitives. You're a Crusader now."

A muscle feathers in his jaw.

"I'll be all right." The lie brings out a horrified snort from him, so I correct myself. "I'll be with my sister. You don't have to worry about me being alone. I'll be with family."

He leans over so our foreheads are pressed together again. I want so badly to kiss him, to feel the irritatingly always clean-shaven face against my own one last time, so that I might die with the thought of something soft and warm instead of the churning darkness festering in my gut.

But Dimitri pulls away without ever glancing at my lips. Gently, he places me back down in the dirt, the ground colder now in the absence of his warm embrace.

Dimitri strides away, toward the other Crusaders. As he passes Alphonse's lifeless body, he glares down at him with so much disdain I wonder if it had been buried within him all this time; he'd just been too loyal to allow it to show. Joining the others, he mounts one of the horses that no longer has a rider, and even as they gallop away, never once does he look back.

I realize with sinking grief that his face will not be the last among my memories. I will never feel his embrace again, never catch his scent on me after a night stolen together.

I'm certain that I've shattered into a hundred, fractured pieces, and that it would take a lifetime just to put me back together again, but then someone lifts all of me into the air. I startle, my hands grasping for anything to hold onto, and finding Ryven's neck.

Someone coughs out of my sight, but the sound is watery, as if they're spitting up blood.

"Piss on a mage," Adrien says, glancing somewhere behind

us. "He's alive." He blows through his lips, exchanging a glance with the others before returning his attention to Ryven. "You have her?"

Ryven's dark gaze burrows into mine, and though he nods, his words are meant for me. "As long as she is with me, she will be safe."

My cheeks flush like a candle held too close to the skin.

"Good," says my uncle. "Take her back to camp. Be swift. We'll be right behind you."

"He's not taking her anywhere," Kalli demands, the fiery conviction of a boiling pot of water bubbling in her words. She challenges anyone to argue with her otherwise.

Ryven's mouth twitches, and before I know it, he spreads his membranous wings and bounds into the sky. May bravery fill his heart and protect his life for whenever Kalli gets her hands on him.

My heart thrills in my chest and I squeeze Ryven's neck tighter. My hand grazes something rough and edged, and I realize with alarming fright that I'm grasping the demonized side of his body. The black spikes along his shoulder fade up his neck, feather-small. I recoil and tuck my arms against myself, only later realizing that I've just reacted the same way Dimitri did when he thought I was a mage.

"I'm sorry," I manage, but my voice is so raspy, it's hardly audible over the rush of the wind around us.

"It's all right. You don't have to hold onto me. I have you."

With another rush of heat to my face, I realize he does have me. I am as secured in his hulking arms as I would be behind a stone wall.

With his wings beating overhead, my eyes slowly flutter shut and I see Dimitri's face. Not the pained expression he wore when I saw him moments before, nor that of the young man I grew up with, but one of my fondest memories of him, the day he emerged from the stairway in the castle the first day we were to train as Crusaders. Bathed and groomed, he looked like a new man. He wasn't the butcher's ward anymore, he wasn't a pitiable orphan boy, but a man, one with convictions and aspirations. I came to know Dimitri more in these last few months than I came to knew him in our entire lives, and should we have survived this together, I would've been honored to remain at his side.

We were meant to right the world together, to protect and save Arcathain.

Hopefully, he can follow through on that dream once I'm gone.

And with that thought, with Dimitri's handsome face still in my mind's eye, I lean my head against Ryven's chest, and let the venom coursing through my veins consume me.

To be continued
Blighted Heart
Book 2 of Primordials of Shadowthorn

PREORDER NOW!

Thank you for reading _Shadow Crusade_!

Leave a Review
Help other readers find this dark saga by leaving a review on
Amazon, Goodreads, Bookbub, or any other reading website.
Even a simple "I loved it!" can really help!

ARC Team
If you're someone who loves leaving reviews and you're excited
by the idea of having early access to all of my books, check out
my website for more information on how to join my ARC
Team: www.jessacawillis.com/ARC

Social Media

And last but not least, if you'd like to stay connected, you can find my social media links here: https://linktr.ee/jessaca_with_an_a

337

mark, or face the consequences of returning to the underrealm empty-handed.

It's no choice at all. She has come too far to stop now.

Besides, no one can outrun a Reaper… Or can they?

~Check out the Reapers of Veltuur Trilogy on Amazon~

Can Sean and three strangers unite the remnants of mankind when everything else has fallen apart? Can they face the darkest horror this new world has yet to offer?

~Check out The Awakened Quadrilogy on Amazon~

ACKNOWLEDGMENTS

Every book takes a team of people to make it what it is, and my stories are no different.

When I started working on *Shadow Crusade*, the only thing I knew was that the world was set somewhere where demons ran rampant. I had no intention, let alone the thought, of expanding the world to include mages, nor the Primordials. I wasn't even sure how I was going to incorporate the raven on the front cover (since I purchased these as a premade set).

As always, **my brother Michael** was the one I turned to for my heavy brainstorming. I don't think even he realizes how crucial he's been to the development of my worlds. I also don't think he realizes just creative his mind is. When we started talking about Qaeus' reign and toying with the idea of a rivalry between the humans and mages, it was his suggestion to have the mages flee with a huge portion of the continent—an idea that I absolutely LOVED, and one that really helped cement the humans' hatred toward magic. Michael helped make this story far richer than it would've been without him, and for that, I am eternally grateful.

Two other people who play significant roles in my work are my editors: **Sandra Ogle** and **Kate Anderson**. I am forever impressed by the level of detail and care they show my manuscripts. Kate herself is also an author, so it's been nice helping one another with our stories.

And of course, instrumental to the very inception of this idea was **Evelyne of Digital Art by Secret d'Artiste**! I don't think I would've ever come up with this story if it wasn't for her breathtaking covers!

Last but certainly not least, it's no secret that **readers and fans** are instrumental in an author's journey, but this was true even more so than usual for me regarding this series. I am open about my struggles with depression and anxiety, and how those impact my creative process, sometimes positively and other times negatively, but I have never been more negatively impacted by my mental health that I was while writing *Shadow Crusade*. With the pandemic, forest fires, a scare concerning my son's health, a scare concerning my job security—this year has been tougher than others for many among us, but one of the things that helped me through some of my darkest days was the support and cheer I received from my readers. Your kind words, your encouragement, your phenomenal reviews on some of my other words is what got me through my days and helped motivate me to keep pushing through some of the challenges of independent publishing. I am forever grateful for your excitement and investment in my stories. I relish every email or message or post that allows us to connect. Thank you for being here with me on this journey.

Sincerely,

- Jessaca

ABOUT THE AUTHOR

Jessaca is a fantasy writer with an inclination toward the dark, epic, and adventure sub-genres. She draws inspiration from books like the Nevernight Chronicles & ACOTAR, videogames like Dark Souls III, and television shows like Game of Thrones and The Chilling Adventures of Sabrina. She is a self-proclaimed nerd who loves cosplay, video games, and comics, and if you live in the PNW, you just might see her at one of the local comic conventions in one of her favorite RWBY cosplays!

www.ingramcontent.com/pod-product-compliance
Lightning Source LLC
Chambersburg PA
CBHW070825190726
48292CB00006B/2111